PROGRAMMED TO KILL

'Get the boy . . .' the old man screamed as the hyena closed in on him. Razz nodded and as the beast sank its teeth into the doctor's thigh she squeezed off another shot, blasting away half the animal's skull, splattering the doctor with blood and fragments of bone. But it made no difference.

Animal and man disappeared in a ball of fire, the old man's scream swallowed back into his lungs, along with mouthfuls of flame. The hyena's jaws had been DNA-coded, its bodypack wired to explode when teeth bit into the right flesh, when the double-helix profile of its target matched that held in the detonator's memory.

It was an old trick but a good one . . .

Born in Malta and christened in the upturned bell of a ship, Jon Courtenay Grimwood grew up in Britain, the Far East and Scandinavia. He currently works as a freelance journalist and lives in Winchester. He writes for a number of newspapers and magazines, including the *Guardian* and *SFX*.

Visit the website
http://www.j-cg.co.uk

Other books by Jon Courtenay Grimwood

neoAddix

remix

redRobe

Pashazade
The First Arabesk

Effendi
The Second Arabesk

Felaheen
The Third Arabesk

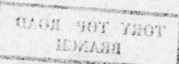

Lucifer's Dragon

Jon Courtenay Grimwood

POCKET
BOOKS

LONDON · NEW YORK · SYDNEY · TORONTO · DUBLIN

First published in Great Britain by Hodder Headline PLC, 1998
This edition published by Pocket Books, 2004
An imprint of Simon & Schuster UK Ltd
A Viacom Company

1 3 5 7 9 10 8 6 4 2

Simon & Schuster UK Ltd
Africa House
64-78 Kingsway
London WC2B 6AH

www.simonsays.co.uk

Simon & Schuster Australia
Sydney

A CIP catalogue record for this book is available from the British Library

ISBN 0-7434-7827-4

Typeset by Palimpsest Book Production Limited, Polmont, Stirlingshire

Printed and bound in Great Britain by
Cox & Wyman Ltd, Reading, Berkshire

The greatest trick the devil ever pulled
was convincing the world he didn't exist.

[Serotonin Heights]

'So, how is his Serene Excellency?'

It was a simple enough question. At least, the silver-skinned bodyguard thought so. Sun glinted off her buttocks as she squinted over the shoulder of a sour-faced Chinese guard busy studying a flatscreen. The screen was staple-gunned to a marble wall in front of his deck. It showed a small blond boy playing a tri-D computer game, badly.

Lieutenant Chang Mao loathed Razz leaning over his shoulder. He didn't approve of swearing, either. And he hated her nakedness. Prissy bastard, Razz reckoned.

Obviously enough, that was why she swore, crowded him and showed the man her bare arse.

Digging deep into the pocket of her Issuki Marino silver jacket, Razz casually palmed two Bayer Rochelle derms and slapped one on the underside of each wrist. Chang Mao sniffed in disgust and Razz grinned. Something else the poor little China boy didn't like. She could have had a ceramic pump implanted into her wrist, but couldn't be bothered.

There was a lot Razz couldn't be bothered with these days. And worrying came high on that list. Crudely put, the derms were synapse-fuckers. Guaranteed to hack out inhibitions, kill anxiety, and reduce the speed at which Razz's brain took back serotonin.

For something that wasn't addictive, Razz sure needed a lot of them.

She'd have preferred to mainline serotonin or take it cold over ice with an olive, but neurotransmitters didn't work like that. None of them did. There was usually a finite loop of the juice: all Razz

1

could do was slow down cerebral re-uptake, buy herself a little time.

The derms 'guaranteed' increased mental stability. Didn't deliver, though, at least not for Razz. Extensive viral rewiring meant her body's core temperature had stabilized at 99.4 and the section of her cortex that granted sleep was toggled to a permanent *Off.* Razz palmed another two derms, flipping them out of the silver bubblepac with one razor-sharp nail and swore darkly.

Three years without sleep – anyone would be stressed.

On the Toshiba flatscreen, the small boy was nodding angrily, blue eyes shut in concentration. Wrapped round his head was a thin gold band, half princely crown/half bleeding-edge synapse link, one giant step beyond basic 'trodes. But no great help if you couldn't think fast enough to flip your way out of trouble, which Aurelio never could.

In front of the kid, balanced on a marble-topped Louis Napoleon table sat a small Sony tri-D showunit. Centre stage, hovering above the tri-D's platform, was a mountain. And high on the mountain's side stood a fuzzy-logic Celtic dragon. Way below, about to fall off the edge, crouched an impossibly beautiful angel with long black hair and snake-thin hips. They were hurling white-hot fire bolts at each other.

The dragon was winning. Which wasn't a surprise. Games play wasn't Aurelio's hot suit. No magic left, almost out of life, and he hadn't even got off the mountain.

'*How is he . . .* ?' Lieutenant Chang Mao demanded, like the answer was obvious, which Razz supposed it was.

'Sulking,' Razz said. She could have added, 'as usual.'

The Chinese techie nodded, his expression sour as he passed one hand over a floating track ball, blinked the cursor into one corner of his screen to cut in on the boy's sullen face. Even cropped in tight, the blond-haired child was too mournful to make usable vid clip. Poor little shit.

Razz's face was bleak as she casually elbowed Chang Mao aside stare intently at his screen. The kid looked tired, upset, all too aware of the cameras watching his every move. Aurelio's reign was coming to an end. A year, maybe two if he was very lucky. Then puberty and enforced obscurity.

'Why the fuck do you think he's upset?' Razz asked. She used Japanese, so did Chang Mao. Most CySat employees did. Come to that, most people did, full stop. That and US English. Razz was so used to both, she flicked between the two barely noticing.

It was late morning and the technician had less than ten minutes to edit together Friday lunchtime's upload of the young Doge at play. All the man needed was one minute of *Lucifer's Dragon* and thirty seconds of smiling child to end newVenice's *good Newz* slot, but Lieutenant Chang Mao had a nasty feeling it wasn't going to happen.

And he knew damn well he couldn't count on the Doge's silver-skinned bodyguard for help. He didn't like Razz or what she represented; an older, more chaotic, overly indulgent way of handling security. Lizard-skin shoulderplates grafted over shark cartilage, for God's sake. Virally-wired exotics were a thing of the past, expensive luxuries for anally-retentive, insecure meta-Nationals. *WeGuard-Beijing* were the future. Now they were here, she should go.

She wasn't needed. When CySat nV put the city's security franchise out to tender, Beijing came up with a package fifty years ahead of the nearest opposition. As of last week, the Piazza San Marco had been quietly, discreetly lined with linkless Brownings spliced into the city's JCIT combat AI.

Done discreetly because CySat might have twice the GP of Imperial France and be the most *meta* of all metaNationals, but it was also known for its trademark liberal paternalism. Linkless Brownings set around CySat's Global HQ didn't sit too well with that image.

That CySat's Council of Twelve felt it necessary to retain the services of a street samurai, even one as famous as Razz was an insult to *WeGuard-Beijing* . . . As was the silver woman's total contempt for modesty. How any female of her advancing age – of any age – could wander the long marble corridors of the palazzo not just with her pudenda showing but wearing gold labia rings, her body hair singed bare, was beyond him.

'Got a problem?' Razz asked suddenly, crowding in on the *WeGuard* techie, knowing he hated the smell of body oil, garlic and sweat on her skin. Disapproval wasn't something she liked. And those derms were getting less and less effective at keeping her aggression levels in check.

Absent-mindedly, Razz fingered the handle of her shockblade. All it would take was a quick flick of its mother-of-pearl button and a high-voltage, low-resistance blast would take the Chinese technician to his knees. Sweet as pie.

Unfortunately she couldn't afford the grief. But it was a close-run thing . . .

'I'm going in,' she said, reaching an off-the-cuff, highly irregular decision. Lazily Razz flexed the claws of her right hand. Razor-sharp molyglass slid out from under each nail, and then retracted automatically when Razz relaxed the *flexor* muscle attached to her fingers.

It was an old, old augmentation, but Razz was still ridiculously proud of it.

The lieutenant was beginning to look alarmed, minute beads of sweat breaking out across the forehead of his round face, his brown eyes widening behind unfashionable heavy-lensed spectacles. The man was *PsiOps*, a data pusher, he wasn't paid to take risks.

'It's not allowed,' he protested, 'you'll get into trouble.'

As soon as the words were out of his mouth, he knew he'd made a mistake. Razz just grinned and nodded towards the door separating Chang Mao's mixing room from the young Doge's living quarters. What people saw was age-blackened oak, festooned with gilded cherubs and inlaid with small panels of tortoiseshell and ivory. What they got was a solid core of standard two-inch-thick bombproof protein/polymer micromesh, fitted on all sides with recessed titanium deadlocks.

It predated *WeGuard*. Hell, it even predated Razz . . .

'Klick the keys,' she demanded.

Resigned to the outsider's arrogance, Chang Mao obediently tapped a numeric sequence into his deck, and waited for the soft thud that signalled the door's electromagnetic bolts had slid back into their sockets. The little shit liked her, anyway. Maybe the bitch could get him to smile. Someone had to.

Chang Mao would have guessed that Razz was good, even if *WeGuard* HQ in Beijing hadn't given him her background (plus the *meme* about a black clinic in M'Dina where 3Razz was on ice ready to receive a mindset already uploaded to a numbered Swiss databank). The woman moved like a cross between a panther and a snake. Just the way she stood said, 'back off . . .' But she was getting old, and old people lost their edge.

Chang Mao risked a sideways glance at the silver woman and wondered if she was as dangerous as everyone said. Then, in the darkened reflection of his Toshiba flatscreen, he caught Razz's sardonic smile as she watched him watching her, and decided he'd better believe it.

Hastily, Chang Mao reached inside his uniform jacket for a Netcard, swiped it through his deck's reader and busied himself calling up a private e-vid mailbox. By the time Razz had pulled open the over-carved oak door, Chang Mao had binned three local vidverts offering him Mitsubishi hovers he could never hope to afford, and was staring at the grainy image of his mother talking that morning from a public-access vidbooth.

Taiyang cong Shaoshan shengi (the sun rises in Shaoshan) read the revolutionary slogan now scrolling endlessly across his screen. It wasn't true. Nothing rose in Shaoshan except dust from the dried-out lotus ponds. These days the birthplace of China's first Marxist emperor was a ghost town. That was the only reason he'd enlisted in *WeGuard* anyway.

The vidbooth quality was even worse than usual, with stuttering bands of interference and enough electronic flicker to make him snow-blind.

It was a bad day and Chang Mao was beginning to get a headache. How much worse it was about to get the *WeGuard* had no idea.

[Ceci Tuera Cela]

Sperm futures were up 129 points on Dow Jones, 151 points on FTSE. Natural fertility was down 0.19% year on year, except in Finland which showed a staggering 1.2% fall. Figures scrolled up the black glass surface of Count Ryuchi's desk, each more or less what he expected.

It was fifteen years since CySat had bought FffC GmB in Frankfurt and franchised a string of *G&Stork* fertility clinics across every major capital. Since then, aggressive marketing had given FffC almost global control of private-clinic IV fertilization. 43% of males in the Western world now went in automatically on their eighteenth birthday for a testicular biopsy, sperm cells frozen for later use, allowing them to father their own children.

Even men with zero sperm count, with no functioning sperm in their seminal fluid could produce healthy offspring under FffC's patented method. Given that 18% of the world's males now counted as zero-rated sperm producers and fewer than one in a hundred couples now met the UN definition of 'functionally fertile' (natural intercourse/natural birth), the Count liked to think that CySat's not-so-recent acquisition counted almost as a public service.

Eye colour, height, EQ, IQ – those FffC could do. That was just basic template work. Of course, CySat didn't let FffC involve itself directly in backing-out genome to produce heavy enhancements or high-level modifications. But its FffC clinics could discreetly recommend smaller, less public clinics that did. From simple night sight to fully functioning, bat-based echo location, it was almost miraculous the sheer atavistic potential contained in junk DNA. And CySat's 39% holding in *WarmWombs* meant it also kept a significant stake in the vast market for external incubation.

'*Bite turns man into werewolf*,' Karo read the heading in disbelief. She was clutching that morning's download of the *nV Enquirer*, words busily rearranging themselves across her page as new stories came in. She should have been reading the second book of Gibbon's *Decline and Fall*, but she was bored with history.

It wasn't possible, of course, to be remade on the spot, but Karo skimmed the story anyway. She knew it was untrue by the time she hit the second par, the one about the rabid mosquito having flown in from the levels, magically passing through the sonic wall, to bite an art dealer from the Rialto and pass infected genome to its unsuspecting victim.

The art dealer's DNA had unravelled on the spot, according to the *Enquirer*, then ravelled back, to leave a shambling werewolf dressed in the dealer's clothes. Karo didn't think so. Not even nanotek worked like that. At least, Karo hoped it didn't.

Karo diOrchi sucked at her teeth in disgust, but quietly, almost under her breath. Enough to annoy her father, not enough to bring down his anger. Between flicking over virtual pages, she polished the brass handle of a Mexican lock knife against the edge of her velvet sleeve.

Its blade had the word *Beauvoir* stamped on it, along with a twist that might have been a double helix, if 19th-century knife-makers had known about such things. The handle was tortoiseshell and brass, worn smooth with polishing. The knife had been her mother's, but her father now used it as his paperweight.

Karo didn't approve. But then she made a point of not approving of anything her father did. *And why should she*, thought Karo. He was cold, smug, hypocritical, dangerous. A politician with no vision. A poet with too few words. An artist with no spirit . . .

Karo diOrchi didn't like her father. But then, Karo knew that was because he didn't like her. Never had done. She was too like her mother in temperament, and not enough alike in looks.

He was onto tri-D soaps now. Karo watched him sit at his *escritoire*, shuffling papers. Written data was an affectation, but his decisions would still decide what a billion people watched next spring, when CySat was due to replace three of its longer-running *novelas*.

Not that she was meant to know that, of course. Such things were business, and so had no part in her lessons. Vivaldi, Veronese, Vitello – why did so much neoVenetian culture begin with a *V*? Even bloody Verdi, and he came from some hick republic in Europe.

Karo shrugged at her own question. Brown almond eyes never leaving the sallow skin of her father's neck, where he bent forward over his rustling laser-printed reports. His narrow back was towards her, the black pin-stripe of his silk Versace jacket hung loose across thin shoulders. It would be simplicity itself to plunge her mother's blade through that expensive cloth into the flesh beneath, but Karo wouldn't do it.

Though, God knows, most days she wanted to.

Karo slid the knife into the sleeve of her simple red jacket, its handle hard against her skin. She was damned if he was going to keep it . . .

'Karo . . .' The girl jumped, almost tripped on the Palazzo's polished marble floor. And the Count sighed, heavily.

'You may go.' Tall, thin, preoccupied, Count Salvatore Ryuchi dismissed his daughter with a wave of one silver-ringed hand, wanting her gone. He didn't want her there in the background when the cameras started. She didn't fit his little gilded study with its ornate marble overmantel by SanSovino.

She was too drab, even though the room was not much more than a Palace alcove to the infinitely more elegant Hall of Council next door. And out there, standing amid the gilded Murano mirrors, surrounded by Bassano's vast mural of popes, hunting dogs and half-naked muses, Karo was lost entirely, dwarfed beneath a huge Veronese ceiling.

'Go,' the tall Japanese poet repeated more crossly, and she went in silence: not even half-slamming the wooden door behind her. Only her flat heels echoing on the white marble floor had a reproachful echo.

Count Ryuchi sighed. Much as he loved his adopted city, it was hard not to regret the custom which banned him from ensuring her embryo had met basic requirements for height, looks and intelligence; never mind adding useful modifications.

Every brat born out on the levels was gene-checked, enhanced or augmented using a pirate copy of the latest mediSoft templates. Hell, with the right wetware and a little nerve, self-impregnation was so simple any thirteen-year-old street kid could successfully do it, before squatting in dark corners to drop her bug-eyed, bat-eared little bastard into some cheap Taiwanese womb for the last few months.

They bred like animals and increasingly they looked like animals. Well, that was over. Or it soon would be. CySat had finally decided to stop shitting on their own doorstep. And what were the levels, if not a century's worth of genetic excrement?

Nietzsche was right, God had died at the end of the 19th century. And by the end of the 20th, socioDarwinists had scanned the soul to death with positron emission tomography. Without God, without soul, was it any wonder the 21st had seen a total eclipse of all values?

Morality so relative it was quantum . . .

And now, in the 22nd? Count Ryuchi turned back to his *escritoire*, tapping impatiently at the black glass inlaid into its mahogany-and-ivory top. Now, at least in newVenice, the planet had an island of elective morality in a sea of dissolution.

The screen snapped alight and the Count was pleased to discover that – as ever – his timing was perfect. At seventy he still had the honed, time-sensitive circadian rhythms of a twenty-year-old.

Noon exactly, that was when CySat documents downloaded to the CEO's desk, ready for authorization. There were no surprises.

Just as well: Count Ryuchi loathed the unexpected, punished it mercilessly. Surprises meant someone had sISOd the Lotus Scrysoft, and he didn't keep an office full of analysts to be given the results of poorly-fed software.

First up was the death of a major Simnet star. Ryuchi checked her ratings and authorized the character's termination without further thought. Her human avatar would have to go too, of course. All actors were obviously virtual, had been since the start of the twenty-first century. But even virtual stars needed human doubles.

Real time/real space events had to be handled live. You couldn't just tri-D the Pope and splice an interviewer in later. The Vatican wouldn't buy it. Like it or not − and CySat didn't − live back-up was sometimes needed.

Still, Sonia Macmillan wasn't, not now. The Count cancelled her contract, having first activated the cameras that would now record him working hard for the good of newVenice. Flicking his thumb against the edge of the glass, Ryuchi turned the page. Oh, yes . . . *Let There Be Life*, religious porn for London, starring Mother F and the Sisters of Perpetual Indulgence. A good franchise, that one.

And finally, confirmation that CySat GmbH had exclusive rights to the siege of Belgrade. London would be upset but Berlin were just sharper, more hungry. Face it, Berlin already had a kid inside the city, wired up to a Zeiss eyeCam and willing to die if necessary to get the shots. Hell, how could you blow out a reporter who has '*If it bleeds, it leads* . . .' tatooed across her wrist, as a reminder of why she was there.

The best CySat B2C could offer was a camera-slung Aero-Spatiale K121 automated drone.

The old man signed, scrawling across the glass screen with an antique Mont Blanc fountain pen. Another affectation. The nib was dry, had been for over a hundred years, but that hadn't stopped his wife's father from using it, or her grandfather either.

Anyway, thought the Count, authorizing his last document, there was nothing wrong with affectation. Most civilizations were built on it; that and decent weapons . . . Closing down his desk, the old man remembered to smile for the cameras before flicking them off.

Hidden behind the two-way Murano looking-glass hung in front of his desk were 9600 pinhead m/Wave Fuji cameras, 80 to a row, 120 rows deep. Each AMC lens was tuned to one of 70 seeds set into the subdermal layer of Ryuchi's face. Seeds tracked by the cameras to create a 2D skeleton of his facial movement, which LotusRendersoft translated realtime into a 3D rendered model.

The changes were subtle: he was less obviously Japanese, less forbidding. That was the beauty of using a ubiquitous, context-free Lotusmorph talking head.

The Count smiled. Besides, he needed to be where he was. Needed to be seen to be here, at work in his office. At least, it was his clique's office this month. Use of the room alternated each calendar month like the position of CEO itself.

Tapping dark powder onto the back of his hand from an enamel box, the Japanese man raised a thin wrist to his nose and sniffed deeply. It was nothing more than Virginia snuff but nicotine imitated the neural effects of choline and that always improved Ryuchi's temper. At least in the short term.

Snuff and chocolate. The only two good things to come out of the New World.

Despite himself, Count Ryuchi glanced at the naked woman in the corner. She was beautiful, thin and high-breasted. Her nipples bud-like, her stomach soft and small, curving down to a discreet bush of fur. The perfect Renaissance figure. No one looking at her would think she had actually borne Karo and then breastfed the brat herself, as if wombs and wetware didn't exist.

His daughter hated the statue, of course. What girl wouldn't? Even at thirty, naked, cast in bronze and dead, Lucrezia put her fifteen-year-old daughter into the shade. The statue had lived in this room since it was first cast, by Ryuchi himself. A talent which had surprised everyone, except the Count, who knew the gap between art and insanity was no wider than that between a single drendritic nerve and its axon.

And few men had been more insane or inspired than he was the night he cast Lucrezia in bronze. Lucrezia diOrchi had been the most beautiful woman in neoVenetian history. Not a smile, not a cheekbone was synthetic or artificially induced. She was that miracle of random DNA shuffle, a genetic masterpiece, a natural, unenhanced beauty from which a perfect Doge should have sprung. Except Lucrezia managed one child only, a girl, before sinking into a hollow-eyed echo of herself.

Anorexia takes will. Starving the body beyond submission into death took all the will that Lucrezia diOrchi possessed. But then awkwardness had always been the one thing Karo's mother had never lacked. What other daughter of a Regent would ever get pregnant by a visiting yakuza grandee, then insist on marrying him?

Ryuchi was no fool. He knew how close he'd come at that moment to being killed. Had he been anything but what he was, it would have happened: a stiletto slipped softly into his heart, or maybe poison into his wine. Something traditional. But Ryuchi was a Yak, a man of rank, rich even by CySat standards.

Besides, his contacts in Edo were good and he learnt fast, integrating himself without glitch into neoVenetian society. When Creutzfeldt3Jacob finally ate the Regent's cortex and lower brain into wet sponge, Ryuchi was ready, already waiting to take his father-in-law's place on CySat's executive.

Which he did, effortlessly, first as proxy, then with full voting rights. But at a price, which was that Lucrezia lost interest in him and in life. But, most of all, in the squalling brat that was her daughter.

Count Ryuchi shook his head sadly, a lion's mane of greying hair brushing the black silk of his shoulders. 'Damn it,' the man tapped black-lacquered nails in irritation against the glass screen of his *escritoire*. No one had asked the woman to fall out of love with him. Or he her. It was just, well . . .

He hadn't realized Lucrezia was so young, so likely to change.

Or to choose death, like that.

Eighteen to his forty-five, he had more than twice her years, ten times her experience. Not hard in a city so resolutely archaic that harpsichord was valued above keyboard, needlework above webweaving.

The richest, most powerful city in the world. A digital data-haven, licencer of off-planet banks, freeport to half the world's luxury drugs, it was also HQ to CySat. Here was where the cultures of the world were *bricolaged*, stripped, fine-tuned. What began as a mere media conglomerate, over a century before, had developed such critical mass that when CSatK Gmb swallowed Sony's SimNet to form CySat no one was surprised. It was the birth of the first true metaNational.

Though what took CySat from simple metaNational to the planet's single richest company was not long-term planning but a single idea, USB. Once hysterical, overpaid live actors had been replaced with streamed, real-time Lotusmorphs nothing but the need for a little extra coding stood in the way of a Universal Sim Backbone.

Birth, sex and death; naked in and naked out. It was all too easy to forget (unless you knew the basic rules) that the Web, CySat and Sims existed not to deliver programmes to the viewers but to offer up viewers to the advertising houses. The USB was merely audience-grabbing in its purest form.

With USB *novelas* could be downsized, to national, even regional levels. Lost virginities, broken hearts, funerals – USB provided the same plotline but with characters tailored for each region. Just code in the preferred Lotusmorph and a hardworking zaibiatsu salaryman with romantic problems in Edo morphed to a fat-but-funny romantically-challenged techie in Seattle or a dour bewhiskered poacher from Tromso with women trouble. In New York, of course, the roles reversed and the salaryman became a Jewish princess with an apartment on West 86th. But USB could handle that, too.

An old Wall Street maxim stated that rich men don't take

hovers, they walk. Well, in newVenice, they sat or strolled through gilded rooms and flower-strewn courtyards. Work itself was delegated, coding to CySat Delhi, character development to CySat TriBeCa, hard news to the C3N departments at CySat London and Berlin, and finance to an off-planet Orbital.

What Lucrezia had wanted from Ryuchi was true simplicity: Japanese wasabi against that sour neoVenetian syrup that demanded Gothic politeness amid exponential architectural extravagance. What she got, Ryuchi realized with regret, picking up a silver-mounted Kodak triD, was a neoVenetian wannabe, already letting his yak-trademark crop grow out into a salt-&-pepper mane by the day of their wedding.

He didn't know that, though, not then. Not what Lucrezia wanted. Though he knew it before the end. But by then it was too late: Lucrezia hated him. Already addicted to crystalMeth, her lovers a string of Arab servants hired from Megrib. Yet it was only after she took out the eyes of Ryuchi's favourite Rodin, turning the dryad's soft marble to powdered calcium with the blade of an antique Mexican knife, that the Japanese count decided she had to go, at his own hands if necessary.

Except that Lucrezia beat him to it.

[Making Now Eternal]

'*Fugu*, for God's sake,' Count Ryuchi sucked at his teeth. It had to be her idea of irony for Lucrezia to poison herself with the raw intestine of a Japanese puffer fish. Not that she'd managed to do it properly. Breaking out of her room to fillet one of his prized fish, only to swallow the wrong piece of its gut. Seven grams of tetradodoxin were all she needed for *ai no nemuri asku*, but Lucrezia bungled even that.

She was dying when he found her that night in his study. She wore his favourite among her nightgowns, the white one with the Maltese lace. Lucrezia's lips already blue, limbs immobile, her body frozen next to his fish tank. Unable to walk, unable even to fall over. Statue-like before he started.

Ryuchi could have taken her to Mount Olive hospital, could have summoned a surgeon, run scans himself using a hand-held mediSoft, but he did none of those things. He didn't regret what he did next. Ryuchi wasn't big on regret. In fact, *unnecessary* regret struck him as one of Europe's less impressive exports.

Ignoring the surveillance cameras – he could afford to: as that month's head of Council only Ryuchi could delete, release or cache the scans, and the recognition software knew he was all-areas authorized – Ryuchi'd carried her dying body down long wooden stairs to the third-floor Armoury Hall, almost running through the deserted corridors in his haste.

The Armoury foundry was empty, its polymer furnaces on standby, ingots of Congo bronze and huge drums of Spanish wax stacked along one redbrick wall. There was UV-sensitive clay too, from Cornwall, a whole marble basin of it, and files, chisels and wooden hammers. All original, all antique.

There was ion-milling apparatus from Mitsubishi, a magnatron fifty-atom splutter-gun for laying down catalytic solder, a Matsui soundsander too, even the latest MIT tek for reversing oxidation, but the Armoury was semi-public so they were all hidden out of sight.

Crafts dead elsewhere flourished under the patronage of CySat. It is the nature of money to buy time. But only the truly rich, truly different, know that the fractal relationship between time and culture can not only be treated and traded like a commodity, it can be suspended, reversed even . . .

But not then.

He wouldn't have saved her life, wouldn't have flushed out her poisoned blood even if he'd had the plasma, drips and tetra-dodoxin-antidote to do it.

Count Ryuchi cut the nightdress from his wife's stiffening body, then pulled her wasted limbs into place, tugging her narrow arms until they hung naturally at her sides. All the while, he rubbed a block of wax into her white, still perfect skin, the wax warming beneath the heat of his fingers until it was pliable enough to smear into or across every crevice or curve of her.

It took the tall man a full hour to rebuild her body, smoothing yellow wax over wasted, anorexia-eaten muscles, building up the *trapezius* of her shoulders, the *quadriceps* and *adductor magnus* of her inner thigh. Stomach and breasts followed, built up with thin strips of wax that the tall man smoothed and pushed into shape until Lucrezia was as he remembered her.

As she once was. As she should have been.

Gritting his teeth, Count Ryuchi thrust an IBM metallurgist's thermometer into her anus – and knew she was still alive from the way her eyelids flickered in shock. Abruptly, he flicked on a nearby screen to check the thermometer was broadcasting and then dug deep into the basin of clay, feeling its oily, slick texture suck against his thin fingers.

The first handful he spread thickly over Lucrezia's mouth. And then the tall man set about finishing the clay cocoon from which his work of art was to arise.

She was dead before he baked her in the oven. At least, Ryuchi assumed she was, for in the final statue her face had softened until its rictus smile was gone and her lips were serene.

He plugged the clay – leaving openings for air, to release the wax or take the bronze – as Jacopo Bellini had first instructed in his banned treatise on bronze work, written 800 years before. Each plug would leave a metal stump that would need filing, either flat or to what ever shape was required.

That he could do later.

Count Ryuchi would have liked the clay case to dry naturally, but that took two days and he had maybe two hours before the Palazzo came back to life. So instead the tall man took a lightwand from a workman's cupboard and ran it swiftly across the outside of the cocoon, making sure light crossed every surface.

It took all of his strength to lift Lucrezia into the idle furnace, more strength than he knew he possessed, but the Count could hardly call for help. So he struggled with her clay cocoon, until it was safely balanced on the furnace's ceramic floor.

Then he shut the glass door to the furnace and set his preferred source of heat from memory, paying particular attention to the readout from the IBM thermometer.

Ryuchi microwaved his wife, radiation setting the clay to a tough shell even as it melted the strips of yellow wax and passed beneath her once perfect skin to melt what little fat anorexia had left in her hyperdermis. Skin bubbled and split like pork rind, dribbles of blood-tinged fat mixed with wax in pools where her reshaped buttocks, hips and stomach had been.

Inside her abdominal cavity, a loop of large intestine ruptured as the intricate loops of her *duodenum*, *jejunum* and *ileum* began to splutter and pop. She was cooking from the inside.

It was – Count Ryuchi realized, checking the temperature – like spontaneous combustion without the spontaneity or the flames. According to the screen's readout Lucrezia had melted like a candle. And like it or not, it was time for the Count to turn off the microwave and knock out the plugs . . .

He did both feet first, suction and viscosity holding in the molten wax, fat and trapped liquid until Count Ryuchi finally knocked out the fontanelle plug at Lucrezia's head, to let boiling grey jelly ooze across the floor of the furnace, slowly at first, then rapidly as an obscene, stinking gush flooded the white tiles with wax, fat and black threads of cooked blood.

Compared with cleaning *that* up, killing his first man had been child's play. Which it was. He'd been thirteen, pissing in a back alley in Sinjuku when a drunken German tourist decided to get over-friendly. All it took was one blow, a razor-sharp *biente-neube* ripped across the gut. Ryuchi could still remember the tourist's look of disbelief as his guts tumbled through the gash in his T-shirt and spilled onto the pavement.

That was the first. Others the Count remembered less well. But this one . . . Oh, he'd remember this one, all right. He might have killed half a dozen people he hated and garotted a woman he never knew. Even, as CySat's Head of Council, ordered the assassination of a man he admired. But killing someone he'd once loved. That was a first.

The Count scooped the congealed, blood-streaked fat into a matter compiler with a spade, where what was left of Lucrezia was swiftly broken down into her component atoms. Let the machine make of that what it would. The Count was sure his wife wasn't the first person to disappear that way.

The Drexie box was discreetly hidden behind a gilded panel, not because CySat's executive disapproved of matter compilers (though they did) but for aesthetic reasons. It was a simple matter of style.

Everything always was . . .

Count Ryuchi shivered, glancing again at the statue. That was how Karo's mother was remembered now. Perfect, naked, cast in bronze in the style of Rodin. Only in the neuron blizzard of

Ryuchi's cortex, in the synaptic fractal flowers that fed his limbic system, did her living skeleton still stand, frozen against a table, one of his prized *fugu* crudely gutted on a marble table.

To the rest of them Lucrezia *was* her statue, its bronze skin warm in the early afternoon light. Even her proportions were perfect, the questioning turn of her head, the uncertainty in her step, the very way she looked almost off balance . . .

A doctor signed a death certificate for a body he never saw, and so signed his own without knowing it. And then Ryuchi had weighed down an empty coffin with his wife's prize collection of antique books and had it buried at San Michele. Her coffin escorted by all twelve members of the Council. To be interred with tears and speeches from Lucrezia's godfather, the archbishop. The ceremony watched over by Count Orsela.

Her brother.

Count Ryuchi smiled. As presiding CySat CEO, current Head of Council and Aurelio's uncle by marriage, he was already late for Friday's formal lunch. Intentional, of course. But all the same, he wouldn't want to miss it, or his weekly feud with Orsela.

Besides, last night Orsela had announced to the Council his plans for handling the levels, as if ditching that floating barrio were really possible, and this afternoon's discussion was likely to prove interesting. Vicious, borderline polite, but interesting all the same.

The *Palazzo Ducale* was officially classified as Byzantine Gothic, but with its marble crenellation and elaborate façade tiled in geometric pink-and-white it came across more like an Arab fort ripped from the sands of the Megrib, set down where the Pacific straddles the Tropic of Cancer, midway between Hawaii and Taiwan.

It looked, as Razz never tired of telling everybody, like a piece of sugar-coated shit.

Inside a chamber hung with age-darkened paintings of plump women with bare breasts, Aurelio frowned as his door swung open. He took a deep breath, ready to shout . . .

He'd been out of sorts since breakfast. Evidence of just how badly the boy was sulking rested on a brass-topped table beside his favorite Moroccan-leather beanbag. *Fugazza di fichi*, uncut, untouched, its top lightly dusted with icing sugar as pure and white as the finest organic cocaine.

'Shhh!' The silver woman had a finger up to her mouth. She checked her pockets, ignored the pearl-handled shockblade and let her fingers close on a Dime bar from a street stall near Maurizio. They'd know she'd been feeding him sucrose as soon as that evening's urine tests came in, but what the hell. It wasn't as if they could do anything . . .

'Hey, Honey!'

Razz tossed the brown-and-black bar into the air.

Aurelio caught it, grinned the grateful, uncertain smile of the over-protected, and ripped its wrapper off with his teeth. He liked Razz. Liked his cousin Karo too, but Razz was funnier. He still couldn't work out why she didn't get cold without proper clothes, but maybe it was something to do with her skin. He'd asked Count Ryuchi yesterday if he could be tattooed silver when he grew up. From the horrified expression on his uncle's face, Aurelio didn't think it would be likely.

As always, Razz had bare legs with a blackglass throwing knife somehow Velcroed in place on her outer right thigh. A floating-breech Browning automatic was hung on a neophrene cord round her neck, and her eyes were hidden behind laser-proof shades. Aurelio was far too young to know what the words meant, but the whole effect was studiedly, pointedly retro.

On top Razz wore nothing under an Issuki Marino bolero jacket that shimmered and changed colours if he looked closely. At first Aurelio had liked to glance at Razz's breasts when she wasn't looking, but now he preferred to watch her strange jacket. Besides, Aurelio wasn't bothered by Razz's nakedness, even though it wasn't like that of the plump women in the pictures. Razz was how she was, he was used to it.

When he'd first asked Razz what it was made from she'd said 'bugs and intelligent spider's web'. And when he'd laughed, she'd frowned and made Aurelio try to tear the cloth. It was soft and stretchy, and impossibly tough. He'd tried cutting it with his toy sword, without effect.

Now he believed her, that lots of little bugs could grow cloth.

'Light,' Razz demanded and the yttrium-hydride windows took up hydrogen atoms, switching to clear as their glass lost its oily metallic sheen. There were curtains, of course, huge swathes of red velvet. But Aurelio preferred gadgets, most kids did. Mind you, so did she . . .

'So tell me, Honey,' Razz said lightly, sinking onto the big red cushion beside him. 'What gives?'

Aurelio looked at the paused tri-D of *Lucifer's Dragon* and scowled. A gout of dragon-flame was stopped in mid-air, which was just as well for the Archangel's will to win was about to flicker and go out.

The dragon didn't actually exist, of course. It was a fuzzy-logic, three-dimensional, digital construct, its design stolen straight from Davioud's huge war memorial at the Place St Michel in Paris and then given a Celtic twist. Not that either of them knew that, or would have cared.

'The dragon's winning.' Aurelio pushed the last of the Dime bar into his mouth, and began to lick slivers of chocolate off the inside of its wrapper. 'And it always wins, stupid shitty thing . . .'

'Shouldn't swear,' Razz said automatically.

'You do,' insisted the boy. 'Anyway,' he added, a fierce frown crossing his narrow nine-year-old face. 'I'm the Doge, I can do what I want.' He rolled sideways off his bag of red quilted leather and went to retrieve his Sega headband. As he did so, a miniaturized Aero-Spatiale K19 camSat whirred gently into life and began to follow him at the prescribed twelve places. If Aurelio knew it was there, he didn't let it show.

Razz shrugged. Courage came in different forms: that was his.

'My hair looks stupid,' the Doge said suddenly. He was back on his bag, cramming the Sega band onto his head, narrow fingers pushing on blond curls which tumbled in a waterfall to the green velvet of his miniature frock coat.

What the boy'd been doing, Razz realized, was checking his reflection in the lenses of her mirror shades. She shook her head. 'No, it doesn't,' she said, knowing it did. A quick glance round the room revealed something Razz should have realized when she walked in.

'No mirrors,' Aurelio confirmed. 'They've gone. I'm not allowed mirrors anymore, in case I get more self-c—' He paused, still ignoring the small, floating camera hovering in the air above him, and the silver woman knew without having to ask, that the kid was terminally self-conscious already. Who wouldn't be with every move recorded to computer?

'It's okay, Honey,' said Razz, watching his eyes fill with tears. 'It doesn't matter. You want a mirror, I'll bring you one.' The little shit deserved a break. It wasn't easy being Doge of newVenice, titular head of the world's only media freeport . . . Which reminded her, Chang Mao should have completed mixing the bulletin.

'Back in a click,' Razz told the boy, rising from his side with the lazy grace of a sleepy predator. 'Then I'll show you how to beat the shit out of that bloody dragon.'

If Chang Mao was worried about getting his bulletin uploaded on time it didn't show as he stood in the doorway of Aurelio's chamber. Nothing did, except the wide glare of his grey eyes and his bared teeth which were drawn back in the rictus smile of the momentarily insane. Drops of sweat oozed from the pores of his sallow face and the air was sharp with the acrid stink of running urine.

He'd pissed himself.

WeGuard or not, she was going to have to slap him. Razz was still staring in disgust at the darkening patch on Chang Mao's clone-cotton trousers when the techie produced a stripped-down Uzi ceramic from behind his back and let rip.

Razz flipped sideways, too late and too slowly.

The first three slugs hit her in the gut, spinning a trail of spider silk after them which any competent surgeon could have unwound to extract the bullets through their entrance wound. If that had been all, Razz might have lived, she might even have been able to fight back using the Browning instinct had already placed in her hand. But it wasn't all . . .

The fourth slug was hollow-point plastic, drilled with a hair-thin phosfex core that ignited on impact. The controlled explosion blew purple handfuls of shredded small intestine out through the lacerated walls of what had been her lower back. Razz could smell the sweet richness of her blood and above it the stench of her own shit. As she hit the marble floor she saw a red cloud growing above her, and without realizing it watched herself begin to die.

'No,' she shouted. Not at the *WeGuard* still busy suffering the full effects of his screen-induced fit-trigger, but at the Doge. But her voice wouldn't come and besides Aurelio would never have heard her over his own scream of fury.

The last thing the silver woman saw before a rush of darkness enveloped her was the Chinese lieutenant lifting his Uzi to the head of the small charging boy.

Then she awoke.

In Zurich.

[Bombing the freeBase]

Reaching the *TripleHelix* meant dodging through the UV-lit reaches of *PolyRiptides*, trying to avoid as many wall-bouncing, out-of-their head drum'N'freebase addicts as possible. Kinetic energy and the laws of Brownian motion ensured this wasn't as many as the girl would have liked. Not when the grooveRyders hit the floor, their heartbeats already running and wired into a floor-to-ceiling B&O betaB sound stack.

And if you didn't feel jungle-sick when you went in, you sure as hell did when you came out. 'Cos the Ryders got off on the dubious delights of 140 bpm sonic cosh, sound waves so fast, so dense that they curdled your cerebral fluid.

Then it was straight up a ladder bolted to the wall, onto a short gantry and in through a steel door open for so long it was rusted on its hinges. Soviet steel was never that good in the first place.

As befit a tek brothel, home to hardwire fetishists, the *Triple-Helix* had walls of buckled steel, an Ultra-tuf vinyl floor sprayed direct onto what had once been a rusting deck and cilia-coated smart tables, whose smartness consisted of an ability to dump their own crumbs onto the floor.

On the wall behind the bar was a carbon-fibre bat, an electronic whip that didn't work and a large, garish tri-D of Santa Passionata, halo of fire round her head, green eyes turned upwards towards the distant stars and satellites.

The room was dirty, noisy and always crowded.

But then that was life on the levels.

The bar itself was sheet zinc, staple-gunned to a hundred-year-old, rock-hard strip of extinct hardwood. Its top was crowded with heavy-bottomed glasses, handblown from pale green re-recycled glass. Most were empty, the full ones were clutched firmly in the hands of the *TripleHelix*'s punters. Two earthenware bowls held what could have been olives. They were dark, vaguely oval and tasted strongly of salt.

They smelt of salt too, not that anyone could identify the tang of brine over the stink of beer, bad cologne and cheap synthetic pheromone, the kind kinderWhores used to pull in trade.

Not that the *TripleHelix* needed to advertise. The number of nervous, slumming CySat suits with *rori-con* complex staggered everyone but Sabine, who catered for all tastes from dark to dangerous. And now the kinder were all over-age what could the NVPD do? What they always did: take a cut.

There were only three windows to the bar, on the long wall away from the entrance gantry, each one small and round, no bigger than a man's head. Someone, years before, had arc-welded them shut and fitted brass bars over the top. Whoever did it needn't have bothered. The ship had once been a Soviet whaler; its porthole glass was two inches thick and would have easily stopped a bullet.

The whaler rested where it had berthed itself more than a century before, bolted to another ship on its landside, its other side still naked to the Pacific Ocean. Occasionally new ships tried to graft there, though not many. Immigrants still came but, by now, most had skimmed the *Rough Guide*'s web-entry to the neoVenetian levels. And if the newcomers didn't know about the *TripleHelix* they learnt soon enough that ships which tried to berth alongside got cut adrift and flamed.

The Countess saw to that. So old that no one knew how old, a Vampyre for so long that some whispered Sabine was real, not genetically elective. Her reputation alone was enough to keep order. At least, what passed for it out on the levels. She was seen infrequently, and when she was someone always regretted it.

Sabine owned the *TripleHelix* and its polyfoam-slabbed row of bedding-stalls in the cabins above, probably owned *PolyRiptides* too, come to that. And she ran not just the Vampyre klans out at

San Michele but the Rori too, kinderWhores genetically-backed-out, perpetual pubescents. Sexual magnets to jaded CySat salary-men, to those in need of innocence. Except that naivety could be broken, wasted or lost – but never willingly sold. By definition, self-marketing commodities cannot be innocent. But that didn't stop Sabine's brothel being one of District III's biggest draws.

Along the water wall, where the windows were, a line of ancient Sega games machines stood flashing and squeaking. Each one with a sensor to alert the machine when a possible punter was passing by. Since the *TripleHelix* was always crowded and the windows' view to the distant ocean outside acted like a magnet to the drunk, dusted-out and homesick, even to those for whom the *Helix* was home, the machines mewled a twenty-four-hour litany of challenges and entreaties. One that the regulars had long since learnt to ignore. Who needed behind-glass graphix when there were tri-Ds to play? Not Paco, who'd been using the *Helix* as home for as long as he could remember, dossing down in the bedding-stalls on a polyfoam slab whenever one became free.

Feet thrust into a pair of Ice-sole ReeBs two sizes too big, wearing fake Levis, a long black Muji T-shirt, cut from paper, his neck hung round with brightly-coloured talismans, Paco was unaugmented, at least so far as anyone could tell. What's more, Paco was a natural, a fuck baby; carried to term, not a rubber womb in sight. It gave him a certain kudos at the *TripleHelix*, enough to get away with using Sabine's bar as the home he'd never had.

Paco shifted on his stool and watched a young, hypertense girl in too-smart street leathers hammer the newest tri-D into sub-mission. Her paper-thin jacket was a tattered mass of zips and velcros, but the scuffs across the back were too regular, too ordered. Paco knew a fake when he saw one.

Not that he'd have said that to her. The aggression radiating from the girl's shuddering body was so palpable it could have had a thousand-year half-life.

The tatty Sony helmet she wore was real, though, but then it came from the bar and had *TriHex* stencilled roughly across the side.

Mind you, that was the only crude thing about it. Upgrade chips and small nuggets of crystal RAM were layered neatly in a row along the front. This was no cheap floating-focus affair from the States: whatever was happening was happening in her head, where the constantly moving images directed straight onto her optic nerve met the lightning-fast reactions of her brain.

But because the machine was fresh, imported from last November's Shoshinkai exhibition in Edo, a hard-edged triD image also played above the console's flat surface, reflected onto holovid screens around the bar, unseen by the girl but watched intently by almost everyone else. In fact, the bar had fallen silent, or as silent as the *TripleHelix* ever got, given the cajoling cries and constant invitations of the other, unused machines.

The low, black Sony was epoxied to a small metal table that seemed to sprout, mushroom-like, ready-welded, from the floor. Behind the girl's helmeted head was a round window showing the steady rise and fall of the sea, but for once there were no dusted-out wave-crazies staring at the swell. Even the hardened regulars were busy watching a wounded Dragon being backed towards the edge of a cliff by a triumphant and bored Gabriel.

'Shit, she's good,' Paco whispered admiringly, more to himself than to anyone else. It sounded the sort of thing an adult might say. Some whore in a sleeveless red-leather jerkin with not much at all on underneath smiled at him, and bent briefly to rumple Paco's untidy crop of fair hair. She was adult, not kinder, but that was fine with him. He had no problem with whores of either kind. As she bent forward, Paco dropped his blue eyes to devour the swell of heavy breasts revealed as far down as her rouged nipples.

'Little sod,' the woman's mothering caress turned into a lazy swipe that the boy dodged easily. She grinned, Paco already forgotten.

'Shit . . .'

A low collective moan went through the room. The Dragon had launched a blinding counter-attack, teleporting in and out of his mountainside in puffs of blue smoke. Appearing first behind Gabriel and then, when the Archangel swung round, behind him again. There wasn't quite fear in the face of the Angel, but the bland arrogance was gone, replaced by grim determination. As the Dragon attacked again, it was the Archangel who fell back, almost tumbling over the edge, feet scrabbling for a grip. Any further back and it would be Void.

'Do it,' Paco urged, rubbing his Izanami talisman for luck. It was used up, dead under his fingers, but he rubbed it anyway.

'Use a special,' Paco screamed. A group of drunken salarymen cursed at him, but Paco snarled right back, wolfBoy style. He had as much right to be there as them. More. He lived in the Third District: suits were just tolerated for their credit. And if any were still around when curfew came down at TwoZeroZero, well, then they deserved whatever happened – which usually involved *throat*, *knife* and *canal* somewhere in the sequence. How else had Paco got his Ice-sole ReeBs?

'Do it, sod you,' Paco yelled, and then the leather-clad girl did, though it was doubtful that she could hear him, or would care if she could.

In a sequence that began with a forward roll and somehow joined together every *Lucifer's Dragon* jinx move Paco had ever seen and at least six he hadn't, the girl hamstrung the Dragon with a short molyBlade, sliced open its chest and then ripped the moly across both the Dragon's leathery wings before breaking its neck with a single scissor kick.

Outright admiration for her skill was tempered by the certain knowledge that newVenice's central games' processor had logged every move, would already be computing a defence. Anyone who tried that exact sequence tomorrow would die.

Lucifer's Dragon was Learning Curve Gmb's best-selling product ever. A multi-level, self-perpetuating, true three-dimensional trawl through the harrowing of hell and the apocalypse.

Its semi-AI, ADLIB9 game engine was coded so the machine learnt immediately not to repeat its own failures. That was why going up against the dragon was so difficult. Anyone who wanted could play *with* the dragon, but to play against the dragon and win you had to play against an echo of yourself.

The number of people who could do that successfully had just gone up by one. That winning sequence would make the Sports section of next morning's newsfeed, but it was probably already circulating in pirate copies, uploaded by Ishies in the crowd. It would be studied and analyzed, until gameheads the globe over knew just how the fuck it had been done. The sequence might not work again; in fact, that it wouldn't was cast-iron guaranteed. But a variation might.

Paco had come in too late to see the girl before she helmeted up. So he was shocked by how normal she looked as she slipped it off and shook out her rough shoulder-length black curls. Brown-speckled eyes, no coloured contacts, no genetic tricks. Lips that were slightly too thin. Skin that was pale, from lack of light, not accident of birth; and not paper-white, like the charnel-house pallor of a Vampyre or drakul.

It was the mole on her left cheek that gave her away. Anyone, even someone as poor as Paco, could afford basic laser surgery, even if it was from some street stall. And Paco changed his hair style every month or so, had been through three eye colours in three years and was as yet undecided whether to go for a melanin-boost that would set off his fair hair or get an all-over skin bleach – something high-Goth.

Either the girl was unaware of the blemish, which seemed unlikely, or was stubborn enough not to mind, which was possible, or she belonged to one of those Midwestern religious sects that proclaimed cosmetic surgery the devil's work and all enhancements vanity. Paco counted out the religious angle. If the Movers and Shakers thought surgery evil, it was nothing to the blind hatred they felt for triDs in general and *Lucifer's Dragon* in particular.

Which left being unaware or being stubborn. From the set of her jaw and the way she glared round at the crowd, it could well be the latter. If Paco didn't know better, he'd have thought she was close to tears.

'Got a fucking problem?' she snarled, her voice amphetamine-rough, like some belladonna street-kid doomed to a tragic end in a CySat sim.

'Got a what?' Paco and the red-jerkined whore grinned at each other. An accent that rough might fool slumming salarymen, but Paco lived on the levels, and most everyone he knew spoke Japanese or an ornate hybrid of alphabet city and hidalgo Spanish. Both were formal languages – it was only the girlKats, the NVPD and the rich who swore with ease.

'Well . . . ?' The kid glared round the room. 'Fucking have you?'

No answers.

She'd long since given up expecting any. What was it Razz said? 'As long as I'm acting I might as well do a good job of it . . .' Well, look where that had got Razz.

Shrugging, the girl slammed a smartcard into a slot in the tri-D. If this didn't fuck-over the Dragon, nothing would . . . Her shoulders were hunched, and she was crying now, openly. The machine blinked and blotted out the Dragon for a second, but her card was accepted. Seconds later, the tri-D spat it back at her, having credited her the money due for defeating the Dragon. And having itself just been infected with a fuzzy-logic subroutine, not so much a virus as Jericho fever. She was going to bring the fucking walls down.

'Shit.' The girl stared around her in open contempt. 'What a sodding dump.' Still crying, she launched herself towards the door, pushing aside punters and regulars. It didn't help that her card was gold, drawn against Hong Kong Suisse.

Show time: Paco could feel it coming. As hot as the tingle from a fully-charged Izanami. He caressed the thin spear point that hung from a cord round his neck. Dead, completely empty – he needed credit to get his talisman refilled. Life wasn't so much fun without hyperfocus. Still, Paco had a feeling he'd soon be able to buy himself a bit more good luck.

Over in the far corner a short-haired black Kat was getting lazily to her feet, stretching slowly, her breasts full above a belly swollen with kits. Not that belly or breasts would hinder her in a fight. Kats didn't give you their names, so Paco didn't know her's, but he'd seen her kill before and it was sweetly violent.

Go with the Kat, go with the girl? The girl, Paco decided. He wouldn't want to risk putting one past the Kat. Paco wondered if the leather-clad girl knew how close she was to getting her throat taken out, and decided not. How could she?

It was time to take the girl down, and in public. As she shouldered past Paco, he tripped heavily and grabbed at the back of her expensive jacket, one scything leg clipping the back of her ankle – dropping her heavily to the steel deck. Even Paco winced at the crash.

Somebody laughed, and the Kat halted, hissed softly and then joined in. The girl was old news. Interest had moved on to a pirate shockjock who'd just spliced himself into newV's main CySat feed, and was broadcasting citywide a rundown of rumours about what might have happened to the Doge.

The police would get him for that, Paco had no doubt. Someone would be backtracking his datastream, chasing it down. And then CySat or *WeGuard* would put a call through to the NVPD. He'd be gone.

Disparu.

Smiling apologetically, Paco helped the foul-mouthed girl to her feet.

'Sorry,' he said, 'so sorry.' With one small hand he brushed at the soft black leather of her coat, cleaning away the dust and grit from the floor. A few more falls like that and the scuffs would be for real.

'That was on purpose, you little fuck!' The girl was furious, tears backed up in her eyes, close to meltdown. Paco worked hard at looking offended, and redoubled his efforts to brush dirt from her jacket. All the while working his hand closer to the purse hung enticingly at her left hip.

Deftly, Paco palmed his blade. And with a single sweep of a ceramic razor severed the neophrene strap, the blade's mono-molecular edge cutting effortlessly through the strap's reinforced mesh.

'Hey, fuckhead . . .' The girl made a quick grab for Paco but it was too late. Jinking sideways, Paco dodged her frantic lunge and slid under a table, rolling out the other side. He was out of there, high-tailing it through the jeering crowd, her curses following after him as he ran for the ladder down to *PolyRiptides*.

Not that he got that far.

The blow that stopped Paco lifted the small blond boy up off his feet and threw him back into the stunned crowd. Half of the mailed fist had caught his chin, the other half had crushed his bottom lip.

'*Owwww*.' Paco could already taste the salt-burst inside his mouth before he even hit the floor. Rolling into a ball, Paco felt at the split lip with the tip of his tongue. It was so numb it could've have been iced-out on crystalMeth, but Paco knew it was just split and getting more bloody by the second.

The boy didn't need to ask who'd thrown the punch. He knew. Towering above him was a blue NVPD uniform. Standard anti-ballistic cloth, a keratin heart-pad bonded across the chest, kevlar-reinforced elbows, knees and turned-up collar. Helmet with its guard up. Neophrene boots studded along the soles with sharpened rivets. An anti-riot baton hung from a belt, a 50,000-volt electric taser held lightly in one leather-gloved hand.

Paco wasn't interested in the man inside: the NVPD uniform told him all he needed to know. He unrolled swiftly and tried to crawl into the safety of the sea of legs surrounding him but managed no more than a few steps before the baton came down, catching him squarely above his hip, sinking deep into the boy's kidney. Paco yelped with pain like a dog, and wet himself copiously.

'Don't,' begged Paco, 'please, don't . . .' He was crying without realizing it.

The follow-up blow never fell. Before the officer had time to bring his baton down again, the girl was in there. One hand reaching up to stop the baton's downward swing, her other back-handing the officer squarely across his mouth.

Everything stopped. Even the cop looked shocked.

[On The Level]

The Zeiss-eyed Ishie camming the scene was so stunned, he shook
his head in wonder, ruining the shot. Not that it mattered. At least
two other metal heads were busy with eyecams, anxious to be the
first to upload their own private news feed.

'*You!*' The girl spat through clenched teeth.

Angeli blinked. Not that anyone noticed.

Me what? As far as Angeli knew, he'd never met her before in
his life. Young, Asiatic, aggressive, half-dressed – Angeli had a
feeling he might remember.

'*Just stay out of my fucking way.*' The girl hissed the words at
him, quietly. But there was enough venom in them to kill a rattler.
She was shaking with rage, real burning anger. Not a dust-out,
because she didn't look the type. But something other than his
slapping a kid around was clicking her synapse at double speed.
There was more. There had to be.

The girl looked the cop full in the face, which wasn't advisable
out in the levels where the NVPD could pull your Social and wipe
your access to free food at a single keystroke. Slop was meant to
be an inalienable right, but people had a way of falling off the
register.

Very slowly, the NVPD officer pulled off a glove and put his
fingers to his lip. It was split. Not turned inside out like the boy's,
but split all the same. The man looked at the red smear smudged
wetly across his fingers and then back at the girl. When he moved,
it was so quick Paco only saw the first and the final blow. The
stuff in the middle was just a blur.

Only nothing landed. The boron-fibre nightstick spun

39

impotently through the air, and every time its weighted end struck at where the girl should have been she was somewhere else. It was the cop who stood shaking when the sequence came to an end. His breath was laboured, his cold brown eyes bitter with rage.

The girl wasn't even out of breath.

Her contemptuous eyes skimmed from his face to the blank space on his collar and the empty slot in his keratin heart-pad. Regulations said all NVPD personnel should be barcoded at all times. Paco could have told her that rules like that didn't apply out in the levels, but he didn't get a chance and she wouldn't have listened.

Karo DiOrchi listened to no one, especially not now. Karo had liked Razz, liked the Doge too, come to that. Even if the blond, blue-eyed little shit was everything she wasn't, starting with wanted.

She knew the man in front of her, even if he didn't know her. She'd left the Palazzo Ducale, run back to her family's own palazzo before this man was summoned by her father; so that Ryuchi could tell both Orsela and Beijing that police had attended the scene of the crime but found *nada*. Because that was what they did find.

Karo felt in her jacket pocket for her molywire. It was there all right, cleaned off after use as Razz had taught her. But the Mexican knife wasn't. Ancient, elegant and now missing, she'd left it stuck into the *WeGuard*. Karo used to wonder when it had last been used. Now, she knew, only too well. Knew, too, the precinct of the NVPD officer patsied by her father into 'examining' the crime scene.

Which was how she found herself a week later in a Sega SimBar, in one of the rougher outer ghettos, an area definitely no-go to girls of her background. Not to mention found herself up against one of NVPD's finest, who had no idea who she was, and judging from the sour set of his bleeding mouth was probably too hyped on NVPD blues to care.

'Your ID number.' The girl demanded coldly. It was bluff, but the NVPD bull didn't know that. She wasn't going to report him when she got home. It didn't take a genius to figure she hadn't got a home to go to, not now. Somehow, meeting her father wasn't the first thing on Karo's mind.

Her street-smart accent was gone, though. Replaced with a voice rich with echoes of those gilded rooms he'd been allowed to visit only as a servant. Its diamond tones whispered of warm wind through secluded palazzo courtyards and cool spray from marble fountains.

The NVPD officer said nothing. But his furious eyes were taking in the cost of her street leathers, her expensive confidence, the fact she wore only one simple gold stud per ear. Echoing through his mind was the cool, dismissive tone of the Count as he thanked the Lieutenant for his time and regretted politely that the NVPD officer hadn't been better able to deduce anything from a murder scene where the marble tiles had already been sterilized to surgical standards.

For once, Lieutenant Angeli Rispoli thought before acting. Mostly he thought about losing his job in the Third District. It wasn't something he was going to let happen.

'Your ID card, please.' He demanded, holding out his hand.

They looked at each other and Angeli smiled. It was meant to be the cold, patronizing smile of a cop who has better things to do than humour little rich kids. Which was exactly how it came out.

Karo flushed. 'Your number,' she demanded, still meeting his eyes.

'Of course,' Angeli said flatly. 'After I've checked your ID.' He held out his hand again. 'If you'd just let me have your card.'

It was a stand-off. And Paco wasn't about to stay around to see how it ended. He had a pretty good idea. The girl would back quietly towards the ladder and the cop would let her. Not that either had much face left to save. Paco would've liked to be there to see the show through to its end, but he couldn't afford to. He didn't want to be around when the girl realized he still had her purse.

[History Happens, Like It or Not]

Santa Passionata protect us . . .

And she did too, didn't she? Angeli sighed and took another hit from a Sandoz inhaler. A strip of clear instant skin ran across the split in his lip, enzymes in its protein/polymer coating already knitting together damaged cells. It was amazing what a difference three days could make.

He was downloading an illegal Sim, *Saints & Synners*. And the sim was good, class coding, near-perfect. It even smelt like history, or at least how Angeli assumed history would smell, hazy with carbon monoxide and clogged with dust. But it still didn't make sense. But then maybe history never did, unless you were there . . .

'*In the beginning . . .*' What? A whole city was built by some spoilt little rich kid? newVenice grew, at the start of the previous century, out of the dream of some druggie New York/West Coast Mafia moll's daughter?

How do you describe that, like shit, CySat just happened: born out of the founding of newVenice, a global accident, serendipity written as fucking code? Especially when the whole world knew this island was the vision of Santa Passionata. Founder, patron of the poor, all-round saint . . .

Angeli sighed and reached into his pocket for a strip of paraDerm, popping one from the pack and slapping it onto the underside of his wrist. In the space of a week he'd been patronized half to death by CySat's executive, caught on *good Newz/badNewz* looking dumb-fuck ineffectual and been shown up by some little electro TKD-trained brat out slumming for the evening. And she *was* out slumming.

43

He could recognize computer-taught Tai Kwan Do when he met it. The clarity of line, the cleanness of her moves let Angeli know she'd been trained not by a human *sensei* but by a computer, in a Fujibishi *dojo*. Every one of her actions scanned by photoelectric cells, the leading edges of her fluid body fed back in a loop to her brain, until her subconscious knew where she was even when she was moving too fast for surface knowledge.

That took heavy credit. In fact, until he'd seen the little bitch in action, Angeli hadn't even realized there was a Fujibishi *dojo* outside the Imperial police compound in Edo. Not that he'd have known if one had reached the city, Angeli reminded himself heavily.

The Chinese guard policed newVenice proper. And that included responsibility for overseeing Niponshi's lumbering airships, the only craft allowed to overfly the city. Except the unloading of pods at Arsenale didn't need overseeing, it was fully automated already. No. The NVPD were just there to keep order in the levels. People like him only got invited into the city if one of the Council thought they might be useful, like last Friday.

Angeli's big chance which turned out not to be. Angeli wasn't stupid. Vicious, addicted to Ice, inured to violence . . . Sure, he accepted that, it went with the territory and at least he knew what *inured* meant. Come to that, he could read and what was more he did . . . But not stupid, he wasn't that.

Maybe that tall Japanese shit in the fancy clothes already knew who'd half taken the head off that *WeGuard* with a moly wire and then knifed the body, and maybe he didn't. Maybe the surveillance cameras wiped themselves and the servants cleaned the floor by accident. And then again, maybe not. The one thing Angeli understood only too well was that he, Angeli, wasn't meant to find out what had happened. No matter what was said, what was promised.

He was there for show only. It hadn't taken much to spot the little comSat that trailed him as he trudged round the immaculate room looking for clues that weren't there. That hung above his shoulder as he examined the man's lacerated neck and cut away the guard's coat to take a mediSoft reading from the stab wound. All of that, all of it, had been part of last Saturday morning's broadcast. CySat's insurance with Beijing that they weren't trying to hide anything. That every effort was being made to solve the crime.

Hell, they'd even brought in a real NVPD officer from the levels, an uncouth, grimy-handed career policeman and made him a Vice-Questore, given him free fucking access to CySat's headquarters, to Santa Passionata's own city. He was the proof.

Yeah, right.

Free access for all of one morning, to a crime scene already cleared, for a murder he wasn't meant to solve. Well, he had news for the fucking Council. He was busy running a polymerase chain reaction on a foreign DNA fragment taken from inside the stab wound. Give him time enough and he'd have not just a DNA profile but a face as well.

Angeli could do it, too. All right, he wasn't good with machines, at least not ones that didn't stun or kill. And it wouldn't be elegant and it wouldn't be easy, but he'd already started to teach himself to navigate the city's datacore. Whether they wanted it or not, Angeli was going to solve this crime. Even if he had to do it long distance, without access to the city itself.

Let *WeGuard* and CySat's department of human resources deal with whatever day-to-day trouble barely rippled the surface of the CySat palazzos that lined the Canale Grande. The crime readout for this murder gave him not just a fragment of foreign DNA but an unusual blade profile. And a molywire wound unlike anything he'd seen. This wasn't a simple garotte: that wire had been in motion when it cut – flicked and pulled.

Blade profile, DNA and moly technique, he'd fed them all to a webSmart, sending it into *nV*'s database to tag whatever looked relevant and bring it back. Murder wasn't difficult to understand. As desires went it was one of the most basic, hardwired human emotions. What troubled Angeli was why the Council didn't want the murder solved.

But then, so did the fact that every time he launched a *smartbot* into the intraNet to get information on that DNA profile it got killed. So he was doing what good officers did when they got stuck: going back to the beginning. Right back.

To a history Sim so illegal it wasn't even listed on the index of proscribed titles. To a Thai street-thief named Kwai and his meeting, over a hundred years before, with Jim Chance, briefly mule for a Medellin cartel.

Lieutenant Angeli hit his choline enhancer again, wished for the tenth time he hadn't given up coffee and restarted *Saints & Synners*. It didn't matter that he was safely inside the grey micromesh walls of the Third Precinct, that there were flatscreens and tri-Ds, floating-focus Zeiss dataspecs, even an old set of Fuji 'trodes.

Angeli was NVPD. He was used to downloading his information from a helmet.

[Santa Passionata/Saints & Sinners . . .]

'Jezussssss . . . Wake up and smell that shit.' Jim Chance was in Bangkok and he didn't like it at all. But then Jim Chance didn't like anything much, starting with the early twenty-first century.

The weather in Bangkok was too hot, the city stank and he was bored. But then, Jim Chance only had another four hours to kill before check-in at BIA for his plane back to San Francisco. So what the hell, he'd live . . .

Strolling across the floating walkways of a vegetable market, it occurred to Jim how he might spend the dollars he'd earned muling blank Swiss bank drafts from Boston to Bangkok.

He'd already bought a gold Patek Phillipe for his wife. He didn't like the bitch much, but then the watch was fake and had cost him less than $20, so that didn't matter.

And there was no point buying her a real one: Kelly couldn't have told the difference anyway. That was one of many things Jim hated about her. That and her whining, small-town Midwest accent and attitude.

Shit . . . If ever a man needed an easy divorce. But hell, no . . . Her daddy was a lawyer. Jim Chance wiped sweat from his eyes and forehead, up onto hair which hung in a limp black ponytail. He had three silver studs in his left ear, two rings of turquoise and Navaho silver on his left hand. He liked silver, and the Navaho rings were large and heavy, good for punching. And punching was what he wanted to do every time he thought of Kelly.

The air was already as hot as an oven, damp like a flannel and it was still early morning. And if yesterday was anything to go by, the humidity was easily going to top ninety per cent. Added to which, this so-called famous market stank like a Louisiana cesspit.

Jim was crossing another walkway, wooden slats held in place on either side by three strands of rope wound in and out like a hundred-yard plait. Walkways criss-crossed the water's dark surface, solid enough when they traversed the deck of a flower boat, but unsteady and nerve-shredding when they dipped down over the oil-stained surface of the basin.

When he smiled, it was the smile of someone with occasional access to large sums of money and a fussy Californian dentist. His teeth were over-white, too neatly capped, and they gleamed in the early morning sun when he grinned. Which he did now. Jim had ideas, lots of them. Occasionally, he even followed one through, if he remembered it later . . .

Genius, thought Jim. He looked round again at the boats, imagining the same thing done many times larger, preferably somewhere civilized like the Florida Keys or Cuba, now it was back under US protection.

Reaching into the inside pocket of his black leather jacket, Jim pulled out his answer to dopehead memory: a brand new Psion organizer, neatly stitched into a red-leather cover, a real one-off. Kelly's Patek Phillipe might be fake but the custom-finished Psion was very definitely the real thing, even though every other stall offered fakes at a fraction of the price.

Fingers stumbling over its tiny keyboard, Jim keyed in his plan. The latest of many. Seven or eight small vessels, each roughly the size of a Staten Island ferry, wired together for stability and let out in small units, say a liquor bar here, an anything-goes cat-house there, with the top deck given over to gambling.

Hell, floating liquor joints had worked back in Prohibition. Why not now?

He knew more than enough people who'd be interested in coming in on a venture like that. But he'd start with the firm he muled for, if only to show them he wasn't the loser they thought. Fuck Cuba. He could even suggest putting the boats just outside the territorial limit of the California courts, make one of them a restaurant, with out-in-the-open, all-areas smoking.

Jim smiled, flicked a strand of black hair out of green eyes and palmed a Lucky Strike, lighting it with a disposable bic. The filter's dry paper glued the cigarette to his damp bottom lip and hung it there, for all the world like he'd been practising. Gunmetal-grey smoke curled up the contours of his face, making his eyes sting, but Jim didn't mind. He had firm ideas about what counted as cool.

Others might think it an insult, but Jim prided himself on still being a slacker long after it went out of fashion, doing what he did best. Living the elegant life on someone else's . . . The thought, which took Jim's hand from picking at one nail to gently patting his jacket pocket, was so instinctive that Jim didn't even know he'd done it. But the boy watching him did, and knew what it signified. Kwai had watched an endless succession of foreign tourists and travellers go through the same revealing ritual. Look around, admire the view, get nervous, tap their wallet for safety.

A remix of Ghost's *LamaRabiRabi* kicking round in his head, Kwai looked critically at the sleazy jumble of boats, their wooden decks splintered with neglect, their garish golds and reds sun-peeled, and wondered for the hundredth time what Americans saw in a market that sold nothing but vegetables that could be bought for half the price at any K-Mart.

Who cared? As long as the market drew them. Night-time saw Kwai working as a desk clerk at Dukes, a no-star tourist hotel three streets back from the floating market. Daytime saw him out wallet hunting, tourists' wallets mostly.

Casually, as if his thoughts were a million miles away, Kwai killed the clattering percussion and temple bells mid-track in his head, put down his Coke and reached for a junked copy of the *Morning Post*, discarded by some businessman on a bench over-looking the market. Flipping it open, Kwai folded the paper so he could skim yesterday's football results, though he knew them already.

Japan got enough fouls past Korea to be embarrassing. That

was good. Kwai'd have preferred to be born Japanese but, failing that, he was happy with Thai. Korean he wouldn't have wanted. In London, a visiting team of Soweto Reds had hammered Spurs, and a game in the Philippines was stopped when a fan shot his opponent's goalie in the leg, just before a free kick. The goalie's team had been awarded the match.

Much as usual. Head down and eyes fixed firmly on the paper, Kwai strode swiftly out onto a rocking walkway, tripped over a broken strut and stumbled straight into Jim Chance. As the American went down, Kwai shot out a hand to prevent the foreigner from tripping over the edge into the filthy water. At least, that was what it was meant to look like. In fact, Kwai's fingers dipped into the American's Levi jacket and grabbed his wallet.

Only things didn't work out as planned. Instead of the embarrassed gratitude Kwai'd come to expect, the American slid from hurt pride into fury when he realized his pocket was being picked.

'Little fucker.'

Kwai nodded politely, kept nodding, kept smiling.

It was a straight stand-off. Kwai stood with the wallet clutched in his hand, but with the American's hand locked tight round his wrist. Kwai's smile remained open, friendly.

At first it didn't occur to Kwai that the American wouldn't be sensible and let Kwai back off, which he was more than ready to do, once the man let go. But then Kwai realized the man had other ideas. Stupid ones. The kind foreigners get when they've grown used to having other people do what they're told.

Maybe Jim Chance would have won on his own territory, but probably not. Kwai'd extrapolated more from life's hard lessons in his seventeen years than Jim Chance had picked up in over twice that time. And although, in all the time that had passed since he left his village, Kwai had never even been further than ten miles outside the city, he'd learnt more about human nature – about when to retreat and when to strike – than Jim had picked up on his entire fifteen-year crook's tour of America, Europe and the Far East.

When it came, Jim Chance's move was slow and hideously clumsy. Embarrassing, even. He'd already telegraphed Kwai his intentions by shifting his weight forward onto one foot, flicking his eyes towards Kwai's wrist and tensing the muscles in his own shoulder.

Kwai ducked the blow, no trouble, leaning in towards the man to stop one wrist being broken, at the same time slipping the twisted zytel blade of a *kris* free from his belt with his other hand. The blade took Jim Chance in the gut, passed neatly under his breastbone and came to rest just below his suddenly-pounding heart.

It felt like a punch.

With a quick flick of his wrist, Kwai pivoted the *kris* so its razor-sharp point scissored briefly from side to side inside the American's chest, severing his gullet and aorta. Blood flooded the man's chest cavity, pushing into the gap between heart and lungs. But it was only when the sticky red liquid forced its way up the man's gullet and began to dribble from his lips that Jim Chance understood what had happened.

Kwai smiled with regret, and stepped back to allow the pony-tailed American space to fall, which Jim Chance did with a slow elegance that seemed barely faster than freeze-frame. If any of the stallholders busy still unpacking their wares for the day thought it unusual for a tourist to suddenly slump on a walkway, it didn't show. Most didn't even bother to look.

Not one of them would call the police, of that Kwai was certain.

All the same, he knelt carefully at the edge of the walkway to wash blood from his hands in the oily grey water. And with that done, Kwai stripped off the jacket, taking Chance's wallet and a gold Sheaffer pen from its inside packet. Then he put one hand under the shoulders of the dead man, another under his hip and rolled. For a second or two, Jim Chance bobbed on the surface, as new bodies do, and Kwai used the moment to punch his *kris* hard into the man's belly and rip it across, stopping to look at the purple guts within. Opening their stomachs was meant to stop dead men floating back to the surface. Kwai didn't know if it worked: he'd never killed anyone before.

With real regret, Kwai let go his razor-sharp *kris*, watching it swiftly overtake the dead American who sank slowly, fading like a ghost.

Inside the wallet was a gold Mastercard in a name different from that typed on the green international driver's licence alongside it. A Bell telephone card and a Sears chargecard sat next to a PCMCIA7 modem. There was a small wad of notes as well. Fifty-dollar bills in one compartment, 5000-yen bills in another.

He was almost on land, Chance's jacket discarded on the walkway behind him, when Kwai remembered to go back for the pretty little toy he'd seen earlier. True, Kwai'd just lifted more hard cash than he got most days, and he could fence that Mastercard in five of the eight local bars, but business was business. And besides, Kwai knew a green-eyed American woman at Duke's who'd undoubtedly over-pay for something as stupid as a leather-covered Psion.

[Santa Passionata/Pya Chakri Dreams]

'*Venice was flooded again in 1966, when wind and water raised a November tide seven feet above its usual level. Italian radio announced this historic catastrophe with the ironic line, High tide in St Mark's Square . . .*'

The ghost girl smiled, even though Passion wasn't there to see her, and Passion was the only one who could, see the ghost girl, that was. The kid looked about six, or maybe eight. It changed. She would have been twelve, had she been born, but that was too old for either of them to manage.

'*Since then, the Palazzo Ducale has been flooded three times . . .*'

The mellifluous, oh-so-English voice issued from a grey JVC microsystem balanced precariously on a cracked basin. Passion loved audio books, they saved her the trouble of reading.

Cutting corners was something Passion had refined to an art form. Usually her 'couldn't-be-arsed' list included swallowing anything not sold in K-Mart or McDonalds, washing and being polite. Though, when fancy hit, Passion could add talking, walking or getting up . . . In fact, the list of things Passion couldn't be arsed to do had been getting longer by the day.

But that was about to change.

Naked and fucked out, with a tumour-sized migraine, the twenty-six-year-old New Yorker stood under a mould-encrusted shower in the corner of a filthy, off-white hotel room and thanked God it was Saturday afternoon. Change over. The last lot of Danes had checked out, the next lot hadn't yet checked in. And with no one else around to demand water, the plumbing actually worked. If you could call a steady trickle of lukewarm water actually working.

The air-conditioning had most probably never functioned. If you wanted air you opened the unwashed window and let in a warm cesspit stench from an overflowing storm drain below. If you had problems with the stench, you kept the window shut and sweated instead.

Duke's was a Patpong dive for sex tourists. 'Rooms by the hour, night or week' read the handwritten card taped behind its front desk. But most guests stayed the full fortnight, booked in by a travel agency in Frankfurt. Duke's took cash only, but that suited its patrons just fine. Most weren't too keen on leaving a trail of credit slips behind them anyway.

Stuck under the trickle of water, washing herself for the first time in a month, Passion wondered briefly why she hadn't thought of having a shower before. But she didn't push the question; most of her cortex was already busy, taken up with ignoring the pain of coming down off freebase.

Her guts were water, her stomach hollowed out with spasms, throat and arse raw with the liquid streams that threatened to dehydrate her into fever. The sensible thing to do would have been to take another hit, to chuck a blue-grey crystal of ice into her little glass pipe and torch it, pull that cold smoke deep into her waiting lungs. But for once Passion wasn't going to cut corners. This was going to be done properly.

Which was a surprise in itself. Not just for her but for Kwai who sat on the edge of her unmade bed, stitching the cuff of an ancient Armani jacket lifted that morning off a clothes stall, while he watched the American woman's stocky body through the frosted glass of her shower cubicle.

Kwai liked her pinkness, the solidity of her shape, her crazy red hair, but best of all he liked the trips she made to American Express to pick up money. Money which until now went into his pocket as swiftly as the ice went from his pocket to her pipe. Little things like that Psion organizer were extra.

Passion without drugs, now that was a thought to worry Kwai. Lazily the Duke's Hotel night porter tossed aside his sewing and pulled himself up off her bed. Reaching for a paper plate of hash cake that rested on a rattan chair, Kwai padded over to the cubicle, pulled open its cracked door.

'Hey, want some?'

Passion shook her head, took the brownie and crumbled it between wet fingers, watching as it hit the puddle at her feet, staining the water brown until it swirled in a circle towards the plug.

'I've given up,' Passion said firmly. Her words were so steady she almost convinced herself.

'Need ice?'

Passion looked at Kwai sadly. Sure, she needed ice. That didn't mean she was going to use it, though. Life was about to remake itself for Passion. The young Thai boy didn't yet know just how much but, to be honest, neither did she. Not yet, not for certain.

'Come here,' said Passion. Pulling Kwai close, she kissed the boy firmly on his lips, ignoring the headache that threatened to rip the top off her skull. Water ran warm down his face, plastering the boy's long black hair tight to his high cheekbones, his white rayon shirt going dark and sheer against brown skin beneath.

Revenge fucks she'd got to an art form. As for consolations and time-killers, she'd tried those two as well, but nostalgia was a new one. But here it was, Kwai and Passion, one last mad sad fuck. Guaranteed.

Passion kissed him again, harder. From habit, the boy's hands reached up to cup her small breasts. Which wasn't the idea. With a shake of her head, Passion prised free his fingers and pushed them down at his side. Shaking so badly she had trouble undoing the buttons of his shirt, Passion peeled back the sodden cloth to reveal Kwai's flat, completely hairless chest beneath.

All her relationships were touch and go: they touched, Passion went – eventually.

Dipping her head, wrapping her arms round his waist, Passion found one small nipple and flicked her tongue across it, then bit. Kwai groaned and Passion sucked his nipple again, biting harder.

Okay, so it was a fucking strange way to say goodbye to who she'd been. But *adios* was what it was. And that was how she wanted it to be.

Anyway, Passion thought, starting on Kwai's other nipple, she majored in goodbyes. People and places, she could do her list of discarded, departed and dumped from heart. Starting with Arthur Avenue in the Bronx, home of her dapper little Genovese cousin. Then Bensonhurst, where she'd stayed with her elderly uncle Vincent. Vincent fed her, looked after her, even respected her in a bizarre kind of way, and she did her best not to return the interest. Now he was dead and she was here.

Water trickled down long trustafarian dreadlocks as Passion sank to her knees and eased Kwai's 501s down over his slim hips. He was half excited, prick curled uncomfortably within his white Calvins. She'd take a bet those were original, too. Stuck right in the middle of ersatz city, Kwai had to be the only man in Bangkok who refused to wear fake anything.

It was one of the reasons she liked him.

Sending his Calvins the same way as the Levis, Passion took the boy in her mouth, pushed back his hood with pursed lips and sucked him from semi-tumescent to hard in under a second. Her head swayed gently, swallowing Kwai whole and then pulling back, swallowing and pulling back.

When his legs were knotted with tension and his breath coming in gasps, Passion slipped one hand up to cup Kwai's balls and squeezed slowly. That was all it took. Kwai literally bounced off the shower glass as he came, pumping into her mouth. For a second, tasting salt and garlic, Passion almost spat into the swirling water, then decided not. What the hell, she wasn't going to be blowing the kid again.

'Your turn,' said Passion. Without bothering to dry herself, she got out of the shower and pulled Kwai over to her bed, hardly even noticing the girl now sitting by the window. Her non-kid. The regret no amount of going to Mass could wipe clean. Kwai, of course, couldn't see the child. No one but Passion ever could.

Grabbing hold of her undersheet, Passion tipped the crumbs, a copy of last month's *Details* and her crumpled top sheet to the floor, revealing a stained cotton mattress. It looked the victim of a thousand messy fucks and a dozen forgotten periods, but it was still cleaner than her sheet. Flopping back on the mattress, the American woman opened her knees.

And when Kwai's tongue had flipped her over the edge a couple of times and her lunging hips had bruised and pounded his mouth until it was raw, Passion took another shower, alone . . .

Later on, she sent Kwai down to the nearest market to buy her black Levis, nail scissors, Covergirl make-up and a basic white shirt. And when he got back she sat newly dressed at her room's tatty dressing table and began trying to unbraid the tangled mess of her crimson dreadlocks.

Passion moved out of Duke's on Saturday evening, the evening she told Kwai sex with her was over. Going east across the river to a better part of the city, where the air at street level still smelt of frying food and too many cars but no longer had the cesspit stink of raw human poverty.

'You come with me, I'm your boss, okay?' Passion was standing outside Duke's, waiting for a taxi. Kwai was considering his options. Neither one was paying any attention to the passing tourists who were watching them both with interest.

'If you don't like it,' said Passion, 'then no hard feelings either way. It's not a problem.'

'And if I come with you?'

'I pay you a good salary. And give you money to buy new clothes . . .'

'Buy them where?'

'Anywhere. Wherever you want.' The American woman shrugged, as if she hadn't given the matter much thought. 'Say Paul Smith – in Tokyo? I'll pay for an air ticket . . .'

That was the point he really became hers.

* * *

Passion smiled. Hell, what was the good of having money if you didn't use it. She was appalled it had taken her so long to buy into the new century's most basic truth. The skin she stripped from a pawpaw with a fruit knife fell in curls onto a white marble table, its sugared juice running stickily across her fingers, splashing onto the open copy of the *Bangkok Herald* on her knee.

Of course, next up Kwai had wanted to know if he could fly JAL and how he'd pay for his ticket. It was when she mentioned a company credit card that Kwai really started to smile. He was, Passion had noticed sadly, really very beautiful. More beautiful than the sad-eyed little girl who'd travelled beside her from Duke's, unseen as ever by Kwai or the taxi driver.

White carpets, gold lampshades bias-cut from shot silk, a framed Hockney that just might be real . . . They were sitting in a huge penthouse suite of the Bangkok Imperium in Krung Thep, the old part of the city, looking down through a vast glass wall at a spectacularly expensive view of the eastern bank of the Chao Phraya river, to where a convoy of open-top boats was carrying sacks of rice along the waterway, brought in for milling from the surrounding lowlands. Half a mile distant was the floodlit splendour of *Wat Phra Kaeo* – the temple of the Emerald Buddha – housed within the walls of the old Grand Palace.

Behind them, looking back into the Saturday-night city, black and white strips of skyscraper window wrote across the distant office buildings like endless lines of bar code.

City of Angels, the real one.

Planned well over two centuries before by the warlord Pya Chakri around a network of canals, most long since bulldozed to make way for the roads and office blocks she could see from her window. There was no reason why Kwai should know, but Passion had a master's in History and Art. A real degree, not some printout from a California-registered diploma mill that only required you to turn up twice, once as a freshman to deliver your cheque and once to cough up again just before you collected your degree.

No, Passion's MA was the real thing. Brain-ache, Ivy League.

Okay, having a Dad rich enough to re-roof the library obviously helped. But then, so did an IQ that let her clock up straight As at thirteen while the rest of her year were struggling to get their blow-addled nineteen-year-old brains round a pass.

But then, at twelve Passion had been wired to a neuroMetric cap for the HIQ test. It worked. Obviously it worked, that's why it was banned. Sixteen seconds staring at a red thumb tack on a white wall, and the cap had measured her hardwired intelligence to within one-half of a standard deviation of what she would score on all eleven subsets of the Wechsler Adult Intelligence Scale.

Passion doubted big-time if she was the first to draw parallels between Pya Chakri's city and the canals and bridges of the serene Venetian republic. But Passion was pretty fucking sure she was the first to decide to take the idea of a city of canals and make it happen – in the middle of the Pacific.

It was the Psion that gave her the original idea, the fact she was sick to the back teeth of bingeing on drugs, sex and chocolate that drove it. Besides, she was a DiOrchi. She needed something to do, and this was it. The only real question was where to begin.

'About my suit,' said Kwai . . .

[Santa Passionata/American Excess]

Out of a cab, into the hot June rain drumming down onto Bangkok's slick black sidewalks, Passion and Kwai ran for a block of offices in the distance. It was Monday morning, and the crowds were as bad as ever.

Pushing her way through the umbrellas, slipping in and out of a wall of tourists streaming in the opposite direction to the one Passion wanted to go, she arrived at the bank's marble-fronted offices. Battling through the steaming rain was worth it, just for the pleasure of walking out of the twenty-eight-degree/ninety-per-cent humidity into the cool, quiet blast of air-conditioning.

Cold as ice, Passion thought bitterly, then caught herself, squaring her shoulders. The need was there, all right, burning behind her green eyes as hunger spun through her head. All it would take to banish the craving was a single rough diamond of methamphetamine, but she wouldn't. Not now, not ever. Passion was nothing if not absolute.

'I want an extra card on my account for this man,' Passion told a cashier firmly. The smartly dressed Thai woman looked doubt-fully at the American and then at Kwai, taking in his overwashed black jeans, his too-tight white shirt and the nervous way he kept pushing a broken pair of Raybans up onto the bridge of his nose.

It shouldn't matter, Passion thought tiredly, but it always did. She was immediately glad that she'd decided to go smart. Yester-day's Levi jeans and cotton shirt were social camouflage to check into the Imperial; classless, louche . . . Today, her white blouse was Thai silk, her chocolate suit a good, toned-down copy of a Galiano/Dior she'd noticed on its first appearance five years before on the catwalks of Paris. She'd ditched the Covergirl lipstick for something bruise-dark from Shu Uemura. Her mascara was Dior.

'I just need to check something,' the cashier said smoothly, disappearing through a swing door, Passion's gold card clutched firmly in her hand.

'You sure it's not stolen?' Kwai demanded.

Passion shook her head, hair brushing her jacket. The Imperial's salon had left it long enough to touch her shoulders. After three years in dreadlocks, her hair's condition was terrible, sure as shit. But the fussy little Australian queen had hacked back the split ends, conditioned what was left half to death with plant oil from some endangered forest, curled it and dyed the final result back to something close enough to North Italian blonde.

Passion smiled. 'Not stolen,' she reassured Kwai, 'and it's out of my trust, not my Dad's account. If it was one of Dad's, believe me I wouldn't use it.'

The cashier came back. She looked flustered. The card was genuine enough, its credit limit several dozen times more than she could hope to earn in a year, even with bonuses, and hers was a good job. There was, however, a clause of small print she was hoping hard to use to cover her back.

The cashier smiled politely at Passion. 'I'm very sorry, Madam,' she said so softly that the American woman had to strain to hear. 'But I'm afraid we can't issue a second card on this account. At least, not without further clearance . . .'

Kwai looked so devastated, it was all Passion could do not to laugh. Transparent wasn't in it. He could see that Tokyo trip going the way of his other dreams. She already knew the answer but that didn't mean she couldn't ask the question.

'Why not?' Passion demanded, catching the cashier's gaze and holding it. There were some advantages to that assertiveness course Vasser had made her take in her freshman year. Passion learning to be bossy: her father had thought it a huge joke and hadn't hesitated to make sure everybody knew about it.

'We would need the approval of your trustees.' The cashier kept her voice purposefully neutral. She didn't like the amused anger in Passion's green eyes.

'You have a vid link?' Passion demanded.

The woman nodded.

'Then this is the code you need,' said Passion, scrawling a West Coast number on the back of a withdrawal slip. California was where he lived these days, where he'd gone after he 'retired' from family business. As if anyone ever retired before someone put them in a box.

Passion checked the code she'd written, and without thinking she added VidPGP code to the slip. 'Ask for Conrad DiOrchi when you get through. I'll take over from there.'

After the glass fountain and marble tiles of the air-conditioned foyer, the offices at the back were something of a disappointment, but Passion ignored the desks stained with ancient coffee rings, the piles of wilting faxes, the empty water-coolers. That wasn't her problem.

If the offices were spartan, the IBM vid-link was anything but. Passion found herself staring at a late model, Malaysian-built Packard Bell with a Taiwanese digital camera built into the top-left corner of its twenty-four-inch Samsung screen.

The cashier keyed in the numbers, her red-lacquered nails flicking effortlessly across a board. Passion had never learned how to touch-type. It was, Passion suddenly realized, something of an oversight. A bit like living next to Henry Ford and deciding it wasn't worth bothering to get driving lessons.

And then Passion had to stop thinking scribble, because her father was on the screen and looking less than pleased at being disturbed.

'Conrad DiOrchi,' he barked. He had his link on sound, not having bothered to switch to sight. Typical that he couldn't be bothered to see who was talking to him. Passion realized she still had time to break the link before he recognized who it was. And looking at his stern gaze, the set of his heavy jaw and the irritated twist of his mouth, she almost did just that.

But that would have been too easy, and Passion was through with easy. Come to that, she was through with talking to her Dad in short, soundbite Tribeca sentences. Her thought patterns might never match his for Byzantine complexity, but if necessary her arguments could be positively Venetian in their sophistication, she'd make sure of it. The tripped-out trustafarian who despised him had gone the way of her dreadlocks. This was a new game.

One she was going to win.

'Daddy,' she said. Passion kept her voice pleasant but confident, as if she was talking to an old, not often seen friend.

Conrad DiOrchi swatted the vision key so fast he might have been reacting to a wasp bite. 'What the hell's happened? Are you in trouble . . . ?'

Passion saw the exact moment that her father first noticed the neat hair, her clone Galiano/Dior suit, the elegant Shu Uemura lipstick. For a second his gruff voice faltered, but he caught himself in time.

'Katherine,' he said smoothly. 'This is unexpected.' One elegantly manicured hand reached up to smooth back his greying hair. The gesture was entirely unconscious, impossibly vain. Despite herself, Passion smiled. Conrad DiOrchi wasn't as ruthless as he would like the world to believe but it was a close-run thing. All the same, her father was actually nervous. When it came to his eldest child, the difficult one, Conrad DiOrchi didn't know what to say.

'Daddy,' Passion said smoothly. He'd obviously picked up her call in the bedroom, but Passion tactfully ignored that. 'I'm so sorry to trouble you, but I need your help.'

'Money,' Conrad DiOrchi said immediately, reaching for a Nokia mobile that sat beside the vidphone. 'How much? Where? I'll wire you funds.'

Over her father's brawny naked shoulder, Passion saw a girl slowly roll over and push herself up off a feather pillow. She muttered some question her father ignored. Like Passion's father, the girl was naked, her breasts small and compact. But unlike

Passion, the girl's stomach was firm and her once-pale skin was lightly tanned. Without looking round, Conrad DiOrchi pushed her back into the pillow.

'I'm still living off last year's allowance,' said Passion patiently. Neither of them mentioned the naked girl. Passion didn't know who it was, but it sure as hell wasn't her mother. Mind you, it wouldn't be – it was over ten years since her parents had split up. But then, it wasn't his second wife, or the one after that, either.

'If it's not money, what is it?' Conrad DiOrchi asked, scowling into the camera. Passion realized with a start he was irritated she'd seen his latest plaything. Still, that was his problem.

'I want to issue a second credit card on my account,' Passion said shortly. 'It's important and I need it done now.'

Conrad DiOrchi's smile was thoughtful. Passion wasn't sure if she liked it or not. 'And you need a trustee to approve the new card,' DiOrchi said shortly. 'And you think I'm the one most likely to say yes . . .'

Passion nodded.

'And who is this card for?' DiOrchi asked. A decision tree of unspoken questions stacked up behind the one he did ask.

'For Kwai,' Passion reached back and pulled Kwai forward a little. The young Thai boy edged nervously towards the screen, his hands clasped behind his back.

Conrad DiOrchi's lips thinned as his eyes flicked between his daughter and the beautiful Thai boy revealed on his screen. Passion hadn't expected him to like the idea, but she wasn't going to give him the chance to say no. Too much depended on it and once she'd let him do that, it would be too late. She knew the man from old.

Christ, he was her father. Where did everyone think she'd inherited her pig-headed obstinacy?

'This is my new personal assistant, I'm not fucking him,' Passion said coldly. Beside her the cashier grinned, then turned quickly away, blushing. But it wasn't humour, it was acute embarrassment that rocketed across her immaculately made-up face.

'This isn't about sex,' Passion said more calmly. 'This is business.'

Now that was a word Conrad DiOrchi could understand.

Naked but no longer half asleep, Conrad DiOrchi looked at his daughter's image in the screen. She was twenty-six, for Christ's sake. Long past the age of marrying, as if her reputation, temper and obstinacy hadn't already made that impossible. She wasn't thin, she wasn't beautiful, and her EQ might be at toddler level, but what she did have was an IQ of over 170 and a strong streak of the DiOrchi steel.

Two years' total silence testified to that. The only way he'd known his eldest child was still alive was the fact money was being drawn in her name, and the signatures on the slips were hers. He knew they matched; he'd had them checked.

It was eight years since they'd last met face to face, when she walked out on him after bringing the restaurant on top of the World Trade Center to a complete halt with her screaming insults. He hadn't been back to *Windows* since. Couldn't face the embarrassment. Even back then, she'd been drinking too much, taking weird drugs, missing Mass, and she hadn't been a virgin, not for a long time.

Conrad DiOrchi smiled. It was, in some obscure way, a compliment that she'd turned to him. After all, last time they'd met her final words had included *skating*, *ice* and *hell freezing over*.

'All right, you win. All right?' Real anger burned in the voice that came at him over the wire and Conrad DiOrchi started out of his reverie to find his daughter glaring at him.

'You were correct,' she said fiercely, 'All right? I agree. Family's important, business is important. There's more to life than alcohol and fucking . . .' She looked pointedly over her father's shoulder, at a empty bottle of Cuvée Napa on the far bedside table and the huddled girl pretending to be asleep under his covers – and DiOrchi had the grace to blush.

'Have the damn card,' he said.

'I will . . .'

They glared at each other, and then Passion abruptly leant forward and broke the link. 'Well,' she said smoothly to the cashier, 'that went rather better than I expected.'

It took ten minutes to complete the paperwork on screen and another half-hour to persuade the bank to rush-issue Kwai's card. Which still left the afternoon for Passion to do some serious shopping . . .

[Santa Passionata/Death and Taxis]

Kwai wanted to hit the clothes shops. Passion had other ideas. Ideas that required a couple of calls to associates of her father. Men she'd promised herself she'd never deal with.

Well, she was dealing with them now.

Kwai in tow, Passion made for an anonymous first-floor office above a sweatshop in Thon Buri. A small door led into a tiny shop stuffed floor to ceiling with bolts of cloth. The air was thick with fabric dust and acrid with incense. Temple music blared from a cheap Aiwa sitting on a battered mahogany cutting-table near the door. On the table lay swathes of Threadneedle Street stripe and Tatershall checks mixed with raw silk run through with gold thread. Passion saw Kwai eye up a length of dark Italian wool and she knew he'd be back here, come what may, with his new Paul Smith having half a dozen more suits made to his own slightly-amended design.

'Madam,' the old tailor bowed. Almost imperceptibly, the man ran his eye over the cut of Passion's silk shirt and almost Galliano jacket. The American girl didn't know it, but in a single glance the tailor took in the stitch count, noted the double hem of her sleeves and checked that the mother of pearl buttons on her blouse were real.

They must have been. For his next bow was slightly lower, and almost without Passion being aware of it, the old man had begun to edge her towards a different, cleaner area of his shop. If he saw Kwai he didn't acknowledge the young boy's presence.

'Later,' said Passion, slipping round the tailor. 'First I need to see Mr Qu.'

'Mr Qu?' The man's brown eyes were blank, his face impassive. Passion smiled. She was getting used to this game. At the far end of the shop was a small door, half hidden by an old batique curtain. And it was towards the curtain Passion moved, ignoring the anxious dance of the elderly tailor as he edged around her, trying to stop Passion without actually touching her body.

Kwai muttered something in Thai, too low for Passion to catch but it made the man laugh ruefully. Around his eyes the skin was paper-thin with age and splattered with pale liver spots. Crow's feet radiated from his mouth like streams in a delta and his hair was almost gone, dusted away to a thin scrub of greying fuzz. But the eyes that flicked across Passion were bright and all too alive.

'What did you tell him?' Passion demanded.

'That you were American,' Kwai said shortly.

'Meaning what?'

'That he should save himself grief and let you go upstairs. Since that's where you'd go anyway.' There was a raw edge to Kwai's voice. Not open anger exactly, but close. And then the boy caught Passion watching him and his face slipped back into a familiar white-toothed smile.

Familiar because it was the expression everyone had worn when she first arrived in Bangkok, stepping down from the air-conditioned luxury of a Boeing 747 into the sticky heat of a wet Thai afternoon.

It said . . . Passion shook her head. How the fuck should she know what it said?

Upstairs Mr Qu sat in a bare office behind a bare office desk, no pens, no papers, not even a basic notebook. Only an old-fashioned Bakelite telephone, the kind with the curly black wire you could buy in expensive shops in London. Up here there was no fabric dust, in fact no dust at all. And for all that the warm rain beat down hard outside, Mr Qu's office was cool and dry.

He was younger than Passion expected. Younger than she'd been led to believe. It was only later she realized this wasn't the real Mr Qu, it was one of his sons, maybe even one of his grandsons. She didn't rate an audience with the old man himself. But that didn't worry her, she would soon enough . . .

What Passion wanted was simple. A shell company, or rather three shells. Companies that were cast-iron and legal, old enough for people to be dimly aware of their existence but obscure enough for the market not to know what each one now did; or rather what it used to do before it was gutted in one of the corporate collapses that followed Beijing's takeover of Hong Kong.

All it took was two telephone calls and then Mr Qu laid out his wares, describing each company's tax history in intricate, mind-numbing detail: manicured nails drumming lightly on his desk's simple ash surface as he outlined the commercial history and final collapse of each institution.

When Passion stood up to go it was as governor of the long-defunct Straits Imperial (Tin) Bank, MD of Siam Securities, and CEO of the venerable Far Eastern trading house of Jardine, Jardine, Chun and Baker . . . A bankrupt firm of rubber planters that had also tried its hand at logging, rice milling and hotel management – and failed dismally at each. Kwai was finance director and head of security for each company. She didn't bother to check if that was okay.

Call one had formed shells to buy shells, to form other shells, setting in motion a complex buying and selling operation that hid the companies inside each other until the end result was virtually untraceable. Call two told Mr Qu that this had been done. And there wasn't much worry either about people knowing what JJC&B used to do or wondering why Passion was busy doing something else: it was over fifty years since the company had traded.

The actual cost to Katherine (Passion) DiOrchi was half her monthly allowance or, put another way, two thousand times the average annual wage of a Thai rice farmer.

Gold Amex swiped through a Matsui card-reader that appeared miraculously from inside Mr Qu's desk, Passion hustled Kwai down the narrow stairs, through the tailor's and out onto a rain-slicked sidewalk.

'Later,' she told Kwai when he tried to return to the shop.

'Where to, lady?' The driver who stopped was old, bald, smiling. More like a Buddhist monk than the owner of an ancient Starburst. Except that his tattered, totally-synthetic blue shellsuit was a million miles in style from the monks' ubiquitous orange robes.

In the back of the taxi, Passion breathed a sigh of relief, ignoring Kwai's hurt silence.

It said something, Passion decided, that the only place she felt really at home was on a plane or in a taxi. When it was leaving the anonymous security of airports that made you feel homesick. She was watching the rain pound across the fractured windscreen faster than the wipers could handle. The summer monsoon was on, overflowing storm drains, making the taxi-cluttered roads even slower.

'Where now?' Kwai demanded. The boy was angry. Passion didn't need a degree in psychology to work that out. He was sitting beside Passion, as immobile as some soapstone statue. Fury burning in the stiffness of his smile, his head obstinately in profile, Kwai's beautiful brown eyes were hard and bright as he stared blankly into the middle distance.

The city proper ravelled back around them, low-level breeze-block and plasterboard slums giving way to rain-softened chrome-hued office blocks and slick black apartment buildings, the financial spore of a Tiger economy.

And all the while silence was stretching out between them, Kwai getting angrier by the minute. She'd been around the boy enough to know when his temper was on a timer, and the clock was practically counting down in front of her eyes. Well, tough shit. He didn't know what went on in her head, she didn't presume to know what was happening in his. But all the same, she was getting bored with his sulks.

'Hey,' Passion said crossly, 'how the fuck can I know what's going on if you won't tell me?'

Kwai gazed ahead. Ignoring the American woman.

Not a clever move. 'You want that fucking Paul Smith suit or not?' Passion demanded, her New York accent getting harder, more brittle. 'You want to go to Tokyo?'

The only sound in the Starburst was the whine of the wipers trying and failing to clear the rain. 'Okay,' said Passion, 'whatever. Don't go . . .' She shrugged. 'Why should I give a fuck . . . Who needs you, anyway? I can pick up ten of you in a morning . . .'

'Really? That so?' Kwai's hand flicked out to grip her left wrist, grinding the eight *carpal* bones beneath his strong fingers, *ulna* grinding against *radius*. 'Then maybe I just take your bag and go, yes?' He twisted, viciously.

Passion screamed, with shock more than pain, and fought to pull her wrist free but Kwai's right hand was like steel, his left already reaching for her leather bag. The elderly taxi driver was watching intently in his mirror, eyes flicking between them and the rain that obscured the traffic ahead, but he made no attempt to stop or interfere.

'Let fucking go,' Passion snarled. She yanked hard at her hand, but Kwai's grip was fixed. Her bag was at his feet now, out of her reach.

'Make me . . .' The boy's gaze was hard, his eyes still on the road ahead, but all his attention was focused on the woman next to him. On her frenzied attempt to twist free of his grip. Passion couldn't do it, he didn't imagine she could.

Fear began oozing from her, sour as rotten milk, rising above the citrus scent of her CK cologne. The driver was really watching now. As well he might. Almost casually, without once looking at the American woman, Kwai swapped her trapped wrist from his right to left hand. Then pulled back the top of the struggling woman's chocolate-hued skirt, scooping his freed hand up between her legs, pushing under the cloth.

Fingers thrust past the static nylon of dark stockings towards her heat-dampened cotton underwear. She felt his fingers reach the gusset and pull at the edge where cloth met upper thigh. Kwai was still forcing his fingers under one seamed edge, busily ignoring the woman's frenzied outrage and pain, when Passion suddenly stopped resisting.

For a split second Passion stopped doing anything at all, even breathing. All her attention was on the little girl who'd materialized on the other side from Kwai, staring sadly at her struggling mother. And then Passion was back in action, free hand already dipping into the side pocket of her silk jacket to come up with a small pearl-handled Lady Colt, which she rammed hard into the side of Kwai's head.

Clothes weren't the only things that credit could buy you at the Bangkok Imperium.

'Five-shot, steel jacket, hair-trigger,' announced Passion loudly. She'd taken the trouble to read the manual. Twice.

The driver hit his brakes, skidding the taxi towards the roadside, wheels throwing up spray. But Passion flicked her gun briefly towards his mirror, just not for so long that Kwai had time to react. 'Keep driving,' she ordered.

The man did. Pulling his battered Starburst back into the tight Bangkok traffic. He wanted to protest, but Passion wasn't having it.

'No, you listen, you shithead.' She was holding his gaze in the car mirror, her Colt still rammed into the side of Kwai's head. 'If you can keep driving while this fuckwit half rapes me, you can keep going while I decide whether or not to blow out his brains.'

'No mess,' the driver pleaded. 'Lady, if you're going to kill him, let me pull over.' Passion could see his point.

The wet street kept unravelling around them, getting ever more affluent. They overshot their original destination, but the driver kept going, weaving his taxi in and out of the early evening traffic. The taxi was a cheap Korean copy of an old-model Toyota without power-steering, which it badly needed but not as desperately as it needed air-conditioning.

Despite the rain, the temperature inside the cab was off the top of the taxi's little red-alcohol thermometer. Either that or the thermometer was broken, which was also possible, even probable.

No one stopped them. No police sirens screamed over the top of the grinding gears and sounding horns. There was no sign that any of the rain-sodden pedestrians – or other drivers, come to that – noticed that Passion had a Colt to Kwai's head.

And even when the crush of Hondas, Kias and Daihatsus ground to an exhaust-laden halt as the wet road narrowed on its approach to Constitution Bridge, Kwai's frightened face did little more than raise a couple of idle stares. For all its noise and crowds, Bangkok was an intensely private city.

'Forget the fucking cavalry,' Passion told Kwai as they pulled slowly away from Constitution Bridge and another Honda Accord edged passed, both salaryman and girlfriend intent on their in-car CD. Early Black Star Liner, Passion decided, listening to the lush Bollywood strings, maybe *Yemen Cutter Connection*.

Passion was finally having fun. Which was weird in itself.

Kwai said nothing. His wide face impassive, his dark eyes still staring straight ahead at rain thick as frozen vodka. Passion would give good money that he didn't know his hand was still thrust rudely between her legs. The boy's whole horizon had narrowed to the small circle of steel barrel pressed coldly against his head.

'Stop the car,' demanded Passion. Faster than that, the driver screeched to a halt beside an overflowing storm drain, ignoring the half-dozen cars which hooted in disgust.

'You both get out here, lady?' The old man sounded hopeful, but the sag of his cheeks showed he already knew the answer.

Passion shook her head, newly untangled hair brushing oddly against her cheeks. 'No way. Not me. But he does . . . that is, if that's what he wants.'

Kwai's face was puzzled, but not as puzzled as Passion's smile was bitter. No humour reached her cool green eyes. In fact, no emotions reached her eyes at all.

'Am I going to shoot you?' Passion shrugged. 'Who the fuck knows? I certainly don't.' She'd had more than enough driving aimlessly around in the rain. The Colt rested heavy in her hand and she wasn't the sight-seeing type; besides, Passion didn't really like this fucking city much even when it wasn't pissing down.

She'd had enough of fucking around and burning out her synapses. She had a life to rebuild, a whole fucking city to create. Kwai's part in that was his choice – but it was a choice the boy'd better make *now*.

Keeping her gun trained on his head, Passion leant over Kwai to open the far door, sliding her hand through the ghost-girl's white dress as she did so. The kid usually sulked for hours when Passion did something like that, but Passion's attention was all on Kwai so she didn't even notice the child vanish.

'I'll take my bag and that gold card,' she told the boy. 'And then you can walk . . .'

Kwai shook his head sadly. 'You're different,' he said bitterly, sounding younger, suddenly afraid. Tears were beginning to slide down over his smooth skin but Kwai kept his expression blank.

'You'd better believe it,' Passion snapped. 'You think I didn't know each time you ripped me off? You think I wanted to be fucked for cash?' Passion kept her green eyes wide open to block tears that threatened to form in the corner of each.

'You don't know what poverty tastes like,' said Kwai angrily. 'Even broke you're richer than anyone I know. Not that I expect you to understand the difference.' He edged across the Starburst's sticky vinyl seat towards the open door, realized where his hand still was and tugged it from between Passion's thighs as if it was on fire.

Behind him, head pounding, Passion tightened her finger on the trigger.

The bald taxi driver was watching in his rear-view mirror, frozen in the face of events like a mongoose before a hooded cobra. He wanted to say something – to act – but didn't dare. At the last minute Kwai halted and turned back to face Passion. His eyes met hers and for a second the boy looked genuinely sorry, truly lost. Passion shivered.

'Do it from the front,' Kwai said, nodding at her gun.

Passion nodded, and pulled back the slide on the Colt as she'd seen people do it on satellite. But she didn't pull the trigger. Instead she placed the pearl-handled gun carefully down on the taxi's filthy floor and slowly buried her head in shaking hands.

'Go,' she said to Kwai, through her fingers. Her voice tired and childish. 'Just go.'

The Thai boy smiled sadly, glanced at the bald taxi driver and shrugged. The driver shrugged back. *Foreigners*. Between them, their shrugs said it all.

Kwai and Passion took a different taxi to the Imperium, Passion having over-tipped the old driver outrageously.

[Santa Passionata/Silicon Alley Blues]

Kwai was along to haggle, though he also took it on himself to make sure no one decided to lighten Passion's pockets by force. He was prepared to accept that the shops would try to lighten them by guile.

The alley was actually anything but. In reality it was a wide, Japanese-owned glassed-over boulevard running both sides of a narrow canal, with even-numbered shops running down one side, odd numbers down the other. Little bridges of red wrought iron tied the two sides of the street together.

It was crowded, but then everywhere was crowded in Bangkok: lack of personal space was endemic. It was noisy, too, the street's cool air blasted every few steps by yet another public demonstration of some Soundblaster-clone soundcard.

'In here,' Kwai instructed ignoring the windows full of new-model Nintendos, Sony PS64s, new Packard Bells and Toshibas, as he stepped sideways and seemed to vanish into a raw brick wall. Following after, Passion found a narrow flight of stairs leading down into a dark basement. Paper dragons with huge, spring-mounted eyes of synthetic pearl hung from one side of the stairwell, as did burnished iron woks and razor-edged kitchen knives punched from single sheets of steel. The other wall was completely covered with metallic prints of coy girls with Thai skin but Western eyes, mixed in with prancing black horses painted onto scrolls made from sewn-together strips of bamboo.

The further down the stairs they got, the hotter it grew and the thicker with incense the air became. Until at the bottom the smell of burning joss was so strong they could have been entering an underground temple. Except that what they were entering was no more exotic than a couple of small, poorly-lit cellars stuffed floor to ceiling with cardboard boxes. One cellar sold kitchenware, the other didn't.

Behind a slab of marble balanced on two wood trestles a thin Australian woman in a half-undone Brooks Brothers shirt was sorting a bag of RAM into three piles. At least thirty seconds passed before she tossed a final chip onto one of the mounds and glanced up.

'Can I help?' Her voice was slow, her face serious.

'We're looking for a telephony card,' said Passion. 'Something . . .' She thought about it, 'Something intrinsically discreet.'

The Australian woman smiled.

Quickly Passion ran through her absolute minimum technical specifications. A 56Kb/sec fax-modem, dual DSP chips, Soundblaster-compatible . . . A minimum capacity of 100 secure voice/data mailboxes and, most important of all for Passion, caller-line identification. That way CLI software could instantly check its programmed list of companies likely to call her and decide instantly not just which department but also which of Passion's 'virtual companies' should receive that call.

'Well, we should be able to do better than that,' the old Australian woman said shortly. Tapping a Lucky Strike from its crumpled packet, she tipped her head sideways quickly as if to check that the cigarettes didn't give Passion or Kwai a problem and then lit up anyway.

Smoke trickled towards the ceiling, lost in the general cloud of joss as the woman ran down Passion's list with her own alternative recommendations. The old woman wasn't even a quarter of the way down the list before Passion realized with embarrassment that she'd based her own requirements on what had been available when she was in her teens, not on what was on the market now.

Whatever Passion needed that cellar could supply: a computer, WebOffice, Netscape vidlink, military-strength crypt. Not to mention a small, discreet Sony relay, tied to a Digidex new low-orbit satellite system, GMPCSes standard.

But then Passion had already stressed that money wasn't a problem – quality was.

Back at her suite in the Imperium, Passion flicked on cable, hitting select until she reached MTV and a classic Underworld remix. It would do. Bobbing her head in time to the back beat, Passion unpacked her spoils. Small flatscreen SSVGA monitor, unbadged grey box, TritonX chipset, MS natural keyboard, Logitech floating mouseball . . .

It didn't look much for the money, but link everything up to the ISDN-30 line she'd had the hotel install and it'd do the job, which was what mattered.

Inside the grey box was an Intel MMX/3, with 32-gigabyte hard drive, 48-speed CD-ROM/DVD and 128-meg memory, upgraded to 320. A radically-adapted Creative Labs WebBlaster3 card was slotted in place and Kwai had asked Passion to buy a state-of-the-art Obsidian XS-700 graphics accelerator.

Passion didn't really play computer games. When she was hooked it was on building ridiculously complex, sub-*Quake* VTML Websites. All the same, she could see how Kwai might get worked up about trilinear filtered texture mapping; because this was a kid who saw Tokyo as little more than a combination clothes shop and games arcade. Already his Rough Guide had heavy circles scrawled round *Wako* in Ginza and *Joypolis*, Sega's game-park at Takashimaya Times Square.

With her computer set up and software programmed to make and take voice and data calls, Passion dialled through to the hotel on an outside line, persuaded the bemused desk clerk she really was calling from one of the Imperium's suites and demanded room service. Always trapped between absolutes, Passion had gone from stuffing her face to eating nothing at all. But then, her life was one long clash between double-thick choc shakes and iced Evian water. Never had been anything in between.

When the *chicken penang* and *pad thai* came up from the kitchens, they filled her suite with the scent of lime leaf and lemon grass. A bit like eating food franchised from *Calvin Klein; the CK cookbook*. But Passion was surprised to find she liked it, even the vegetables.

Supper done, Passion hit the shower, letting bursts of scalding water thud onto her body, feeling the last of the dirt wash free from her skin. Outside in her room, the sad-eyed kid was still sulking, sitting as always, her long childish legs folded under her on the window ledge. Kwai sulked too, only in his own room next door.

Kwai's problem was he didn't want to be in his room, he wanted to be in Passion's room with its oversized waterbed, giant TV and fully-stocked minibar. Only Passion had already told him no. Though at least this time she didn't need a gun to reinforce her message.

So Kwai was camped out in a small breakfast room, reading up his *Rough Guide to Tokyo*, not really believing a word about air-conditioned, strip-lit, twelve-floored underground shopping complexes or about high-rise offices held together by sheet glass, high-tension wire and advanced mathematics.

All Passion had to work on was an idea, a new computer and a back-issue of *Time* with an article on the demise of the ex-Soviet whaling fleet. Plus, of course, some interesting facts and figures from associates of her father and a healthy disregard for international law.

Two hours later Passion was still in the shower, cleaner than she'd been for years. But at least she finally knew where to begin. At the beginning, with a call to Moscow.

'General Zublovsky?' Her question was fractured into binary, crypted using DES, re-encoded, then bounced in digital scribble off a low-level comsat from a Triad mailhouse somewhere in Hong Kong. From there the signal hit a relay, did a high-speed/highly illegal receive-and-bounce off a US warship, was switched to Helsinki via clearing houses in Geneva and Naples and finally reached Moscow along a private optic landline which crossed the Baltic seabed. There were simpler ways to route a call, but not many were more secure.

'Yes?' The voice that answered was gruff, suspicious. Not least because the call had come though to the general's Moscow house on an unlisted number. Zublovsky had been chosen because he spoke good English, was a fervent believer in the free market and had gambling debts totalling several times his legal salary. It had taken some slick social engineering from Passion to get the unlisted Karensky Prospect number out of an English-speaking assistant at the Kremlin.

'General,' she said confidently, helped by the fact that her soundcard was configured to add an edge of age and authority to her usual voice. 'This is Catherine Chun. I'm the chief executive of Jardine, Jardine, Chun and Baker. You've probably heard of us . . .' Calling herself Chun was a touch of genius. At least, Passion hoped it was. Passion left a brief space, into which the general muttered something non-committal.

'I gather that your department is responsible for the Federation's Pacific ports . . . and that this includes the old whaling fleet, what's currently left of it.'

There was a silence. If Passion had been called on to describe it, she might have called it bitter. Whatever he was thinking, the General didn't think it necessary to add anything to the conversation.

Passion glanced at the magazine open on her knee. Photograph after photograph showed rusting factory ships moored offshore from Vladivostock and the Othotsk ports. Ancient and almost derelict, the whaling fleet was still there, but the whales were not, at least not for the hunting. The Whaling Commission's total moratorium on commercial catches had just been extended for another fifteen years.

Following that vote, *New Scientist*, *Scientific American* and *Nature* were confident the blue-whale population could be rebuilt to sustainable numbers, just as Russian, Japanese and Norwegian economists were certain the vote meant economic death for their fishing industry. And further economic disaster was the one thing Russia could ill afford.

Passion skimmed the article. Rampant inflation. Rigged elections. Local capitals overrun by Chechen mafia. The rebirth in St Petersburg of the fascist Black Hundreds. It was more than a mess, it was Princip and the Archduke, a world war just waiting to happen.

'General,' Passion said. 'My company would like to buy the whaling fleet that currently sits rusting and worthless on your Pacific coast. Obviously, our offer would be based on its real worth following the Commission's recent vote.'

'It is a priceless national asset,' the general said firmly.

Passion laughed. Not much, just enough for the general to hear. 'Seventy per cent of those ships were built during the last days of the Soviet Union. Half of them are no longer seaworthy.' She plucked figures from the air. They might be accurate, they might not. The only thing Passion did know was that the general would know no better.

'And even those ships that are seaworthy can no longer be used for their true purpose . . . At least, not for the next fifteen years.'

'They are an asset,' the general repeated firmly. 'I'm not sure that it would be in our national interest for them to be sold. We have enemies everywhere,' he added darkly. 'Who knows when we might need those ships'

Passion smiled to herself. Zublovsky was every bit as Ruritanian as a quick scan of *Krokodil's* Webpage had led her to believe. But the very fact he was still on the other end of the line meant he was at least interested.

'Invade anyone using those ships,' said Passion briskly, 'and you'll sink before you get halfway. Most of them are death traps. You might as well torpedo yourselves.'

All she got from the other end was an offended silence. Passion shrugged. She knew as well as the next person when to bait the hook. 'I can pay you in any currency, with the money wired to any bank your ministry might select.'

Passion paused. 'If it's advantageous,' she added, 'the money could be split, with the bulk paid to one account and whatever percentage you chose paid into another account.' She left it the general to work out why that might be an advantage.

From the steady breathing at the other end of the link, Passion got the feeling that he was thinking it over. 'Let me give you a number,' she said, reading off digits from her screen. 'This will take you through to my office. The line is guaranteed secure. Please think over my offer and then come back to me. That is . . . if your ministry is interested,' she added politely before breaking the link.

It was difficult to say how it had gone. But the idea had been planted. Now it was time for her to come up with the bait.

Raising credit wasn't difficult. It never was if the seed money was big enough. First Passion dialled up her own account in San Francisco to check her current status. By anybody's standards it was extremely healthy, but there certainly wasn't enough to buy a whole factory ship, never mind an entire whaling fleet. Not unless Zublovsky was feeling particularly philanthropic.

Which left her trust fund in the Caymans. That too looked good. Her father might not have been talking to her, but it hadn't stopped him topping up her list of securities on a surprisingly regular basis. Passion did a quick calculation in her head, rounding up or down to the nearest one million dollars as required. This time there was enough to get started.

With a grin Passion activated the software that called up the virtual office of the Straits Imperial (Tin) Bank. As Conrad DiOrchi she signed over her total trust to Straits Imperial. And then, doubling as Catherine Chun, Passion went into the open market and secured lines of credit against the total worth of the borrowed securities from a finance house in Sydney, and then again from a house in New York and another in Bogota.

Rome, Tokyo and even Moscow followed. Within an hour and

a half she'd secured five-year lines of credit worth ten times the actual redeemable value of her entire trust. It was a frighteningly large amount.

Dialling up a bank in Zurich, Passion signed herself on as the chief broker for Siam Imperial (Colonial) Securities. It took another five minutes to create a deposit account and then she was done. By the time anyone worked out what was happening it would be too late. At least, she hoped it would.

There are few cities that night cannot improve and Bangkok was no exception. Lights from office windows made pixelated patterns across the cityscape, the distant bridges looked like huge necklaces strung with lights. Lines were softened, architectural arrogance dimmed. Darkness and snow are the only things that can render urban sprawl almost beautiful, and snow was out, at least in Bangkok.

Night had even hidden the thick fog of pollution that hung in the narrow canyons of the streets. It was still there, of course, but now it acted like a photographic filter, diffusing the vast flickering neon signs that demanded she drink Coke, use Fuji, buy Honda.

Sipping at her iced Schlitz, and picking fitfully at cold noodles, all that remained of her *pad thai*, Passion listened to the squeals coming through the wall. The low thud of flesh, the muffled grunts of desire. Either Kwai had someone in there or he had spliced into a porn channel. Either way, it wasn't Passion's business, not any more. And besides, she had another call to make.

If Moscow was tricky, Brunei was no problem. But then, dealing with representatives of the world's richest man simplified things, particularly when he also ruled his own country as sultan. The assistant under-minister listened politely to Passion's offer, said nothing to commit himself either way and promised to get back to her swiftly.

Within twenty minutes she had a return call. There were thirteen possible tankers moored off Brunei's coast. Seven were in excellent condition, regularly maintained and not for sale – even if the bottom had dropped out of the oil shipping business. The other six had been seaworthy but were so no more. They were, the under-minister wanted her to know, single-skinned, without modern internal buoyancy tanks, and were decades out of date in their design. Unless extensively modified, it was unlikely they would pass the latest set of UN safety standards. They were for sale, for scrap only, if she was still interested.

She was.

[Santa Passionata/Bar None]

Passion dragged Kwai from his room, ignoring the stink of sex, the empty crushed cans of Tiger and the frightened-looking young Phillipina who was curled up naked in his bed. Ordering Kwai to hit the hotel pool for a workout, she told him to follow it with a cold shower to kill his hangover. She paid off the Phillipina from her own pocket.

It was the next day and they had work to do. Ships needed crews, and the crew needed for what Passion had in mind would have to be more than just flexible in their interpretation of international law.

By the time she'd finished her croissant (no jam, no butter) and drunk two cups of hot black Java coffee, Kwai was back upstairs and dressed. White shirt, red tie, black suit. It wasn't real Armani, but it was a good copy, lined in red and cut from heavy black silk. The jacket hung loose around his shoulders. The waist of the trousers was cut slightly wide, but given what she remembered of the snake-like thinness of his hips Kwai could get away with it.

Topping it all off was a new pair of wrapround Raybans. He looked young, but not as young as he was. And he looked both elegant and dangerous. It was, Passion realized, impossible to tell from looking at the loose jacket whether or not he was carrying her gun. She'd offered him her small Colt yesterday, when they got back from Silicon Alley. And he'd taken it with a smile. That was as close as either was going to get to an apology.

Kwai smiled, turning to show her his suit. 'Good, no? Made by the tailor in the foyer. It was done while I . . . slept.' He grinned at the last word, but Passion smiled right back and it was Kwai who looked away first.

Their first call was out at the oldest part of the port, where the concrete quays were too short and the draught too shallow to take the new container ships. It was an area even the *Lonely Planet* guides suggested people avoid.

At a small waterside bar overlooking the run-down docks, a woman sat out front, staring silently at a rainbow slick that topped the dark water of an empty berth. The concrete along the berth's edge was cracked and pitted with chemical blight, gone soft as chalk where the aggregate had degraded. She didn't look up when they passed.

The bar fell silent the moment Passion and Kwai walked in through its swinging sheet-steel door. Behind the zinc, a fat Australian pushed a Yankees cap further back on his cropped skull and frowned, meaningfully.

'We're closed,' said the Australian. If he'd had a flick knife he'd probably have been using it to clean his broken nails.

As best she could, Passion kept the suddenly-rising fear out of her green eyes, forcing herself to gaze slowly round the room instead. She could have done with a pair of Kwai's new Raybans.

If Kwai was afraid it didn't show.

'Hey, two Singha,' Kwai ordered, glancing briefly at the chalk-scrawled tariff behind the bar. The Australian did nothing.

Kwai smiled, that embarrassed, apologetic smile Pacific Rim Asians sometimes adopt when someone else has forgotten their manners. 'Two Singha,' he said again, more softly.

'Didn't you hear me?' said the Australian. He wiped his huge hands on his gut and leant across the bar, bringing his face close to Kwai's. 'We're closed. And you know what?' he said. 'Even if we weren't, we'd be right out of everything.'

'That so?' The young Thai boy stepped back from the filthy counter, as if uncertain what to do next. Shrugging apologetically at Passion, he looked briefly at the door and then glanced round at the silent seamen and dock crew watching him.

When he moved again, it was fluidly, almost effortlessly, pivoting on the ball of one Gucci-clad foot. Kwai's drop kick shocked Passion nearly as much as it stunned the Australian behind the bar, except that wasn't really possible.

The boy had swivelled from the hip, his foot easily clearing the top of the zinc as it sped towards the Australian's heavy face. There was a muffled crunch as the man's jaw cracked, and then a howl of agony cut suddenly short as Kwai chopped the man lightly across the throat, not quite crushing his larynx.

The entire 'fight' was over in less than three seconds.

After that, Kwai strolled over to an old chrome jukebox, punched in the code for a dub electro/Japmix of Motorhead's 'Killed By Death' and wandered back to the bar to wait for the fat bartender to pick himself up off the concrete floor.

Then Kwai reordered his beers. The Australian's hands were shaking but not so badly he couldn't flick off the bottle tops.

A Singha clasped in one hand, his other thrust deep into the pocket of his black silk jacket, Kwai made a round of the tables with Passion in tow, fixing for each of her ships to receive a skeleton crew of Thai, Malay and Chinese sailors who knew the waters. Chances were some moonlighted as pirates but, as Kwai had already pointed out, that could only help.

At least they'd know which straits to avoid. At Passion's insistence, Kwai also let it be known he needed two mercenaries per ship, promising them hand-held grenade launchers, infrared-sighted sniper rifles and long-magazine Uzis. The payment for mercenaries and crew would be in US dollars – a third up front, the rest on delivery of the Brunei tankers to a place to be specified by Passion.

That done, Kwai led Passion back to a yellow taxi that had been waiting for them, its nervous driver standing chain-smoking by the cab door. 'Take her back to the Imperium,' he told the man.

'Where are you going?' Passion demanded. There was something in his manner that worried Passion. But she couldn't pinpoint what it was, because she didn't recognize the way physical age can conflict with experience. Kwai'd never been as young as he looked, even when he looked older than he was.

'Hey? Me? To the airport.' Kwai pulled a JAL ticket and a new passport from his inside jacket pocket and grinned. Pausing only to push his new Raybans further up onto the bridge of his nose, he politely opened and then shut the cab door for her.

Passion couldn't tell if she was being mocked or not.

[Santa Passionata/New Prospekts]

General Zublovsy didn't return her call that week, or the next. But equally he didn't sound surprised when he realized who it was on the phone.

And the first thing he said was, 'I had your firm checked out.' Passion held her breath.

'Very old and very quiet,' the General continued, apparently not noticing her silence. His voice was gravelly, sounding like an elderly American actor impersonating a Russian general. Passion wondered if he, too, was using software to boost his voice.

'We prefer discreet to quiet,' Passion said and the general laughed.

'So discreet that no one quite knows what you do . . .' He coughed, a depressing smoker's hack and Passion decided that maybe the gravel in his voice was for real.

'We do many things,' said Passion smoothly, 'most of them secret. The fact you haven't found anything out about us is an indication of our success, not of our failure.'

There was a long silence from the other end and Passion suddenly realized that she'd offended the general. She just wasn't sure why.

When the general was certain the woman he knew as Catherine Chun understood his displeasure, he spoke again. His words came clear and precise down the line. 'On the contrary, we have found out all there is to know. You deal with mercenaries, you have just bought ships from Brunei – in even worse condition than ours – and you have extensive lines of credit. You, personally, are on the board of two other companies . . .'

So far it was as it should be. Passion had left enough conflicting markers in the Web to make searchers want to draw their own conclusions as to who and what she was. Not the least of her markers was a recently planted backdated cryptic reference in a human-rights newsgroup that added ten years to her age and closet-linked her with the CIA.

'So,' Passion said, 'do we have a deal?'

The general said nothing, so Passion said nothing back, concentrating on the slightly sweet taste of her cold Kirin beer and the far-off lights of an old Boeing 747 circling the city. Kwai was still in Tokyo. He hadn't called her but he was busy using his gold card. Passion knew that for certain.

'If not a deal, then the basis for a deal?' she asked at last. The general undoubtedly knew the extent of the credit line allowed her by the Swiss bank. That's what it was there for, to allow him to know. By now he must have worked out what proportion of the money he believed he could get for himself. Fifteen to twenty per cent, Passion reckoned. Any more would be dangerous, but the general's greed wouldn't let him settle for less.

'We have a problem,' the man said slowly, his voice as gravelly as a dry river bed.

That wasn't what Passion wanted to hear, but she kept silent. If he had a problem he could tell her about it.

'Here in Moscow we have big trouble. So big that nothing can be done, nothing can be decided until . . .' He let his words trail away.

Passion didn't know what was coming, but she was willing to bet that she wouldn't like it when it came. She didn't.

'You've heard of the Black Hundreds?'

Of course she had. Everybody had. Photogenic, dashing, handsome. Also anti-Semitic, nationalist, pro-Mother Russia, pro-Tsar. A few were still drawn from genuine *stepnoy*, Christian Cossacks, but most were disenfranchised, unemployed factory workers. Their uniform was a knee-length black coat, with a row of black-metal bullet cases across each breast and a curved *shasha* sabre carried at the hip. Their self-proclaimed *ataman* was Colonel Volkonsky, an ex-film star whose stable of *kabardin* mountain horses commanded huge stud fees throughout the equestrian world.

It was the Black Hundreds who'd fought the Muslim *Kavkassky* Cossacks to a standstill, massacring the survivors in a bloody fire-fight on the banks of the Don. The Black Hundreds who now demanded that Volkonsky be given the post of Secretary for War in the new Duma.

The world was fragmenting along religious fault lines, and it was the humanists, the non-aligned who were going down before religion's seismic blast. CNN had run a report that month about Volkonsky's plan to impose an 'anti-crime' curfew on Moscow and St Petersburg, to be policed by his own men.

'I can see that the Black Hundreds could be annoying,' Passion began – and was rewarded with a snort of disgust from the general.

'The man is a lunatic,' he said shortly.

'But the Chechen mafia, isn't that your biggest problem?'

The general sighed. 'Between a rock and a hard place, as the Americans would say. Who knows which is worst? The Chechens are everywhere, like lice. Even returning their own mudhole to them wasn't enough to scrape them off our backs. But to get rid of the mafia, it would be like shooting pigeons in Red Square, there are too many. As yet the Black Hundreds are not that widespread . . . yet. Dangerous, yes. Widespread, no . . .'

Passion waited. Slowly sipped at her Kirin and wondered what was coming next. Whatever it was, she could wait. Fingers suddenly brushed her arm, cold as wisps of wind. The ghost-girl stood by her, watching Passion quizzically.

'Go back, I'm still talking,' Passion whispered. She wasn't. She was waiting for the general to break his silence.

The girl smiled sadly and returned to her corner, crawling under a silver, rattan and glass table to reach a battered brown-skinned Barbie. She'd stripped herself down to white pants in an effort to get cool, folding her small white dress and socks into a neat pile. Barbie was naked, her clothes folded into an even smaller pile.

* * *

Once the girl had been a sad thought, a regret. Something that might have been. But slowly she'd become more real. Until now Passion couldn't shake her loose, at least not when she was sober. Oh, Passion didn't regret what had been done, spread out on that table. Girls of thirteen don't deserve to be, shouldn't be pregnant. Even her father believed that. It was her mother, smile ice-cold, who reminded her every now and then how old the child would have been, until eventually the ghost child turned up to remind Passion herself . . .

Crossly Passion ditched her lukewarm bottle of Kirin and grabbed another, colder one from her icebox. Not for the first time, she seriously regretted giving up meth. What Passion needed now, what she really wanted was a line of freebase. Or even a good long line of grit-grey cooking sulphate.

Instead she shook out a 250-mg tablet of choline, 25 mg of powdered dhea and a 750-mg capsule of L-Argenine from a pill box, then swallowed them all with one gulp of chilled beer. All were medical-grade pharmaceuticals, and anyway amino acids didn't count as drugs, at least not to Passion. But then, nor did the .75 mg of melatonin she used each night to reset her body clock just before she went to sleep . . .

Passion sighed. The line was open, but the only thing being crypted and bounced between satellites was their silence.

'General,' Passion said finally. 'What exactly did you have in mind?'

[Santa Passionata/Rag Time Ratio]

Kwai wasn't impressed to be dragged from his huge, very American bed at the Ginza Plaza by the incessant double buzz of his Nokia mobile. He was particularly unimpressed by the fact it was three in the morning.

Passion was equally unimpressed by the girlish giggles in the background, giggles that came in stereo. Pointing out tartly that if he tried going to bed alone he might get to sleep more easily . . .

For his part, Kwai didn't bother to tell her his night hadn't even really started. In fact, he'd only just arrived back at the Ginza Plaza after an evening cruising the finest bars that Nishi Azabu had to offer, not to mention red-lantern establishments in Shinjuku and Shibuya, and at least five nightclubs in Roppongi. It was the night he felt he owed himself after a second hard week's window shopping.

He didn't tell Passion, wouldn't even have admitted it to himself, but the reason he was looking not buying was that Takashimaya, Isetan, Seibu and the *departos* were just too daunting behind their spotlessly clean sheet glass and polished marble.

Tomorrow would be different, though: he was going to do a trawl of Ginza, gold Amex at the ready. But adapting had taken him longer than he'd thought, much longer. From the weird, capsule-like 'hotels' to the electronic boutiques of Akihabara, Tokyo was a city from the future. Its people, too. Very neat, very clean, very fast – and very, very expensive. If this was the future, Kwai approved: it was just taking him a while to get used to.

'Got the crypt turned on?' Passion demanded.

She could hear his sigh bounce off some comsat but didn't care what she was interrupting. 'It's important,' said Passion.

'Yeah, right.' The connection went dead and then Kwai was back on line. 'So tell me,' he said, 'what's so important?'

Passion told him, in detail. Outlining her conversation with Zublovsky, ending up with the general's final demand. Could he? Would he? It wasn't a question Passion knew how to ask.

She'd seen the knife Kwai carried, run her fingers over the ridges of razor scar that slashed across the lean birdcage of his ribs. Hell, she'd been there when he took the offered Colt from her, turning it over in his hands, caressing its barrel with his fingertips.

Passion might be American, rich and spoilt, but she sure as fuck wasn't as naive as Kwai believed. But she wasn't as experienced as she believed, either. Still, she was getting to know her own limitations – and there weren't any. All Passion need do was frame the question.

'I'll do it,' Kwai said shortly, before she'd even brought herself to ask.

It would cost her, a lot. He didn't know what, not yet. That could come later. Meanwhile he wanted to know exactly what Passion hoped to achieve, and what resources he had to do it.

She told him, in short clear sentences, spelling it out to herself as much as to Kwai. And at the end of it, Kwai's only question was, how soon? When Kwai discovered there wasn't a time limit, he suggested softly they increase both the complexity and possible reward of their hit. What he actually suggested was that Passion should milk Zublovsky for all she could get. But the meaning was the same.

Why just take out the Cossack *ataman*? Kwai wanted to know. Why not do something about the Chechen mafia as well? What were they but street gangs writ large – and there was little Kwai didn't know about power struggles on the street.

Briefly, abruptly, Passion and Kwai agreed that Jardine, Jardine, Chun and Baker would take care of both Zublovsky's problems. In return JJC&B would want more from him than just the rusting

Pacific whaling fleet. Passion would demand the assets of a bankrupt, government-backed Moscow telecoms group, NovCom3.

Spectacularly bankrupt or not, NovCom3 nonetheless owned a chain of still functional if dormant low-orbit comsats: numbers 11,320–11,349 in the SC Registry of 13,423 bits of logged and recorded space junk. And the comsats were good for maybe another ten, twelve months before they wobbled out of orbit and burnt up on re-entry.

Because what the fuck was the point of faking a multinational, diverting billions to create an artificial island to act as the world's first video/data/drug-design freeport, if you didn't have a LEO satellite system, operating line-of-sight on Ku, to broadcast the stuff when it was finally up and running?

Kwai sighed and clicked off his Nokia. She'd get back to him with the details . . . Yeah. No doubt she would. He looked at the two Japanese girls still sitting half-dressed on the end of his huge bed. Between them was an empty bottle of Chablis (genuine, from France) and a small bamboo box with a woven lid. Until recently it had held tiny cubes of grilled eel, sticky rice and pickled radish. The Plaza's kitchen had sent up food as requested, but the girls had only picked at it. So, in the end, Kwai'd swallowed the lot, in about three bites. So that was sushi. He still couldn't see what all the fuss was about.

One of the girls was obviously beautiful, with a heart-shaped face framed by long jet-black hair, parted neatly in the middle. She was the expensive one. Her eyes were deep chestnut, her cheekbones high and her skin good enough not to need the thin veneer of make-up that covered it.

Her figure would have had Passion sick with envy, and Kwai was strangely glad he and Passion hadn't been using a vidlink. The Japanese girl had a narrow waist, boyish hips and high, apple-like breasts with small nipples that pushed hard at the silk of her short Versace chemise. Her sex was completely bare, either depilated or shaved, Kwai didn't know how to tell.

Silicon and surgery were in there somewhere. The girl's beauty was too Western, too much of a cultural compromise. Even her wide-eyed air of innocence was the result of a neat snip and resew carried out by a very discreet, very expensive plastic surgeon from Shinjuku. Those kind of looks were expensive even in Bangkok. Kwai didn't want to know what she was costing him here.

The other girl was older, less manufactured. Her nose slightly snubbed, her face round, almost flat. Serene or emotionless, depending on how you looked at it. Her hips were wider than the other girl's, her legs slightly too short and muscular. From what Kwai could see of her breasts, lit by backlight through a thin cotton vest, they looked good. Not too large, not too pointed but just beginning to lose their battle against gravity.

Which made her maybe early twenties . . . at least, that was what Kwai decided. Her hair was short, also black but not as well cut or conditioned as the first girl's. Which made sense. Hooker One came from the foyer of the Tokyo Hilton. The second he'd picked up on a street corner, on his way back.

'You,' he said, nodding at the older girl. 'What's your name?'

She smiled. A bright smile that didn't quite reach her brown eyes. 'Whatever you want it to be.'

Kwai shook his head. 'No,' he said, 'your name?'

'Sasumi.' Her English was calm, untroubled. Maybe she often found herself entertaining teenage boys in over-priced Ginza hotels: Kwai didn't know. Nothing about Tokyo would surprise him.

'You. Please stay.' Kwai walked over to his dressing table and pulled open a drawer, reaching for his wallet. Returning to the bed, Kwai handed his gold card to the younger, prettier girl.

'Hey, take your fee from this.'

Beautiful and wide-eyed, she looked from Kwai to the older girl, and then reached for a hotel dressing gown, wrapping it tightly over the top of her silk chemise. Her unspoilt face was full of questions, but she asked none of them. Not that Kwai would have answered if she had. Silently she pulled a small card reader from a shoulder bag and swiped Kwai's card through its central slot.

Kwai didn't even bother to ask how much she was taking. It wasn't his money.

Her fee paid, the girl retired to Kwai's tiled bathroom to dress. And having dressed came out of the bathroom, collected her coat and left, without looking back and without saying goodbye.

'She was more beautiful,' Sasumi said, not stirring from where she sat at the end of Kwai's bed. 'Why send her away . . . ?

'I'm not complaining,' she added almost apologetically, with a small quick smile.

There are a dozen ways to insult someone unintentionally, Kwai knew that. The most common was pity. That knowledge was wired into his brain, burnt there by memories raw with the corrosion of other people's casual charity. Including Passion's . . .

And yet, Kwai knew without telling that Sasumi needed the money. Where the first girl wore Chanel and Versace, Sasumi was dressed in an off-the-peg suit from some cheap department store. Her clothes looked fine from a distance, but the closer you got the more loose threads you noticed and the worse the finish became. Details like that were second nature to Kwai.

Besides, her eyes were tired, red-rimmed with screen burn from a day working at some VDU. And her nails might be neatly filed and varnished in blackish red, but they were cut short not to catch on the keys of a keyboard. She wasn't rich enough or tough enough to be a real Ginza professional.

'Don't do this full-time, do you?' Kwai asked her.

Sasumi looked at him and then slowly shook her head. 'I could tell you this was the first time, but I won't . . . I do it now and then, once a week, maybe twice when I have to . . .'

Have to.

That need drove a lot of things, Kwai decided, as the girl picked at the crumbs he'd left in the sushi box. The radish was sharp, raw. Absent-mindedly, she picked up a toothpick. Even these were elegant, turned on a lathe to resemble little wooden banisters sharpened at one end and varnished at the other.

Kwai sighed. Maybe he was out of his depth in this city, where even the whores had impeccable manners. All the same, he could use her, that much was certain.

'How about earning some real money?' Kwai asked suddenly.

'Doing what?' Sasumi's question was as guarded as her voice was flat, but she couldn't keep hunger out of her eyes. Kwai'd no idea what had put it there, didn't want to know. Sasumi was part of his plan.

He didn't need to know she was supporting some sick sister, looking after a father too drunk to work: or, worse still, sending money back to her village, if they had villages in Japan.

'Hey,' Kwai smiled. 'Nothing dangerous. I just need a girlfriend. For a month. I'm going to St Petersburg and Moscow. We can stay in the Metropole, overlooking St Basil's, where Lenin held his first provisional government.' Kwai'd got that last bit from a cable travel show on Discovery, but he wasn't about to tell Sasumi that. 'You don't have to do anything except stay with me. I'll be out during the day, but you can go shopping.'

Sasumi looked doubtful.

'I'll get you a credit card,' Kwai promised.

'A month?'

Kwai nodded.

'What are you paying?' Sasumi's smile was apologetic, as if it wasn't a question she should have asked. But Kwai knew it would've been his first question, too.

Kwai mentioned a sum that sounded astronomical, even to him: even after seeing what Passion had spent on computer hardware while setting up her virtual empire. It sounded astronomical to Sasumi, too.

'Just to stay at a hotel?' Her voice was amazed but still doubtful, as if she was looking for the catch. 'But you'll want sex?'

Kwai looked at her like she was mad. 'Of course I'll want sex . . .'

They had sex then, too, to seal the deal, Kwai stripping off while Sasumi rummaged quickly for something in her leather bag.

It was a Gucci copy, cut from poor leather, badly dyed. She palmed something, hiding a foil packet in her fingers as she retrieved a small sandalwood candle and a flip-top box of matches.

Ripping free a match, Sasumi lit her candle and placed it carefully on Kwai's glass-topped dressing table. Heavy scent filled the room, drowning out Sasumi's perfume and the sour smell of the empty sushi box.

Sasumi killed the overhead light, throwing the room briefly into darkness, Kwai's eyes adjusting as candle flame suffused his room, lighting Sasumi's face. She looked sad and more than a little lost. It was a mixture Kwai'd always found inviting.

Pushing himself off the bed, Kwai walked over to where the young hooker was standing. Young by the standards of her world, that was. Not by his. He'd already decided she was older than him by a good two years, maybe three. He knew women of that age back home who were practically grandmothers. They didn't look like Sasumi though.

Kwai's fingers dipped into his pocket and found two small white tablets. Sasumi looked suddenly uncertain, but she took the *e2* anyway, downing it with water. But only after Kwai had swallowed the other. Passion had introduced him to pure MDMA, and now Kwai used it from choice. It made sex like dreaming in colour. Not as elegant as monochrome, but a lot more interesting.

'Hey,' Kwai said, because that was what he always said: and then felt stupid, not knowing what he should say next. Nothing was needed. Sasumi lifted her round face, eyes swimming, and Kwai kissed her. Softly at first, his lips just brushing until desire hit and Kwai pushed her mouth open with his lips. She tasted of mint. When she'd vanished to his bathroom it hadn't been what he'd thought; she'd gone to clean her teeth.

Then Sasumi broke free and gently pushed Kwai back so that he sat on the edge of his bed. 'Show time,' she said softly. In the light of her scented candle, with the night-time laser-and-neon cityscape of the world's most modern capital held at bay by red velvet curtains, Sasumi began slowly to remove her clothes.

Kwai's gut tightened as she folded her hands across her front and gripped the edges of her white vest, pulling it up over her head to reveal full, softly curved breasts. Kwai was still staring when Sasumi dropped her vest to the carpet in a heap. Tights followed, and then she stepped out of her brief slip and stood there in only a pair of cheap white pants, the kind you get from station vending machines.

Turning her back on Kwai, she slipped down her white pants, bending slightly as she stepped neatly out of them. Kwai watched, drugged by the smooth lines of her back, her soft bottom and legs. Then she stood full height again and swivelled to face him, one arm folded half-defensively across her breasts.

'End of the show. You like?'

He was in an expensive hotel, with a beautiful girl. And she was naked, eyes glazed on *e*, waiting on his pleasure. Kwai nodded, not trusting himself to speak. He liked, all right. Sure, this was a credit card transaction, nothing more; definitely not the time to go soft, get sentimental.

All the same, he kept his brown eyes fixed on her round face, watching the way her top lip was a little too short, which gave her a permanent pout. And then his gaze dropped, his eyes lingering down her narrow shoulders and soft full breasts, lowering to take in her dark twist of body hair.

'Come here,' Kwai said.

She did. Standing there as he wrapped his arms tight round her soft waist, burying his face in her smooth stomach, running his hands slowly over her back and hips to cup her soft buttocks. One hand moved in between her thighs, caressing, and then Kwai's fingers crept up the back of her leg, until a fingertip brushed against skin, wet and warm under his touch.

Kwai sighed, burying himself in her smell.

Musk filled his nostrils and Sasumi sucked in her breath as he rubbed his fingertips against her, one finger sliding deep inside. Sasumi pushed Kwai away, but gently, back onto the broad expanse of his hotel bed, and crawled over him, knees straddling his legs.

Dipping her head, Sasumi lent forward, her short black hair falling over her face, brushing his thighs. Her mouth opening to take him between her lips.

It was like being buried in warm liquid. Kwai groaned despite himself and Sasumi smiled, pulling her mouth away, white teeth nipping at him.

He wanted to grab her shoulders, to pull her mouth down onto him, but Sasumi shook her head, hands already reaching under his body, pulling him upright.

Maybe it was the scented candle or the night held at bay outside, or it could have been Kwai's knowledge of what he'd offered to do for Passion. Or maybe it was just the MDMA messing with his serotonin levels, but Kwai suddenly felt he'd never really known what sex was, until now. Pretty dumb for a street kid who'd lost his cherry to a retired thirteen-year-old whore in the back of a rice warehouse.

He wanted to own Sasumi, to taste her, to force himself inside her. Still kneeling, Sasumi reached for Kwai, squeezing softly until pleasure ripped through every nerve. Slowly she spread her legs to let Kwai reach forward and touch her, too. Maybe it was fake. But he sure as hell couldn't tell the difference.

And as Kwai licked his fingers and then moved them across her open vulva, feeling the lips swell, Sasumi gripped Kwai's rigid penis, easing the skin back and forth.

'Now we fuck,' Kwai announced, putting both hands on her hips, ready to stretch her out on his bed. He wanted her, all of her.

'First you wear this,' Sasumi said suddenly, producing a condom packet she'd palmed earlier from her bag. Her voice was confident, her eyes weren't.

Kwai groaned.

'Please?' Sasumi said. For a second she sounded almost afraid, but that vanished when Kwai nodded, his lips twisted into a half-smile.

Deftly Sasumi ripped open the packet with one hand, and less deftly rolled the condom onto his shaft. She'd practised opening foil packets, Kwai realized with surprise, she just didn't yet have the experience putting their contents on. Maybe she really was the amateur she said.

'*Now* we fuck,' said Sasumi. Kwai nodded.

Lying back on the imported Spanish lace, her pale body lit by the light of a scented candle, Sasumi pulled a feather pillow under her buttocks and slowly parted her knees. Steadying himself above her, reaching down to position himself against her open sex, Kwai thrust slowly up into her tightness, feeling Sasumi's hips coming up to meet him, her legs hooking over his. With the entry came an incredible sense of calm, of release. He would keep her when it was all over. If Sasumi wanted to be kept.

Her full breasts swayed under the shock of his thrusts. Each thrust sending a small *tsunami* up through her body to ripple her skin. Dipping his head, Kwai halted one rocking breast with his mouth, trapping her nipple between his lips. He sucked gently, then harder, swallowing her hardening bud until Sasumi pushed her breast up at him, squashing it against his lips.

Hungrily, Kwai moved a hand to her other breast, squeezing until its flesh strained beneath his grasping fingers. Finger and thumb closing on an already taut nipple.

Sasumi was groaning now, slow steady moans as her mouth reached up for his. His fingers still tugging softly at her nipple, Kwai bit into Sasumi's lower lip, feeling her buck beneath him, hips punching up, arms linked tight across his back to give herself leverage.

Kwai could feel the need in the way she ground her hips against him, in her hot wet tightness. He would have thought it an act, and a good one, but Sasumi was crying, silent tears that rolled down her wide cheeks.

Guilt, fear or just the *e2*? He wanted to know why but didn't know how to ask.

Instead he settled on giving her what her body so obviously wanted, if he could. Shifting a little, he drew slowly out of Sasumi until the head of his penis rested just outside her, unmoving.

Sasumi looked up at him, suddenly worried, but Kwai grinned. And then he went into her on a long slow thrust, feeling the quick tug as his penis slid through the tight entrance of her vagina. Kwai held himself inside her, letting the soft mound of her *mons* push hard against the base of his penis.

Sucking his fingers, Kwai slid one hand down from her breast, smoothing it over her hip and round under her buttocks. For a second, his fingertips brushed against her wet and swollen lips, and then Kwai shifted his hand until he found the crease of her arse and, very gently, pushed one wet finger deep into her anus. It was enough. Sasumi gasped, almost wide-eyed with embarrassment, and then she was bucking under him, her face pushed tight into his shoulder to drown her own sobs.

Afterwards Kwai watched her in the candlelight, seeing her tears dry in tracks down her flat cheeks, smudging the porcelain finish of her cheap face powder. But he still didn't know how to ask the right questions.

And later still, when shards of light had begun pushing through the velvet curtains, Kwai took her again. From the back, so he didn't have to see the bolted-down sadness in her eyes.

[Santa Passionata/Stage Diving]

The two weeks were up and Saturday was his final day in Tokyo. So, while Sasumi slept, Kwai took himself down to the litter-free exclusive-shopping zone of Ginza, to tread the sidewalks of the most expensive real estate on the planet. It was like walking into an elaborate marble, glass and concrete canyon. Daylight banished to a strip of sky high above his head, as straight and narrow as the street below.

The nervousness, the sense of not belonging, not knowing the rules rolled in on Kwai once again as he watched small, elegant cars slide in and out of the morning traffic, every third one looking as if it were an expensive toy escaped from a Disney cartoon.

And what kind of city had its taxis display red lights when they were *empty*, and green lights to show that they were full? Here was none of the noise of Bangkok, none of the smell of burning noodles, joss and bubbling black Java. He would never have imagined he might, but part of him already missed the smog, the stink of the canals, the noise and chaos of jaywalking pedestrians as they forced traffic to screech to a halt.

Retracing his steps, Kwai stopped briefly to look in the windows of *Wako* and *Mitsukoshi*, drank an overpriced double latte at a café on the *Yon-chome* crossing, where *Harumi-dori* and *Chuo-dori* intersected, and then backtracked to find the shop he was really after.

A gutted room, stripped beech floor and a vase of wild scrub bamboo. Clothes hanging from haphazard chrome rails. He found PS/T without trouble and was seen by a very serious young

Japanese with slightly too long hair and a little too much Calvin Klein aftershave.

'Sir?' The man's eyes flicked over the Thai boy's dark suit, with its single stitching and slightly asymmetrical lapels. His face didn't change but Kwai was sure he stepped back a little, distancing himself.

Kwai frowned. He loved that suit, it was his pride and joy. Or it had been until last week when he first walked through Ginza, stopping every few paces to marvel at the sheer elegance and élan of the garments in the shop windows. And then he'd known the difference between a Ralph Lauren copy, even a good one, and a Purple Label original, between clone Armani and the real thing. No contest. Not one of the suits in any of the windows had a price tag. Which told Kwai all he needed to know about what they were likely to cost.

Sighing, Kwai hitched the Raybans up onto his nose and pulled out a red lizard-skin wallet, slipping his gold card discreetly onto a glass-topped counter. It was elegantly done and Kwai was ridiculously pleased with himself.

'I need a suit,' he said in English, 'Off the rails, *prêt à porter*. Something dark. Loose cut, almost baggy,' he added.

The assistant looked as if he might protest, politely, but Kwai held up one hand. 'Loose,' he said firmly, 'and baggy under the arms.'

Kwai knew that wasn't the fashion. He'd picked up a copy of *Esquire* at Narita airport and knew suits were being cut tighter. But you couldn't hide a Colt under the armpit of a tight jacket, any more than you could throw a decent kick in an overtight pair of trousers. Besides, tight clothes might work in Tokyo, but the weather in Bangkok was as erratic as the air-conditioning.

The polite young man eventually found something to satisfy them both, and discreetly swiped Kwai's card through a reader. With the suit, Kwai took six shot-silk shirts and a red silk tie. As looks went, it was already dated in Milan and New York. But Kwai wanted something classical, something that whispered postmillennial without having to spell it out. To the Japanese man's horror, Kwai refused to have the clothes sent to his hotel and insisted on wearing the suit and having the shirts wrapped to take with him. The Thai boy smiled slightly as the Japanese shop assistant meticulously folded the shirts, sliding them into two elegant carrier bags as he tried hard not to crease the already fashionably-crumpled material.

It took all Kwai's will not to point out that he was about to fly to Moscow, and carrying the clothes back to his hotel was nothing compared to subjecting it to seven hours on Aeroflot, even travelling executive class. But that wouldn't be discreet, and Kwai was giving himself urgent lessons in discretion.

He followed buying the suit with a new haircut, something English and floppy at the front. It went with the new clothes and made him look not older but ageless, the way that certain Englishmen were ageless. Kwai liked it. He added two pairs of black leather shoes with metal heel plates, good for kicking, a leather belt, dark wool socks and a set of new Calvin Klein underwear.

Then Kwai took a detour to dump his shopping off in the foyer of the Ginza Plaza, leaving instructions with a pock-marked porter that they be taken immediately to his room. That was when his day started to go seriously wrong, though Kwai didn't yet know it.

All he knew was he didn't like the way the uniformed boy refused Kwai's tip. Not insolently, not quite, but totally without deference. As if Kwai should have known tipping was banned. As if being a porter at the Ginza Plaza was automatically better than being an ignorant guest.

Kwai let it pass, time was counting down, and went instead in search of what he really needed – a new identity. Ameyuko market under the elevated track that ran from Ueno to Okachimaci JR station was excellent, if you wanted dried soup, shelled groundnuts or a new ignition system for the latest 750cc Fireblade, and Takeshita-dori was good for clothes and crowds of pushing, chattering teenagers, but it was at Tsukiji he found what he wanted, in the back room of a sushi bar overlooking the fish market. How Passion knew it was there Kwai didn't want to know: there were depths to the American woman's friends he hadn't even guessed at, dangerous ones.

It took Kwai most of the morning to negotiate and haggle, but by lunchtime he'd got a new passport, Japanese no less, and a selection of cashcards all made out to his new name but with their digital strips programmed to draw only against his gold Amex.

He didn't look Japanese, of course. Not really. Certainly not to someone from Tokyo, but hell, hicks from Okinawa didn't look Japanese to people from Tokyo. And he'd get by in Moscow and St Petersburg, where anyone who had his cheekbones and almond eyes had to be Japanese if they weren't Chinese or Mongol.

Kwai'd done his research. Japanese was good in Russia: it spelt money, technology, respectability. It also, unfairly or not, spelt a gut-level right-wing bias and a belief in monarchy, in social deference. Kwai needed that. Well, he did if he wanted to get close enough to the Black Hundreds to take out their leader.

With the cards came an international driving licence, grey laminate with a new photograph, and a US pilot's licence even though he'd only ever been in a plane once, and that was the Boeing on his flight between Bangkok and Tokyo.

By lunchtime, Kwai'd found the last item he needed, a new blade. He didn't mind what make, but the knife had to be ceramic or glass throughout. There was no point getting a glass-bladed flick only to have some internal metal spring trigger an alarm at the first airport security monitor.

What he got was a gravity blade and, as added precaution, a tiny black punching knife that slotted into a sheath behind the buckle of its accompanying belt. It had a flat neophrene T-handle and an inch-long blade that curved in on both sides towards the handle. Basic and lethal, it came without instructions. None were needed. Rest the handle in the palm of your hand, wrap your fingers round the stem of the zytel blade and punch, hard and fast.

It wasn't the first one Kwai had owned, though it was the most expensive. With speed and determination, a good fighter could get in four or five lethal punches before a victim even realized his attacker was carrying a knife.

'Where were you?'

Sasumi's voice was raw, her words thrown at Kwai as soon as he stepped through the door. She was standing by his dressing table, fully clothed, her small black bag tucked protectively under her arm. It looked like she'd been about to leave.

'Out shopping,' said Kwai. Given that his bags had been dumped in a pile on the bed, he'd have thought that was obvious.

Sasumi said nothing. She didn't go, she didn't relax either, just stayed silent, unmoving; radiating bitterness.

'What's wrong?' Kwai asked, talking a step towards her. Only to halt when the young prostitute stepped hurriedly back. Sasumi's eyes were red, her mascara smudged dark across her flat face. Even a thick layer of foundation couldn't hide a bruise that hadn't been there when he left.

'Tell me,' Kwai demanded, but he already knew.

'*They* came up with your shopping.' Sasumi's voice was filled with loathing, her words brittle as glass, as if Kwai was somehow responsible. It took Kwai a second or two to realize it was taking Sasumi every ounce of effort not to cry.

'The bell boys?'

'I was in the shower,' the young prostitute said bleakly.

Kwai knew the rest. Prostitutes didn't do well in the flash hotels of Bangkok either, no matter what tourists thought. God alone knew how they fared in Tokyo. Especially a Japanese girl with a Thai. It didn't bear thinking about.

'What did you say?' Kwai asked, buying time, running possible responses through his head. Sensible was out, his gut reaction was a toss-up between dangerous and idiotic.

'That I was waiting for you . . .' Sasumi delved into the side pocket of her black jacket to drag out a packet of Lucky Strike.

Viciously she tapped one free from its packet and put it between quivering lips, ignoring the room's prominent *No Smoking* sign.

So badly were her fingers shaking, it took Sasumi three attempts to light the thing. But she brushed away Kwai's help, swatting his lighter aside.

'It was the truth,' Sasumi added fiercely. 'I *was* waiting for you.' Not that the truth would have made much difference, they both knew that.

'And then . . . ?' Carefully, Kwai slipped his false passport, the credit cards and the ceramic gravity knife into the drawer of an ornate bedside table. When he glanced up the Japanese woman was looking at him in silence, waiting for his attention.

'What do you think?' Sasumi asked coldly. 'They said I must go . . . you wouldn't want me still here when you got back.' Sasumi shivered. 'They threatened to call the police.' Hunching her shoulders inside her cheap jacket, she folded one arm tight across her body, the other lifting the cigarette to her lips. It could have been smoke putting tears in her eyes, but Kwai knew it wasn't.

'And then . . . ?' he prompted her, stepping round Sasuni to get a pair of black boots from his wardrobe, folding them in tissue paper, then placing them carefully at the bottom of a leather case. Kwai wasn't ignoring her, he was still thinking . . .

'They . . .' Sasumi clenched a fist. 'Oh shit, you know what happened,' she said furiously. Even with her face turned away, Kwai could tell she was crying openly. Not dramatically like on cable, but silently, the way real people cry, privately, so he wouldn't hear. It made him angry, but not with her: it made him feel protective. Those weren't good emotions for someone in his line of work.

'Who?' Kwai asked, then answered his own question for her, because he already knew. 'The pockmarked one, and the older man with sideburns . . . ?' The two he'd told to take up his bags.

Sasumi nodded.

Anger, real anger. Kwai recognized it for what it was, and was still surprised. Total cold fury wasn't an emotion Kwai knew well.

In his full seventeen years, it had come maybe twice, three times. But it was there again, in a cold, clean adrenalin rush; in the hard beat of his heart, in the extra oxygen that began to pump though his blood.

Unbuckling his old belt, Kwai fitted the new one in place. It was perfect, exactly the right width for the loops in his suit trouser. What's more, the leather was good quality.

'Wash your face,' Kwai told her. 'Then get your bag, order yourself a taxi.' He pushed an Aeroflot plane ticket and a thick bundle of yen at her. 'Find some new clothes at the airport. Oh . . .' Kwai paused, 'and get those two porters to collect my bags. Make sure they're the ones who came up earlier.'

Sasumi stared at him.

'Do it,' said Kwai gently. He took Sasumi by the shoulders. 'Look,' he said, 'they won't expect you to tell me what happened. And anyway, why should I care? You're a whore, I'm just passing through . . .'

The Thai boy zipped his bags and dumped one by the bathroom, another by the open window. The room's red velvet curtains were already open so Kwai hooked back the nets as well, as if he was letting in fresh air. And why not? Tokyo wasn't brilliant for pollution control but it sure as hell beat the air in Bangkok.

Sasumi left, still shaking, looking nervous. Wide dark eyes set in a flat face. He liked her, more than he had intended. More than he liked Passion.

Having moved his first bag from outside the bathroom to just inside, Kwai killed time flicking through the cable stations. The Ginza Plaza was too upscale to have porn channels, so instead he clicked through a dozen Saturday-afternoon kids' cartoons, *Dragon Ball Z*, *A-Ko*, *Lum*, watching each in five-second bursts. He had no trouble keeping track of the plot lines: boy meets girl, girl turns into monster . . . they were pretty standard.

Before the bellhops even had time to knock, Kwai told them to come in. He'd been tracking their footsteps in the corridor outside. They came in, looking not nervous but wary. Eyes skimmed the room, taking in his packed bags and Kwai sitting on the huge bed watching kids' TV. And both of them relaxed, as they were meant to do.

Kwai nodded to the window. 'Over there,' he said, then walked to the bathroom, 'and here one.' The younger bellhop smirked at his atrocious accent, at the jumbled order of his Japanese.

'The bags,' Kwai said, flushing.

As the elder one got the bag by the window, Kwai followed the younger into his bathroom. Grabbing the pockmarked boy by the back of his head, Kwai slammed him once, face forward into the white-tiled wall. Blood splattered, tiles cracked and then the man slumped to the floor without a sound. His nose broken, tongue bitten through.

'All right here?' Kwai asked, stepping back into his room. Still smiling, he walked swiftly across to the window, one hand resting lightly by his side, T-bar blade folded back inside his closed fingers. Not that Kwai intended to use it, not unless things went badly wrong.

'What happened?' The older man made to push past Kwai, but never got the chance. The punching knife was at his throat before the bellhop knew it.

'No sound . . .' Kwai moved its zytel blade up towards the man's eye. The blade wasn't impressive, not like the *kris* Kwai had used on Jim Chance back in Bangkok, but the bellhop still got the message.

Deftly, Kwai dropped his other hand to the man's hotel-issue trousers, unzipped the fly and thrust twisting fingers into the older man's crotch. Closing his hand over a testicle, Kwai twisted, ripping veins, fingers digging through coarse cotton to crush the delicate, nerve-rich tissue.

The man choked on his own rising spray of vomit. Only the knife at his face kept him from howling in agony. Swiftly Kwai released his grip, thrust his hand through the fly of the man's Y-fronts to yank out his fear-shrivelled penis. And then Kwai tipped him roughly backward, through the open window. The man fell in silence, landing with a muffled thud on a flat roof below. Someone would spot him eventually, but Kwai was prepared to take a risk it wouldn't be for an hour or two. And Kwai would be long gone before anyone thought to pin anything on him.

To start with, three of the walls facing into that inner well were blank, while the other wall had nets over each of its windows. And a flat roof housing the hotel kitchen's air-conditioning unit wasn't a view guests would want to examine too closely anyway.

Time to finish it. Moving towards the muffled whimpers coming from inside his bathroom, Kwai pushed open the door. The younger bellhop was up on his knees, kneeling over the lavatory, his head deep in the bowl, with blood dripping from his nose and vomit running in thin sticky trails from his swollen mouth.

For a second, Kwai was tempted to stamp the bellhop's neck into the clean white edge of the porcelain, but that didn't fit in with what he had in mind. What Kwai wanted was to walk away from the Ginza Plaza leaving no trace, and no reason why anyone should want to trace him.

The bellhop's name was Micky Onada, he was twenty, originally from Osaka. He'd worked at the Plaza for three years, that much Kwai deduced from looking at his identity papers and staff pass. Also in his hip pocket was a packet of Durex condoms, a subway ticket and a small French penknife with a wood handle.

That knife was an unexpected bonus. It meant Kwai didn't have to sacrifice his new ceramic blade as evidence at the scene of the crime. He had an old *NYPD Blue* repeat to thank for his knowledge that violent death without visible weapon automatically counted as murder not suicide.

Hoisting the boy into the bath in one quick move, Kwai turned on both taps and then slashed three times across the boy's wrists, the Opinel's blunt blade raising stark but ineffective weals as it pulled against tendons. Amateur night . . . Then, with the bath half full, Kwai sat on its edge and grabbed the bellhop's hand, yanking his arm out straight.

This cut was going to bleed. Kwai didn't know how much. But

enough to need mopping up. Still, one towel should do it, Kwai thought wryly, especially given the thickness of the ones they provided at this hotel.

Folding the towel so it covered his own legs, Kwai gripped the small lock knife so its blade faced towards him and then dug hard into Sasumi's attacker's arm just below the elbow, raking the cutting edge along the inside of the bellhop's arm towards his wrist. It took a stab to punch the blunt blade in through his skin, but brute force did the rest as a long wound ripped open like obscene lips along the boy's forearm.

Blood pumped out, turning the warm bath water bright red, then gurgled away as Kwai pulled out the plug. Pint after pint of blood swirling in a circle before vanishing. It was hard to tell when Sasumi's attacker died. His moans had long since ceased and his skin had turned pale the moment Kwai slammed his head against the wall.

One body dead on the half-roof below the window. Another with its wrists slashed in the bathroom of an empty hotel room. Let the police make of it what they would. The Ginza Plaza at least would do their best to hush it up. Not least because of the unzipped fly of the bellhop with the sideburns.

Kwai pulled the bathroom door closed behind him, having already shut off the taps, washed his hands and wiped his prints from the taps. Then he hooked shut the window, pulled the net curtains neatly back into place and checked that the room was tidy.

[Saints & Synners]

So, Lieutenant Angeli thought to himself as he broke the connection, letting Kwai fade away like a ghost, newVenice was founded by the dusted-out bulimic daughter of a West Coast crime boss. With help from a Thai street thief.

Interesting, not to say improbable, but ultimately, so fucking what? Of course, that DVD wasn't downloaded from CySat's official site, because *S&S*'s take on newVenice wasn't the official version. That was *St Passionata's Passion*, a we-took-on-the-world (and won) epic that formed one of CySat nV's longest running exports.

But *Saints & Synners* was another matter. Primitive and crude, but real. It's V-actors, levels and music had been coded in entirety – years back – by a Belfast boy name of Declan, who knew Passion before newVenice was founded, or so Angeli had found out.

And Declan had made the *S&S* V-actors look like real people. Or at least, real people back then. Fat/thin, crook-nosed/broken-toothed, not smooth as heroes or slick as gods. What's more, *Saints & Synners* was never uploaded. Which in Angeli's book was a sure fucking sign it got closer to the truth than any official version.

He'd got the pirate DVD disc from some Ishie he'd pulled in for splicing his 'fight' with that girl into the evening newsfeed, run the disc through a Sony RomReader wired straight to his NVPD helmet, played it out inside his visual cortex. Getting the tiny silver disc was a straight favour for a favour. The Ishie found Angeli *Saints & Synners* and Angeli agreed not to pull the kid's slopcard.

But did it tell Angeli anything he could use, anything he didn't really know? Angeli wasn't sure. He wasn't good at unaugmented thought but, much as he'd like to, he couldn't risk borrowing an official NVPD neural net to help him on his way.

And without authorization Angeli couldn't pass through a safe gate in the sonic wall, couldn't get back inside the city proper. He'd tried, only to be turned back at the Third District gate by a smirking member of the *WeGuard*. Officially withdrawn or not (and it hadn't been) it seemed the usefulness of his acting rank of *Vice-Questore* was at an end. But Angeli still had DNA fingerprints from the stab wound, not to mention a neat, ray-traced reconstruction of the blade.

And then there was that little shit Paco, out getting information from punters and slummers, scum who'd have clammed tight in front of Angeli, or else gone scuttling back through the electric fences to the safety of their palazzo. And, according to Paco, word on the levels was that the Doge was missing, word in the city was that his bodyguard wasn't around either. No one in the city was too distressed by the idea.

[Dancing The Apocalypso]

The plane came in low over Lake Zurich, the tips of its squat up-flipped/down-turned wings skimming inches above the flat calm of the cold pale water, never quite breaking the surface. The plane was dark silver, though it reflected blue in the washed-out azure of the lake's mirrored surface. It was small, maybe even a single-seater, with a long wrap-round windscreen of smoke-coloured plexiglass that doubled as the walls of the pilot's pod.

Looking out at the lake, Razz had already decided the approaching craft was a plane, though it could have been a speedboat with wings. Or maybe some kind of skirtless hovercraft. In fact, it looked like nothing so much as some giant flatfish caught by an underwater photographer in the middle of its downward flap. That was if you could overlook the two huge propellers to the rear of its strange wings.

Whatever it was – and actually it was a prototype, Lugano-made wing-in-ground Honda personnel carrier – the craft was coming in low and fast over the narrow waters of Lake Zurich in a way that left Razz feeling decidedly uneasy.

But then a lot of things had been leaving Razz feeling uneasy, not the least of which was that she didn't know where she was. Though, strangely enough, the most obvious cause of her distress was that she smelt. Not of perfume or chemicals, nor rank and unwashed, but with a warm animal smell that radiated from her every pore.

Razz knew scent was a straight chemical reaction, like thought and memory, no more than molecules acting on nerve receptors within the olfactory epithelium. She just wasn't used to being aware of her own smell.

And there were other scents to disturb her: mud-like richness from roasting coffee creeping thick and heavy under her door, the distant scent of a wood fire, the sweet corruption of black orchids set in a vase in the corner of her bathroom.

Maybe she'd had a new neural enhancement to update the potency of her epithelium nerves? She considered and immediately rejected the idea as the real answer became clear. She hadn't had her sense of smell enhanced at all. She'd merely had it restored.

It was years, Razz realized, *years* since she'd been conscious of how objects smelt. Unless you needed smell for tracking, scent was a distraction, a waste of neural resources: a candidate for deletion to heighten those senses that remained. Her ability to detect smell would have been removed years before, in that black clinic in Budapest probably, when she was still little more than a kid.

The plane had banked now. Still low over the water, it swept along the bay below her hotel window. It *was* a hotel and a good one, Razz decided. She'd yet to step outside her door, but knew already from the expensive anonymity of the heavy oak furniture, the neat but soulless brushed paths outside and the snow-covered lawns. All displayed a complete lack of character. A Conrad maybe, or one of the better Hyatts. Either that, or it was an upscale clinic of some sort.

Looking at the WIG as it spun back out towards the middle of the lake, Razz realized something else. The plane couldn't leave the water and that realization reassured her. All the same it was now banking above the waves making ready for another inward run. Instinctively, Razz stepped back from the window – and like in a dream became conscious of her nakedness.

More shocked by that than anything else.

She was naked. That wasn't unusual. Little more than expensive and lethal pets, exotics were expected to be naked. Just as they were expected to be thin and fit, to have viral enhancements that made this happen. No, what was strange about Razz being aware of her nakedness was that self-consciousness was a failing she'd had whipped out of her.

But that was long ago and in another life.

Walking over to a huge antique Louis XV mirror, Razz glanced in, intending to take a long hard look at herself. She never got beyond the first glance, the one that told her that her silver flesh was now pale brown and her nipples mahogany-dark, that her hips were wider than she remembered, her breasts not yet starting to droop. That she had body hair, deep dark-red body hair unaffected by radiowave electrolysis.

What knocked Razz flat, crumpling her unexpected, unrecognized body into a heap on the expensive Persian rug, was simple shock: cocaine-pure and twice as cold. Okay, so the person in the mirror was young, maybe a good thirty years younger than Razz was: and the body really was hers, Razz realized, though she'd always thought herself thinner at that age. But that wasn't the shock, not the real one . . .

No. Two things clicked out Razz's neural paths, knocking her unconscious. One was seeing herself totally unaugmented. No claws, no shoulder armour of lizard skin layered over shark cartilage. The other was the sudden, sickening realization that she didn't know what had happened to Aurelio.

She hadn't the faintest fucking idea.

The Doge could be dead, of course, Razz realized in the split second it took her to hit the floor. But then, she'd been dead too. And dying wasn't something she liked, never had done. Someone somewhere was going to . . .

[SnowBlind in Zurich]

'Razz?' There was a soft double-knock at her door. And when it wasn't answered the double-knock came again, harder this time. It had taken longer to land that fancy plane than Alex, Lord Winterbrooke had hoped. Most planes flew-by-light, a few, a very few, still flew-by-wire. Alex Gibson flew by thought, operating the controls by neural link. It wasn't as easy as it should have been. But then, there were reasons for that.

His brain was wired through with bioClay. Within his cortex he held a whole simulacrum of the Cy; hardwired neural templates filled in what few synaptic gaps viral rewiring had left unaugmented. He could, and did, taste digital data the way countrymen tasted the wind, instinct fine-tuned to coming changes.

But still he forgot to eat, to sleep.

'Break the door down,' a voice ordered impatiently. But it was ignored. So were all the other voices who instantly agreed. Alex knocked once more and then, when that failed, reached inside his tattered jellaba for a small matt-black box. Taking a thin laminate from the box, the tall man swiped it once through the hotel door's lock, then watched a set of numbers flick into life along the card's surface.

'Got it,' he said with satisfaction, putting his thin hand over the lock.

'Sweet Jesus,' a voice snapped in his head, 'just kick the door in, and get on with it.' But Alex did nothing of the sort. He enjoyed being slow and methodical, not least because it wound up his 'partner', if Alex Gibson could use that word about the tall Sicilian prince who occupied the wastelands of Alex's brain.

So, instead, Alex thought hard, his fingers against the door, and breathed a sigh of relief as the electronic tumblers clicked into place beneath his touch.

'Patience,' he told the other voice softly, and then laughed at himself. *Breeding, courage* and *obstinacy*, all those were cardinal virtues according to Prince Sabatini, but *patience* would never be among them.

Part god/part lunatic, patience still came naturally to Alex Gibson. Once he'd been an evidence chaser, tracking down trials for CySat. A man with a gut feel for what made a good show. But these days he was contracted to the Church of Christ Geneticist. Stuck out in the desert like some Byzantine anchorite, telling the truth to people who didn't want to hear it. And patience was a luxury he could ill afford. Alex's periods of sanity were becoming briefer and this one was almost over.

Hard, luminous edges had already begun to build up around everyday objects and the splutter of bright sparks had begun to flicker behind his haunted eyes.

The man (and there was only one) walked slowly into the room where Razz lay knocked unconscious with shock. Stepping neatly over her naked body, he searched the suite swiftly and efficiently, checking for evidence of foreign DNA. There was none. So far as Alex could tell, no one other than Razz had recently been in either the bedroom or bathroom.

There were no bugs, no miniaturized cameras. The transparent fooler loops he'd ordered slicked over the inside of each window were there in place, ready to scramble input to any distant parabolic microphone, their sub-miniature batteries busily recharging themselves in the Swiss sunlight.

Alex Gibson hadn't expected to find signs of anybody else, but he checked anyway. He was like that. It was why he was still more or less alive, which until very recently Razz wasn't.

Alex needed something from Razz. He couldn't order Razz to track down the Doge. For that, he'd need leverage he didn't have; and besides it was a long time since anyone had tried to give Razz orders. And he wouldn't ask her – or, maybe, it was that he couldn't. Ask her, that was.

But deep inside the jumbled howl of voices that passed these days for his mind, Alex Gibson knew Razz would do it. It just had to be her throw, or not at all.

Swiftly he put a visiting card onto a window ledge. The card was studiedly old-fashioned, *Prince Sabatini* embossed in swirling black onto its china-clay surface. Above the title was a baroque coat of arms, with an elaborate twisted coronet poised above a shield divided into sixteen. Draped behind the arms was the vast ermine *manteau* of a ruling prince.

With a sigh, Alex flipped over the card and scrawled what looked like (and once was) a random mix of twenty-nine letters and digits, followed by the initials *HKS*. Then he scrawled *Doge?* and as an afterthought he added *Alex*, then a swift cross.

Looking at the written kiss, Alex wished he could take it back. But it was too late, or rather it wasn't, but Alex couldn't be bothered to extract another of the Prince's ridiculous cards and go through the effort of calling up the HKS digits from the scrambled recesses of his memory.

Alex was gone when Razz awoke. His Honda wing-in-ground had been dumped at the other end of the cold blue lake where a stealth-laden Sikorski j-jet waited to carry him south over the toe of Italy, low over the swell of the Med and back across the North African littoral to the headquarters of the Church of Christ Geneticist . . .

Refraction, Alex thought happily, looking at the blue water below. Waves of light in conflict with hydrogen and oxygen molecules, the water stripping blue out of the spectrum to let the rest pass through. Like life, really, or memory; how events appeared depended on what you filtered them through.

Zurich was gone. Already forgotten. And so was he. Alex had made sure of that. The last thing he had done, before Lake Zurich vanished like a sliver of silver behind him, was to stop at a public holovid, punch in the access coordinates for the hotel's security system, slick one end of a trode over the microphone and jack the other end into a ceramic wrist socket. In less time than it usually took Alex to remember his name he would wipe clean the whole day's record.

FujiLara would have claimed their camera system was uncrackable, but Alex had hacked it from habit, without having to think about it. Which was just as well, because by the time he'd reached his HondaWIG, the lightning in Alex's head had grown so bad he wanted to die.

Digital flicker was breaking up his vision so badly Alex couldn't tell what was neural white noise and what was actual falling snow. Two Swiss minders had helped him out at the other end of the lake, taken him to the vidbooth as he'd demanded, then strapped the staggering tramp into the waiting Sikorski.

Over North Italy Alex started seeing people he knew were dead, because he'd killed them. By the time the Sikorski passed unseen through Sicilian airspace, Alex was raving, blood running from his bitten lips. Alex passed through mania into a grinning catatonic trance long before his j-jet reached that high-rise strip of ribbon development that signified the beginning of the North African littoral. Gods were useful, even minor ones like Alex, but they weren't easy to live with.

Her first problem, Razz realized as she picked herself up off the expensive Persian rug was finding something to wear. She wasn't going to get far wandering stark naked round wherever this was. The second – Razz checked there was a second problem and there was – involved getting out of the room. Its door might be laminated in burr walnut, hung on noiseless hinges and polished to an unnatural shine, but it was still locked.

As it turned out, clothes weren't a problem at all. Having wasted five minutes standing in front of an oak wardrobe ordering it to open, Razz discovered the brass handles actually worked. And knew just how expensive a hotel she'd found herself in. Only the very rich or very sophisticated would do things in such a resolutely old-fashioned way. But then, only they had the time or inclination.

Razz opened another wardrobe at random, finding it full of clothes, all of which looked as if they would fit. Razz tried on a spider's-silk body and it did, perfectly . . . The tailoring was immaculate, tight across her gut, cut neatly around her thighs. Someone, somewhere had fed a scan of her new body into a SingerSoftCut, the ubiquitous *virgin's friend*.

A must for women who could afford perfect, made-to-measure clothes but didn't want to get touched by human hands in the process, the SSC sold well to husbands and fathers in Saudi Arabia, not to mention the US Midwest.

Razz slid back the door of a third wardrobe to find more clothes, different style. Five wardrobes, five styles. She chose the silver jacket with neophrene elbow pads, a short skirt cloned from maroon ultrasuede and black knee-length boots with spiked kitten heels. They fitted perfectly, and looked absolutely ridiculous.

It's down to colouring, Razz decided with a frown. She should stop trying to colour-match clothes to her silver skin, not least because it wasn't there any more . . . Razz tried on something in a vat-grown sharkskin/lizard mix, same style but in hues that went better with the rich tan of her face and legs.

Zip, neit, nada . . .

Still wrong, fuck it. But at least the wardrobe operated manually. The last thing Razz needed was this year's sodding Zanusi Stylemaster offering this season's bland style advice.

She was worried her skin was back to natural, not least because when Razz took out that cloning policy with First Virtual she'd been obsessively careful to specify the exact Pantone match for the silver she required. But her new skin wasn't the real problem, at least not fashion-wise. The real problem was her age.

Five years younger than her actual age at termination were the terms of her policy. Certainly not practically back to fucking childhood. It hadn't been that much fun the first time round: Razz had no great interest in repeating it. And it wasn't just that this wasn't the skin tone she'd ordered. Razz wasn't even sure it was a genuine clone.

Standing in front of an ornate mirror, Razz took a long hard look at her new self, considering. The face was young, slightly too pretty, with high cheekbones and lips that weren't exactly full but had more than a hint of slight pout. But her gaze was firm, her eyes brown and clear, her nose broad but not wide, and at least her chin was firm. It was a good face, a strong face, but Razz already knew what was lacking. What it missed was experience.

Life codes itself onto the human face as certainly as lasers write to disk. Except that, unlike data, experience couldn't be completely erased, or so Razz had always believed. She was the sum of her old face, its silver skin stretched too tight over enhanced cheekbones, tiny fault lines radiating out from the edges of her lips, tension inherent in her dark gaze. Even her last clone had adapted on start-up to the emotional dictates established in her cerebral download.

This face was missing all that. No matter how hard she looked, Razz couldn't find herself in the wide-eyed girl who stared intently back. The outward signs of her character had been erased. Not from her mind, but from her face.

She was, Razz realized with a start, somewhere around sixteen, about as old as that shit DiOrchi's daughter. It was hard to be exact, she didn't have enough data to judge against. Razz wasn't one to waste time with the pampered, protected offspring of newVenice, her tolerance was too low. Though she made an exception for Karo, always had done. Otherwise Razz wouldn't have taught Karo the things she did. Wouldn't have . . .

Hurriedly, Razz switched track. Only problem was, Razz realized, her memories were catty-corner to her body's age. And her experience was older still. It was an ugly thought, to be filed in the back of her mind. Let the different bits of her subconscious fight it out later. She needed to dress.

Eventually Razz chose something almost understated (which was a shock in itself) but obviously expensive (which wasn't).

She ditched the white spider's-silk body for a black thong, red silk shirt with dark pearl buttons (both cloned), a long black skirt of wafer-thin ultrasuede and a black velvet jacket.

Feet, Razz thought, running her eyes along a long multicoloured line of boots, shoes and pumps. In the end she chose a pair of round-toed back boots, short at the side with sharp titanium reinforcements to the toe and heel. It was Razz's one concession to the silver-skinned exotic she'd once been.

She looked good. No, Razz grinned at herself in the glass, she looked way more than good. Young, true. But stylish, still slightly dangerous. Razz had a feeling she might get to like understated.

The wardrobes might have been manual, the door to her room wasn't. As far as she could see, it wasn't meant to be opened from the inside. There was no handle, no self-illuminating touchpad, no slot for a smartcard. Razz tried again to make it open, ordering it in everything from a whisper to a near-shout. Briefly worried the hotel software might not understand English, Razz dredged up rudiments of German and French. No success. The door still refused to budge.

Which left Razz with the windows. It was while she tried each one in turn that Razz discovered the visiting card, its bottom edge not quite touching but precisely parallel to the window ledge. Obsessive wasn't in it. And that meant Alex. Which, these days, meant the howling horde in his brain as well.

'Prince fucking Sabatini,' Razz almost spat in disgust, then caught herself. Spitting was out, it didn't fit with *understated*, it went with silver skin and reflexes wired tight enough to let you drop kick the shit out of anyone who thought to object.

What fighting skills she still had left, Razz didn't know. But she'd already worked out that if her body wasn't augmented then chances were her reflexes weren't wired either. These days if she went up against someone, it was going to be on equal terms; which wasn't a thought Razz found reassuring.

Flipping over the card, Razz read the message scrawled on its back. HKS was Hong Kong Suisse, the twenty-nine-character/

digit figure the crypt key to some account, or so she presumed. These days, who knew anything where Alex was concerned?

Razz returned to the burr-walnut door, tried one final time ordering it to open and then gave up in disgust. No voice-recognition facility, no handle and so far as she could see no manual override. Razz was still leaning against the wall, worrying at the problem, when her brown eyes glazed over and she began to deconstruct, too fast for the human eye.

Not into corruption or bruised and broken flesh, but into invisibility as her body disappeared into fractal wisps of grey smoke. The change began at her fingertips and once it reached her wrist her clothes too began to unzip molecule by molecule, millions of fractured atoms breaking away only to reassemble on the other side of the door. Dust to dust, copy to copy. It was over in a nanosecond, as Razz vanished from one side and reappeared on the other.

Razz blinked. Spat. And sat down on the floor. 'Sweet Nazarene,' she muttered, staring at the locked shut door behind her. 'How the fuck did I do that?'

It was a good question . . .

[Searching For The Edge]

Herr Garibaldi was a small man. He might once have been termed a dwarf, but that word was in disuse. And had Razz ever been bothered enough to look it up, which she wouldn't have been, she would've found it used only in relation to small fictional beings found mostly in Scandinavian myth.

Razz could have asked why a man with an Italian name and a German accent was head of a Swiss bank, but she didn't do that either. It would have involved too much history. Razz wasn't big on history at the best of times, and this seriously wasn't one of them.

She'd drunk more hot chocolate than one person could stand. Refused the offer of custard cake and insisted that, no, she didn't need to use the bathroom.

It didn't help that Herr Garibaldi was treating her like a small child. All right, so she was wearing the body of a teenage girl, but the way he was talking to her she could have been seven.

Leant over Herr Garibaldi's desk, her face pushed close enough to his to smell garlic on his breath, Razz shook her head impatiently, a cascade of dark copper hair sweeping across her hunched shoulders. 'I have the key,' Razz said crossly.

The elderly banker nodded, his slightly too bulbous eyes flicking nervously between her face and the small visitor's card she held firmly in one hand. He didn't know the digits or letter written there. What he did know was that the girl had just punched these into a keypad and the bank's central computer had accepted them as valid.

It was obvious Herr Garibaldi was unhappy. Equally obvious

that he didn't appreciate Razz's stubborn refusal to sit. This left him pressed back in the depths of an impressively old green leather chair, staring anxiously up at a girl whose face was now only inches from his.

She looked too young, too innocent to be the kind of girl who enjoyed violence, but something about her manner suggested otherwise.

'You have the right numbers,' he agreed reluctantly, looking at the card clutched tightly in her hand . . .

'And all I need to access the deposit box is to know the numbers?'

He nodded, his large head bobbing nervously up and down, his eyes never leaving hers. *Which of us is the snake?* Razz wondered. As if it mattered.

'I have the numbers. The numbers are correct. I would like the box,' explained Razz patiently. She already knew Hong Kong Suisse took money mostly in the US and the Far East these days, that this was one of its oldest accounts. And that, to be honest, HKS had long considered this a frozen account, its rightful owner long lost in the dust of history.

He was big on history, was Herr Garibaldi. He'd already told Razz far more about Napoleons III, IV and V, and about Swiss banking law, than she'd ever wanted to know. Far more than anyone *needed* to know, either, unless they happened to run a venerable financial institution, which of course he did.

Razz sighed. 'Let me have the box,' she suggested, leaning in even closer until Herr Garibaldi could feel the back of his chair pushing hard against his own spine. Her eyes were wide, almost childish, her brown pupils speckled with a fractal dust of darker chestnut. But they were also confident, determined.

Herr Garibaldi nodded, admitting defeat. Levering himself out of his chair he reached up to a mahogany-and-brass humidor on his desk and chose a Partigas, which he lit defiantly with an antique lighter. The offending cigar was rolled from a single, sun-dried Cuban leaf and looked oiled and vaguely obscene thrust between Herr Garibaldi's small fingers.

Unexpectedly, the smoke reminded Razz of autumn, of thyme-scented bonfires ... Before she could help herself, flashes of memory had downloaded, fractured and incomplete but still staggeringly clear. A smoking fire, a small child and an old man with dark eyes and a greying walrus moustache.

Her grandfather, bullet cases strung in rows across his chest like medals. The little girl was her, Razz realized. That bonfire, the last-ever autumn clear-up on his tiny farm. The last clear-up before winter. It killed him, of course, relentless blizzards finally achieving what mere old age never managed.

'Are you all right, my dear?'

Herr Garibaldi was staring up at her, cigar forgotten, worry written quite clearly across his round, anxious face.

She was crying, Razz realized angrily. God knew when she'd last done that: not this century, anyway. An old woman had come in from the village below their small farm, fighting up the mountain path to lay out her grandfather, cleaning his stick-like body and washing his hair. That was when Razz discovered that the man's hair had long since gone as white as the snows that killed him. He'd been dyeing it in secret, probably for longer than anyone still living could remember.

'I'll take you to the vault,' said Herr Garibaldi hastily. He reached into a desk drawer and took out a large iron key.

Despite her tears, Razz almost laughed. The key had to be for show. It was centuries since banks had used anything except electronic locks, retina readers, time codes or encrypted passkeys. Most money was virtual anyway, always had been. Half the world's wealth was now stored in orbital banks. No one would leave valuables to the mercy of a single locked door. No matter how complex the lock or how thick the door.

'We have a contracts policy,' Herr Garibaldi said, catching her glance. He coughed hesitantly, twisting his cigar nervously between his fingers. The Partigas crackled, like old paper. It didn't take the world-weary assassin inside Razz's new body long to know what was coming next. Or to recognize his words for the warning they were.

'Contracts?' she said, rubbing her eyelids crossly as she followed Herr Garibaldi down to the HKS vault.

'Three times we've been robbed,' said Herr Garibaldi. His words were soft, almost sad. 'Three times in fifty years. In every case the thief – and his family – met an unfortunate accident afterwards, usually within hours. Though it took two days the first time.' Herr Garibaldi shook his head in disgust. 'Before my time. Obviously the bank then put its security contract out to re-tender.'

'Obviously,' Razz said, ignoring Herr Garibaldi's sudden sharp glance.

The vault was just that: a vault. A simple semicircular tunnel below Bahnhofstrasse, cut into rock and lined with red brick. There was only one entrance and that was behind a black molybdenum door, worked to look like ancient wrought iron. The temperature in the vault was way below freezing, Razz knew that from a read-out on the wall. But then, that wasn't surprising; outside, the whole of Zurich was being steadily buried under snow.

Sure enough, Herr Garibaldi's key fitted the door, turning effortlessly in its vast lock. But Razz noticed what many others wouldn't . . . Optic-fibre pin-lens Fujis, semiAI-controlled, on both sides of the lock. And two paces back from the door, just about where she stood, two bricks at waist height that had been replaced sometime in the past. One on either side of her. Their colour was almost right, as was the texture, and someone had dusted their rough surface with a mixture of dust and broken cobweb, but the bricks were still too new, too recent.

Protection against someone marching Herr Garibaldi down here with a gun in his back. Fine-focus claymores, Razz decided, that section of her cortex devoted to munitions cycling swiftly through the options.

BioSemtex core, probably, wrapped around with a dozen metres of self-fragmenting steel wire, so thin a single strand was almost invisible to the unenhanced human eye, not to mention to something as crude as a hand-held battlefield X-ray.

There'd be a trigger somewhere. Probably the *lack* of something. SemiAIs were still lousy at knowing when something extra had been added to a visual mix, but the current models were red-hot at spotting when something was missing. Provided, of course, that whatever was missing was large, had clean edges and a clearly identifiable shape.

The key . . . That was why it was so large, so simple in structure. So even a semiAI couldn't fuck up.

Inside the new Razz the old Razz grinned, impressed despite herself. At this distance the claymores would have torn her in half before she even knew it had happened, without even grazing Herr Garibaldi. Sweetly beautiful.

She'd used something like it once during a corporate heist in Guatemala. But then she'd had to take out the whole line. Armaments sourced from Bogota weren't so finely tuned they could wipe one person and leave the rest still standing. But then this was Switzerland: if the Swiss couldn't precision-manufacture smart weapons then who could?

'Yours is box number forty-three,' Herr Garibaldi said solemnly, handing her a small white-metal key. He dragged heavily on his Partigas which still looked like the oiled, snub penis of some endangered animal. A snow leopard, Razz decided, thinking back to a crowded medicinal market in Lhasa.

Standing beside the molybdenum door, Herr Garibaldi gestured vaguely at a small brass button set in a polished circle of mahogany. 'Push this when you're ready. I'll be in my office. Oh . . .' his green eyes flicked towards two other bricks, set this time on the inside of the vault. 'Don't try to leave alone.'

'I won't,' Razz assured him.

And then she was on her own in the vault of one of the most exclusive banks in the world. True, HKS kept open its Swiss office only for the status value it conferred on the company, but all the same . . .

What Razz had been expecting she didn't know. What she got

was a wall of row upon row of small metal doors, each embossed with a number in blue enamel. She found her door without trouble, keyed her crypt into a keypad and waited until she heard a small click.

Behind the door was a long box of green metal with a flap at one end that Razz opened with shaking fingers.

Shaking fingers . . .

'What the fuck?' Razz said, mostly to herself. This was Razz, the original 'Stepping Razor' feared by governments and meta-Nationals across most of the Western world. Not to mention being wanted dead by half of them. Why else did that stinking *WeGuard* think she'd accepted the newVenice job?

You name it, she'd done it, probably in slo-mo animated-action replay. Razz didn't get nerves, she didn't need to. Maybe it was her new body, maybe it was losing those augmentations. Either way, the idea of losing her edge worried the fuck out of her. And as soon as she could, Razz was going to down an ice-cold Stolie and think this thing over.

Until then, she'd better find out just what the hell Alex had in mind. She had a Doge to find and at least one Chinese techie to kill.

It wouldn't be true to say that the box was empty. The thing just wasn't very full, and what was in there didn't seem worth hiding.

'If I knew why it was here,' Razz muttered bitterly, 'then just maybe I'd know what it meant.' She turned the little tray over in her hand, tracing the tunnel that snaked down its middle from what looked like a pinhole at one end to a small circular aperture cut into the surface at the other. *Self-lighting*, read the die-stamp on the underside, *piezzo-electric, copyright Ronson Electronics, Amsterdam*.

Along the top, wrapped around the small meshed hole, was the word *Apocalypso* stamped into cheap white metal and then filled with something that just might have been genuine red enamel. And that was it: apart from the souvenir, the HKS box was empty.

Why? Razz wondered. The thing was a freebie . . . a giveaway.

This deposit box might have been opened in another century, but things hadn't changed so much that Razz couldn't recognize a club freebie when she saw one.

Maybe it had sentimental value. Not a concept that appealed to Razz, but she'd been around enough to know that people placed a value on the strangest things – so why not? But a deposit box, in an exclusive Swiss bank?

So what else was she meant to be looking for?

And where was it hidden?

Whoever put the object in the box couldn't be that clichéd, could they? Or maybe it was irony, who the hell could tell? On instinct Razz thrust her hand deep into the box and felt for the back. Paper crinkled beneath her touch and Razz groaned aloud. And then she was ripping a small package off the rear wall. It was a letter, tightly folded, the cheap paper yellow and brittle, not even in an envelope. Crude strips of tape running top to bottom and left to right across its surface.

Hesitantly, aware she was almost certainly being caught on camera, Razz unfolded a sheet of writing paper. Except what she held wasn't a letter at all. *Hotel Imperium, Krung Thep, Bangkok* read the heading. On the paper was scrawled the deeds for a holding company, with details of how the business was to be managed and who had the right to make what decisions. And then there was a crude fractal equation outlining how branches were to be weighted in any decision tree.

The name of the company was *Passion Splash*. Razz couldn't make out the names of the three people who'd signed. Their signatures were smeared with a dark brown stain that might have been blood. But, this being Switzerland, it could equally well have been chocolate.

'*Apocalypso*?' Herr Garibaldi said, meeting her at the door of the vault. 'Of course I know it, on Neiderdorf.' If he found Razz's question odd he didn't let it show.

'What is it?' Razz demanded.

'As its name suggests, a bar . . .' The dwarf raised one shaggy eyebrow. 'It's quite famous, like Florian's in Venice. But, of course, you haven't been to Zurich before . . .' He let his words hang in the air.

'No,' Razz said flatly, 'I haven't been to Zurich.'

Herr Garibaldi smiled. 'You're still young, there'll be time enough for bars and travelling later.'

Razz considered drop kicking his pumpkin-like head off his thin shoulders, just to check that she could still do it, but common sense prevailed. She had more important things to worry about. Lack of money for a start. But hey, she *was* in a bank.

'How do I arrange a loan?' It was a simple enough question, or so Razz thought.

'From us, from HKS Zurich?'

Razz nodded.

'You don't.' Herr Garibaldi gave the girl his fondest smile. 'We're not that kind of bank . . .' His shrewd eyes flicked over her body, leaving Razz uncertain whether to be furious or embarrassed until she realized he was sizing up her expensive velvet jacket, her beautifully cut black skirt. The man was putting a value on her clothes.

'You could always try your family?' Herr Garibaldi suggested gently. Razz could swear that had he been tall enough he'd have tried to pat her head.

[Petite Mort]

If the headquarters of Hong Kong Suisse were old, it was in a discreet, oak-panelled Bahnhofstrasse kind of way. In contrast, the Bar Apocalypso had ossified into a flamboyant elegance as studied as any courtly minuet.

Tri-D posters, laser blades, ancient M-16s, a black Les Paul, the teardrop tank of a chopped Harley, even an antique Kalashnikov minus its curved magazine. From Dublin to Durban, Razz had seen it before – trash culture frozen into timeless respectability. The Apocalypso's walls were thick with the cultural detritus of the previous two centuries, all lovingly labelled and dated and safely preserved behind sheet plexiglass.

Friday night, so the place was packed, the crackle of conversation almost drowning out the heavy riff and retro beat of crash&burn. Anorexic models, CySat stars, minor nobility crowded tightly around obsidian tabletops supported on welded legs of sandblasted industrial steel. Razz hated them on sight; she didn't think much of the tables, either.

This was international chic. Razz doubted if anyone of them had ever eaten anything that wasn't naturally grown, never mind slop from a Drexie box. Chemical-free glacier water imported from Antarctica, organic vegetables, meat taken from live animals – the only synthetic thing about them was the crystalMeth that kept them corpse-thin. That and their monthly Bayer-Rochelle laserPeel facelifts.

In her past life, the only time Razz would have walked into a place like this was to kill someone. But these days she was just too young, too soberly dressed and, if nothing else, too fucking poor to feel at home, even among Eurotrash.

It didn't matter that she had fuck knew how many million credits uploaded at the Edo branch of HKS, that she had a fall-back account in Grand Cayman and a permanent line of credit from the Prince Imperial's own bank in Paris. Razz, this Razz, couldn't get at them. The accounts were DNA-logged, tied to her double helix and the fractal pattern of her neural net.

Like, they would buy that she was her, but in a different body? Razz wasn't even going to try, not until she'd talked to Alex. Always assuming he was sane. No. For the immediate future Razz was broke, and as far as the digital world was concerned she'd just fallen between the cracks. She wasn't even her.

'Madmoiselle?' The maître d' wore a white coat of genuine sharkskin, black trousers and black shoes that actually had laces. He might have been Italian or Hispanic, or maybe even Levantine: it was hard to tell in the dim light. But he had the proud and arrogant sneer of head waiters everywhere. Dark eyes skimmed quickly over her dress, flicked to her wrists and fingers to check for jewellery – noting the lack of both – and then stopped dead, so that he seemed to be looking at her but was actually staring at a neutral point a hand's breadth in front of her face.

'This is the Apocalypso?' Razz demanded, even though the name had been written over the entrance in heavy Gothic lettering across a sign made from original perspex.

The man nodded.

'As in, this Apocalypso?' She tossed her trophy at the man and was glad to see him fumble the catch. The maître d' turned her metal square over in his hands and strode quickly over to a crowded glass case fastened to the wall with ostentatiously large brass screws.

The maître d' scanned along the contents and then stopped. It took Razz a moment to work out what he'd been looking for and then she saw it too. Like hers, but very slightly different in design.

'This is version one,' the maître d' said carefully, holding up the small object that Razz had tossed to him, turning it over between beautifully manicured fingers. 'Obviously,' his voice was unemotional, but he chose his words carefully, 'this is of interest to the bar. Are you thinking of selling?'

'Maybe, maybe not . . .' Razz shrugged. 'I'll be at the bar,' she said, her voice more confident than she felt.

And even that brittle confidence didn't last. Before she'd killed her first Stolie, Razz knew sitting up at the bar had been a bad mistake. It put her on view to the clusters of rich Eurotrash camped out around the metal-and-obsidian tables. And Razz didn't like being looked at.

Carbohydrate dulled her edge and besides she wasn't even hungry, but Razz still picked at the dish in front of her. Recently-shelled Brazil nuts bright with the sheen of natural oil mixed in with almonds fried in virgin olive oil and dusted with crystals of rock salt.

Stolie after Stolie arrived, each one in a chilled, freshly sterilized glass, and Razz drank the lot. All the time eating the almonds, chewing hard on the salt, wishing to fuck each small grey crystal she cracked between her teeth really was the wizz it looked like. It was hours, probably days since she'd last had a hit. In fact, it was a miracle she wasn't huddled in a corner somewhere with the shakes.

Things looked pretty *crash* on the face of it, Razz realized. She was in Zurich, with no money, no lines of credit and no wizz. The hotel had told her, very politely, that her room had been paid for for last night only. After that, she was on her own, literally.

On the *burn* side, she was still alive, even if less than half the age she had been when offed by that *WeGuard*. True, she was unarmoured, but she was also without her trademark silver skin. Which, when Razz came down to it, was probably a serious bonus if she really was going after whoever had Aurelio . . .

Razz ran that back, thought by thought. There was no *if* to it. She was going after that *WeGuard* chink, just as soon as she could suss what had happened. The way Razz saw it, the techie had offed her to get to the kid. Control the kid, control newVenice.

That was, if the sainted Council of Twelve cared as much for him as they claimed. Which, when she came to it, Razz seriously doubted.

She could see the temptation, though: controlling the city meant global control of CySat, which ate up world events faster than cancer corrupted healthy cells. Whoever had the Doge had a serious plus when it came to bargaining, whoever they were bargaining with. As she saw it, version 1.0 was to get the Doge back. Version 1.1: kill whoever had ordered her killed. Version 1.2 was to get a life. But first she needed to see Alex, find out what the fuck that letter in the safe deposit box meant.

Which was easy to say. But she still had to get to him and that was going to take credit. Something she seriously didn't have. Hell, she wasn't even carrying credit enough to pay for the iced Stolies that kept materializing in front of her every time she emptied her shot glass. Unless the maître d' reckoned they were in return for that little electronic bong, in which case Razz wasn't getting the best of the deal.

Razz needed a card and fast.

In the old days, she'd have dodged round that revolting ice Herm with its vast penis, wandered over to one of those crowded tables and enforced a quick loan. But, even drunk, Razz knew that wasn't going to work, not tonight. It was one thing to be suddenly faced up by a semi-naked silver exotic, razor-sharp glass nails flexing casually, quite another to be approached by a soberly dressed young girl. What she needed was another approach.

Razz hit back her fifth iced Stolie and took a deep breath, dragging alcohol-laden vapour deep into her chest, letting Stolie hit the millions of alveoli lining her lungs. Her head swum before she even had time to breathe out.

'Enough,' she said quickly, as a North African barman reached for her glass. 'More than enough.' Razz flicked her eyes over the noise-glazed, late-night crowd. She still had the attention of an occasional few, their eyes meeting hers as she looked them over, but most of the room had already long forgotten her.

The lights were down, dimmed almost out of the visible spectrum into an edgy *Mazda ultraviolent* that gave even the most pallid an ersatz ski-bum tan. It was hot in there, humid. Rank not with sweat but the stink of money corrupting, with sex waiting to happen. Well, she could do without the sex, but that was more than she could say for the money.

And in the end, the one usually went with the other. It was time to go hunting. Or it would have been, if Razz hadn't just got the idea someone had already marked her down as prey. Late thirties, weapons-trained, minor viral enhancing . . . At least she hadn't lost her ability to read the signs. Crop-haired, blond, North European in origin, the man sitting alone at a table in the far corner was more interested in her than he wanted to admit.

It was too dark, too distant to clock his eye colour or pupil size, but Razz could bet he wasn't dusted out. He didn't look the type: too health-conscious, too scared of losing his edge. Besides, he was working, an open smartbook on the table next to a glass of what looked like real orange juice. What was more, the bowl of salted almonds next to his glass was untouched, which didn't surprise Razz at all.

Given the hollow tautness of his face and the whipcord-thin wrists that protruded from his black jacket she'd have guessed he was a man who avoided empty calories, probably obsessively.

Standing, not steadily, Razz stepped carefully down from the bar and threaded her way between the tables, ignoring slurred invitations and hands pushed out to stop her.

'What are you selling?' the blond man demanded before she'd even had time to pull out a chair. He spoke in English with a Texas accent.

'Myself,' Razz announced baldly, her gaze holding his. He had pale blue eyes and she was right, he wasn't dusted out at all.

The blond man smiled a thin smile. Up close, he wasn't as young or as handsome as she'd thought, but his teeth were his own, his nose wasn't caved in with freebase and at least his cheekbones were real, which was more than she could say for most of the men in the room.

'Yourself?' the man said, sounding amused. He gestured at a thin blonde woman and a small dark man, 'Well, I suppose it beats swapping freebase for a dubious title.'

'And you?' Razz asked, 'What do you sell?'

'Security.' He said it shortly, his dry clipped voice swallowing the middle syllables.

Razz smiled. 'Whose?'

He stared at her, cold-eyed, until Razz's gaze faltered and she almost looked down at the table's shiny surface. His face was the kind Lotusmorph coders might steal from a good plastic surgeon, if they couldn't be bothered to do their own design work. Handsome without being pretty, hard but not ugly. But if it was elective, why leave a pale scar that creased his face from left eye to left ear, as if someone had tried to blind him and failed?

'Whose security?' Razz asked again.

When it became obvious he didn't plan to answer, Razz pushed back her chair, but she never got the chance to leave. His grip on her wrist was tight as a pair of smart cuffs, his fingers digging hard into the pressure point between her wrist and hand. She was right, he was virally enhanced.

Without having to think about it, Razz pivoted her arm, twisting swiftly against the blond man's grip until her wrist should have pushed out between his thumb and fingertips, breaking his hold at its weakest point. But as she twisted, so did he. Her move ended where it began, with his fingers locked tight on her wrist, except that now she had skin burn.

Their eyes met and the man smiled, thinly. Obviously surprised by how close she'd come to making a successful counter-move. She was surprised too. Though actually Razz wasn't so much surprised as totally wiped, mainly to find that she hadn't succeeded.

'Shit for brains,' Razz shot at him from habit.

The man grinned coldly, and then tightened his grip. Razz could tell he'd just started to enjoy his evening. It was equally obvious, at least to Razz, that something had to give and at the moment it looked like being the bones in her wrist. Still, as Miyamoto Musashi pointed out in his scrolls, what you can't do with force can sometimes be done with guile.

'Hey,' Razz relaxed, looked the man straight in the eye and smiled. 'Forget security. You tell me what you're buying, I'll tell you exactly what it is I'm selling. Who knows . . .'

She smiled again, sweetly. She'd kill him, of course, when it was all over. A kind of self-reward. But until then . . .

So he told Razz what he wanted, as if she hadn't guessed; and she told him what it would cost, and enjoyed seeing his eyes widen. A full platinum Amex was a very high price, Razz agreed. Particularly for a snotty-nosed kid. But he was rich – the man didn't deny it – and, anyway, she was worth it.

And then Razz told the Colonel why . . .

Virginity. Provable, quantifiable purity. In an era of retroVirus 3/c, she was offering him the ultimate in vacuum-packed safe sex. No disease, zero psychic blowback, pretty much as safe as taking yourself in hand. Wouldn't he agree?

[Still Life with Ice]

Colonel Carlos Don Carlos folded a miniature lie detector back into its small box. He punctiliously checked the DNA read-outs of a disposable SKleinB haematrometer, rechecking them for evidence of disease, T/count or immune-system weakness. There were no flaws, no problems, no warnings.

Somewhere in her new make-up Razz had a subcutaneous contraceptive pump. She'd no idea who had put it there but it was there all right: the fourth diode along lit green as did all the others.

Colonel Carlos Don Carlos didn't seemed unduly surprised: maybe he just figured Razz had responsible parents. Hell, the lie-detector read-out hadn't even flickered at any of her answers, but then they were all true, sort of.

Sex and death were all she had to offer and the Colonel was well capable of doing his own killing. And even if he wasn't, how could he know Razz was for hire? *What* had never really been in doubt, *how much* was now agreed, which just left *where . . .*

Razz was expecting a hotel. A Hyatt or a Raddison, something large and anonymous where neither of them would be recognized. Not that this was likely to be a problem in her case, not these days when she could have walked past herself in a mirror and not noticed.

Or if not a Raddisson then maybe, if she got really unlucky, the snow-cold doorway of some shop or up against the rough wall of some slush-filled alley out of sight of the city's security cameras. What she got was the frozen metal floor of a Chrysler armoured personnel vehicle/hover.

The APV/H was huge, a dark-green ceramic/polymer monstrosity as tall as a man, as long as an eight-person Honda ultraglide. It lit up at the Colonel's approach like a dumb dog, hissing and whining as one side-panel slid back with a rough hiss. Razz couldn't tell the APV/H's front from its back; the bloody thing was double-fronted, both ends wrapped round with black plexiglass.

Getting close, Razz could see that the windscreen was strengthened with nearly transparent layers of clear tightly-woven fabric.

'Lockheed laminate,' the Colonel told her proudly, tapping the shiny black surface with his nails. 'Fifteen layers of perspex shatterproof, five of polarized light-sensitive glass, five of laser-reactive synth/polymer and five of woven, vat-grown spider's web. Each screen costs several times what I'm paying for you.'

'Maybe I should up the price,' Razz said shortly.

The Colonel's answering smile was hard, his lips thin. 'And maybe you should shut the fuck up.' Time, space and tolerance got eaten up from there on in.

Luckily, or maybe just intelligently, Razz had demanded the Amex in advance before they left the Apocalypso. It was a First Satellite issue, unused and unregistered. And while the Colonel had busied himself retrieving his coat from a half-naked hat-check, Razz had quietly used the neon light of the bar's entrance to let the card's wafer-thin digital camera record her coronal flare and register the Amex to Razz's eye-pattern alone.

On her way out she scored two twists of wizz cut with synthM2DA and a strip of paraDerm. She had a nasty feeling she was going to need both . . .

'Lose the seats,' the Colonel ordered, and the APV/H obediently folded them back with a low hiss, clearing a strip of space down the centre of the vehicle.

'How about a blanket?' Razz suggested, looking at a metal floor cut into hundreds of small rough squares. Great for stopping soldiers from slipping around if the APV/H was awash with blood, just not so hot for lying on.

'Oh, I don't think so.' Colonel Carlos Don Carlos glanced

around at the clean, almost clinical interior of the APV/H and smiled slightly. Absent-mindedly he shed both jacket and leather coat, then crossed his hands over his gut, gripped both sides of his black spider's-silk teeshirt and peeled it off over his head in one fluid movement.

A ten-digit number and a small, neat barcode were tattooed in red ink into the top of his arm. Someone else with a cloning policy at First Virtual Insurance. Razz just hoped that 1stVI did a better job for him. Well, actually she didn't . . .

'No heat?'

His expression wasn't kind, but then it wasn't meant to be. He probably spent hours in front of the mirror practising it; jutting his chin forward, half-closing his eyes. Needless to say, his figure was neurotically perfect, lean and lightly tanned without an ounce of fat. Another bloody, brooding self-obsessive, Razz thought tiredly. She'd been there, knew that score. The man's six-pack was so clearly defined Razz could see where one band of muscle slid neatly over another. He had small flat nipples and no visible body hair. Either that, or he went in for regular laserwave depilation.

Razz shrugged. 'Whatever you want,' she said grimly. If he wanted to freeze his butt off in the middle of a Swiss snowstorm that was his business.

The Colonel stopped unbuckling his belt long enough to nod. 'You've got it,' he said, going back to his belt.

Seconds flickered by. Razz sat cross-legged on the floor, quietly waiting, her dark eyes never leaving his impassive face, her hands folded neatly. She looked to the Colonel like some rich kid out on the lam from an overpriced Swiss finishing school. The idea didn't worry him.

'You,' he said, looking up from folding his clothes into an impossibly small, impossibly neat pile. 'Get that top off.'

Razz pouted at the naked man. 'Don't you want to take it off yourself? I mean . . .' Her eyes held his and for a second the Colonel almost shivered. 'This *is* my first time.'

'Strip,' he ordered roughly. 'Now.'

Razz did what she was told, taking care to place her small black bag with the credit chip out of his way under her velvet coat and red silk shirt. She could tell he was impressed with what he saw. Hell, so was she. Her breasts were full and firm, her small dark nipples puckered and erect; though even he must have realized it was the cold, not sexual readiness that made them that way.

It didn't take a trained psychologist to read the hunger in his face. It was almost as naked as he was.

Party time. Razz split open a twist of wizz/synthM2DA, slitting the packet with the edge of her nail. The crystals were bitter, burning the back of her throat before they hit properly, making her temples pound in a sudden rush of blood that mixed uneasily with the alcohol already in her veins.

Unfastening the last of the small jet buttons that ran the length of her ultrasuede skirt and still wearing a thong, Razz knelt up to fold the skirt neatly on top of her discarded silk shirt.

'Hold it there.' The naked man leant over, gripped Razz by her shoulders and toppled her back, hard. Her head hitting the floor with a heavy thud.

'Hey,' Razz shouted, but it was way too late.

With one hand, the Colonel flipped two ampoules onto the cold metal floor above her head and stretched out her right arm, banging it down hard against the floor so the back of one hand cracked open both bubbles. Deftly, the man grabbed her other hand and brought that up as well to touch the drying puddle.

GripoxE: Razz would have known its eye-watering stink any-where. Chemical restraints, developed in New York and briefly issued to the NYPD instead of self-sealing polymer cuffs. Razz couldn't remember which of its several side effects had led to *GripoxE* being withdrawn.

'Any trouble,' the Colonel told her, 'and I'll cut your throat and piss in the slit.' He meant it, too, his expensive wolf-like smile revealing two sharp upper canines, replaceable ceramic implants. The bastard probably had a pair for every occasion.

'Like the teeth,' Razz said sweetly. It took effort to sneer with both hands epoxied to the floor of an APV/H and a naked, anally-retentive West Coast psycho crouched above you, but Razz managed it anyway.

His slap back-handed her face, splitting Razz's lip wide open and crushing Razz's nose. For a moment the Colonel looked irritated and then he shrugged. The APV/H was designed to be hosed down. Full of shit wasn't in it, Razz decided. For all his knife-you-soon-as-look-at-you attitude, the Colonel was a distance killer. Deadly from the bubble of some copter or wired into this geeky little APV/H. Close up and dirty, he'd be as panicked as the next man. At least, she hoped he would.

Razz smiled grimly. Decades of close-combat injuries had left Razz with a unerring grasp of what wounds she should worry about and what she could let go. Blood might be flooding from her battered face onto his floor, but it wasn't enough to worry Razz. Not yet.

'You're a sick shit,' she said.

The blond man nodded and knelt between her legs to lower his mouth to her cold breast. His lips were dry as he tugged softly, but as her dark nipple softened to his touch and then hardened again as his tongue rolled softly across it, his rough lips softened too, closing over her whole areola, sucking her nipple deep into his hot mouth.

Razz smiled as her body began to respond to his touch. That was the thing about synth, it could make almost any sexual encounter erotic, even this one. Despite herself, Razz groaned, and the man bit hard on her breast, making her gasp with pain.

As if the bite had never happened, the blond man went back to sucking her nipple, running his tongue in circles around the dark target of her puckered areola. She tasted of salt, though how much was blood and how much fear the Colonel didn't know. Nor did he care. He only noted her taste the way he might log the scent of an animal he was hunting or the sourdough tang of bioSemtex.

The man fucked infrequently, and then only on his terms in his territory. It wasn't that the Colonel didn't like sex – fucking was a hardwired biological imperative – he just didn't usually allow himself the indulgence. He was a good fundamentalist boy.

Moving his mouth, the Colonel slid his tongue down into the deep valley between Razz's breasts and then bit gently under her left, feeling its taut skin swollen beneath his teeth. Twenty-five per cent. That was the maximum increase due to arousal and, despite herself, Razz was aroused. Unquestionably furious and almost afraid, but still definitely aroused.

Razz wasn't sure it was a feeling she liked.

She bit back a groan, stayed silent as his mouth searched for her other nipple, rolling it between his lips. But when one hand smoothed its way down her stomach to stop between her legs, Razz instinctively thrust her hips up towards the Colonel.

The man stopped, dead. Staring down at her, his pale blue eyes as hard as the thin smile that crossed his scarred face. Razz froze, collapsed back against the cold floor, her dark face instantly impassive, eyes fixed at a neutral point over his wiry shoulder.

'You learn quick.' He said it casually, but the hand that reached up to wrap itself in the thick tangles of her hair said she didn't learn fast enough. It hurt. Razz was in no doubt it was meant to.

'I like silence,' he said. Lazily the man bent, kissed the red trickle running sluggishly from her bruised lips. Then, just as suddenly, he slid his blood-slicked mouth down her body, until his face was lost again between her young breasts. Fingers snaked out to grip both, squeezing each to bursting point as he pushed into the tightness between.

Razz said nothing, did nothing, just listened to his ragged breathing. She felt cold and irritated. She'd have liked to say she didn't feel afraid or worried, that however young she looked on the outside, she was way too old at the core to be fazed by another blond freak with thousand-klick eyes. But it wouldn't be true. Not quite . . .

Razz wasn't terrified, she certainly wasn't trapped in anyone's headlights, but she didn't need to check her heart to know it was taking an adrenalin hit. And it sure as hell wasn't from sexual excitement. Not after that business with her hair.

Staring at the grey ceiling with its recessed safety lights and reinforced air filters, its micromesh roof and zytel struts, Razz decided that being young again wasn't so hot; not if it meant being glued to the floor of some APV/H without her biotek rewirings. She'd have killed to get them back – quite literally.

'Hey, bitch.' The blond man wasn't usually given to frowning. The scar on his face was one reason, another was the certain impassiveness expected in his job. But he frowned all the same. From the tension leaching out of her body, it was obvious she'd stopped paying him any attention at all. And that wasn't what he was paying for.

There was no denying she was pretty, in an over-lush kind of way, but he expected more than just youth for his money. Huge hands gripped one breast until it felt as if it might burst open. Crushed fruit, he thought grimly. And then his mouth was on hers, his teeth biting at her split lip.

One of his hands moved up to her head, fingers twisting tightly into her hair again: the other pushed roughly between her legs, his hand cupping her sex, the heel of his palm pressing tight over her labia, the tip of his index finger reaching round between her buttocks.

And even as Razz winced, as his finger caught against her dry anus, the finger was gone, sliding over the raised ridge of her perineum towards her open vulva. She had a hymen, Razz realized with a shock as the Colonel's fingers found it and moved round its membranous edge. She met the Colonel's gaze. He was amused all right, but his amusement was shot through with bitterness, as ironic and sour as wizz cut with strychnine.

He took her almost every which way, thrusting himself inside her with no effort to make her wet or ready. No KY spray, no Durex cream. And it was only when he tried to flip Razz onto her stomach to enter her at the back, that the blond American realized that maybe gluing her wrists to the floor hadn't been so bright after all.

For a few sweaty minutes he grappled with her cold legs, trying to push them far enough up to raise her buttocks. But he couldn't get a grip, and Razz's skin was already too slippery with sweat, blood and bodily fluids.

The man wasn't pleased. And he was busy finding a way to show it.

Razz wasn't sure if hookers could be raped under Swiss law, and that was what she'd made herself when she took his chip. Or maybe whoredom was what random change gave her. That's what Alex would have reckoned. Either way, it probably wasn't rape, not if she'd been paid in advance.

Not that she was planning on going to the law anyway . . .

The Colonel was above Razz now, punching himself into her with long vicious strokes that drove her across the studded floor, twisting her arms and lacerating her back until she slammed up against a bulkhead and had to twist her neck to avoid having her skull cracked against the armoured wall. Huge hands gripped her shoulders, nails biting through her skin as the strokes grew faster and ever more frenzied. And then he was done, all his effort released in one strangled grunt.

Petite mort, the French called sex. And that's what that was. Murder without the death. By the time Razz'd winced, sworn, pushed herself away from the wall and opened her dark eyes, he was already knelt back on his heels, his breath steadying. Perfect fucking physique, shit personality. *Story of my life*, Razz thought with a grimace, spitting blood onto his floor.

The wizz was already wearing off, following the MDMA into burnout. Seventy-two per cent pure, she'd been told in the cloak-room of the Apocalypso. No way. Razz shook her head: fifteen per cent, maybe twenty per cent at the most.

'I suppose you want your hands back?' His voice was cold and even, not a tremor or muffled gasp to reveal the physical workout he'd just given himself using her body.

'That would be nice,' Razz said and smiled sweetly.

For a second it looked like he was going to backhand her across the face again, but instead he just shrugged and reached for his leather coat, fingers dipping into a side pocket to come up with a small bubble pack. He tossed it at the girl and watched it fall uselessly beside her head.

Razz shrugged. The Colonel had that real psycho stare, the full thousand-klick monty. When she looked up again shit-for-brains was gone, zoned out. Dug down somewhere inside himself. Which was fine with Razz: she wasn't going to miss his company.

There'd been a time when stressflash wasn't treatable in advance with betaBs, when ready-made, blood-hued flashbacks weren't thrown in for free with cheap, edit-it-yourself tri-D software. When that stare wasn't taught in *psyque 101* at every hick security school, when it was the visual barcode of the walking wounded.

His was that.

Real.

She was cold. Everything hurt, but mostly her back which felt blood-raw. Blood pounded like a living headache in her temples, and the shakes vibrating her teeth were not just from the sub-zero temperature of the APV/H. Razz was scared. Whatever was loping past the inside of that man's eyes, Razz didn't want to wait around long enough to become part of it.

So she began to concentrate on the bubble pack resting inches from her face. It hurt but, by twisting her head, Razz could bring her face close enough to the pack to move it with her nose, except there wasn't enough free movement to get it anything like close enough to one of her glued hands.

Helplessness wasn't a concept Razz liked. Winning wasn't about being stronger, Razz knew that. Shit, everyone knew that. It was about ignorance of fear, negation of ego. Zen combat turned on not knowing you were beaten. Ever. And she wasn't.

Razz had zero illusions about her ability to duck shit. That Chinese techie had offed her with a ceramic UziMicro, the kind brats from the Harlem barrios picked up before hitting their mid-teens. If they ever did: hit their mid-teens, that was. It was years since she'd last been to the Sprawl.

Shit happened. That was practically a *koan*. And it didn't just happen to Razz: she'd made a living handling it before it could happen to others. Well, she needed a way out of the shit, starting now . . .

And then she had one, in a single, simple memory . . . That boat skimming inches above the cold pale water, the tips of its squat up-flipped/down-turned wings never quite breaking the surface, gliding effortlessly above the choppy little waves.

Razz looked at the twist of bubble pack near her face and then at her trapped wrist. Ten inches between them at most, and over a metal floor studded with molybdendum rivets that looked like waves. Well, they did if you stretched the point.

She blew through bruised, bleeding lips towards the bubble pack, not at it but under it until the pack rose off the floor and quivered on a cushion of air. For a nanosecond it seemed the pack would spin off in the wrong direction and Razz almost choked. Instantly, the solvent fell back to the floor.

It was possible: it was enough to know that much. She was still Razz, still the Stepping Razor. If something was possible, then Razz could do it. Softly, as silently as she could, the girl blew along the floor, lifting the bubble pack back onto a cushion of air. Letting it hover there until slowly it began to move as it was meant, edging towards her trapped wrist.

Almost. She was running out of breath, hissing spits of blood from her lips as she emptied the last of her lungs. And then the bubble pack was there. Savagely Razz twisted her torso to one side, tearing skin as she brought her wrist over the fallen pack and banged down, squashing a bubble of solvent. It burst, flooding the personnel carrier with a sharp chemical smell.

'What the . . . ?' The Colonel was out of his loop even as Razz got her wrist free. But one free wrist was all she needed. Ankle sweeping him to the floor, rigid fingers catching him in the throat, under his Adam's apple, half-crushing his larynx.

Ignoring the gasping man, Razz scrambled with her free hand for the bubble pack, found an unused bubble and popped it, breaking the *GripoxE*. Both hands now free, Razz chopped the Colonel across the throat again, once more for luck, then smashed his nose with the heel of her hand, flattening bone the way Chinese cooks flatten Peking duck.

Razz grinned. She was too young, her tits were too big, her back felt like it'd been whipped, her hand hurt like fuck where strips of shark cartilage should have cushioned the blow, but what the hell . . . Maybe street fighting was like riding blades: some skills you never lost, not even if you changed bodies.

For good measure, Razz took the man round the throat with both hands and launched herself to her feet, carrying him with her. There was a satisfying crack as he came upright. His neck wasn't broken, unfortunately, but his head looked decidedly lopsided. And the shock in his blue eyes had to be seen to be believed.

Digging rapidly around inside the pocket of the Colonel's black leather jacket, Razz found another NYPD restraint kit, grabbed a strip of two-part chemical handcuffs, cracked a *GripoxE* bubble between her fingers and spread the slimy liquid evenly across the palm of her right hand. Then she quickly dipped her fingers and caught the Colonel by his testicles.

He winced. It was instinctive and unnecessary. Not that Razz wasn't tempted, but she did nothing more painful than smear chemical across his scrotal sac. By the time Colonel Carlos Don Carlos understood what was happening it was way too late. A grinning Razz had flipped the second part of the chemical cuffs to the floor, smashed its bubble with her bare heel and neatly drop kicked the Colonel's legs out from under him, watching his fall.

The *GripoxE* bonded into new, stronger molecular chains and the man was suddenly stuck, really stuck. Glued by his balls to the floor of his own APV/H. Razz grinned, flicked him the finger and reached for her clothes. 'See yah . . .'

He stared at the girl, not seeing her nakedness or the blood that ran from her bruised mouth. All he saw was himself in her eyes, trapped, humiliated. It wasn't a pretty sight, but then it wasn't meant to be. Razz grinned.

'I'm going to kill you,' the Colonel promised.

Razz grinned again.

'I wouldn't count on it,' she said, and trod into his groin on the way out, heel twisting on crushed flesh.

[Nzigé Unbound I]

'Anyway,' Alex said, 'there was a goddess called Alex who . . .'

'She wasn't called Alex.' The Prince's interruption was abrupt and unforgiving, his voice as sun-stripped as the desert around them. 'And she wasn't a god, she was a sub-Sahal earth spirit. Her name was Nzigé.'

'Nzigé is a lake in lower Sudan,' Alex said crossly. His throat was parched. As well it might be: whole weeks sometimes went by before he remembered to drink the water left each day by acolytes at the tiny entrance to his mud-brick hut.

Razz sighed.

Not for the first time, she wondered if she'd really crossed the Sahara by Seraphim 4track for this? To sit on a mud floor, dressed in a dirty jellaba, listening to the ravings of a drug-mad anchorite, a man with more ghosts inside his head than there were names of God. While cool showers, a pool, and freshly-made beds waited in an air-conditioned complex less than a hundred yards away.

Vast, mostly buried beneath the sand, everybody knew the San Lorenzo Complex was where the Church of Christ Geneticist hoped to clone the Messiah's DNA. Their trademarked cross-and-double-helix was as familiar as the 'M' of McD's. Their very name, *Geneticist*, was the third most recognized word in the world, coming after 'Coke' and 'Hi'.

But all the same . . . And only people who'd been out to the Geneticists' sprawling ferroconcrete HQ knew how difficult it was to reach. Razz had picked up a copter at Mitsubishi AirHire, Zurich, a black two-seater with MS AeroR/Soft and a human pilot.

The pilot was an indulgence. She didn't expect to need him but she wanted someone other than a computer to talk to on her trip. Besides, she could sure as hell afford it. She chose a Brit in his early twenties called Rupert. (Razz liked the English, they were so Japanese.) Unfortunately, Rupert turned out to be a profiler, neurotically sneaking glances at himself in any shiny surface. And it certainly didn't help that Razz was busy avoiding her own battered reflection.

At Mitsubishi AirHire (Mitz were Japanese, they insisted on keeping a human/customer interface) the manager had glanced once at her recently stapled lip and the bruising along her jaw, then pointedly ignored it. Letting Razz get on with the more important business of choosing a machine and passing over her card.

Razz purchased 176 hours of pilot time, to be taken in blocks of no more than six hours at any one go, over a period of no more than three weeks.

The RouteSoft came with sixteen frames of Microsoft small print. She signed without bothering to read it. Everyone did. Pilot and MS licence were expensive, but not as expensive as hiring a new two-seater Mitz: the black copter made more of a dent in her Amex than Razz had expected. But even then, Razz was still left with more spare credit than most of the North African city states she'd be flying over – except M'dina, obviously.

It was half an hour before departure, when Razz demanded that Rupert fly her out to San Lorenzo, that the floppy-haired Brit decided that Razz wasn't just a spoilt little rich girl, she was certifiably mad. They were in a glass-walled bar at Mitsubishi AirHire. The place was safely anonymous, pink carpet, wipe-clean surfaces. A bored teenage girl with bleached blonde hair stood behind the bar laced into Swiss national dress. She was waiting to serve them.

Around her, the air smelt of alpine flowers, schnapps, roast coffee and fresh bread. Only the coffee was real, and even that wasn't as fresh as it smelt.

They took two lattés anyway.

The first thing Rupert said was, 'Sorry, but I'm afraid you can't get your money back.' And without stopping for breath, he ran point by point down the International Aviation contract. As he said, there was no break clause.

'I don't want my money back,' Razz kept her voice calm. 'I want you to go to San Lorenzo.'

'No can do,' Rupert replied.

'You have to. It's an emergency.'

'Look, have you ever visited San Lorenzo?' Rupert asked heavily, brushing back his floppy fair hair. With his dark blond stubble, pale green eyes and white aviator's silk scarf, he looked almost as good as he thought he did.

'Of course I've fucking been to . . .' Razz snapped, and then caught his look. Profanity in public was a fineable offence in Switzerland. And, of course, she looked about sixteen . . . Or maybe she really was seventeen. How the hell should she know which . . .

'What's the date?' Razz demanded suddenly.

He told her. It was a month and three days after she'd been shot, after she'd blown it for the Doge. No sooner had Razz thought of Aurelio than a grab of him that final afternoon pulled itself out of her memory. The ridiculous velvet suit, the stupid haircut. His irritation at not being able to beat the dragon. Of course the kid couldn't. He was a child, the dragon was a fuzzy-logic construct created from Aurelio's game-playing weaknesses. *Lucifer's Dragon* wasn't designed to be beaten. All the same, Aurelio might have got off the first level . . .

Without intending it, Razz found her eyes filling with tears. One of which slid over the edge of an eyelid and began to trickle down her battered cheek.

'Hey, look here,' said Rupert hurriedly. He leant towards her, but Razz backed away. She didn't want him to touch her. Hell, she didn't want anyone to touch her. But she didn't want to have to hurt him, either.

'Look,' Rupert said. Blue eyes met hers, and for a second he looked genuinely worried and not just about his pay. 'I don't know what you imagine, but no one flies over San Lorenzo. It's an open fucking invitation to get yourself killed.' He glanced behind to a crowd of Italian Suits quietly nursing their shots of schnapps in the booth next door, but no one showed the slightest interest in their destination or in his language.

'I used to fly in,' Razz said shortly.

Rupert looked doubtful. 'Must have been when you were sprog-like. Lorenzo's been dead airspace for as long as I can remember. Actually,' Rupert looked embarrassed, 'I think it got closed down before I was born.'

Razz glanced at his unlined face. Not a pockmark, not a scar, not a single sign of elective surgery or a lazer skin-peel. He really was as young as he looked. But the eyes were even more recent.

'I was born blind,' Rupert's voice was calm, unfussed. His face was impassive under her stare. 'My father insisted on bio-optics, floating read-out, autofocus infra-red, the lot. Hardwired direct to my optic nerve. I got rid of them last year, as soon as I was old enough . . .' He paused to check his reflection in the black-glass wall of their booth. 'This is me,' he said firmly, nodding at the silk scarf, the pale fawn polo neck. 'Not that other person I was. It's okay,' he shrugged, his voice studiedly languid, 'I don't expect you to understand.'

Razz smiled, catching her own reflection, watching the girl who smiled back at her. 'You don't have to believe it,' she said, 'but I know exactly what you mean.'

They settled on the city state of M'dina as their destination. From there she could hire a 4 × 4 Seraphim to take her out across the Megrib. Rupert and the Mitz would wait out the rest of her three weeks at M'dina until she returned. Razz got a definite feeling the young Englishman wouldn't be holding his breath for that to happen.

Rupert brushed a strand of hair out of his beautiful blue eyes and looked up from his Toshiba smartbox, ignoring its flash about fundamentalist rioting in Algiers. 'I'm sure you know what you're doing,' he said politely, sipping at a frosted glass. 'But the Geneticists don't exactly welcome visitors with open arms.'

'Look,' Razz said. 'You fly and I'll worry about the Geneticists, got it?' She stood up, clapped the Englishman briefly on the shoulder and walked towards the leaving gate. Rupert was still staring after her as she disappeared into a sonic sterilization booth . . .

[Nzigé Unbound (I]

'As I was saying,' said Alex crossly, 'and this is important, so don't interrupt.' He wasn't talking to her, Razz knew that. 'Once, so long ago that all oceans were still desert, an African water spirit called Nzigé was unhappy. She would sit in the desert and the sun would dry her up, she'd sit in the shade and animals would drink bits off her. And if she hid underground, bushmen would probe the dry red earth with hollow sticks until they found her.'

Razz nodded: it seemed appropriate. Though trapped in the smoky darkness of Alex's hut she had no idea if he could see her. Probably could, if he wanted to . . . Most of the time, Razz had no idea if Alex even knew she was there or not. In the days since she'd arrived at San Lorenzo he'd done nothing but tell folktales or argue bitterly with himself.

A quick scan with a (highly illegal) hand-held Charcot neuroscanner showed ninety-seven point two per cent synaptic activity, which was impossible. Most unaugmented humans were lucky to reach neural levels of twenty-five per cent activity, and even implanting bioClay gates between the left and right cerebellum rarely kicked the ratio above forty-five to fifty per cent.

The only problem was, about eighty per cent of Alex's brain activity seemed to be involved only with itself. According to the Charcot, Alex's brain operated as a sealed unit. It was like having a hover with two engines. The smaller one struggling to keep the hover off the ground, while the other ran at full capacity, with no one knowing what the fuck it actually did.

'One day,' said Alex into the darkness, 'Nzigé was so unhappy she decided to let everyone drink her to death. So she pulled all of herself together, which wasn't very much, and trickled out into the Kalahari.

'But the sun wasn't yet up and the moon walked the edge of the sky, for neither sun nor moon yet lived high in the firmament. Now the sun was glorious, brave and stupid, but his wife was . . .'

'More intelligent,' Razz said as she settled herself back against a mud-brick wall. A cushion would have helped, a quick hit of ice would have been even better. But no luck. These days San Lorenzo was drug-teetotal. The crop-haired, jellaba-dressed goons at the gate had left Razz with the new floating-breech Berretta she'd picked up in M'dina and stripped her of anything resembling wizz, ice or synthMDMA. Pretty funny, for what used to be one of the world's hottest drug-designing concerns.

Razz sighed. Everything told her that it was going to be a long, long day.

'It may not be very interesting, but at least try to listen . . .' the Prince suggested, his words hissing snake-soft from the lips of Alex. Other voices agreed, but then some things never changed. In death as in life, when the Prince spoke there were always people to agree.

But that wasn't the reason Alex had originally killed Prince Sabatini, drunk his tainted blood and taken the Prince's memories. So that viral rewiring had ripped through his own body, all those years before, remaking him as something more than human.

No. Knifing the Prince had been a mistake, an accident. Alex had intended to kill the man standing next to him. He always was careless.

Alex shuffled uneasily in the dirt, his thin buttocks pushing against dry earth as he tried to get comfortable. Raw sores covered his body, mottling his arms. *A bath might be a start*, Razz thought. And some kind of sound treatment to kill whatever lice colonized his ragged beard. She could smell the man's sweat from where she sat, not that his hut was big.

A bath, a haircut and some new clothes: that would do for a start. The torn and tattered cotton jellaba that Alex wore in public did little to hide his whipcord-thin body; it was more holes than cloth. Still, Razz doubted if the world's only living god noticed, never mind actually objected.

Alex was muttering crossly, something vituperative in a murmur too low to catch. Once again, whoever he was talking to, it wasn't Razz. 'So,' Alex said, as if he'd never interrupted himself, 'Nzigé told the moon how lonely she was. Now the moon, sun and animals slept together in one house. Even the bushman made his bed there, though no one ever saw him come and go. Only Nzigé slept deep in the earth, alone.

' "Live with us," said the moon. "We won't hurt you." Now Nzigé didn't believe this but she went with them anyway. And that was when the trouble started . . .

'For the small water spirit, who was now no longer small, grew to fill first the cellar, then the ground floor as well, and all the animals, the bushman, the sun and the moon had to move to the top floor. They were pleased Nzigé was happy, but worried she'd get so happy there'd be no space for them. So they tried to drink her smaller.

'But it was too late and Nzigé grew without stopping until the day came that the sun and the moon and the animals were pushed out to the roof, while Nzigé filled all of the rooms below.

'And the moon looked at the sun. And the sun burned with anger. And the moon said, "I will take the sky and the animals and bushman can have the roof." So she leapt into the void and the sun leapt after her. And the roof became the land and the rooms that Nzigé occupied became the oceans around the land. And no one could remember how it had been before.'

Clearing his throat, Alex spat expertly in the darkness. Where or at what, Razz didn't know. 'Have you noticed,' said Alex, sounding exactly as he used to sound before he became a god, 'how like running water static can sound? Sort of high noise, zero signal?'

Razz looked blank.

'Nzigé's a metaphor,' Alex said flatly. 'Not that Nzigé knows that, or would give a fuck if she did. We need to talk, you and I. And there's something I need to give you . . .' Razz suddenly had an unmistakable sharp feeling of being watched, which is exactly what was happening, as Alex's eyes scanned Razz in the darkness, optic nerves effortlessly readjusting to infra-red.

'Like that new body,' Alex said as he flicked through the frequencies of virtual light until he hit m/wave. Razz's clothes fell away from her as if she'd stood up and stripped. Then Alex fine-focused and took a quick look through her. For a second, at least through his eyes, she looked translucent, somewhere between ice and a live TC scan.

Brain, liver and lungs were viral-wired with a narcotics bypass, enough to kick strength down to twenty-five per cent. Alex wondered briefly if Razz knew and figured not. If she did, she'd be a lot angrier than she was. And anyway, what was the point telling her? She'd work it out for herself soon enough.

He could identify tissue damage to her groin, and an extensive criss-cross network of fibrin and thrombocytes across her back, indicating scabs. One side of her mouth and the back of her hands were also scarred, and her nose was a recent rebuild, but he didn't really want to know about all that.

'You know the real problem?' Alex asked her suddenly.

Yeah, Razz thought, *too right I know. I'm hungry, I'm dirty, I've just spent three shit days driving across the Megrib in a Toyota Seraphim 4 × 4 when I could have done the same trip in twenty minutes using that overpriced Mitz. My mouth hurts, I'm out of paraDerm and I've got cramp and PMT bad enough to take your fucking head off . . .*

She shook her head

'There's just too much noise,' said Alex.

Razz said nothing. She'd like to think it was because she didn't want to add to what he was complaining about, but knew really she just couldn't be bothered.

When Alex was sane he was boring. And when he was mad, Alex was brilliant but unhelpful. The Doge wasn't dead, Alex almost admitted as much. newVenice was still operating out there in the middle of the Pacific, churning out its daily diet of holoporn, tri-D soaps and MTVids. It still controlled the ratings, still ate up most of the world's advertising budget.

CySat just happened to have a complete news blackout on events in newVenice itself. Not open, not announced, but closed and subtle. The media-machine still produced to schedule, but optix in and out were being filtered, satellite downlinks were blocked. In desperation Razz had tried getting through to Karo via an anonymous voicemailer in Finland. Nothing. The Webware worked perfectly, the line just didn't connect. When it came to tightening the digital sphincter, even closed-down, anally-retentive little Singapore didn't come close.

Razz had no illusions about neoVenetian politics – there was one family who would have been distraught if the young Doge had been killed, and eleven who would have been delighted. She just didn't know what they had to do with an African water spirit called Nzigé.

'Too much noise,' Alex insisted. 'Too little signal. That's the real problem. It stops me thinking, and that means I can't do my job properly ...' He sounded remarkably sulky for someone widely believed to have a mind equal to the most advanced Magnus Imperial AI.

Alex staggered up from his corner and clattered across the hut, his hand rifling through a pile of rubbish for a large wooden ladle. He found it eventually and then Razz heard the splash as Alex dipped his ladle into a wooden bucket. She knew what was coming.

Very carefully, so that his shaking hands didn't spill more than half its contents, Alex carried the ladle across his small room and tipped urine carefully onto a pile of red-hot stones. Acrid steam billowed up, a taste like chlorine catching in the back of Razz's throat. She coughed, and then swore under her breath.

Brilliant: 2,000 litres of blood a day passing through his kidneys so he can tip his own piss onto hot stones.

Alex chuckled.

When Razz had first entered his new mud-brick hut, which was even smaller than his previous stone cell, she'd thought the thick steam was for religious purposes. Steam baths for inner cleansing, for inducing dreams or conquering spirits were a West Coast fad. The Navaho/Blessed Way model had even reached newVenice. But that wasn't it. No, Alex was cold.

In the middle of the Sahara, sitting in a small, airless mud-brick hut, Alex was so cold he used urine and red-hot stones to stop ice from eating into his bones.

'You know what's happening in my head?' Alex asked her.

'Do I, fuck . . .' Razz answered. No one knew what was happening in the head of Alex Gibson, except maybe Alex himself. And Razz wouldn't even count on that. The man was half downloaded memory, half human, half divine – and Razz knew that added up to one half more than it should have done. She'd been there in the catacombs of Paris when it happened. When Alex knifed the Prince and absorbed his powers and memories, burning into a full viral rewiring at precisely the point biochip tracery inside his head fused with the Cy.

'Lucifer's Dragon,' Alex said.

Razz looked at him in surprise. Looked through the impenetrable grey filter of steam to where his hunched figure sat, wrapped in his filthy jellaba.

'Addictive, demanding, rewarding . . .' Alex smiled, sadly. 'World without end. It's a religion, you realize that, don't you? That if you create spirits you have to honour them or they get lonely?' He shrugged. 'What no one understands,' said Alex. 'What even *I* didn't realise when I started, is that the Dragon's truly without end. You see my problem . . .'

No, Razz didn't. She shook her head.

'I can't win,' said Alex, sounding almost surprised.

'Then stop playing,' suggested Razz.

'He can't.' The Prince's words came hard from Alex's mouth. More angry, less urbane than usual. 'He's addicted, just as the game's addicted to him. Of course, he *could* win if he really wanted . . .'

'Then why . . .' Razz wanted to ask, but Alex was back.

'How can I cheat?' Alex demanded.

The Prince sighed, the heavy, heartfelt sigh of a ghost completely out of sympathy with the times in which he had manifested. 'How can you not? As far as I can tell from that jumble of pitiful responses you call thoughts, the Dragon's begged you to take that option.' Prince Sabatini's voice was dark, sardonic. 'Didn't I hear you both discussing *godMode* . . . What could be more appropriate?'

Alex was silent.

'You want the Doge. He needs a divorce,' the Prince told Razz. 'He could do it himself, of course: God damn it, he's quantum. But he's too squeamish to rewrite code on the fly. You, however, could pull the plug . . .'

'First I find the Doge,' said Razz. 'Then we talk about that bloody game. Okay? Get me out to newVenice and as soon as I've got the fucking Doge, I'll cut wires, bomb databases, trash whatever connections you want. After I've offed that shit-for-brains from *WeGuard*.'

The Prince's laugh was sour, his voice contemptuous as he rolled her swear words back at her.

For a second, Razz considered taking out one of his eyes as an object lesson, but it would be Alex she'd hurt. Not that losing an eye would bother Alex much. Where better to be in need of a vat-grown optic than sitting in a hut on top of a thirteen-level arcology dedicated to gene, clone and transplant technology? Not to mention the glory of God.

She spat in the dirt. 'Just get me out to newVenice.'

But Alex held up one tired hand. 'The Doge isn't in newVenice. I know, I've looked. You think I haven't ripped through every data path, ghosted every web? He's not there.' Alex sighed heavily, his head beginning to droop onto his chest. The air was thinning as steam condensed on the rough mud-brick of the walls, running in uneven streams down the baked clay of the hut's building blocks. 'Nzigé's got him . . .'

Great. Razz waited, but there was nothing to wait for. If not actually asleep, Alex was no longer interfaced with the world she occupied.

'Prince?' Razz had no idea if Prince Sabatini could manifest while Alex wasn't there. But even if he could, he didn't. She crawled fitfully around the hut, cursing every time her hand hit discarded food or worse. Whatever Alex intended to give her didn't appear to be there. Though what he had that she might want, Razz couldn't say.

This was the man she'd loved, whose life she'd saved, cutting the throat of her owner rather than letting him kill Alex. And now beggars were better dressed: drunks, fundamentalists and dusted-out streetpunks made more sense . . .

Razz knocked back a tear with her hand and crouched down beside the huddled figure. He slept like a snake, with his eyes open, his gaze fixed somewhere in the infinite distance. Something to tell her, something to give her. Half from instinct, half because she noticed that the fingers of one hand were tightly clenched, Razz began to prise open his grip.

[Santa Passionata/Watarishu]

As *Saints&Synners*'s primitive voiceSprite pointed out to Angeli, it was a uniform to kill for. Which was just as well, because Kwai had . . .

Kwai swaggered across Marinsky Square in a black tunic decorated at the shoulders with silver scales. A heavy silver chain swung against his side, starting at a pocket over his heart and vanishing under his arm. Silver bullet cases adorned each breast, clinking against the silver chain as he strode through the crowd which opened before him.

Behind him, his black cloak flapped dramatically as a warm St Petersburg wind blew in from those mosquito-infested marshes on which Peter the Great had once, long since, decided to build his city. Finland was across the horizon, but Kwai could have been 1,000 miles to the east and a hundred years in the past.

Double-headed eagle banners hung from the façade of St Isaac's Cathedral. In the centre of the square, Baron Klodt's prancing equestrian statue of Nicholas Pavlovich I was freshly gilded, huge on its pedestal of granite and marble.

Kwai's cloak was high-collared and lined with red silk. Useless against any cold but dashing, dramatic, like the huge cobbled square through which he strode.

At his left hip Kwai wore a curved sabre in a simple scabbard of black leather. At his right hip was a lovingly-restored 1906 model Kriegsmarine Luger, loaded with 9mm bullets, newly re-blued by a Black Hundred gunsmith. He looked dashing, dangerous, slightly deranged. In fact, he looked just like all the other officers who strode arrogantly through the crowd of 20,000 potential new converts to the cause of steppe Cossack Colonel Volkonsky.

But Kwai was different, and the wary expression in the faces around him acknowledged that. It might have been the enamel-and-gold double-eagle insignia on his collar that marked him out as a half-colonel in the Black Hundreds, a half-god among lesser mortals, or it could have been the crested gold-and-cornelian signet ring of a Cossack prince. But Kwai knew, just as the milling crowd that opened to let him through knew, that what really impressed them was the body of an infantry major sprawled, broken-necked, on the cobbles behind him.

He'd had no alternative but to kill the man. The major had interrupted Kwai's Zen-like concentration, disturbed Kwai's iron control over the patterns of his own body. And that was something Kwai couldn't afford, not yet. It hadn't been quick thinking that had caused Kwai to reach casually up to the officer's neck and snap his spine like a twig, it had been Kwai's awareness that his own heart-rate was rising dangerously. Blind panic wasn't an option, not even when stopped a hundred paces from his destination by a barked demand for his Black Hundred card.

The Hundred might be techno-revisionists, they might even be as neo-Luddite as the Mullahs, but they sure as hell still believed in smart cards. Fingerprinted, photo-carrying, here as almost everywhere else on the planet, smart IDs were the smart way to reveal who and what you were. Designer labels for humans, Passion called them. As pointless as they were apparently important.

Kwai didn't have one, of course. Or rather he did, but the face on it belonged to someone else and the thumb print that activated the card was in a small pocket in the lining of his flamboyant cloak, along with the rest of the man's thumb.

Besides, Kwai couldn't afford to be stopped, not with eight sausages of condom-contained Semtex lining his gut like a fat, deadly tapeworm. Sasumi was gone, that was fact one, killed when a Black Hundred-inspired anti-foreigner riot had ripped apart the Vasilevsky district of St Petersburg four nights before. Fact two was that Kwai intended to go face to face with the man responsible, even though he would die in the process. Maybe this was what they called love: Kwai didn't know.

But he knew only too well that he wouldn't have done what he was doing for anyone else. Not purged his gut and then locked his bowels with kaolin, solemnly ingesting Semtex until his gut was packed at both ends with enough explosive to rip him and everyone around him into shredded meat.

The detonators were simple, wired to blow when his pulse hit a hundred. He'd buried one in the centre of each condom, surrounding it completely with explosive. The switch itself was a pulse-counting Casio sports watch strapped tight to his left wrist.

It was always going to come to something like this, Kwai decided, warm wind pulling tears from his eyes as he made himself march ever closer to the podium on which stood the Black Hundreds' *ataman*, Colonel Volkonsky.

That brief section at the end, with Passion and then Sasumi, the Paul Smith suits and the Loebe shoes, that was just a coda, a codicil to the real plot of his life. A thread that began with a Khmer-controlled mountain village high in the Golden Triangle and ended here, surrounded by the cold neoclassical architecture of Enlightenment Europe.

What was it his grandfather had always said? *Nip the buds, kill the kids.* Coca Cola and cocaine, gangs and drugs. It hadn't been a good life, few were. But there'd been moments like that first girl behind the warehouse, when he came south to Bangkok. She'd been beautiful, believing the easy lies that already tripped off his tongue, words stolen from some soap about inner-city kids.

Not that it mattered now.

There'd been others, of course. None so special as that, not until he met Sasumi. Bought her, rather. Calling things by their name was a strength, a form of power. Why else did the gods of every creation myth name things?

Kwai stuck out his chin, and tipped the fur hat lower over his brow. With his wide almond eyes, high cheekbones and weathered skin he could pass for a steppe Cossack in a way Sasumi never could. Maybe if he'd been there he could have protected her from the riot. Maybe not.

God knew, Kwai realized he was stupid to get upset about someone he'd paid for. But with her it hadn't been about money – at least, not for him. It hadn't even been about power. She'd been happy, he really believed that. Tears ran freely down Kwai's cheeks now and not from the wind. People took surreptitious glances at his face but looked away long before his troubled gaze could catch theirs. He was at the podium now, past the Cossacks hidden in the milling crowd and the CIA-trained anti-explosive sniffer dogs, carried safely through the mass of people by the emptiness etched on his face and his stolen double-eagle insignia of rank.

Volkonsky was standing on a small wooden podium, surrounded by his sullen bodyguards, an elderly, bearded patriarch by his side. The *ataman*'s narrow face was turning rapidly in all directions as he sprayed his ideas out at the crowd, one clenched fist beating rhythmically at the palm of his other hand, stressing the importance, the weight of his words.

His eyes caught the red silk of Kwai's cloak and Volkonsky smiled in recognition, but then he shifted his gaze and his deep eyes finally met those of Kwai. Void staring into void. For a second Volkonsky's booming voice faltered. And while his bodyguards were still trying to work out from which direction danger had come, Kwai leapt up onto the podium.

His mind was completely clear now, purified. He had Sasumi to avenge and a job to complete. Not in the way that Passion had intended, but it would be completed all right, and in a more thorough manner than any assassin could usually hope to achieve.

The crowd had fallen silent, the bodyguards uncertain, halted by the authority of the double eagle on his shoulder. Kwai turned to the crowd, removed his fur cap so they could finally see he wasn't from the Steppes and opened his mouth . . .

Three things happened simultaneously. Kwai's cry of '*Chechnya*' rang out across the shocked square. All four bodyguards raised their pistols. And, in that Zen-like gap in time, Kwai looked into the small black circle of a gun barrel's mouth and allowed himself to panic.

By the time the first bullet took him through the jaw, splintering his mandible, Kwai's pulse had broken a hundred. It would have made one-fifty but as it hit the double-nought a switch on his wrist kicked in and tripped the detonator . . .

Deep inside the compacted explosive that stuffed his duodenum, the electronic detonator's instant reaction shredded Kwai's stomach, liver and central vertebra. Ribs splintered outwards, shards of bloodied bone scything through the air, ripping like shrapnel through the flesh of the appalled onlookers.

Volkonsky was gone, not even just fatally injured but *pulped*, as fragments of Kwai's spine ripped through his body like frag from a claymore. The shock wave burst the Cossack's eardrums, turning his eyes to jelly. It would have broken his neck had the Semtex not already twisted the *ataman*'s head from the top of his spinal column. A distant camera caught the exact moment his head landed, deaf and sightless, in the panicking crowd.

CNN had scooped everyone else as usual.

But Kwai felt nothing, remembered nothing, not even Sasumi. His final thought, as pure and as honest as any he'd ever had, was the sudden overwhelming adrenalin rush of blind panic.

[Fear Feathers]

No longer blinded by steam, Razz crouched over Alex and tried to prise open the man's clenched fingers. Her dark eyes still stung from smoke that spiralled from an iron bucket of coals in the corner of his tiny cell. Blood pounded in her temples; every time she turned her head it felt like her brain rattled.

She was out of everything. Patience, adrenalin and paraDerm. All she wanted was to be gone, but first Alex had something to give her. That's what he'd said, the shit-for-brains. Something to help her find the Doge. And, try as she might, she couldn't recall the name that Alex had been going on about, Nizee something. She'd remember it, though, and track down the Doge. God knew how, but she'd do it.

She was holding her breath, not just against the smoke but because of the rank stink of shit and sweat that attached itself to Alex's wasted body like some hellish cologne. The man was muttering in his sleep, some loop-like mantra in no language she knew.

Once getting whatever it was would have been simple. All it would have involved was cutting off his hand or breaking his fingers. But now, without her claws, her viral enhancements, she didn't have the strength or the will. And besides, strange as it was even to her, Razz didn't want to hurt Alex. So she worked slowly, pushing the carpal pressure point until his *flexor digitorum* muscles slowly loosened of their own accord and she pulled open his hand to touch a red feather.

Panic rocketed through her, like pain. And went just as suddenly, when she dropped the feather. Even putting her hand near it made her afraid. Ripping a strip off her jellaba, Razz tried picking up the feather, using the cloth. Nothing. Not the slightest fear. Whatever it was, it needed direct skin contact.

Except it wasn't a feather. At least, she didn't think so. No bird had flown with it, that was for sure. The shaft was gold, the actual feather vein-like and silicon-thin, its edges fractal in their repetitive complexity. Whatever, she thought, it wasn't a feather. Razz nodded: at least she agreed with herself on that.

If the object was like anything organic, it was most like a leaf. OrganoSynth? Nanetic Art? Could be . . . A gold stem with a leaf of ruby shot through with an intricate tracery of silver thread. It looked like . . . Hell, Razz didn't know *what* it looked like. A blade, maybe, from a spear almost too fragile to handle, never mind use in battle. So intricate it had to be organic or machine made, its complexity and intricacy way beyond the skill of human hands.

Maybe Alex had made it? Razz shrugged, running her hands over Alex's sleeping head, then just as quickly wiping her hands on her black jeans. Pity wasn't an emotion that came naturally to Razz.

A year or two running the streets of Moscow, a couple more as a freelance hacker in London, then practically her whole lifetime as an exotic: those were the kind of credentials to burn pity out of anyone's circuits. And Razz didn't go too much on the milk of human kindness anyway. Never had: from what she'd seen, it always turned sour pretty early on.

But Alex . . . Ignoring his stink, she leant over the man and tried to straighten out his twisted body, but it was no good. Every muscle was locked tight, twisting him until he could have been someone caught in the middle of a seizure or flash-frozen.

Even his eyelids had locked open, so that try as she might Razz couldn't close his blind, staring eyes. Not that it mattered much, thought Razz, looking round at the darkness of the cell, lit only by the coals in the brazier. It was like eternal night in there. And who the hell knew what it was like wherever Alex really was?

[Dusting Out the Devils]

It was a strange vehicle, but that didn't mean Nzigé hadn't seen one before. Nzigé wasn't her real name, of course, but as a girl the old woman had gone travelling, north to where the desert was sand, not stone like here, yellow rather than rough red. From the yellow sand, she'd gone east, crossing borders, avoiding soldiers, the basic moves of bushman life. Ending up high in the blue mountains near the start of a great river. That was where the real Nzigé had come to her, laughing in a dream. Telling her that she, the world and all those in it were just mathematics, which some people called poetry.

Of course, that was years ago, but that was when Nzigé had first seen a craft like this one. Low, lumbering, passing slowly over the broken ground without ever touching it, leaving a trail of dancing red dust devils in its wake. Devils that danced and died, just like the real ones that spun across the wastelands of her home.

If this was like the ones she'd seen before, then that meant this craft was very old too, maybe as old as Nzigé. Because Nzigé knew that machines changed their shape every few years. Animals and humans remained more or less the same, except those that died, but machines changed. They grew themselves now, effortlessly. Change, update, augment. She knew this was true. Alex had told her so, but Nzigé had also seen it clearly in a dream.

Grey with black markings, and a huge cross in red. The ones Nzigé had seen years before had also had red crosses – the ones that didn't have red crescents. There was another craft, too. But where the large one rumbled like an angry animal over the cracked and uneven earth, fixed at the height of a man's waist, the second craft hung in the sky, tiny and silent, its wingspan no bigger than that of a large vulture.

It was invisible, too. Though that wasn't quite accurate because Nzigé could see it if she tried. But it worked hard at not being seen and Nzigé had to concentrate to empty her old head of the thoughts that seemed to fill it every time she looked in the craft's direction.

And though it was the hover that stirred up her memories like dancing dust devils, the voices in Nzigé's head warned her the second craft was the one she'd been waiting for.

Razz would find Nzigé, Alex had been certain of that: he'd make sure of it. And the old woman was to be there to meet her, waiting on the cracked earth, where the Kalahari desert slid into the hill lands.

Just when Alex had first appeared in the dream lands Nzigé wasn't certain. If you asked Alex, he'd say he'd been there forever, but he hadn't. There had been a time before. There always was.

All that fuss down there with the hover would be about the little blond boy Dr Schwartz was meant to heal. Story was, the boy lived out on the Edge, had been thrown from a horse. But it wasn't true, couldn't be. No one lived out on the Edge any more, not since the last temperature hike. Even the meerkats had moved.

Men were taking a bodypod from an old Chrysler hover now, lead by old Dr Schwartz and his houseboy whose name Nzigé didn't know. The houseboy didn't like Nzigé but the old woman didn't mind. She could have told the houseboy that she too, when she was young, had worn smart clothes and travelled in Boeing BWBs and airships. She'd travelled beyond the earth, up to the Disney Voertrekker ring colonies, to where the new cities were being built.

Only the poor and the really rich now remained in Namibia. The first couldn't afford to live in orbit, the second could afford to build the world they wanted where they already were. That was the nature of money.

But Nzigé hadn't stayed. She didn't like flying machines. If she had to, she could travel in them, but she didn't want to live in one. Especially not a NASA-designed ring that hung in space like some silver doughnut. No, she didn't want to drink other people's piss, eat their shit, breathe the air someone else had only recently breathed out, no matter how well it was all scrubbed.

Razz saw the small, almost naked woman watching the mission. If she hadn't known it was impossible she'd have thought the old woman was watching her as well. Every so often her dark eyes would flick in Razz's direction and her battered face would look vaguely puzzled. Then she'd shrug and smile, and the worry lines would fall away, though that still left a face more crumpled than a piece of bark paper.

'Crazy old fu—' Razz began changing it to something less . . . couldn't think what and let it ride. She grinned. Being young again was fine, or so Razz was coming to think. She'd never really felt old, except right at the end when she took on newVenice as a way out of the loop. But all this trying to be polite, she was the wrong generation for that.

Razz's mouth twisted into a sour grin. Was that crazy old bitch down there Alex's water spirit, her guide through the desert? A sag-breasted old woman in faded khaki shorts, nothing else, tightly curled grey hair gone white at the temples, black skin burned as hard as leather?

Maybe she was. She was certainly waiting. At least, that's what it looked like on Razz's Nikon screen. Not that she could *see* the screen, of course. Except at the back of her eyes where a hairline laser wrote across her cone cells what it read from digital cameras slung beneath each wing. The BAero3z came with an auto-focus Nikon 2D mounted on a gyropod. It moved when she did, looked where she looked and when she blinked hard did a 180° flip to show Razz whatever was right behind her.

Which was great. But whoever'd designed the pod hadn't taken flying over the Kalahari into account. Or maybe there was an auto-polarizing filter for the pilot's bubble, if she could only find it.

'Shit.' It wasn't even as if Razz could ask her computer. There wasn't one. The blond American's card had stretched pretty far, but not that far. Zurich to San Lorenzo via M'dina was pretty much it. So she'd stolen the plane from the Mufti's own air force, but that was a whole other story. And not one she wanted to make public.

Still, she had air-conditioning and a water recyc, even if she didn't have a semiAI to hold her hand. Razz banked hard into a thermal as it hit, using the sudden updraught to take her higher into the African sky. She had a Lockheed fU/zon engine for emergencies, but most of the time she relied on a propeller fixed to the back of her pod. The prop fed off amorphous silicon in the skin of the wing, and the BAero3z's wings themselves were multipurpose. Not just photovoltaic, but designed to ride thermals and take pressure off the prop or fusion jet.

It was a beautiful plane, small and sweet. Too bad she was going to have to junk it. But junk the baby she would and soon. Because sweet as it was, it did everything except land vertically – and that was what Razz needed now.

The Kalahari below her was a fractured marquetry of red dunes, gravel banks, obsidian-smooth rock and cracked earth. There was nowhere down there flat enough to land, except maybe the concrete area in front of the mission. And the over-square Chrysler hover was hogging that.

'Take me on roller coaster, take me on airplane ride . . .' Okay, so her BAero3z didn't have semiAI but it had on-board sound, retro-fitted for CD, DAT and DVD, and back in Zurich Razz had invested heavily in European classic. Too bad she was going to lose that, too.

'Okay, let's do it,' Razz told herself, pushing back her visor, letting autopilot cut in.

Pulling her plane out of its spiralling thermal hike, Razz paused to catch her breath and then quickly primed her parachute. One after another, she checked the neophrene straps holding her into her bucket seat, then shifted uneasily to pass another strap up between her legs and slap its end against a black plate over her diaphragm. Plastics fused and she was bonded into her chair.

Ready to roll, more or less.

Hanging from a silk lanyard next to the black plate was a cutter, its razor-sharp moly blade safely concealed at the bottom of a ceramic vee. All Razz had to do if she wanted out of the chair was ram the edge of a strap into that vee and pull: the moly-wire blade would do the rest. Satisfaction guaranteed.

'Get on with it,' Razz muttered crossly. And despite everything she'd read in the instructions, hunched her body as she reached down with one hand, flipped up the safety cover, grabbed the manual eject on the side of her seat and gave it a good yank.

She rocketed. For a second Razz blacked out and then the BAero3z was way below her and she was frozen in space, completely motionless, not yet started on her fall. A muffled thud from her seatback told her the tiny canister holding her pilot chute had blown and the fabric was billowing up over her head like the flame of a candle.

Then her main chute caught and filled out until it looked like a huge, almost transparent box kite. Her trode box disconnected from the side of her seat and fell away, starting to burn, not hot and red but cold and white. A catalytic conflagration designed to stop it falling into enemy hands.

'Sweet fucking Nazarene.'

The first thing Razz thought, when she stopped being shocked at having just flown 2,000 miles wired into a box designed to burst into flames, was that she should start steering her chair. The second was that she was dangerously, maybe lethally, over-dressed.

Ripped free from her air-conditioned bubble, Razz could feel heat close instantly around her, like the outblast from an oven door or a burst of flare magnesium. She knew heat. Christ knew, as the silver-skinned thug she'd flown, driven, even sand-scooted out to see Alex, and you didn't get to cross the Megrib without meeting heat. But this was something else. And that had been twenty years ago anyway, Razz realized sadly. She couldn't even remember when she'd stopped visiting him.

It was heat like panic, an amphetamine rush that would have knocked Razz off her feet had she been standing. Sweat beaded her hairline. Her neck went slick and Razz felt a first runnel of sweat begin down her side. And then her body was leaching moisture, perspiration beading across her shoulders and in the small of her back, between her legs and at the back of her knees. She was broiling in her own sweat.

Maybe it was her new body, Razz thought, maybe heat had always been like this and she'd lost her defences along with the years. Who the hell knew? And retro 501s and a Free Mexican Airforce flying jacket might have looked neat when she bartered for them up at the glass-roofed souk in M'dina, but in the middle of the Kalahari they were terminally stupid, an instant invitation to cook. Which was what she did. Razz was unconscious long before she hit the sun-baked ground . . .

She was lying on a wooden table, a dust-grey canvas awning rippling above her in the afternoon breeze. Someone had cut off her flying jacket and her boots.

'Hot as hell,' the old man said when Razz opened her eyes. Then reflexes hit, and Razz flipped her body sideways off the table. Except she didn't, her body was too weak, too tired. The man's arms might be thin, flesh creased with age and skin scar-blotched with melanoma, but for all the strength Razz had, she might as well have been pushing up against steel.

'Lie still,' the man said gently. 'It's the heat that gets you.' He reached over for a green glass and brought it carefully to her lips. 'Drink this,' he ordered.

Razz twisted her face away. 'Is it sterilized?' she demanded.

The old man's eyebrows were white, like an albino bat's wings, scraggy, a bit unlikely. He raised both and then smiled, not that kindly. 'Sterilized? Out here?'

Razz said nothing. She couldn't think over the pain in her head.

Light burnt her eyes, her vision was an out-of-focus flicker and blood still pounded inside her head. She saw him, dimly, standing over her, an old man in a stained lab coat, cheeks hollow with age, a heavy moustache died yellow with nicotine.

The old man held the glass up to the light, examining its bubbles and flaws. 'Washed in clear water, dried in the sun.' He coughed, carefully turning away to cover his mouth with a fist. 'Heat sterilizes, so does light . . . Drink it,' he insisted, and Razz did, letting the sips of water run down her throat, cold and welcome.

'Two sick children in one day,' was the last thing she heard the old man mutter, and then there was darkness.

When Razz next woke it was evening and she was naked, in a metal bed with one white sheet covering her sweat-slicked body and a large, slow fan that revolved steadily overhead.

'How are you feeling?'

'Fucking terrible,' Razz said, then flushed when she traced the voice to a white-wimpled Sister of Mercy sitting on a wooden stool in the corner. The nun said nothing.

'Oh, Christ,' Razz said, and flushed again. 'I'm sorry.'

The nun said nothing but picked up her sewing and quietly left the room.

'Fucking great,' muttered Razz and sat upright, letting the cotton sheet drop down around her soft waist. She was still sitting like that, examining the heat blotches that ran raw across her breasts and gut, when the old man came in, another glass held tightly in his hand.

Without thinking, Razz grabbed the cotton sheet and yanked it up to her chin. Then she grinned, idiotically. *Shit*, she thought. Intimations of modesty, her!

'No problem,' said the old man, turning away as Razz reached for a paper gown left neatly folded at the end of her bed. 'I'm a doctor *and* a priest.' His sardonic voice was almost too soft to hear, and he spoke with an accent she couldn't place. 'Actually,' he said sadly, 'you're triply safe . . .'

Razz looked at him and the old man smiled.

'I'm also dying.' He said it as if it should have been obvious.
Razz blinked.

'I'm old,' he said, 'that's what happens. Or at least, what's meant
to happen.' The priest coughed again. 'Two years, maybe less . . .
Either way, I won't be sorry. Who wants to be a plugged-in block
of ice?' He fumbled in his pocket and came up with a packet of
Chinese Marlboro. Tapping one out of the packet with his nail, he
had it lit and a cloud of smoke billowing up towards the fan before
the packet was even back in his coat pocket.

'Want one?' he asked suddenly, fingers moving back towards
his coat.

Razz shook her head.

'Bad habit,' the man agreed, 'and anyway, you're too young.'

If only . . . Razz thought. But it was strange. Her body no longer
felt such a bad fit, and she was getting used to catching sight of
her new reflection and seeing herself look young again. Maybe it
was true, maybe she really was younger, because she sure as hell
was losing her edge. Anyone tried to hold her down like that and
she'd have ripped their throat out with her teeth not too long ago.
Instead, she'd drifted back into sleep.

'So which is it?' the old man asked, pulling up a three-legged
stool, its wooden seat black and slick with years of use.

'Which is what?' Razz asked, watching him carefully. Just
because he looked like a sweet old man didn't mean he was. If
there was a double game in play, she'd find it.

'Well,' said the old man. 'Are you running or looking?'

'This is the Kalahari,' he added, when Razz looked blank. 'If
you're not escaping from something, then you're looking for what
you haven't found elsewhere. You look too young for the first and
. . .' He paused, his small green eyes looking into hers.

She shivered and the old man suddenly smiled.

For a nanosecond Razz was left with the sensation of having
gazed into a bottomless well, and then it was gone.

'No matter,' he said lightly. 'You can tell me later.'

'I'm looking for a goddess.' Razz said shortly. 'It seems I've got something she needs. Oh, and I'm looking for a small boy,' she added, feeling stupid.

The priest raised his bat-wing eyebrows. It was a reaction that Razz was beginning to recognize. 'Ah,' he said with a softer smile, 'I may be able to help you there.'

[Digital Dust]

Lieutenant Angeli Rispoli was where he wanted to be, back inside his NVPD helmet, skimming tri-D reruns of the pirate DVD. He couldn't help it. Crude coding or not, *Saints & Synners* was just more interesting, more real than taking kickbacks and cracking heads together outside in District Three. *S&S* also made a hell of a lot more sense of politics up in the Suites. Didn't solve the murder of the *WeGuard* techie, but Angeli knew he wasn't meant to solve that anyway.

Which was why he still intended to do so, and from a distance if needs be. Angeli blinked his cursor onto reverse, skimmed back to the opening grab of Colonel Volkonsky on the podium and began a rerun of Kwai's final moments. Tragedy, bravery and irony, whoever the fuck Declan really was, *Saints & Synners* included the lot. For a start, Sasumi wasn't dead, she wasn't even in that hotel when the crowd torched it to ash and rubble. She'd been in a bar, on line to the Kremlin finalizing details with the General. The first she knew about Kwai's death was when she saw it on a news flash . . .

CNN had a field day, the best since Alaska tried to declare independence. For seven whole days, CNN grabbed the world by its throat and kept its attention. It didn't matter that the Ogoni uprising in Nigeria had entered a final, deadly phase. That the *fascisti* government in Ankara was bombing Kurdish children. Only in London and Hollywood did CNN's grip slip slightly, when the Prince Regent and Courtney Love both held press conferences, the Regent to announce his impending engagement and Ms Love her candidacy for President.

The rest of the world watched in shocked fascination as the Black Hundreds rose like a deadly wave in Moscow, Kiev and St Petersburg to gun down the Chechen mafia. Buildings burnt, whole streets were gutted-out to empty, blank-windowed movie lots. Thousands, tens of thousands died in a hail of 7.62 mm, .357 and 9 mm bullets as Volkonsky's Black Hundreds tried to wipe clean his death with everything from Saturday-night Uzis to Heckler & Koch SD3s.

History repeated itself first as deadly farce, then as tragedy. Serbia and Mali were dropped as Russia's tragedy split into digital packages to navigate the web, then flicked at light speed down the threadworms of the planet's fibreoptic cables to spill out on screens the world over.

Always the same tight-cropped pictures: wide-eyed little boys, terrified young girls, sobbing grandmothers, mixed with the unshaven, sullen, shocked faces of once-ordinary men who'd had their very normality stolen by the requirement to kill. Every cliché, visual and verbal, spilled out on the screen.

Stock footage of Colonel Volkonsky addressing his troops, footage of his funeral – which was State in all but name – crowded out heavily-edited camcorder shots of the first riot in Smolensk, all the more brutal for being cammed by amateurs while the rat-pack professionals were still split between Moscow and St Petersburg.

Not that CNN minded running amateur vid, or the world watching it. The world didn't give a fuck whether the man on the ground carried a union card or a cheap Sony, as long as he got in there. News was suddenly news again, and media fasting went from West Coast hip to dross in a matter of hours, as millions mainlined on satellite news. Moscow, Kiev, St Petersburg – it was like watching the Ku Klux Klan take on the Colombian Cartels. And about as edifying.

[Santa Passionata/Suits & Shades]

The footage from Russia, watched anxiously in the Oval Office and 10 Downing Street, was the same as that broadcast to the Bangkok bar where Passion sat, drinking Rolling Rock from the bottle, picking unsteadily at a sticky dish of beer nuts. Not tasting any of it.

Salt was crusted across her lap where it had fallen through her shaking fingers to stain the chocolate cloth of her no-longer-new suit. There were empty bottles stacked up in front of her. How many, Passion didn't know; she couldn't see straight enough to count.

Passion's recent diet was shot to hell. McDonalds, Hersheys, deep-pan double-cheese – she'd been bingeing solidly since word of Kwai's death first came through. So, the junk went straight down her gullet, until her bloated gut stuck out below her tits like a ledge. Passion knew that. She just didn't care. A quick trip to the loo, two fingers down her throat and she could start again.

The kid was finally gone, though. They'd been ignoring each other since the news came through, the child growing more ghost-like each hour, less real. Maybe Kwai's was one death too many. Maybe Passion didn't have space to feel guilty about two things at once, she didn't know. Didn't care much, either. From the day she walked out of the clinic, she'd carried that ghost with her, from bed to bed, restaurant to bar. It was enough to make anyone drink.

'Still not doing drugs, though . . .' Passion announced, to no one at all. Which was just as well, as no one answered, though the barman looked anxious and a German tourist sitting next to her shifted uneasily in his seat. No drugs: Passion was proud of that.

True, tears ran down her wide cheeks and her blue eyes were bruised black with lack of sleep and smudged mascara. But she'd refused the hotel doctor's offer of Prozac or betablockers. And why the fuck not? Passion wanted to feel what she felt, which was novel in itself – given that she'd spent most of her teens trying to prove money couldn't buy happiness, and most of her early twenties hitting Valley clinics to prove that, in Passion's case at least, it couldn't buy a cure either.

The American woman's throat was raw from vomiting and she'd coughed up so much bile the back of her teeth were etched yellow, but Passion had no intention of stopping, not yet. Not by a long shot. And it wasn't as if the fucking plan needed her: everything was all going like clockwork, if anyone still knew what clockwork was.

Another thirty-one million pounds sterling had just bounced through her Swiss account, feeding into subset offshores in Grand Cayman and Panama. And the credit didn't even come from her own borrowing. Passion had branched out. It was trash money, paid out by a noted merchant bank in London's square mile. The bank had a 280-year history, a marble-floored, Wren-designed mansion headquarters and a director who was first cousin to the Prime Minister, but it still didn't have the faintest when it came to security.

Passion drained her beer and banged down the Rolling Rock bottle just a little too hard, its crash reverberating round the bar. But no one met her eye. Office suits, resting whores, off-duty police, all pointedly looking away.

'Yeah, right. Just another spoilt tourist . . .' Passion nodded fiercely in agreement. And why not? She was spoilt all right, ripped through the middle and trashed round the edges. Story of her life. Crap little Catholic girl. Shit hot, 2600-class as a hacker, though.

The way it worked was basic. Passion chose a target, something venerable, beyond reproach and tek-illiterate, and then ripped through their accounts and trading database, winkling out double accounting, identifying star traders who were actually busy hiding from their own bosses ten years' worth of losses on Tokyo metal futures, the New York zinc market, whatever . . .

And then the bank paid her five per cent of one month's trading figures for not going public and another five per cent for not trashing the database. As she said, trash money. And this was the third – and smallest – European bank she'd hit that week. It was old, all right, but in global terms it was also second-rate and Passion had only turned it over out of bloody-mindedness, after seeing it mentioned in *Newsweek*.

Okay, so she had other reasons. Though it probably wasn't his fault the man in the *Newsweek* photograph wore a well-cut blue suit or had hair greying at the temples. Nor that he sported understated spectacles and a discreet Rolex. But, fault or not, he still looked like her Dad, and that was reason enough. Not that his bank would agree.

Passion didn't need that money; she'd already repaid her trust fund, tidying it up round the edges until no one could tell money had ever been borrowed. The SI (Tin) Bank, Siam (Colonial) Securities, even Jardine, Jardine, Chun and Baker had been swapped up, traded, sold on to act as someone else's shell. No. Passion's money was now self-creating, as she bought and sold, gathered interest or hit metaNationals for more cash.

Digitized, flicking though binary byways, encrypted and with enough firewalls for an Aboriginal corroboree, enough credit surged in and out of Passion's account in Zurich to buy Panama. Money just bled into that account from all round the world, like she'd leeched into some global financial artery – which, come to think of it, was exactly what she had done.

'Well, why not?' Passion demanded loudly.

Sheer fucking spite, anger, sadness. She could run a list off the top of her head without even engaging her brain. But they weren't the reasons. Not the real ones . . .

Passion glanced up at the flickering Sony that someone had glued to a metal plate welded to one end of an iron teebar. The other end was plastered roughly into the wall. Electricity and a scart cable hung in a loop between wall and TV. Cheap, makeshift and ugly, but entirely functional. Much like life.

On the screen Chechen guerrillas were sniping at Russian civilians in between politely answering a BBC journalist's endless questions. Overhead, Russian MiGs left vapour trails in a dead grey sky, counting down the minutes until the camera crew's Toyota pulled out and the jets went in. Over a sniper's shoulder, the city was burnt out to a concrete lot. Passion didn't know its name, but she wasn't alone in that. No one in the bar knew. Somewhere in Chechnya or Russia, or somewhere like that . . .

Somewhere it snowed in July.

'Ash,' said a drunk behind her. 'Not snow, ash . . .' Passion turned to find pale blue eyes staring at her from a drink-ravaged face. 'It doesn't matter,' he added quickly. 'It's just, it's not yet winter over there . . .'

'That so?'

The man nodded.

Passion smiled and slid clumsily off her chrome bar stool, nodded back at the ravaged face and headed for the door. She was out of there. There was a private jet waiting out at the International, always assuming she could find a taxi interested in taking a food-stained, drunken American woman.

Waiting for her at the airport would be Declan, the man with the guns. At least, she hoped he would. She'd spent enough on flights and bribes getting him there. With his green eyes, freckles and ridiculously beautiful brown hair, Declan could have been a twelve-year-old altar boy. Passion knew, she'd seen the photos. Except that Declan was actually in his early twenties, a Dublin boy, but with a past in Belfast he didn't talk about.

Large amounts of cash had been spent to ensure the Irishman decided to double as her armourer and bodyguard. His impossible good looks got thrown in free.

'Too much beauty's dangerous,' Passion told the third taxi driver, the one who actually took her to the airport. Her words were meant to sound wise, but just came out slurred. She was drunk, Passion knew that. Only drunk would she think about beauty, remember things best forgotten, like the hut where she used to watch endless reruns of Leo Di Caprio in *Romeo & Juliet*, the rock video version.

It wasn't the film she remembered, though: it was getting fucked by her mother's lover. His eyes weren't green, they were the colour of flint. And he had stubble like sandpaper and tightly-curled body hair that ran from his groin to his shoulders, but he was thin and beautiful, and he knew what he was doing, all right. Which was more than Passion did.

It had been smooth, inevitable. Unfolding around her in a small reinforced hut at the DiOrchi entrance gates. Tall, Raybanned, with cheekbones to die for. Even the blue security-guard uniform somehow looked good on him.

He'd led her on, but she'd been willing enough to follow, at least at first. As friendly chats about school turned into a sympathetic arm around her shoulders and quick hugs spilled over into a first consoling kiss. That was when it went into freefall. Serious kissing, heavyweight petting, tentative oral sex. Then the real thing and, later on, a little pure Colombian rubbed around her anus, so he could finish off her education.

She'd followed that man round like a puppy for three months, more than willing to roll over every time he asked. And then her mother dropped by Bel Air, on her way from the Upper East Side to her new house in Mexico, a faithful copy of a design Frank Lloyd Wright had tossed aside as too ludicrous to make real.

Her urbane, polished, oh-so-polite mother had slapped Passion silly. Not the usual mother-to-daughter violence, but hard, claws-out, woman-scorned stuff. The punches bruised, but that wasn't what hurt. What hurt was Passion realizing afterwards that it was the only time her mother'd ever touched her.

Next morning, over fresh orange juice and toasted bagels, they'd had a short, strained chat in the white breakfast room. Too brief even to be a chat, really. Immaculate, packed, ready to go, the woman had stood behind Passion and, as the young girl ducked to avoid another blow, her mother had leant politely over her shoulder and placed a gold credit card next to Passion's untouched plate.

'If you're old enough to fuck,' she said, 'then you're old enough to learn it isn't as good as the real thing . . .'

[Santa Passionata/Sprezzatura]

There were a thousand ships, more or less, so inevitably some classically-educated retentive at the *New Yorker* nicknamed her Helen. Not that Passion's face would have launched anything, she knew that. What power she had was in her lines of credit. Her mother was right about that. Same as it ever was . . .

The name didn't stick. Too many people on board the SS *Karensky* knew her as Passion, though back in Moscow and over in Washington the spooks knew her as Katherine DiOrchi, hippy daughter of a Mafia boss. She was watched, of course, every grinding nautical mile of the way. Day in, day out, the whole bloody Rainbow flotilla was watched. Not that it took a string of geo-stat spySats to spot a thousand ships ploughing their way across a sea that was anything but wine-dark.

The Pacific was pale, sun-blinded, hardly rocked by waves at all. And her ships weren't even a proper flotilla, not as a navy might understand it. They were a one-fifty-mile string of rusting tankers, decommissioned Peruvian aircraft carriers, and tiny whale hunters still hanging parasite-like round the bloated mass of near-derelict, long-ex-Soviet mother ships. Crude tin cans baked in the blazing sunlight.

There were even two battered Polarises, bought for next to nothing from a receiver at Scotland's base near Faslaine. They'd have dived to escape the heat, but their captains weren't sure the ballast tanks were in good enough condition to get them back to the surface.

And then there was the Press, following after in hastily-hired yachts and fishing vessels. Not to mention three boats from

Greenpeace, not yet certain if Passion's flotilla was a blow for freedom or an ecological nightmare waiting to happen. As far as Declan was concerned, what he'd been told was a mission was becoming a circus.

Ships that could ploughed north into the Pacific towards the tropic of Cancer, while the rest ambled after or else floundered as their turbines gave out or they shipped too much water. By the end of the first week a tenth of all the ships had been abandoned. Within a fortnight the wastage figure had doubled.

Aboard the *Karensky*, crouched in a sliver of shade on the front deck, a couple of Australians from Port Moresby were using an Apple to try to pinpoint the currently watching spySats. BillE was reading coordinates aloud, while Karla tried to position a reflective screen they'd designed between them. Karla's reflectors were supposed to catch the sun's rays and reflect them back at the spySat, throwing out its sensors and blinding the camera.

Given that CNN, NBC, the BBC and every other media acronym known was buzzing them in light planes or copters, finding the flotilla wasn't going to present the UN with a problem. Still, wrapping the ship in foil kept them both out of trouble, and amused her Malay crew who moved silently round the baking decks, keeping the huge Russian whaler on the move.

'How much further?' asked Passion. She was standing in the bridge, gazing through cracked glass at the water ahead. Declan had already answered that question a hundred times before, but she couldn't help it. They were so close to the Meldarin ridge that it hurt.

'Five hours,' Declan announced casually without glancing up from his Dell laptop. *Minding* wasn't all he did: he'd majored in systems at Trinity in Dublin, when he wasn't playing keyboard at a pub in Temple Bar. And when that was over, he'd put in a year in Tokyo. As he pointed out, weapons had stopped being a skill and become a science, like music.

'Five hours!'

Declan nodded, ran one hand though sticky brown hair and

smiled. At least, it might have been a smile. It went by too fast for Passion to be sure.

She didn't know whether to be delighted or furious. The last time she'd asked, his answer had been three days, and that couldn't have been more than four hours ago.

The Irishman shrugged, gave another half-smile and then looked quickly back at the read-outs scrolling up one side of the Dell's screen. And he turned up the sound on his Sony Discman, to make sure she got the point.

The flotilla had bought their own satellites. Or rather, Passion had hired time from a French commercial operation, and Declan was checking the Rainbow flotilla's length. He measured it not in distance but in time, making it four days from end to end. Which meant the *Karensky* might arrive in five hours, but a hundred hours had to pass before the last ship was in place. A hundred hours, during which they would be at their most vulnerable. During which any nation could attack, or even all of them, if the afternoon UN meeting in New York went against Passion.

She was a strange one.

Declan glanced across at the girl. Middle, maybe late twenties. Strong jaw, broad face, olive skin. Sensible clothes of the kind that said *rich*, but not too loudly. And dark green eyes that held their gaze . . .

Controlled rather than inherently strong, Declan decided. Emotionally self-taught. He knew the feeling. Maybe that was why she picked him. Throwing cash in his direction until he couldn't refuse. He liked her, liked her strength: liked her body, even if she didn't.

Somewhere on the flight from Bangkok to Jakarta, Declan had decided that, if Passion was willing, once she was over her obsession with this flotilla, he'd like to take it further than business. And yeah, he knew who her father was. But then, shit, he always had lived dangerously. Check out his stint as a fixer on the Falls Road.

She was a living nightmare, of course she was . . . In a world where the richest forty-three people owned more than the poorest two billion, how could Passion be otherwise? At the last count *Fortune* had come up with 159 US billionaires who, if not all actually alive and well, were at least alive and plugged into the best life-support machines money could buy. And among those 159 were five members of Passion's family, including her father, her uncle and her aunt. Against odds like that, Declan decided, it would be impossible not to be spoilt.

And why not? Only someone coming from where Passion DiOrchi came from could think it sane to build a new country because she didn't like the laws, regulations and morals of the ones already on offer.

'Bastards,' Passion said, more from habit than real irritation. She was glued into Sky News, watching a report on that afternoon's UN meeting in New York called to deal with the flotilla.

Declan looked up.

'Bastards,' Passion said again, more loudly.

'True enough,' Declan said, turning off the Discman. His voice was as soft as Passion's was strident. 'But it's all talk anyway, that lot.' And it was, for the moment.

For a start, none of them knew what Passion intended, though suit after suit stood up to present opinion as fact. The Vietnamese, the Philippines, even the Chinese had declared states of emergency as the flotilla neared their waters and then quietly stood down their élite forces as Passion's raggle-taggle fleet sailed by.

Only Jakarta had attacked, right at the start. A mistake as costly as it was stupid. Passion's crew of Malay pirates and Comoros mercenaries fought back happily, not least because Declan had armed the flotilla with the very latest in surface-to-surface missiles.

Five Indonesian Navy ships later and the Rainbow flotilla steamed on, having bought time at the cost of a thousand Indonesian lives and having lost only one vessel, an Indian frigate even Passion had thought twice about buying, or so she later told Declan.

Declan got the feeling that thinking twice was a luxury Passion didn't allow herself. Not that she needed to, when it came to her ships. All she intended to do with any of them was scuttle the rustbuckets over the Meldarin Ridge to create foundations for a new city. *All!* Not that the UN knew that.

'It's not insane, is it?' Passion asked, but Declan didn't bother to reply: he didn't even bother to look up from his screen. Besides, she wouldn't like his answer.

'It's not,' Passion insisted. But they both knew it was. As surely as she and Declan knew that, according to messages tapped from CIA Langley, the only thing stopping Passion's flotilla being considered a real threat to 'world order' was the fact she hadn't purchased maritime concrete.

Up on screen, a thin Englishman was outlining reasons why the UN should halt the flotilla. Words like *colonial* and *gunboat* came swiftly back from Nicaragua's UN ambassador. But the American representative said nothing, just sat there shuffling her papers and nodding in silent agreement.

Trouble waiting to happen.

Her own people were going to be a problem, Passion just knew it: had known it all along, if she was honest. But as yet the White House hadn't worked out her purpose. There were rumours, all right. A floating island, a city undersea, even the occupation of Hawaii. The web was awash with rumours. But only she and Declan *knew*. No, not quite true. Waiting on a rig somewhere over the Meldarin Ridge, Sasumi *knew* too. But that was it, no one else, not yet.

So, according to the *New York Times*, her flotilla was a shipping hazard. The BBC had them down as a health hazard. *La Monde* thought 720 rusting ships were an environmental catastrophe in the making. In their own way, all of them were right.

But that was it: hot air, nothing to really worry the politicos. Not yet. But then, Passion had gone to a lot of trouble to hide her shopping list. Which took her back to concrete, and her lack of it. Because a Rainbow flotilla was one thing, an artificial island quite another.

It wasn't just tons of concrete that a city would need, or even hundreds of tons, but tens of thousands, and a sale that big would have left electronic slug traces to be found by the boy hackers at Langley. But they hadn't found it, because she hadn't bought concrete. Instead the hold of her ship was filled with research-grade coral crystals, bought through fake research labs and suspect bioTek start-ups, but mostly though the back door of a government agency in Mexico.

Freeze-dried coral: Passion owed the idea not to *Nature* or *New Scientist* or any encyclopaedia she'd ever skimmed, though in the last two months Passion had scanned dozens of DVDs, copying sections that interested her. No. Her impetus came from a recent paper on marine biotechnology, cached at the website of the Japanese imperial family.

It went without saying that what Passion knew about marine bleaching could be written on the flap of a Rizla packet. But the theory went something like this . . .

Three-quarters of the planet's surface is deep sea. Inhabited by primitive micro-organisms, some of which can thrive in habitats as inhospitable as deep ocean vents or survive temperatures that range from 105°C right down to 5°C. But coral isn't one of them. Coral is different. It needs shallows, sunlight and stable temperatures.

Without shallows, coral can't get a grip. Without sunlight, it doesn't grow. And if temperatures fluctuate too rapidly, coral bleaches as carbon (and the algae that gives coral its colour) is expelled from the coral polyps.

The end of the twentieth century saw coral bleach from Java to Costa Rica, from the Persian Gulf to the waters around Polynesia. In the very early years of the next century, Friends of the Earth launched its campaign to save the 'Marine Rainforests' but by then it was more or less too late.

Or it would have been, except a marine biologist at UVI in the Virgin Isles came up with a genetically-modified coral, designed to survive temperature fluctuations brought on by *El Niño*, the current circulating in the Pacific. Bayer-Rochelle bought the UVI patent outright, and augmented UVI's coral until the new, carbon-stable 'bioCoryl' was created. Two years later, someone discovered that, with only minor modifications, bioCoryl could be freeze-dried.

Passion had her foundations. The moment that Japanese site started unfolding into frame after frame of research, Passion knew it. Knew it as video streamed through her modem, to explode into a living marine forest across her screen.

Add Bayer Rochelle's own growth enhancer, back it up with a couple of ex-BayerR bio/tekkies sick of suits and bean counters, and who needed concrete anyway?

'Coffee,' said Declan. He passed Passion a tall glass swimming with crushed ice and Java. 'And then you need to change for the cameras. Take a shower, we can afford the water now.'

Passion nodded. 'How long?

Only this time Declan knew she meant how long before the last ships arrived? Not to mention how long before the crews could leave? Because it was the ships that Passion wanted. She'd promised the Malay and Thai crews that she'd return them home. They were going back on the only two really seaworthy vessels in the flotilla, and both of those had been leased, not bought.

Planning ... Everything was thought through to the last set and subset. Passion was proud of herself and Declan was openly impressed. Well-thought-out planning did that to him: it was the coder coming out. And Passion was right, the bioCoryl was a neat twist, it also sure as hell beat oak piles driven into mud, which was what the original city of Venice was supported on. But then, Passion had no intention of letting her city slip gracefully, century by century, inch by inch, below the waves.

[Santa Passionata/Cathedrals In Steel]

The two rigs were waiting, baking in the July sun. So vast they now towered Baubourg-tall, sheet-steel cathedrals above the SS *Karensky*. Once they'd sat like mosquitoes on the Fortieth Parallel, sucking up crude oil through a vast proboscis that cut through the Japanese seabed to the oil traps below. But the bed was empty, the company only too willing to offload its rigs to the first person willing to take on the grief of decommissioning them. And the first person was Passion. Hell, Passion was the *only* person. No one else was that stupid.

'Mother of God,' said Declan, when they finally stopped in the welcome shadow of the rigs. 'Will you look at that thing . . .' He stared up at the platform that towered a good eighty metres above, Press copters buzzing it like flies round a corpse.

'Yeah,' said Karla. 'Who says size doesn't count?'

Passion smiled. She'd changed her loose cotton dress for a black DKNY teeshirt and an old wrapround in rainbow silk from Anna Sui, but sweat was already staining the cloth under her arms.

'Don't suppose they've got air-conditioning?' Declan asked hopefully.

'Fully functioning,' said Passion, not taking her eyes off the huge rigs. Up on one platform, Passion could see small figures pointing her out, camcorders already whirring, and one of them waved. Passion waved back, unhooked a flyweight Sony geekmike from Declan's laptop and flicked her fingers over the Dell's keys. Minimizing their navSat programme, Passion double-clicked V/Con, then launched a video encrypting program. The call she put through was to the captains of the surrounding ships.

'Stay back,' Passion ordered. Water churned as the first wave of the flotilla put its turbines into reverse. And then the ships began to halt, but slowly, their critical mass way too big to stop easily. 'Go round if you need,' said Passion, 'but give the rigs a wide berth.'

'What happens next?' BillE asked.

'Watch,' said Passion, sounding more confident than she felt. This part of the idea had been Kwai's, and it was a beauty if it worked. Passion crossed herself, then flicked her fingers rapidly over the board: she was better at hotkey combinations than giving mouse. Switched to voice/video link, Passion called up the rig and a young woman appeared on her screen.

Japanese, soberly dressed in Western style, mostly black, and with make-up that was subtle but immaculate, only Sasumi's eyes and their grief-dark shadows said how badly she still took Kwai's death.

'Sasumi . . .' Passion tried to keep her greeting light, but her tone made little impact on Sasumi. Why should it? Beaten up, unconscious within minutes of running from that bar, Sasumi'd come to in a St Petersburg convent, only to find the city still in riot – and her lover still dead. Right from the start, from that night in the Ginza Plaza, he'd refused to tell Sasumi what he'd be in Russia to do. But killing himself didn't seem a likely reason. She still didn't know why Kwai had done what he did, the way he did. And Passion wasn't about to tell her.

'Hello, Passion,' Sasumi said.

'Ready to roll?'

The Japanese woman looked startled.

'Not literally,' Passion said hastily. 'I mean, is everything up there ready to go?'

'Of course,' said Sasumi. 'We're ready when you are.'

'Okay,' Passion flicked over to her spySat link, clicked in tight on the location of her lead ships, judged their distances from the rigs and decided everyone was far enough back.

'Do it,' Declan said.

Passion nodded, passing him the keyboard. 'Put Sasumi up on the big screen,' she suggested. The bridge was getting packed. Even the crew had stopped to watch, gathering in a silent little crowd at the bow.

'Do it now,' she told Sasumi, and held her breath. For a second nothing happened. And then the sea beneath one rig began to boil as ballast tanks in its six huge 109-metre legs blew their valves.

'Slowly,' Passion demanded.

On the screen Sasumi nodded, and said something over her shoulder. The sea beneath the rigs slowed to a slow roil. Very, very slowly, legs thicker than the vastest sequoia shortened, the huge overhanging platform getting closer to the water.

'High point of the ridge,' Passion told Declan, but he already knew. He'd worked the positioning out with Sasumi over a secure vidlink.

'Water here's only 115 metres, the legs are 118 metres.'

He knew that, too. If everything happened as it should, both rigs would ground safely on the bottom, their main platforms almost level with the sea.

Of course, if it didn't work . . .

'Then I've wasted a hundred and fifty million dollars on useless rigs,' Passion said shortly, 'not to mention the billions spent on derelict ships.' She pushed a sun-bleached strand out of her eyes and wiped her hand on her black T-shirt. If the US didn't extradite her, the Thais probably would. And the banks might not be able to prove anything, but they'd sure as fuck try . . .

'This will work,' Passion told Declan, then grinned. '*I have a dream* . . .' She gestured wryly at the catamarans, fishing boats and yachts crowded alongside. Her flotilla had been attracting hopefuls the way sharks attract remora. Not that Passion minded. The hired crews might be returning home, but there was no point having a city without inhabitants.

And an immigration policy was the one thing new Venice wasn't going to operate. If you'd been prepared to work passage or attach your own vessel to the flotilla, that was fine: you qualified. Even though none of them yet knew what they'd qualified for . . .

Declan didn't like that bit, but then, Declan wasn't running the show.

It was like watching an iceberg break off a glacier and sink into the sea, never knowing if the huge mass was going to tip over on top of you. Except the sun was too hot and the sea too blinding to think seriously about icebergs.

'They're shifting,' Declan said in alarm. And so they were. Even as the vast platforms sank evenly into the waves, the distance between them began to narrow.

'Attraction of ships at anchor,' Passion said smugly. 'Shock waves between floating bodies cancel out, the calm area draws objects towards each other. Old naval rule . . .' Passion shrugged nonchalantly. 'Apparently it works on a subatomic level too.'

Declan just smiled.

'Okay,' Passion said crossly, 'so I read it somewhere.'

The two rigs came down slowly. Like watching the descent of a giant lift, or seeing New York's World Trade Center collapse through a sidewalk on the downstroke of an invisible piston. It was . . .

Hell, it was what it was. Two rust-bucket, derelict rigs being sunk below the waves. She just knew she sure as fuck hadn't seen anything like it before. And it was an odds-on bet, too, that no one in all those Press copters buzzing them, on one at Langley, GCHQ or the Pool in Paris . . . in fact, on one at any of the spySat bases, monitoring the earth's surface for governments or profit, had seen anything like it either.

'Metal ballet in motion,' Declan said, and it was Passion's turn to grin.

Both rigs hit the sea bottom within ten seconds of each other, the sound reverberating like a double bell through the struts, tubes and decks of the vast steel platforms. All around, crew and passengers covered their ears in shock before they even knew they'd done it. Hell, let the UN make of that what it could.

'All legs down,' said Sasumi. Her face on the screen was pale with strain, her lips tight with worry. And despite the rig's air-conditioning, her wide forehead was beaded with sweat. Behind her stood a silent crowd of technicians, their eyes either glued to the camera above Sasumi's computer or to Passion's face on their screen.

Passion smiled. 'Excellent,' she said. 'I'll be aboard in a minute.' Turning to a dreadlocked refugee from Bayer Rochelle, Passion gestured at a hatch on the *Karensky*'s main deck. 'This is where we stop. If you seed bioBoryl now, how long . . .'

'Two weeks at least, maybe three,' the man said, staring around him in disbelief. 'You want to put a reef right round the rigs?'

'The rigs and the ships,' Passion said. 'Round them, under them, through them. Tie everything up solid, use all the coral you've got.'

'I'll need help,' the man said at last. He couldn't think of anything else to say.

'You got it. You . . .' Passion turned to a nearby man in khaki uniform. 'Get your men to help set up the hoists.' Large, bearded and bear-like, the man nodded, his face impassive, brown eyes direct and unflinching. The Major didn't like taking orders from a woman. It didn't take a psychic to know that. But Passion had never yet met a man who did. And anyway, he was getting paid enough to live with it.

The Major wasn't going to be part of newVenice either. Nor were his Comoro mercenaries. They were muscle for the voyage, bouncers to keep the uninvited out of her party. She had them scheduled to go home, get fat on her money, just as soon as her own defences were in place.

'Some of you could set up anti-aircraft guns,' Passion suggested. 'Mount surface-to-air missiles around the rigs.' Holding measures, the lot of them, third-world armaments. As primitive as a flick knife against a mugger with an Uzi; not great and not sensible, but marginally better than nothing.

Declan was erecting the real weapons system, up on the rig. Pulse weapons, laser radar, the lot. As well as that year in Tokyo, he'd done three months at Beirut's Hezbollah University in the practicals of electro/optical warfare. And he'd learnt fast; how fast she'd discovered back in Bangkok, flicking through an MoD database of suspected terrorists, a database stored at Victory House in London.

How else did Declan think she'd found him?

Passion went down the rope ladder without hesitation, without once faltering. Of course, with the rigs now resting squarely on the Meldarin Ridge, it was the *Karensky* that towered over the rigs' largest, lowest decks.

'Come on,' she said to Declan, and was over the side and halfway down before he'd made a move. Casting his eyes to heaven, Declan followed.

Passion was aware of other eyes, of cameras watching her as she stepped onto the rig and strode across the vast steel platform, its surface clanking beneath her shoes. She could hear Declan behind her.

'This way . . .' A young Japanese technician materialized at her side.

'I know,' said Passion, punching the button on a lift. But she smiled quickly, to take the sting out of her words. She did know, too, probably better than he did. Nights sitting up in her suite at the Bangkok Imperium learning the floor plan meant she could find her way round this rig blindfold. She'd even run up a five-storey, 3-D walk-through of the living pods and storage areas, navigating through the sim, level by level, corridor by corridor, until understanding its maze of ladders and lifts was second nature.

What hadn't been coded into her program, though, was the static: the sheer stink of warm oil, the thud of winches – that, and the dirt.

Sasumi was waiting in the Ops room. At least, that was its name these days. Originally it had been reserved for the rig's Captain and was on the fifth and highest level of the living pods, with its own copter circle on the roof. Up there where Declan planned to put his weapons system.

'This is it,' said Passion. She was grinning.

'Upload?' Samumi asked.

'Yeah, do the website,' Passion announced, tossing Sasumi a DVD that flicked across the ops room like a silver frisbee. It went straight into the slot of a small Packard Bell stuffed under an aluminium table in the corner. Glued to the wall above the table was a custom-made flat screen, its non-reflective black surface as large and as epic as any late Rothko.

'And take a look at the UN,' Passion told Declan. Reaching into a nearby coolbox, Passion tossed the Irishman a Pepsi Max without asking and offered one to Sasumi, who refused with a polite smile.

In New York the summit had gone into evening session, trying to cope with the sudden news of the rigs' sinking. Sky News had a camera cut in tight on the US representative who was on her feet, a sheet of fax in one hand, papers stacked on the table in front of her. She was reading some kind of prepared statement.

'In the opinion of our government, based on information supplied by our own intelligence services and those of our allies . . .' She broke off to nod to both the French and the UK representatives, 'the so-called Rainbow flotilla constitutes an act of aggression towards the legitimate states represented by this organization. These ships are operating under no national flag, not even a flag of convenience . . .'

Behind her delegates were nodding, even the Russian delegate. Agreement between Moscow and Washington was still new enough for the on-site editors to feel it worth emphasizing with a replay.

'The flotilla has been clogging the shipping lanes, unflagged and uninsured. And now we have word the leading ship has stopped and lashed itself to a sunken oil rig, confirming what our intelligence services already knew. As the civilized world acts to bring the Internet under control, an outlaw flotilla plans to establish not just an offshore virtualBank but also secure data-havens for those who can afford their services.'

She glanced darkly towards the delegates from Syria, Iran and Iraq who stared impassively back. 'We have to ask ourselves how has this operation been financed, which governments will benefit from the inevitable destabilization of the free-world economy?

'We cannot be expected to sit by, while a pack of pirates endanger the seaways. If the UN cannot muster a deterrent force, then responsible nations must.' She paused, and glanced slowly round at the assembly, trying to gauge their mood. 'Under a UN mandate, obviously . . .'

'Shitheads, the lot of them,' Declan announced, crushing his Pepsi can and tossing it towards a trash bin. It landed with a bang.

Sasumi shook her head. 'There has to be a vote first.'

'Vote!' Declan's scowl was sardonic. 'Sweet Jesus, the bastard plans are already made. All that . . .' he gestured dismissively towards the screen, 'is so much window dressing, always has been.'

'There'll be a vote, all right,' Passion said. 'But it won't make a blind fuck of difference. We all know the result . . .' She reached for an infrared keyboard, fingers flicking effortlessly across the keys. 'The site goes up now.'

'Too early,' Declan was on his feet, moving towards the stack.

'Leave it,' Passion snarled. Her green eyes locked with his, meeting his glare without flinching. 'You do the weapons,' she said, 'I do the planning, okay?'

The Irishman said nothing, and he didn't drop his gaze either. But it was obvious from the scowl on his lips that he'd have walked out on her – had there been anywhere to walk to.

Sasumi watched with outright interest, but Passion was too busy outstaring Declan to notice. The Japanese girl nodded to herself: so that was the way it went. Well, it was bound to happen sometime. She coughed, and when that didn't work, she coughed again, louder. Only Declan had the grace to blush.

'It has to go up now,' Passion said, as if she'd never been interrupted. 'We were safe while they thought we were a bunch of ecoWarriors. A bit of force, a few casualties, we'd soon be back in our box. But now they know we're putting down roots . . .'

Passion walked over to the window, looked at the black specks on the horizon, her flotilla struggling in, hours, maybe even days away. 'They'll be planning the attack. Dotting the *Is*, crossing the *Ts*. We need the NV site up and we need it up now. It's not just the best bluff we've got, it's the only bluff.'

Declan nodded.

'And we need those weapons operational as well,' Passion said. 'Okay?' She was looking at Declan, who smiled sheepishly, flicking dark hair back out of his eyes.

'I'm on it,' he said, and slid out of the door, blowing Passion a kiss on his way. Seconds later they both heard his boots clanging on the copter pad overhead.

Sasumi sighed, heavily. 'I just hope he's good in bed.'

Passion shrugged, 'I wouldn't know.' And then she too was gone, leaving Sasumi looking after her.

[Santa Passionata/Code Warriors]

nVTv, newVenice's streamed web TV, made pick of the day on US, UK, Japanese and French *Yahoo*. In fact, by the time Sasumi picked up long-distance radar warning that ships were gathering over the far horizon, nVTv's hit-counter had blurred to a whir.

Since the Rainbow flotilla still streamed up from the south-west, if that raggle-taggle collection of boats could be called a stream, and the dots gathering on radar were to the east, Passion immediately announced over the tannoy that a US/UN battle fleet had been detected.

'We don't know that,' said Sasumi as Declan came storming into the room, an inch-thick Lockheed manual clutched in one hand.

'Check it, then,' Passion suggested and Declan spliced into their satellite link to make sure, burning up bandwidth and Passion's dollars as he demanded finer and finer resolution.

Three carriers, a handful of destroyers, two frigates and a mine layer. Passion keyed something in on her own keyboard and seconds later Declan's satellite grabs had been uploaded to the NV website.

'Set up a permanent link,' Declan suggested, indicating the satellite pix. Then turned to go back to assembling his weapons system. Passion did.

To see what she was getting, Passion pulled up the newVenice site and flicked through its frames, until she hit one showing a high *pov* satellite shot. The two rigs looked like tiny architect's models. Streaming in towards them from one direction, hundreds of small ships were strung out across the sea like beads. Hanging back to the other side were the carriers. Miniature aircraft were being lined up on miniature decks.

'How soon?' Passion asked Sasumi.

'Counting down, I think.' Sasumi stood in front of the flat-screen, still neat in her dark clothes, her straight dark hair held back with an Alice band. 'The Press planes have gone . . .'

They had too, Passion suddenly realized. So had the Press launches, falling back from the rigs. That alone told her what she needed to know.

'Five-mile exclusion zone,' Passion announced. There was a fax waiting to go out, on newVenice paper, claiming the sea around the rigs as territorial waters. It banned all other shipping from the area and prohibited use of newVenice airspace. Now was the right time to send it.

'The UN have passed a vote,' said Sasumi. 'We're outlaws. They say we don't just have computers and weapons, we hold enough drugs equipment to flood the world with cheap amphetamines ten times over . . .'

Passion looked embarrassed. 'They're jealous,' she said hastily. 'Anyway it doesn't have to be speed, we can synthesize dhea, dmae, choline, ginko, you name it.'

'If we don't get these defences up soon,' Declan said, ducking under the low doorway, 'we won't be producing anything.' Through the glass of the Ops room, Passion could see the Portuguese Major far down on the main platform, getting his men to position sandbags. 'That lot couldn't fix a piss-up in a brewery,' Declan said, nodding at them. 'I'd better boot up the JCIT, you keep spinning that web and Sasumi . . .'

'I'll get everyone under cover,' Sasumi announced firmly.

'Then get the Major in, too,' said Declan, 'I don't want him messing things up. It's going to be sweet murder as it is.'

'Tell him we're keeping him in reserve,' said Passion quickly. Seconds later they could hear Sasumi's voice over the sound system calling everyone except Declan's combat team off the decks.

'So,' Passion said slowly. 'A third of the ships are in. What do you reckon for the others?'

'Evens,' said Declan, 'better than that if we tie up those carriers.' He checked the radar, the spySat and read-outs from his Dell all at one go and frowned, checking it all again. 'Oh, fuck it . . . I'm reading surface-to-surface, laser lock-on for the two largest oil tankers.'

'Women, kids, refugees,' Passion's voice was bitter.

'Terrorists, drug dealers, hackers,' replied Declan darkly. He put up a hand to stop her protest. 'Maybe we should concentrate their minds,' Declan said, his voice as soft as it was deadly. Green eyes met hers and then he smiled, reaching for his Sony fly mike.

'Do this,' he said, 'and there's no turning back.'

'I know.'

For a second, Declan thought she'd say some more. But when Passion didn't, Declan flipped his fly mike into place, ducked his long body under the door's steel lintel and stamped up the ladder out onto the copter pad, like a rock star walking on stage.

Pausing a fraction, as if for applause, Declan reached for his sunglasses, made a brief bow to the rig's security cameras and stalked centre stage, to stand in front of a thin black desk that perched on metal legs. Thick wires from the desk ran across the deck, then vanished down an air duct.

Fingers hit its obsidian-smooth surface as if playing an invisible keyboard and thrashing chords echoed through the rig's tannoy. 'Christ,' Passion muttered, 'he's wired the fucking thing for sound.'

Behind him stood a metal spider built of ceramic, glass, crystal and five different alloys. It came shielded, to protect its wiring, but had been stripped back to bare metal bones. Where the spider's body should have been was a heavy five-foot black tube and inside that other tubes. Declan knew exactly how it worked, he just didn't know why. But it did, it worked perfectly. He'd read the test reports.

Operating Declan's spider and three others was Declan's table. It might look like a Roland, but it was really a third-generation Joint Combat Information Terminal, semi-AI. And though it had emergency override and took direct human interface via a simple inset touchpad, the 928-page instruction manual stressed that if override was needed the battle was probably already lost.

Declan had spent three days training the JCIT's speech module to his voice. If necessary it would take orders from Passion or Sasumi, but he was logged in as the primary user. It was Declan's accent, Declan's tone that the machine recognized.

'Well?' Declan said into his fly mike.

'Do it.' Passion's voice shook and her face was hollow, at least that was how it looked to Declan in the viewscreen of his deck. The Irishman knew exactly how she felt. Spending money was easy, and enough of it had come his way from Passion to make him rich for life, if he still had a life when this was over. But killing people was something else again. He knew that, too. That was why she'd selected him for this job. Hands-on killing and computing skills made for a rare cv.

'I'll take out the sat and the UAVs. We don't hit soft targets unless they do. Okay?'

She could pretend the decision was Declan's, but it wasn't. This battle might be his show, but she was the producer, sponsor and artistic director. She nodded slightly, watching as his elegant fingers passed swiftly over touch-sensitive diodes.

'Subspace grid,' said Declan, his soft voice oh-so-Irish. Passion smiled. His shades were black-lens Armani, polarized against the glare, and Declan had the geek phone bent in close to his mouth so he looked like an angler fish.

His head was bent over the deck as line after line scrolled up the glass, the weapons system scanning the upper sky with laser-Radar, waiting as the deck made primary and secondary passes across objects found in low orbit.

Search over, the black glass erupted into miniature pictograms. Not what Declan wanted. 'Use words, you fucker,' he ordered the deck. God knew, he might only be in his twenties but he was still too old to have learned to read fluently in icon.

It was more or less what he expected. Three military satellites, a spySat tentatively matched to a US model and two low-orbit UAVs. There was also the French commercial spySat Passion was spliced into. Declan left that out of his calculations.

'Take them when you're ready,' said Passion, 'I'll start running the NV-Sim.' Her fingers hit key combinations as she loaded, then executed a new DVD.

'Running,' Passion announced.

In the viewscreen on Declan's desk, the two rigs, the *Karensky* and the scattering of surrounding tankers, whalers and tugs began to morph into a city that looked like Manhattan with canals. The spaces between the ships filled with plazas, green parks unfolded where in reality waves lapped over the first seedings of coral. Gun turrets and anti-aircraft missile pods suddenly assembled themselves on the rooftops. Small *vaporetti* could be seen ploughing between bus stops on the main canals.

If nanotechnology had already existed, this was what it would have looked like. Self-constructing buildings, organic matings of steel and concrete. It took Declan a moment to realize Passion's sim was being loaded to the NV website, seamlessly replacing the video stream from the French spySat. What's more, the sim was being boosted back to the now-jammed satellite to replace the original feed.

Looking down on the rigs, real time, Declan saw a marine metropolis expand and bloom like an opening poppy. In place of the rusting hulks stood a city for the next century. Rich, prosperous, protected. Gone was the rig on which he stood, gone was the ancient Soviet whaler that had carried them out to this site.

In its place was a capital city.

'Seeing's believing' said Passion and Declan snorted, then turned back to running his fingers across the deck, pulling out complex chords, arming weapons. He'd split the deck's functions. Its main task was as a weapons system, its secondary function to act as his synth, but not play music at the cost of lowering combat efficiency. He'd made sure the system understood that. At least, he hoped he had.

'CPB lock-on,' Declan ordered and waited as a metal spider behind him swung in its computer-generated arc until it was pointing to the heavens.

'Arm and fire, all targets.' Inside the spider an accelerator whipped up an electron beam, the beam director focused it to its target and then the CPB let loose three pulses, almost at light-speed. The first ignited the air it cut through, creating a reduced-density, heated-air channel through which the second pulse passed, extending the channel even further. Its hole-boring process complete, the CPB's final pulse deposited its lethal energy squarely into the centre of a spySat, which exploded to dust, littering the lower orbits with shrapnel.

The deck played itself a long and baroque drum roll.

'One down,' said Declan and waited as the low-level tracking laser on the CPB shifted its aim. The second charged-particle-beam sequence came a few seconds later, and the third sequence a few seconds after that. One by one, six satellites blinked out of existence.

On the deck's side screen, newVenice had grown to the size and complexity of Manhattan and, boxed out in a web frame, Declan was shocked to see himself, a miniature figure in front of what looked like a large keyboard standing as if in the centre of Battery Park.

'Might as well give them a target,' Passion said with a grin. The nV sites were taking hits so fast, global bandwidth was locking solid.

'If they can, they'll take out the newsfeed,' said Declan into his fly mike. At least, that's what he'd do in their position: hit the propaganda first, then deal with the facts. If Mao didn't say it, then it had to be Goebbels.

'Not possible.' Passion's reply was firm. 'We're shielded and mirrored. Even if they hit newVenice and take us out, this is still what people will think we looked like . . .'

'Incoming aircraft.' The JCIT deck's interruption was flat, unemotional.

'Direction?'

'Due east.'

'Type?'

Lockmart fighter, thirteen items, third generation, fly by light. Laser/G air-to-surface missiles. Combat-hardened electro/optics, on-board computer.'

'Small arms?'

'M9 Volcano, rotary doubled-ended feed, hydraulic drive, linkless ammo, 7,500 shots per minute . . . Hostile weapons systems in readiness.'

'Shit,' said Passion, and she meant it.

'They're not going to get close enough,' said Declan, already hunched over his deck, checking readbacks from the rig's laser-Rader. He nodded once, dark brown hair spilling over his satisfied face, and turned to a screen insert of Passion pulling up close-focus grabs of incoming combat planes, V-tailed and black-skinned, skimming low over the water. With a shock, Declan realized she was busy loading images to the NV website.

'Do we kill?' His soft voice was almost as flat as that of the JCIT deck.

'No.' She shook her head, not taking her eyes from her own screen. 'Not first, not unless we have to. Can you take them out without killing the pilots?'

'I can try.'

'Then try,' Passion said.

'Field of fire?' Declan asked the machine. He'd read the answer ten times in the manual, he just wanted to hear it anyway.

'Safe elevation plus ninety and minus five: azimuth plus or minus eighty without tracking change.' It was way more than enough, a wider horizon than he needed.

'Hostile missiles launched,' announced the JCIT. 'Missiles jammed, missiles destroyed. Basic-level DEW.'

Both Passion and Declan drew breath at the same time. From inside the pods they could hear muted cheering as the deck gave itself another roll of the drums. The battle had drawn its own local audience. The planes that had been coming in low and hard, skimming the waves, banked sharply and flipped into evasion mode, thirteen shock waves shaking the rigs as each plane emerged from, then went back through the sound barrier

'Praise God and keep your powder dry,' said Passion happily. 'Oliver Cromwell.'

'If there's a hell, may that man rot in it,' Declan snapped. Quoting Cromwell to a Catholic was Declan's idea of bad taste. Especially when that Catholic was busy protecting you.

Passion grinned.

The two oil rigs were stacked with high-level armaments, most of them not yet assembled. HF/DF and COIL lasers that operated in optical, infrared and UV/X-ray bands, tuneable high-power mWave and bBand 'directed energy' weapons.

But the Lockmart lightning throwers, the electron-beam guns that Declan was using, were the most deadly. Add a JCIT deck which could operate its own smart jammer, identify hardware/software components of incoming missiles and use tailored in-band jamming to break the missiles' own lock-on, and you had as good a defence system as money could buy, anywhere. There was even a JCIT-controlled DEW solid-state laser to take out the missile itself.

It was hard to see how Passion could have bought much more. As it was, there'd be half a dozen Balkan self-styled warlords going green with envy.

'Are you going to fire that fucking thing or not?' Passion asked suddenly.

Declan checked his screen. The planes had circled round to the west and were approaching the rig from the direction of the convoy, screaming over the heads of the small ships as they roared in for the kill.

'Fry the electronics, not the pilots,' he told the JCIT hastily. 'Fire at will.' Servos whirred as the four CPBs sighted rapidly. Accelerators powered and the CPBs unleashed thirteen lightning bolts, each one tied to the fast thrash of a guitar chord. Declan was grinning fit to split his face.

At that distance, hole-boring was irrelevant: a single pulse was all that was necessary. As the machine would have explained, had Declan been bothered to ask, the CPB bolts passed close by each nose cone, generating ionizing radiation that caused transient upset to essential electronic components.

What actually happened was that memory chips fried, CPUs developed new and unhelpful circuits and the precious, essential packets of data passing both ways through the optic veins buried in each fighter's single skin turned to gibberish. Thirteen pilots ejected simultaneously, as each on-board computer admitted defeat before that possibility even occurred to the pilots.

'Get them out of the water, and get them up here,' Passion ordered into her geek phone, shouting over Declan's crashing chords. 'No one's to get hurt . . .'

Neophrene-skinned boats immediately zipped away from the edge of the other rig. Sasumi had her end of the operation firmly under control.

'What do you think they'll do now?' Passion asked Declan. She'd come up the ladder, too impatient to wait for the lift. From the look on her face, she didn't know whether to grin or cry.

'Take a break, I imagine.' Declan said. 'Maybe get new orders . . .' He shrugged, looking down to where black dots skimmed out over the water, going to fetch the pilots. 'Okay,' he said to the deck, 'watch those carriers.' And then turned his attention back to the American woman. She was standing close, at least close enough for Declan to smell her CK, and under that a faint scent of fear. 'It's going to be all right,' Declan promised, one hand reaching out to brush hers, not taking it, just touching it quickly.

Passion jumped.

'Hey,' Declan said, 'it's okay. We're winning.' He smiled, took her hand properly. Passion looked surprised, but she didn't protest. 'Let's finish this off. Can you get a flat screen up here?'

'Sasumi,' Passion began . . .

'Heard him. We're already on it.' The Japanese woman's voice cut Passion short and less than a minute later, Karla and BillE staggered out of the lift, carrying a huge ToshibaFlat that they lent against a railing.

'Right,' said Passion, 'Let's see what they're saying about us . . .'

It went without saying, the first place they found themselves was on CNN, where a serious-looking woman was standing outside MIT, talking to the camera. In the corner of the screen was a box-out, of Manhattan-with-canals, spliced direct from the spySat feeding the nV website. The city looked bigger than ever. The woman was talking about sudden, shocking advances in nanotechnology.

'Shit, Passion,' Declan said.

Passion smiled. 'Beautiful,' she agreed. 'The French spySat records us, we capture the recording, run it through the sim, then upload for the satellite to broadcast to everyone else. Total penalty, a three-second time loop. Neat, huh?'

'It's better than neat, it's brilliant,' said Sasumi, stepping out of the lift with a wet, bedraggled Air Force Major in tow. Sasumi had the pilot's flight helmet in her hand. The pilot scowled around at them all. 'Meet,' Sasumi glanced at the woman's name tag sewn onto her flightsuit over her heart, 'Major Gore. She's not very happy.'

An understatement if ever there was one, thought Declan, eyes flicking between the pilot and BillE who'd thrust a 3VJ-Cam camcorder close to the pilot's face. Sasumi, Passion or Declan would drop in an appropriate background later. The crewcut Canadian looked as if she'd quite happily kill the lot of them, except that her hands were locked behind her back with a pair of black plastic cuffs, the self-tightening kind.

At the sight of the four Lockmart lightning throwers, the woman's eyes widened.

'Yeah,' said Declan. 'Computer-sighted, reactive CPB, with laserRadar, run through a JCIT deck. You never stood a chance. Didn't they tell you?'

The pilot shook her head, unable to keep her eyes off the deck Declan stood next to. 'They said you were a bunch of hippies.'

Her voice teetered somewhere between bitterness and disbelief.

'They lied,' Passion said firmly. 'They knew exactly what you were up against.' Which was rubbish, of course: she'd spent months making damn sure they *didn't* know, but Passion wasn't going to tell the pilot that.

Passion walked over to stand in front of the woman. 'We can keep you locked away or we can leave you free to wander, it's your choice . . .' Passion looked impossibly relaxed in her black T-shirt and silk wrapround, more like someone on holiday than a rebel leader.

'We're not going to hurt you,' she said. 'We're certainly not going to kill you. We're not even going to question you.' She looked the pilot direct in the eyes. 'We don't need to. There's nothing you can tell us that we don't already know.'

'You're American,' the pilot protested. It was a straight accusation, said like she couldn't believe it.

'I was,' Passion corrected her. 'Now I'm neoVenetian, like everybody else on this rig except for you and those people down there.' She nodded down to the main platform, where grinning Comoros mercenaries sat against a sandbagged gun emplacement, a stack of battered *Hustlers* scattered at their feet, a pile of empty Bud cans testifying to just how heavily they'd been drinking.

'And between you and me,' said Passion, 'both lots of you will be going home, just as soon as we can arrange it.'

Other pilots were appearing now, to be paraded before BillE's camera. Passion watched, a sardonic smile on her face, feet apart and arms folded while other UN pilots stepped out of the lift onto the copter pad. She looked, Declan decided, hollow-eyed and hawk-nosed, a bit like the emperor Napoleon in the days when he was still a general. Impressive, though.

Suddenly uncertain, aware of a prickling feeling at the back of his neck, he glanced to one side to find Sasumi watching him watching Passion. Sasumi smiled wryly.

In her hand, Sasumi held a Panasonic 3VJ-Cam identical to BillE's. Passion had picked both up second-hand in New York.

They looked like short fat pieces of grey tube, bent in the middle. Each time a bedraggled pilot clambered up the steel steps, trying hard to look steely-eyed and confident, Sasumi or BillE would grab footage, to capture the exact moment when the pilots first stared around in puzzlement.

Part of it was the contrast between the weapons and the people.

The leaders of the flotilla didn't look like dangerous terrorists. But then, it was hard for the sunken rig to look like an international crime base when the first thing the pilots saw, after Declan stripped to the waist in black Levis and Armani glasses and Sasumi behaving like a Japanese tourist with a camera, was a bare-breasted Australian woman trying to launch a Batman stunt kite, while her three-year-old kid tore round the deck on a yellow tricycle, wearing a pink Osh Kosh dress and red knickers.

At Passion's nod, the cuffs were removed from the flyers and Karla tied her kite to a rail, then stepped alongside a young, mustachioed Argentinian pilot to lead him below. But the Argentinian didn't move, he just stood there swaying in the afternoon heat.

'You okay?' Karla sounded suddenly worried.

Instead of answering, the pilot crumpled sideways and fell in a heap, cracking his head on the metal deck.

'Medic.' About ten people shouted it at once, but it was Declan who bent his geek phone back into place and sent an emergency call echoing through the rig's sound system. Two paramedics and a lightweight stretcher materialized on the copter deck and the airman was bundled, swiftly but carefully, onto the stretcher and down to the hospital bay.

'Fucking brilliant,' Passion hissed to Declan, nodding towards Sasumi who was busy catching the last of the shot. 'Put in a background, get it out to all the networks . . . Fucking brilliant.'

An Outsource of Options

[If It Bleeds, It Leads . . .]

Violence sells. An adage as old as advertising. But so too does sentiment – and so does compassion, if only for its rarity value . . .

newVenice set an instant record in the history of media studies. That snatch of the pilot hitting the ground took the biggest cut of the world's audience ever. Ninety-three per cent of those on the planet with access to TV watched it, seeing the city around him rise from the waves like that naked girl in the Italian painting, the one standing on a shell.

And in the century that followed, no one came even close to taking that share of the audience. Maybe it was proof television had finally gone global. Or maybe it was just that, even in those early days, nV had a bloody hot syndication department. Whatever.

For one time only, every major channel on the planet led its evening bulletin with the same story. The destruction, without loss of life, of every single UN plane sent against newVenice.

Time and again, the handsome young Argentinian twisted sideways, his dark fringe flopping over his huge brown eyes, his childish lips twisted into a puzzled *moue* as he fell towards the ground. Time and again, concerned news readers and anchorwomen assured viewers the pilot was just suffering from heatstroke, that he was being carefully looked after at Mount Olive hospital in newVenice . . .

Lieutenant Angeli Rispoli smiled, in spite of himself, as he examined a still of the hospital ward downloading itself onto his smartbook. Smiling didn't come naturally to Angeli, but this time he couldn't help it. The ward was huge, impossibly hi-tek, in that retro way people always assumed the future would be.

This city had never been even close to the Manhattan-with-canals of Passion's original sim. Passion's intention was always to have a perfect reproduction of the real Northern Italian city of Venice where her paternal grandfather had been born. And it had taken fifty years to complete her dream, not the minutes and hours which nano could now do.

Angeli knew that, he'd checked. There wasn't much the Lieutenant didn't know about the city he wasn't considered important enough to enter. He might be no closer to solving the murder, but he hadn't forgotten.

Angeli was naked, except for his NVPD helmet. But then, the air-system was erratic, increasingly so. Though not as erratic as the weather. Even in late April it was too warm for uniform inside the Precinct House.

Walking the station naked didn't matter, there was no one there to see him. No one but NVPD got inside a Precinct House, anyway, unless they were under arrest. And if they were under arrest, then they didn't matter. Besides, Angeli didn't even let people he'd arrested into his precinct.

Criminals he put straight in a holding pen, which could be reached from the alley *via* a separate metal door. And there was a meshed-off alcove at the front where Angeli could deal with the public, if any of them were stupid enough to come bothering him. Here, inside the Precinct, he could do what the fuck he liked, wander naked, crap with the door open, access stroke-site holo-porn, whatever . . .

Suction-pegged to the wall behind Angeli, hanging loose, was his standard-issue anti-riot baton and 50,000-volt electric taser. Tossed beneath them was Angeli's blue uniform. Standard anti-ballistic, helical-chain cloth, keratin heartpad to fix across the chest, kevlar reinforcements at the elbows, knees and turned-up collar, the usual.

His neophrene boots had been flung in a corner. They stank. A century of smart clothing, endless tests with purified carbon and sweat-eating nanites and the NVPD still couldn't provide boot linings that didn't rot . . .

With a sigh, Angeli turned back to his history of newVenice and Santa Passionata. God, she'd been good. Obsessive, neurotic, totally insane by the end, but good. And anyway, it was a given that insanity and genius were flipsides of the same chip. And it definitely took genius to put together a scam as huge, as flawless as newVenice.

To ream out the banks like that, but leave no proof: to bluff the UN as successfully as she did. And God knew how many generations later, half CySat's global audience still believed the island looked like Manhattan-on-the-Pacific.

Everybody knew Santa Passionata, half the levels carried her amulet. But there were . . . Angeli thought about it, maybe five people who could actually tell you who *Passion* was. Who she'd really been, how she fitted into history.

Up on the original rigs, which Passion had flattened, paved over and done out in mock Byzantine Gothic as the Doge's Palace, there might be fifty people who still knew the truth behind the shrines and the tri-D posters. There could be none. Angeli couldn't say.

Mind you, if anyone knew, it would be the DiOrchis. Angeli scowled, stamping his way round the empty precinct, butt-naked, book in hand, and thought about Count Ryuchi. These were dangerous waters.

The NVPD answered to the Council, just as the levels answered to the Suites, but in practice the levels were self-governing, cut off from newVenice proper by a sonic fence that ringed-in the city. CySat might govern in theory, but the NVPD did the real governing for them, if banging heads together could be classed as such. But then, the levels weren't really part of newVenice, at least not according to the NVPD rule book, which NVPD regulations demanded be carried on duty at all times, uploaded to his helmet.

Angeli tapped the bottom left corner of his page, and his Sanyo

Librox smartbook flicked back a couple of screens, until it reached the part Angeli was after. He'd already read the section three times, but wasn't sure he'd taken in all the information.

There'd been a second attack on the city. Only this one hadn't been televised. In all probability, it had been organized by the CIA, certainly not the UN, at least not officially. Enzymes had been released down-current to kill the new city's living foundations. But Passion's pet refugees from Bayer Rochelle had been ready for that, pumping tons of enzyme over the reef's disintegrating edges, stabilizing the bioCoryl to a land mass twice the size of Gibraltar.

(It seemed that what really upset the President was Passion buying a desalination plant from Iraq and installing it on one of the rigs.) As news of the second attack went out, a second flotilla of smaller boats set out from the Pacific Rim: reinforcements, volunteers, exiled militia. Pretty soon newVenice was overrun with would-be inhabitants, members from Cult Arum, Montana freemen, dispossessed Hong Kong Triads. And as the coral mass got ever more crowded, Passion issued an ordinance stating newcomers had to live in their boats until new land could be grown.

To make it stick, members of the Montana militia were recruited wholesale into a makeshift force, the NVPD. Both this, and living in the boats, were meant to be temporary measures. But it didn't work out that way. The boats were still there, strung together, boarded over, lower holds pumped full of expanded polystyrene to stop them sinking.

Miles of wire and optic cable now knit them into a complex spider's web. Alleys and walkways spinning round the city on five or six levels, joined by ladders, planks, spiral steps, whatever had been at hand. And running out from the edge of newVenice, cut through the decks, were alleys radiating like spokes from the city proper.

Not that these got used much. NVPD cameras watched them constantly, feeding back to a central control. No, the inhabitants had long since lanced doorways into the sides of their ancient vessels, just above water level, letting inhabitants step from ship to ship without ever needing to leave the shadows.

According to Angeli's uncle, apart from crossing the estuary that led into Sabine's *TripleHelix*, it was possible to walk right round the levels without once ever going up on deck to be fried by the solar panels. Angeli had never tried it, he didn't have the time to waste.

'Fuck it.'

The Casio inset in Angeli's wrist was peeping every thirty seconds. Time for his next shift – and he wasn't even in uniform. Angeli had no reluctance about going, he wasn't afraid of anyone, not even the Kats who'd taken to straying into his precinct. In fact, he hadn't been afraid at all since his uncle died – Angeli just wasn't ready.

'Plans,' Angeli said aloud, blanking the Casio. Instantly the smartbook changed frames, showing an aerial shot of newVenice, in which Angeli could trace the revered silver S of the Grand Canal as it twisted up from the original two rigs, round the edge of what had once been the SS *Karensky* – before it was set in coral, cut flat and replaced with the synthetic stone of the Palazzo Reale.

Five other mother ships and several ex-Soviet oil tankers formed the sides of the Grand Canal. Cut flat at deck level, they provided stable foundations for the rest of the Grand Canal's elegant palazzi, with entrances not just at water-level where waves lapped gently over steps cut from dark coral but up high, where an endless succession of little bridges arched over the water of the side canals. The *Pte dei Sospiri* might be the most famous, but truth to tell, the Bridge of Sighs was just one of hundreds.

It was easy, Angeli reminded himself, looking at the gentle lap of the water and the steady bounce of *vaporetti* over the waves, to get lulled by the beauty of it all. But Angeli was NVPD. Better than most, he knew what darkness and greed lurked in the steel circle set round the city's elegant confectionery centre. And if he couldn't prove it lurked too in the palazzo, that was because he wasn't allowed back into the city and never would be, if Count Ryuchi got his way.

Whatever Santa Passionata's Serene Republic now was, it wasn't serene and it certainly wasn't a republic. Just what it was, Angeli was going to take time to find out.

'Shit,' Angeli said abruptly as his Casio began to bleep again. His smartbook blinked. There was no relevant section for shit, so the book left its screen blank. Angeli sighed.

'Waste disposal,' he said, wondering despite himself. Fed into matter compilers, which shouldn't have been a surprise. The city's internal economy and ecosystem were tightly tied: limited-function Drexie boxes constructed and deconstructed, using the same atoms in different orders as circumstances required.

Maybe a neoVenetian bar somewhere off the Rialto actually sold fresh fish, instead of textured protein, grown as slabs in some ceramic vat and then flavoured, marinaded, basted and grilled until what was pulled off the cast-iron skillets might as well have swum in the sea for all anyone could say. Maybe, too, there was someone who could tell the difference: Angeli doubted if he could, doubted, too, that he'd ever get the opportunity to try.

'Water system,' he tried, but the book just pulled up plans of the old desalination plants and shots of sunken gathering tanks that collected rainwater runoff from the solar panels out on the neoVenetian levels. The city's water system was closed, like most of its systems. Which didn't stop chilled rainwater selling at a premium in some of the fancier bars lining Fondamente Nueve.

Whatever Angeli was after, it wasn't there, but then he shouldn't have been surprised. All books in the city fed off the central library, the Libreria Veccia up at the Suites. Maybe there really was a second, secret library as his uncle always used to insist. Or maybe it was just that access got restricted. Either way, Angeli wasn't going to get the information he wanted.

There had to be tunnels beneath the city itself. How else could that girl get out to the levels, through the sonic wall surrounding the city, without using a safe gate? And she hadn't . . .

Because, *one*, he'd checked the visuals on who got issued safecards on the nights she appeared at the *TripleHelix* and she wasn't in there. And, *two*, the little bitch was a palazzo kid, not a zaibatsu suit: she wouldn't have been given a pass anyway. Not even if she was fucking a gate guard. The guy wouldn't have dared go up against her family, whoever they were.

But still, she came, she went. Frequently now, sometimes out all night. Flashing her tits at punters in the *TripleHelix*, as she hammered the tri-Ds. Though with the dragon down, she still hadn't yet come close to making it double, beating the Archangel. Mind you, the whole game got more fucking erratic by the week. And not just the game, the whole city.

No matter how hard he tried to keep track, Angeli knew the little bitch was the one keeping track of *him*. She was playing games with the NVPD and Angeli didn't like that. He felt, strongly, that someone should teach her a lesson.

He rather hoped it might be him.

Angeli slid into his black combat trousers, feeling the cloth mould itself to his legs. Running a finger lightly up the fly of his trousers, Angeli fastened its velcro zip. Then twisted his lips into a wry smile as his body quivered. Now wasn't the time. Anyway, he had enough trouble keeping his mind *off* her breasts and *on* the threat she presented. And she did pose a threat. His NVPD file had been accessed three times in as many days, straight in through the firewalls.

He had his own primitive *bot* out there, watching NV Intranet traffic for items mentioning him by name, and the simple-minded avatar was near meltdown trying to keep track, because someone inside the Suites was pulling together a full profile.

And he was past news where the Count was concerned, so it had to be the girl.

'Bad move,' Angeli said aloud, and meant it too. If she was out to get him, then Angeli had no alternative but to get her first.

Pushing his arms deep into the sleeves of his flak jacket, Angeli felt the material tighten itself. The kevlar weave was force-sensitive, able to distinguish between the low-level threat of a batten blow and the incoming danger of a bullet, and react accordingly. Which meant stiffening into ridges like armour or loosening, layering, polarizing its fibres at ninety degrees to each other to muffle a shot.

A nice idea, but Angeli still never ventured out without first slapping his self-sealing heartpad into place. 'Heartpad' didn't really describe it. The thing was bigger than that, designed to seal off a sucking chest wound.

Thursday night, and here he came. Angeli slammed the keratin pad into place, picked up his baton and taser, and pushed his helmet down over his head. A map of the levels flicked into focus in front of his eyes: he was the orange dot at its edge.

The dot could have been an avatar, any avatar, his choice. His uncle had some toon called Bugs, but that wasn't Angeli's style. Might be the NVPD's, but it wasn't his. Angeli was happy enough being an orange dot, or as happy as he could be about anything, with some smug little shit from the Suites sitting on his tail.

Oh, come on, Angeli told himself. On one side you had Lieutenant Angeli Rispoli, aged thirty, fifth-generation NVPD. Briefly, very briefly Vice Questore for the city of new Venice. No girlfriend, no good memories but a small apartment overlooking the actual edge of the real city, sea-side from S. Francesco della Vigna. Thirteen years with the service, his record so clean he wondered anyone at the Council of Twelve had even heard of him. Three kills, all justified, no demerits.

Against what? Some tits-out kid of sixteen or so in expensive street leathers. He should just kick her ass. What the hell could she put up against him?

Angeli knew exactly what, that was his problem. You could start with birth and wealth. Access to archives, the ear of the powerful. Inbuilt arrogance . . . though maybe it was just guts. After all, she'd been alone, well off her own territory, when she first tried to face him down. And it still took something, to go up against a fully-armoured member of the NVPD, even if your father was more than just a CySat suit, and Angeli was willing to bet that hers was, way more . . .

The hacks to NVPD's database always came on the evenings he'd seen the little bitch, and she'd seen him. And they were high-level hacks, which meant she had access somehow to the NVPD passwords. And putting it all together, that meant . . . Angeli ticked his conclusions off on one gloved hand.

One, her father didn't know she visited the levels. (But he'd take the girl's part against Angeli, if that's what it came to.)

Two, she either had no mother, or her mother took too little notice of the girl to notice her evening absences.

Three, she either had high-level access to the Libreria Veccia or a staggering, make that unlikely, level of hacker skills . . .

Angeli was already late beginning his rounds, a fact NVPD Central would undoubtedly notice. But he needed to think this through, and there was a fourth blindingly-obvious conclusion outstanding, one he couldn't, shouldn't avoid.

It was personal. She could have withdrawn from the Third District, found another Simbar to infest, but she hadn't. Her visits were a taunt. If she didn't hate Angeli, then she feared him, and Angeli didn't think that likely. Not given the scar on his lip.

The big question was, would she come clean to her father about visiting the levels? Actually, there was another question. Did she come from a family powerful enough to do him serious damage, and could he take the risk she didn't?

The answer to the first was *maybe*. To the second it was *no*.

He was going to have to arrest her for something. Underage gambling, illegal drugs – there were drugs that were illegal, Angeli just couldn't remember which ones they were. And if that didn't work, he could always try for theft, provided that little sneak-thief Paco could be relied on to set a plant up properly.

Whatever, Angeli needed some leverage.

'Okay, fuck it,' Angeli said and swatted his Casio implant into silence. 'I'm out of here, all right?'

Stopping only to crunch a couple of NVPD blues and check his image in the video, Angeli squared his shoulders and stamped out of Precinct House3. Outside on the levels, he pushed through the early evening crowd, heading out towards *PolyRiptides* and the *TripleHelix*.

A grey-furred wolfBoy muttered when he thought Angeli wasn't looking, and some drunk little kinderwhore swatted a mosquito off her arm and spat at his feet. But every one of them moved out of Angeli's way.

[Hexed In The TripleHelix]

She was there all right, beating hell out of a Segasim booth, its cracked polycarbon sides almost too scratched to let others see in. Which didn't matter, because its frame was studded with cameras, feeding through to an editing deck. VJ SlyMix over in the corner was mixing the screens, and she featured heavily; dancing, whirling against her unseen enemy.

A battered black helmet obscured the girl's head, its opaque visor coming right down over her face, but Angeli knew her from the street-samurai stance she always adopted, and the casual way one hand dipped blindly for a bowl of vat-grown olives between bouts, sliding an olive under the visor into her mouth. The bowl was by her feet, and for all the girl's rapid twists and kicks, she never touched it. That took class, or arrogance or both . . .

A lot of punters were watching her, placing bets. She was up against the Archangel. Since taking down the Dragon, she'd been going for the double. This week should see it happen, if she got lucky.

'How long's she been here?' Angeli demanded, materializing at Paco's side and resting one heavy hand on the boy's shoulder. Immediately, the street kid seemed to wilt under its weight.

'Well?' Angeli could check it with the NVPD scans, pull her out of that night's *TripleHelix* upload in the time it took him to frame his question, but he'd rather ask Paco. The street kid and Angeli were coming to an arrangement. Angeli said jump, Paco asked how high.

He wasn't sure what Paco thought of the new arrangement: not much, judging from the pained expression on the kid's face, but that suited Angeli just fine.

'Hour,' Paco said reluctantly, 'maybe more . . .'

'You trailed her in?'

The kid nodded, hunched inside a quilted red jacket several sizes too big. He smelt of cheap cologne and had rinsed his head so his blond locks were no longer so matted. He'd recharged his spearhead Izanami talisman too, but Angeli knew he wasn't meant to notice that. Izanami and Cú Chulaind, Angeli believed in neither. Didn't believe in Santa Passionata, either come to that. But Paco did, following *the lady* as he called Izanami, and not just for the neural buzz her talisman offered.

'And you picked her up where?'

A worried look flicked across the boy's narrow face, though he did his best to block it. *Okay*, Angeli thought, *so I'm not going to like the next bit.*

'Tell me anyway,' Angeli demanded, his fingers tightening on the kid's shoulder until Paco went rigid under Angeli's grip. If anyone saw tears start suddenly into the child's blue eyes they sure as hell didn't let on. Wearing NVPD uniform had that effect.

'End of the Rio dei Mendicanti, just before the Fondamenta.' The boy twisted sideways out of Angeli's grip. It was neatly done. As Angeli made to grab the kid Paco shook his head. 'Please . . . don't.'

'Why not?'

'Why?' Paco leant his head sideways, blond curls touching the shoulder he still held hunched with pain. 'Where am I going to go?' Paco demanded flatly. 'What am I going to do? Hire a lawyer?' He sounded so wrung out for his age, Angeli wondered briefly just what he'd seen so far out on the levels. Rape, murder, theft . . . It couldn't have been much more than the usual.

'Where did she appear from?' Angeli demanded, but this time he kept his hands to himself.

'You know the Fondamenta?'

Of course he knew it; the Fondamenta Nuove was the northern edge of the coral mass, Rio dei Mendicanti a fat canal that ran out to meet it. Sixty yards in from the Fondamenta was the sonic wall, invisible but there, broken by stone gates that stood alone and ludicrous, the only safe crossing between the two cities.

Dead birds on the cobbles were the only sign the wall was there. And even the feathered corpses had become rare, as birds learnt to fly high over the area.

'Where on the Fondamenta?' Angeli demanded.

Paco named a narrow strip where canal and city's edge intersected. Once it had been the deck of an oil tanker, then it had been sunk into growing coral and coated with asphalt. Later still, someone had it cobbled with round grey nuggets of stabilized, sterilized compacted shit. It was a Japanese idea. Most of Shinjuku had been paved over in a similar fashion before Passion even thought of new Venice.

About fifty years after that, someone had slammed up a Greek Orthodox basilica during one of the religious revivals, but the God rule hadn't lasted. These days, the basilica's bronze doors were green with age, its domed roof glued into place with zytel scaffolding and half the mosaics of the sad-eyed Christ were gone, cut out for souvenirs by kids who used the abandoned church to drink and fornicate.

Angeli knew the place. At eleven he'd thrown up behind the old broken altar from one too many beers, at twelve he'd nearly burned out the back of his throat with three rough diamonds of wizz nicked from his uncle's NVPD coat and a year later he'd lost his virginity to a kinderwhore from this bar. True, she'd overcharged him outrageously, robbed him of his new jacket and threatened to go to his uncle if Angeli complained, but apart from that it had been great.

Angeli grinned at the memory. Good days. 'Yeah, I know it.' Only thing was, it was just outside Angeli's precinct, which could be a problem. 'You saw her cross the strip?'

Paco shook his head.

'Okay,' Angeli said, trying not to let it spoil his mood. 'When did you spot her?'

'At the Fonda bridge,' Paco repeated. 'She wasn't there and

then . . . You know, she was still lacing up that black . . .' Paco was still searching for a word when Angeli nodded. Hell, he wasn't sure what to call tonight's outfit either. Except, maybe, a death wish on wheels.

'She just appeared?' Angeli asked, trying to get it straight. 'Still lacing up her clothes when she hit the levels?'

Paco nodded, looking nervous.

'No, that's fine,' Angeli reassured him. 'That's good.' Angeli dipped a hand into his coat pocket and closed his fingers round a shockblade. Synthetic mother-of-pearl handle, cheap electrics, put together in Shanghai. He'd lifted the blade from a spitting ginger-furred girlKat a couple of night before. It was tat, as likely to shock its owner as his prey, but what the hell . . .

'Here,' Angeli slid the blade into the kid's hand with a nod. 'Don't let me see you carrying it, don't let me see you using it.'

Paco grinned in disbelief and hefted the blade in his hand, as if to judge its balance, then stuttered brief and embarrassed thanks and slid swiftly away before Angeli had time to change his mind.

Karo DiOrchi was winning. And although she didn't yet know it, her booth was the centre of attention in that bar. If it was just the game, that would be acceptable, Angeli decided. After all, half the slumming suits had heavy side bets as to whether the Segasim booth would go live with a death match. But it wasn't just the game.

The attraction was her, and that dangerous mix of sex cut with violence that radiated from her fluid, rapidly-moving body. The girl had all the front of a true exotic, with none of the augmentations. She moved like a natural.

The game would go live, though. Cutting VJ SlyMix out of the loop. Gone live, a game took over all screens, that was the house rules. And it would go, any second now, Angeli judged from the determined way she held her body, shoulders slung low. Her hands spinning round each other in a blur, operating weapons no one else could see, or would see until the *TripleHelix*'s vast tri-D screens lit with close-ups of the Archangel's actual defeat.

Karo was in black leather again, tissue-thin, bonded with polyvinyl to make it cling to her body. The girl seemed to have a thing for black. The leather was real, too, Angeli decided. Imported probably, not clone-grown and stripped off a skin bank.

Clothes weren't Angeli's thing, but he could still tell the outfit was expensive designed to look cheap, not the other way round. It looked like a fancy jump suit. No one on the levels could afford clothes like that, but even Paco would have recognized it for what it was, *haute couture* Issuki Marino. Similar outfits featured every day on *MyFortune* or the CySat soaps.

The legs looked normal, if tight cut. And she had a narrow half-belt, sewn to the back of her tight trousers, with a small pouch attached. But it was the top that had everyone watching. The garment had a full, high-collared back but at the front it was laced from her bare neck to her pubic mound, revealing a long strip of soft olive flesh as wide as Angeli's hand.

Her belly-button was studded twice, her breasts squeezed by the lacing and her pubic hair had been plucked or singed. Not that Angeli, or anyone else, could actually see Karo's genitals: the jump suit was too well designed for that, its soft black leather coming discreetly together in a vee a finger's width above her clitoral hood.

That was the trouble with rich kids, Angeli decided. They just didn't get the rules, and that meant trouble, always did. The code in the *TripleHelix* was short but tight, and to trash it got you into deep trouble.

Don't kill (unless you have to).

And don't pretend to be something you're not.

Male or female, whores dressed like whores, kinderwhores like kinderwhores, Kats spat and wolfBoys skulked. Ishies took the pictures. That way everyone knew who was who, what was for sale and what came free, it wasn't problem. That crazy bitch Sabine took ten per cent off the top of whatever anyone earned in her bar, Angeli took another ten per cent and everyone was happy.

What Angeli didn't need was some rich kid slumming it,

dressed up like the presenter of *LateNite Sex/FactorE*, upsetting Sabine's punters by not knowing her place.

Whoever the fuck she was, the girl didn't realize how dangerously she was living, which made her the only one who didn't. Because Paco did and so did Angeli. So, too, did every everybody else in that bar – whore, vampyre or what passed for normal.

If Karo hadn't been so bloody good at that game, she'd probably already be dead, or at least have had her face redesigned without the aid of mediSoft.

'Stripe,' Angeli demanded of Lucy, the kinder/Vampyre cross who doubled part-time as Sabine's bargirl. She looked eleven and was going on thirty-five, maybe older, but then that was her choice. And there had to be worse ways to scrach a living, though Angeli couldn't remember what.

The red can hit the zinc, frosted at the sides and so cold Angeli could feel the chill through the leather of his reinforced gloves. All the same, the beer hardly touched the sides on its way down.

'Again.' Angeli tipped a second beer after the first and settled his back against the edge of the zinc, glancing slowly round the crowded bar. It looked as it always did, as it had looked when he first came in as a kid. Roof too low, walls of buckled steel, conversation drowned out by squalling machines and the drunken thud of drum&bass from *PolyRiptides* next door.

Maybe that was it, Angeli thought. Maybe it was a bar for people who didn't want to talk or couldn't afford to hear themselves think. All the *TripleHelix* had going for it was reputation, Segasim booth and its Sony tri-D. That and the bedding stalls upstairs

Angeli didn't really like the place, probably never had. He didn't like the filth, the crude stink of pregna-4 pheromone or the way everyone, from slumming salarymen to Paco's kinderwhore friends, watched him from the corners of their eyes.

He could have been out on the gantry, checking out the flesh at *PolyRiptides*. Come to that, he could have been upstairs in the stalls, taking a freebie. But he just wanted to be here, right here, when those screens lit, the house lights cut out and that little bitch went in for the kill . . .

But Angeli was wasting his time, because tonight it wasn't going to happen.

The NVPD officer was positioned to get a good view of the booth. Actually, he'd positioned himself to get a good view of her breasts, or as good a view as you could get through the Segasim's scratched sides. Which meant he was in the right place to spot Karo's first stagger as the fight turned against her. That was fuzzy logic for you, it could fuck you over bigtime if you were feeling too literal.

Karo locked her shoulders, head hunching forward. Without even realizing it, she shifted from attack to defensive. Whatever the fuck went on inside that helmet, the girl's nervous system didn't like it. She still moved, kicked, danced on the spot as she dodged the Archangel only she could see, but Angeli saw the exact moment she lost her nerve. And then everyone in the place knew the girl was in trouble.

The screens weren't going to light, not tonight, not for her.

'Stupid little shit.' Lucy's comment was low but clear. Next to Angeli, a woman who looked old enough to be Lucy's ma but was probably really half her age, muttered agreement and her nervous CySat suit nodded intently. The same snide glances and vicious glee manifested right across the bar as the regulars realized Karo DiOrchi had finally met her match.

The magic was off. Angeli sighed: this was going to be messy.

The girl was staggering now, her hands fumbling against nothing. She looked stupid, like some carnival puppet with half its wires cut. Twenty seconds to go, Angeli decided. Maybe only fifteen . . . She lasted thirty, then her body jackknifed to the floor as if hit by *grand mal* and Karo was scrabbling to get the helmet off her head. She'd almost managed it when the crowd closed in around her.

That was when the lights went down, came up, went down, throwing the bar into flickering darkness. Even the noise from *PolyRiptides* next door was stilled.

'Second time in three weeks,' Angeli heard Lucy say. It was, too, and no one could remember a brownout happening before. 'Weird or what . . .'

Angeli pushed himself up off his seat and flipped down the visor of his helmet, switching to night-sight. 'Stand back,' he ordered, his voice deepened by a chip in his throat-mike. Simultaneously, Angeli's order was broadcast over the *TripleHelix*'s sound system as his helmet decided this was an emergency and operated an aural over-ride.

And then the lights went back up. A couple of CySat suits at the edge had faltered and fallen back. But not the regulars, though they looked less strung-out crazy than they'd been. All the same, a dark-eyed Edgar Allan and a heavily pregnant, black-furred girlKat were busy trying to pull Karo from the booth, egged on by a nervous crowd.

Shit, fucking, fucking shit. Late on patrol and now the makings of a riot. NVPD Central was going to love him. Zero tolerance was the NVPD motto, ZT to everything. Angeli smiled grimly and slipped his Colt from its holster, taking aim at the middle porthole. He'd always wanted to do this. Dropping to one knee to give himself an upwards angle, Angeli squeezed the trigger.

A flechette smacked into the glass, shattered it and fragmented back over the top of the frozen crowd. One shard took out a Sega machine before burying itself in the wall. Most just scythed overhead. For the first and probably only time, there was utter silence in the *TripleHelix*. Impossible as it seemed, even the games machines had stopped their chatter.

'I said . . . stand back,' Angeli announced, moving towards the Kat and the chalk-faced Edgar Allan who had the girl gripped between them. Move back they did, dropping Karo roughly to the floor. Quickly, Angeli scanned the crowd, letting his gaze assess the danger and damage. No one dead, no serious injuries. Sabine would be pissed about her broken Sega machine and the white-faced Edgar Allan would have a fresh scar when he finally pulled the slivers of glass from his cheek, but other than that, no problem.

As for the exploded star splintered into the porthole, Angeli shrugged. This was the *TripleHelix*, they'd be telling punters about that for years to come. There was only one thing left to do, and that was get out of there, fast.

'This woman is under arrest,' Angeli said firmly. Ignoring NVPD regulations that stated weapons must be holstered immediately after use, Angeli held his Colt pointing upright, its barrel parallel to his cheek, combat style. The stance wasn't lost on the crowd, who stood away.

The girl was still on the floor, crying. The girlKat had split her lip and her scalp was badly torn, but she was more or less unharmed, if you ignored the ripped-out lock of hair still gripped in the Edgar Allan's hands.

Angeli knelt, hooked his fingers roughly into the laces that criss-crossed her squashed breasts and yanked the girl to her feet. An elderly whore sniggered and even the girlKat gave an evil grin.

'Give her one for me,' a voice in his ear said loudly.

It was Lucy. In one hand she swung a carbon-fibre bat, in the other she held a chilled Stripe. Flipping up his visor, Angeli took the can, letting his fingers brush the kinderwhore's as he did. He owed her.

Draining the Stripe in one, Angeli shifted his head slightly to one side and nodded to the bat. 'Didn't know you played,' he said lightly.

The crowd grinned and Angeli could feel tension sparking off into laughter. 'Work to do.' Angeli pulled a card from his coat pocket, folding up one corner before beginning to read the girl her rights. Twisting the card activated a chip recorder. It also overrode any Third Precinct m/wave security camera, forcing it to upload a file into the Third District's computer showing him doing the same.

Live by the book, get protected by the book. His uncle had drummed that into him, mostly with clenched fists. But the old bastard was right: do it by the book, because this was going to be difficult enough as it was. And as his uncle never stopped telling him, right up to the day he took a blade in the guts, a cop's most important job is to cover his back.

Angeli was about to slide her now-recorded arrest card into his smartbox, when the girl began to twist in his grip. As one, the crowd growled.

'Don't move.' Angeli's voice was harsh. It allowed for no challenge but she faced up to him anyway.

'*You again*,' she spat the words. 'Touch me and I'll . . .' Her voice was hard, ripe with bravado, but Angeli could hear an underlying worry. He grinned.

The girl didn't like it. So she fell back on what she understood: privilege. 'You know who I am?' Her wide face was impassive, her almond eyes cold. Whatever street accent she'd affected had just fallen away. Angeli could recognize the cut-glass accent of the Suites and so could the rest of the *TripleHelix*.

Trying to face him down was arrogant, but mostly it was just blindingly stupid. For a second, as Karo caught the expression in Angeli's eyes, she understood what she'd done. And then the crowd were moving in again.

Lifting his gun, Angeli didn't fire into the air or at the spitting girlKat moving towards him. Instead he chose a spot on the girl's skull, just to the side of her forehead, and clubbed hard. Metal split skin, as the gun's handle bounced off her skull. And Karo DiOrchi buckled, a dead weight in his arms.

[Ripped Out At Rip Tides]

'Back off,' Angeli ordered, falling back again on NVPD procedure. 'Stand away.'

He glared round the room, gun raised to his cheek, combat-style: fingers still hooked tight into the laces of the girl's leather top. 'This woman is my prisoner. This arrest has been taped. Interfere with the course of the law, and you'll be dealt with accordingly.' It was all cliché, older than the hills, but then NVPD training taught Angeli to use the familiar. It was what the public wanted, and it was what worked.

The crowd was muttering, but even the girlKat stepped back, which was all he'd been waiting for. Hoisting Karo over his shoulder, Angeli marched out of the bar, trying not to think too much about her hip against his helmet, or the leather-clad buttocks resting under one gloved hand. It took him several minutes to clamber safely down the ladder into *PolyRiptides*, changing rungs with a clumsy one-handed hop rather than risk dropping her onto the near-naked dancers below. And by the time he got the girl to the bottom, Angeli had quite an audience, but no one tried to stop him and no one stood in his way.

Paco was waiting. That was a shock in itself. The boy was sitting on a narrow walkway outside *Riptides*, polishing the mother-of-pearl handle of his new knife with a scrap of dirty rag. His feet were over the edge, kicking his ridiculous ice-sole ReeBs back and forward over the dark water.

'You want to see where I first saw her?' The boy breathed heavily onto the shockblade's handle and wiped it over again. 'I mean, so you can send her back.' Paco's voice was serious as he fell neatly into step beside the NVPD officer. The boy took it for granted Angeli wouldn't be so stupid as to arrest a girl from the Suites, not really arrest her. Paco had a point.

'Show me,' Angeli said without breaking his stride and together they cut across a metal-railed walkway that led from *PolyRiptides*, ducked into a covered market past stalls grilling strips of indeterminate protein rolled in satay, then crossed a low wire bridge where water lapped darkly beneath them again, and then climbed up to a narrow gantry which sloped away towards the Fondamenta Nuove.

120-volt electric mesh closed up the nearest safe gate, but on the other side of it was newVenice in all its glory. As exotic and unreachable as Beijing, at least for Paco. Angeli had been there. It wasn't an experience he was going to forget.

'Here,' Angeli said. He gave the boy a small grey box, no bigger than a cheap toy hover. Three diodes lit in rapid succession, a fourth pulsed faintly. 'Fooler loops,' Angeli said, using an old term. 'Scramble the cameras.'

Angeli took another, his backup, and flicked it to life. Fooler loops weren't perfect, but they were sure as fuck better than nothing. Paco, Angeli and the girl had reached land now. That was, there was coral beneath them, rather than water and metal. And the long, low warehouses were faced with red brick. There were other differences, too. The ground no longer swayed for a start and the water in the canals had started to stink.

It was an irony of newVenice that its floating ghettos were kept clean by the sea on which they floated, while the expensive, increasingly exclusive areas of CySat's central city sat the other side of micromesh nets. Nets designed to desalinate the water that passed through. Only the nets were clogged, the water in the real canals brackish and stinking. Not to mention clogged with rubbish.

Rubbish was meant to be recycled, certainly, but somehow the rich had more trouble than the poor getting their heads round that idea. Nanites had been tried in the main canals, of course, as had a nightly crew of semiAI drones. But the nanites couldn't tell the difference between rubbish, silt and coral. And the drones blocked the canals for hours at a time, bringing evening traffic to a halt. So the canals stank and Matsui did brisk business in air-purifiers.

It made Angeli glad he lived in a poor district on the edge of the city, where the tides still reached. Yeah, really . . .

'Okay, where?' Angeli demanded, lowering the girl to her feet. She'd been groaning and wriggling under his grip for the last minute, but then maybe his hold on her hips had been a little too tight.

'Here,' said Paco, stopping by a stone bridge that led over the Rio dei Mendicanti towards a deserted strip. The derelict church was where Angeli remembered it, a hundred paces away on the other side. The NVPD officer tried to remember the position of the street cameras but couldn't. It wasn't his precinct. He'd have to rely on the fooler loops. The idea didn't make Angeli happy.

'It was here,' Paco insisted. 'Like magic.' The boy clutched at his Izanami talisman and rubbed it quickly.

Angeli grunted. People didn't just appear: they had tunnels, secret doorways, safe houses. It was just a question of sweating out some answers. 'Hey, you.' Angeli cuffed the girl across the face, reopening her split lip.

Karo spat at him, bloody spittle missing his eyes, smearing his cheeks. And Angeli gut-punched her for good measure. Now he was going to have to get a retroVirus booster.

Karo's response was to throw up over his boots, then try to kick him in the groin. When that failed, she spun in a half-circle, pulled a wire from the pouch on her half-belt and flicked it at his face. It was slickly done, but Karo was too weak and anyway Angeli was faster, though the wire caught his helmet, opening a shallow cut along one side. *Molywire*. She didn't look old enough to remember that. Angrily, Angeli caught her wrist, twisted slightly and stopped as he felt the bones stress to breaking point.

'Jesussss.' She dropped the wire onto the cobbles, her curse little more than a hiss of pain.

Angeli released the pressure on her wrist slightly, but not enough to make her dangerous, dipping down to fetch the wire. It was professional quality, able to go from fluid to solid in a single flick. Useful if you wanted to nearly take off someone's head . . .

'Well now,' Angeli said, letting his gaze linger on the laced-in curve of her breasts and the soft swell of her naked stomach. 'What *am* I going to do with you?'

Karo flushed and instinctively tried to cover herself, bringing over her free hand, but Angeli grabbed that too, twisting it. He was smiling.

'I thought we were letting her go,' Paco said hurriedly.

'We?' Angeli looked at the boy, who stepped back.

'I couldn't do that . . . Anyway, how could I get her back to the Suites? You think they're going to open the safe gates at this time of night, to us? Or maybe she could try walking through the sonic wall?'

'You can't keep her,' Paco protested.

Angeli dropped one of Karo's wrists as his own hand rose to slap Paco, but he stopped himself. The kid wasn't worried for himself, he was worried for Angeli. Just what Angeli needed, a self-appointed sidekick.

'Why not?' The NVPD officer demanded.

'She comes from the Suites. You don't know who she is,' Paco was whispering. 'Her father could be . . . he could be a member of the Council.' The boy said it as if it was the most outrageous thing he could think off. It was. But from the sudden stillness of the girl's body, Angeli knew Paco'd hit the mark.

'The Council . . .' For a second Angeli's voice sounded almost worried, then he grinned and his Colt was out, the diode on its barrel lit red for loaded, its muzzle pointed at the side of her head. 'Shit,' said Angeli. 'Can't keep her, can't give her back. Not too many options left.' His finger tightened on the trigger and even as Paco convinced himself Angeli was about to pull it, Karo spoke, her words spilling out in a terrified jumble.

'There's a door, a subway,' she said frantically. 'Maglev trains, always running, always empty. I can show you . . . It's true.'

'Trains?' Angeli looked at the girl in astonishment. He was so shocked, he forgot to keep hold of Karo's wrist. Half-frozen with fear, the girl was still deciding whether to make a bolt for it across the darkened square when Angeli thrust his Colt back in its holster.

'How come no one knows about it?' Angeli demanded. It was an obvious question. He just knew he wasn't going to like the answer.

'They do.' The girl sounded embarrassed. 'My father knows. So do other Counc—' Her words trailed away and she looked nervously at Angeli. But instead of asking the obvious question, Angeli glanced round him, thoughtfully.

'There's an entrance near here?'

'A service entrance. Over there.' The girl nodded towards the Church.

'The Savanarola revival.' Angeli smiled bitterly. 'A dozen churches thrown up in as many days around the city's perimeter, then left to fall derelict.' He caught the girl's stunned glance. 'We can read, you know, some of us.'

Karo had the grace to look ashamed.

'So why not just put up stations?' Angeli asked.

Karo thought about it. 'You know Passion vanished . . . ?'

Vanished, turned up a year later in the US with her own show, then vanished again. 'Of course I know.' Angeli didn't say how recently he'd found that out. But then there were a number of things he wasn't saying, at least not yet.

'After she went, the Council spent years debating building the stations she'd planned.' The girl's expression was embarrassed, but she still met and held his sardonic gaze. 'They decided not . . .'

'Even then, they didn't want to encourage movement towards the centre. Right?' Angeli nodded. That made sense. The barrier between city and immigrants hadn't always been as literal as the sonic wall. Which wasn't to say a barrier hadn't been there from the start, one way or another. 'Are there stations out at the levels?'

'No.' Karo shook her head. 'Only as far as the coral's edge. Passion looked at running tunnels under water, but it never came to anything.'

'Okay,' Angeli said. 'These tunnels, show me.'

Paco, Angeli and the girl walked over the bridge towards the derelict Church. When they reached the portico, Karo dipped her hand into the pouch on her belt and pulled out a smart card. Moving lightly towards a shadowed wall, she slid it at shoulder height into a crack between two marble blocks and swiped down. Silently, eerily, one of the marble blocks slid back maybe two inches and then slid silently sideways. They were left looking at a small unlit lift.

'Night lights,' said Karo and the inside of the lift lit softly in response.

'This will get you back to the Suites?' Angeli asked.

'To the Palazzo? Yes.' Karo nodded. 'If that's where you want to go.' There was something about her words Angeli didn't like. He looked at her, but her face was impassive.

'But won't you get caught going back?'

For a second, Angeli thought she was going to say something useful, something real. But she just shook her head. Whatever was worrying her, she wasn't telling him.

'But they'll notice that.' The NVPD officer indicated her split lip, the blood matted into her black hair, where he'd clubbed her with the Colt. 'What are you going to tell them?'

Again the hesitation, then Karo shrugged. 'I'll think of something, if I need to. A fall down the stairs, maybe. That was always my mother's favourite . . .' A tiredness was in the girl's brown eyes, and the hand's breadth of bare skin which ran down her front was rough with goosebumps. Stress, Angeli decided. The night wasn't cold enough for it to be anything else.

'Are you sure you won't get caught?' he demanded.

'I've told you, no . . .'

Angeli looked at the lift, at Paco and then back to the young girl. He nodded slowly. 'Just for the record, your father *is* a member of the Council.' It was a statement, not a question, but the girl answered it anyway.

'Yes, he is.' Her smile was twisted as she glanced around her, then slid to a halt on Angeli's face. 'For the record . . .'

'So you have access to the Palazzo Ducale?'

Karo nodded, her face tired.

'Right,' Angeli said reaching for his Colt. 'I'm arresting you on suspicion of murder.' Angeli pulled the molywire from his pocket. 'I have reason to believe this matches a wound profile for a murder committed eight weeks ago at the Palazzo Ducale.'

She was staring at him in disbelief. 'You can't . . .'

'Shut it.' Angeli thrust the gun under her nose and when she flinched he pushed it even further. Out of the corner of one eye, Angeli saw Paco begin to back away and grabbed him just in time.

'I'm arresting you, too,' he told Paco. 'For being in possession of an illegal weapon. Namely a pearl-handled shockblade I have reason to suspect is hidden in your back pocket.'

Tears welled up into Paco's blue eyes, but Angeli met the young boy's gaze without hesitation or shame. 'Of course . . . I could let you go.' Paco stopped looking hurt and started looking hopeful. 'But I'd need you to do something first.'

Paco nodded.

'Use that lift, take a train to the other end, then come back and tell me where it comes out, how many other entrances there are, everything . . .'

'He'll be killed,' Karo protested.

'Not Paco,' said Angeli, glancing down at the boy. The boy looked at Angeli in disbelief, and kept on looking that way, until Angeli agreed Paco could have his blade back and keep anything he found at the other end. Then, the girl's card clutched safely in Paco's hand, Angeli watched as the marble slab closed and the deserted portico fell back into darkness.

Overhead there were a million stars scattered like dust across the sky, five ring colonies and more satellites than anybody could count. Insects buzzed low over the water, and in the distance spotlights revealed the church of San Zanipolo.

But none of these were what held Angeli's attention. He was

looking at the girl. The bruised, vomit-splattered half-naked daughter of a CySat executive. And he'd got her under arrest for the murder of one of CySat's own security guards. It didn't bear thinking about.

[Crash & Burn/the reMix reEdit]

Razz didn't see the Hondas coming out of the desert. No one did, but then Colonel Carlos was nothing if not professional. And anyway, it was hard to see APV/Hs in full stealth mode.

She'd been sitting with Dr Schwartz on the wooden verandah of his mission hospital, looking out at the impossible beauty of night in the Kalahari. The old man was dodging her questions about the blond boy he'd operated on that morning.

As ever, he was charming and unfailingly polite, but determined not to tell her more than he wanted her to know. Which was less than nothing. Not where the boy came from, not why he had had to operate. It was the Doge, Razz was certain of that. Alex wouldn't have given her the coordinates for this place if she wasn't *meant* to be here. And the only reason Razz could think of for being there was to protect the blond boy from futher damage.

But how the fuck could she do that, if the old man wouldn't tell her anything?

Time was, she'd have leant over, gripped the priest by his larynx and throttled the truth out of him along with his breath, but she just couldn't bring herself to do it. Not here, not now, sitting on his verandah in a canvas chair, chilled water in her hand, listening to the old man switch between calling her *My Dear* and *My Child*.

Cognitive dissonance, Alex would have called it. Razz was having trouble remembering her real age, her profession.

These days, when she got up and looked at herself in the flyblown shard of glass that passed as a mirror at this mission, she *expected* to see a young girl staring back at her. The lack of silver skin, the vanished shark-cartilage shoulder plates were as welcome

. . . no, even more welcome than the lack of lines around her dark brown eyes. Somehow, somewhere, she'd been given another chance.

Razz liked the old priest, was pretty sure he liked her in return. Oh, he didn't trust her, but he hadn't pushed his questions as to why she'd turned up alone in the Kalahari. Where she'd got the plane. He'd even listened patiently while she told him of her need to find Nzigé. And while Dr Schwartz took leave to doubt that either Nzigé or Alex was an actual god, he was prepared to believe both might know things denied to normal mortals like him.

The old man even admitted Nzigé was not an unknown name to him. He just wouldn't say any more, not yet, not until he'd finished healing the boy. And sitting there, looking out over the red desert, drunk on desert air and the smoke of a burning mosquito coil, Razz finally let her defences down.

It was to cost the old man his life.

They came in from the front, two dust-red APV/Hs, bristling with laser radar, armed to the teeth with g2g missiles. The mission had defences, of course, but the Church Anchorite weren't the Geneticists, and their defences were primitive: a simple anti-missile laser, which the lead hover blew out of synch by a single pulse of RF. There were electric fences, too, ringing the whole mission, but the hovers just ran straight through them, bursting the wire apart in a shower of sparks.

The world lurched.

One minute Razz was sipping water, the next the doctor was begging her to take cover even as she sprinted up the steps into the mission to look frantically for a weapon, any weapon. She found a Braun cancer scalpel and a bolt-action .762 mm Sig Sauer, which was great if you wanted to keep wild dogs in check. Simple Quarton laser sight, ceramic barrel. It wasn't much, but it was what she had.

Throwing herself behind a window, Razz squinted at the on-coming hovers, trying to remember anything about Hondas, recent issue. But it made no difference how new or outdated they were, hovers were more than one notch up on the defences of the hospital, which was all that mattered.

God might not be on the side of the big battalions, but that was sure as fuck the way to bet. Razz sighted her Sig Sauer, took aim at a weak spot where the semiAI beltless gun pod fitted into the turret, and fired. Nothing.

She slammed off another shot, saw the priest looking behind him in horror and signalled him to get down. The old man was standing there like a walking target, an expression of disbelief written across his face as he saw flames begin to twist up the walls of his hospital. He was still looking in horror when Razz first saw the hyena, loping in towards the priest through the red dust.

She flipped out through the window, rolling in the dirt, Sig Sauer clutched tight. She came up kneeling, the rifle already sighted. Shit. So that was what this was about. Razz pulled back on the Sig Sauer's bolt, pulling a new round into its barrel, and squeezed off a shot. It missed, God help her. Without enhanced reflexes or night sight, Razz was no better at this game than the next person.

'Fucking concentrate,' Razz told herself, re-sighting the Sig Sauer. She didn't fire until her breath was stilled, half in/half out, her heart steadied. Her next shot took the hyena in its shoulder, but the animal's muscles kept pumping as it ploughed on towards the doctor, locked onto his scent as surely as those missiles had locked onto the hospital buildings.

'Get the boy, my quarters,' the old man screamed as the hyena closed in on him. Razz nodded and as the beast sank its teeth into the doctor's thigh she squeezed off another shot, blasting away half the animal's skull, splattering the doctor with blood and fragments of bone. But it made no difference.

Animal and man disappeared together in a ball of fire, the old man's scream swallowed back into his lungs, along with mouthfuls of flame. The hyena's jaws had been DNA-coded, its bodypack wired to explode when teeth bit into the right flesh, when the double-helix profile of its target matched that held in the detonator's memory.

It was an old trick but a good one. Rapid polymerase reactions boosted target DNA until it could be pulled through a molecular maze. The whole process took fractions of a second. There were a dozen different ways to set up the targeting, though from the way the hyena had homed straight in on the doctor, Razz knew this was something simple and Pavlovian.

Razz was dragging combat knowledge up from her memory, except that the facts didn't belong to her, they belonged to the silver assassin she'd once been. The killer whose swift, lethal reactions she no longer possessed.

Shit. Razz rolled sideways in the dirt, and squeezed off another shot at the nearest hover. Nothing. It was like blowing peas at an armadillo. And she didn't even have time to improvise: there was the boy to rescue. Always assuming the little shit wasn't burnt to a crisp in the fire behind her.

Flipping from side to side, throwing herself behind rocks, rolling into disused, irregular ditches, Razz bolted for the old man's quarters. Wild thorns ripped her legs, stones twisted her ankles in the dark, one of her hands was raw but not bleeding. *Burnt not broken*, Razz thought, caught in the first magnesium flash of the hyena.

She was there now, pounding up wooden steps towards a doorway that vomited smoke into the warm African night. Someone was in her way, a black soldier in combat fatigues, the boy tossed across his shoulder. Without breaking her stride, Razz put a scalpel into his throat, hearing his scream sink to a hollow burble, blood spreading down his chest, dark red blooming suddenly across his green-grey uniform.

That was the Doge he was holding. Her child, her charge.

Reaching for the Braun, Razz ripped it brutally from the soldier's throat, dropping it as she burnt her fingers on the red-hot blade. She didn't want heat sealing the wound, each terrified breath was meant to pull blood and air deep into his struggling lungs, drowning him. If he'd let go of the boy, Razz might have let him be, but the soldier wouldn't.

Angrily, Razz flicked sideways and bent up one leg. Pivoting on the spot, she stamped down hard on the man's knee, hearing it rupture with a ugly pop. Wide-eyed with shock, already choking on his own blood, the man finally dropped his prize into the dirt, and scrabbled for his holstered pistol.

It was way too late.

Leaning forward, Razz gripped the soldier's wrist and flipped him round towards the burning building. But instead of sending him into the flames, she kept a grip on his wrist, twisting as the soldier pulled up short with a thud, his shoulder dislocating with an ugly squeal of tearing muscles.

He was finished, she knew that. Anything more was an indulgence. All the same, Razz drop kicked him in the stomach while he was on the way down, kicked out his other knee and then snapped his spine with a single swift stamp of her heel. What she left twitching in the dirt might once have been human but it wasn't now.

Grabbing a moly knife from his belt, Razz reached towards his neck. The figure shrank back from the high-tension cutting wire, not realizing Razz had no intention of delivering a *coup de grâce*. She wasn't that merciful. Razz wanted his uniform.

The moly edge sliced open his combat jump suit, from neck to lower back in a single stroke, and then she was stripping it swiftly off his twitching body, like the shell from a chrysalis, leaving broken pulp within. Razz stripped to her pants, discarding jeans and T-shirt, struggling into the blood-soaked jump suit, tangling herself in its sleeves she was in such a hurry.

It took control to make her slow down, but anger gave Razz the strength to manage it. Anger into control, fire to ice, no one lasted long as a street samurai if they couldn't manage something that simple. Razz laughed, harshly, rolling out of the way of a falling beam, watching sparks flame up around her. There was fire all right.

Where was the ice?

Fucking great, thought Razz. A street samurai in the desert. Without armour, without viral enhancers. All she had was instinct, and even that didn't seem as sharp as it once was. Still, at least the nearest hover was doing what she'd hoped. It'd spun rapidly round the corner of the burning hospital and swung to an uneasy, rocking halt. The way hovers did, even expensive battleship models from Japan.

It was waiting out there, a hundred yards away, ready to collect the boy . . . Time to make her move. Not that there was any other decision events would allow her to take.

Taking the man's helmet and nightsight RayBans, Razz velcroed two grenades to her belt, hoisted the kid onto her shoulder and sprinted for the hover, head down. The jump suit's cut edges flapped open, exposing her naked back, but they couldn't see that. At least, Razz hoped to hell they couldn't. Razz was counting on them taking her at face value.

Sure, they'd scan her when she came within range, that was why she'd taken the jump suit: its recognition chip was in a sealed ceramic block sewn into the shoulder.

The hover's Browning was turning towards her. For a second, Razz thought the hover aimed to take her down, but when the semiAI fired it was over her shoulder. Razz turned her head in time to see two hospital orderlies fall in a mass of broken limbs.

They'd been trying to save the boy. Probably didn't know the old man was already dead, or maybe they just felt they had to retrieve his patient. Razz tried not to worry about it.

Without viral rewiring, she was practically dead on her feet, her breath rasping in her throat from the effort of carrying the unconscious boy across open ground. A few paces more was all she needed.

That, and some self-welding nickel/aluminium tape. The magnatron 50atom splutter-gun kind that flicks from twenty-five to 1,600 degrees C in a couple of milliseconds, repairs an axle, melts ceramic, instantly welds shut a hover door, with the enemy still inside it . . .

The hover swung from side to side, rocking a little as the gyros cut in and out to hold the machine in place. Somewhere inside, a soldier hit a button and then the hatch was opening, two inches of titanium-polymer laminate lifting in a smooth hydraulic sweep. Right hand already balancing the boy across her shoulder, Razz used her left to flip down the control-pad cover of one of the grenades and set its timer. She was so close to panic, she wasn't even sure which side of the line she was. Sweat rolled down her naked back, the skin prickling as if caught in a thousand laser sights.

'Report, fucking report . . .' Inside the hover a soldier demanding something, his words screaming inside her helmet. But Razz couldn't concentrate enough to work out what he was demanding.

The grenade was busy counting itself down, still velcroed to her belt, but that was a risk Razz had to take. No options. Climbing onto the hover, Razz hoisted the blond boy off her shoulder, as if to bundle him head first down the hatch and then, as rough hands reached up to grab him, Razz leant in and shot the soldier directly below, then blew away the hatch's manual override using a Glock taken from the first soldier. The one whose throat she had re-arranged. Ripping the already-blinking grenade from her belt, Razz flung it into the well of the tank.

Given the option, no one but a moron would choose anything but nickel/aluminium foil to weld a hover hatch shut. But all the same, no matter what manufacturers claimed and soldiers boasted in the dark, cluttered gloom of *Last Boer* merc bars, it wasn't possible to lift a hover hatch with someone lying across it.

Although they tried. Razz gave them that. She felt a thump, as the grenade fragged, its blast lifting her and the boy into the air. Not enough to throw them off the top of the hover, but enough to rip a shock through them both. Enough to stun the boy awake. And Razz suddenly found herself staring into irises of the deepest, purest blue. She felt like crying. Which wasn't a surprise: these days she spent too much time on the edge of tears.

'Who are you?' the boy asked politely as she rolled off the burning hover, taking him with her. Razz fell to the ground, feet first, and then she was running, boy in her arms, away from his question, away from the burnt-down mission towards a dark line of distant hills.

'Get cover,' her brain said, 'get cover.'

It was difficult to dodge and weave carrying the kid, but Razz made herself do it anyway. She had to. The other hover was still out there, armed with laserRadar, guided by satellite tracking. It wasn't an even match.

'Who are you?' the boy asked again. His thin arms were wrapped so tightly round her neck, Razz felt like she was choking. But every time Razz tried to pull loose, the boy tightened his grip again.

'*Who are you*?' Aurelio's voice was still polite, but impatient, almost worried. Except that he wasn't allowed to show it, poor little shit.

'Honey, I'm Razz,' Razz said.

The boy looked at her in disbelief. It didn't matter about the helmet or the night glasses covering her face, he was close enough to see her skin was dark, not silver, that she had curves and flesh where she should have had muscle and biotek armour.

'No, you're not,' said Aurelio crossly. 'I should know.'

[Hip & Run]

The levels survived on a diet of soaps, Rai and rumours – plus cheap ice and Drexie-box alcohol. As the joke said, ninety per cent of Levellers had permanent headaches, the other ten per cent were unconscious.

The word was the Doge had been kidnapped, that he'd been shot through the head, that Count Ryuchi had murdered one half of the Council, that *WeGuard* had taken over the Palazzo Ducale, CySat was about to blow up the levels . . .

So when news broke that Aurelio was alive, safe in his chambers, busy battling the Dragon, word spread like wildfire. Except wildfire wouldn't have spread. It's hard to burn brothels, markets and bars when they're made of steel, when their furniture is *bricolaged* from fragments of fire-resistant polymer and non-flammable ceramic.

But if the levels were fireproof but unprotected, the palazzi of the city proper were a bonfire waiting to happen. But they, of course, were guarded by semiAI anti-fire systems, designed to protect CySat's collection of Third Empire, Victorian and US colonial furniture. Not to mention its classic West-Coast Hockneys and mid-period Pollocks, along with dark, age-cracked oils so ancient the artists' names were lost.

There were Italianate landscapes, filled with flat castles and oversized angels. Pictures of miniature crowds skating over frozen canals. Out-of-focus boats fashioned from thousands of different coloured dots, like someone trying to paint pixels. And then there were the nudes.

Right from the start, even before he became Aurelio, it had

struck Paco as odd to have so many old pictures of naked people.

Struck him as odd too, that all the naked figures were women or young boys, mostly with wings. Even odder that all of them were pink. Maybe the naked small girls and grown men had got lost. Or maybe they were in another room. It was true, there were naked men, but the only ones Paco had seen so far were bad life-sized models in the corridor where he'd come up, stepping out of a small lift onto a checker-board marble floor.

Some of the models were missing arms or legs, and not a single one had proper eyes. Instead they stood and stared down at him, blank-eyed, from the little boxes they perched on.

The train worked, as the girl had said it would. Though she hadn't said it wouldn't touch the ground, or that its doors would hiss at him when they opened. And she definitely hadn't said down there was where she was living, either.

But it was. Paco knew a *bash* when he saw one, and hers was a tiny room right below the basilica, with a basin and a fecal recyc at one end. The floor was strewn with satay sticks, empty bottles of water. There was an old smartbox, still whirring unhappily, wired crudely into an optic line. But mostly the floor was littered with clothes, black street leathers and a strange blue velvet dress.

Paco should have gone back to tell Angeli about the bash, instead of going on, Paco knew that. Knew, too, that Lieutenant Angeli was going to be cross if he was gone much longer. But he wasn't ready to leave yet.

Paco was staring at a naked girl. She was young and a bit overweight, lying face down on a large bed, one leg draped over the edge, just touching the floor. Paco liked her on sight. From the broad grin on her wide face, she looked like she'd just slunk in from the levels, was trying the bed out for size. Hell, give him a year or so and he wouldn't mind trying it out with her.

Paco was still grinning at the thought when a *garotte* went round his throat, pulling him backwards. He would have fallen, but the strand of monofilament also held him up, so instead Paco's body cannoned into a black-suited *WeGuard* standing directly behind him.

Chinese, Paco thought, *neat uniform* . . . And that would have been the last thought to enter his head, if a cool, oh-so-polite voice hadn't spoken.

'Let him go.'

When the guard hesitated, the polite voice spoke again, its tone a little sharper this time. A thin ring-covered hand gripped Paco's shoulder, and the guard stood back hurriedly.

'Good,' said the voice.

Even choking, Paco was impressed. Quiet, polite, dangerous, all in one word. That was real training. The hand on his shoulder tightened, long fingers digging into Paco's thin shoulder.

'Breeding, you little thug . . . Not training, breeding.'

Paco wasn't aware he'd said anything. Apart from anything else, his throat was too raw to speak, his breath rasping between quivering lips.

'You didn't speak.' The voice was still polite, but now it was amused as well. *Psi*, Paco realized with shock. He was with a psi. Paco decided to stop thinking and concentrate on the *garotte* still wrapped loosely round his neck.

The tall man ordered the guard to release his monofilament and Paco smiled at the frustration in the *WeGuard*'s eyes. Not clever. A savage blow to Paco's kidneys dropped Paco to the corridor floor. A kick would have followed, except the *WeGuard* was stopped by a single glance from the tall man.

'Wait,' said the man. 'Let's see what we've got first, shall we?'

He could have been Japanese, but he looked too tall.

Shiny black jacket, white shirt with pearl buttons, a fat belt made of purple cloth and another piece of purple tied round his neck, in a small bow. Grey hair fell in a waterfall onto his shoulders. His trousers had a shiny stripe down each side, and his shoes shone so brightly Paco could see his face in them as he lay on the floor. The tall man looked as if he'd walked out of a painting.

No one asked Paco how he got there. Paco thought it must be because they already knew. He didn't realize they didn't care. Most of those who tried to reach the Suites swam up the Grand Canal,

to be killed by pulsed ultrasound as they reached the desaliniza-
tion nets. The half-dozen or so who stumbled on the tunnels each
year and actually got inside the city also ended up dead. As Paco
would have, had it not been for his height, weight and eye
colouring.

'Can you play Lucifer's Dragon?' The tall man had knelt beside
Paco, one hand resting on the boy's shoulder, lightly this time.
Looking at the boy's filthy face.

Paco looked back in blank amazement. It was like asking if he
could breathe.

'Do you do it well?'

Paco remembered the girl Angeli had arrested. Thirteen death
bouts in just over three months, one dead Dragon and nearly an
Archangel. 'No,' he admitted hoarsely, rubbing his Izanami amulet
for luck. 'No . . . Not that well.'

The man shrugged. 'Doesn't matter. Nor did Aurelio.'

It took Paco a second or two to realize that the elegant man was
talking about the Doge, and was talking as if he knew him.

'He's missing, that's what people say,' Paco said, his raw voice
faltering at the thought. 'He hasn't done his mix this month. People
are worried. He's all right, isn't he?'

An expression Paco couldn't identify flicked across the man's
thin face, and Paco had seen most expressions in his eleven or so
years. But this was fixed somewhere between contempt, amusement and worry.

'The levels are worried that the Doge is missing?' the man
asked Paco.

Paco nodded seriously.

'How sweet. Then they'll be glad he's been found, won't they?'
And as a hand closed again on the boy's shoulder, Paco realized
the man was smiling, not at him, but at the *WeGuard*.

'Well,' the tall man said, shrugging. 'We don't want the levels
worried, do we? Certainly not yet . . .'

[Up Close & Personal . . .]

Something inside was burning her up, but it wasn't his questions. And she was anxious, but about time running out, not about the fact that Angeli intended to charge her with murder. Most killers couldn't keep their eyes off his face when it got to reciting the charge. Either that, or they stared at the floor.

The girl did neither. She didn't even try to cut a deal. Karo just couldn't keep her eyes off the clock.

The molywire tested positive for DNA from the dead *WeGuard*, the girl's fingerprints were all over the wire, and worse than that – at least for Karo – there was a clear, provable match between her prints and the *WeGuard's* stab wound.

Stab wounds close up, everyone knows that. Flesh locks around a blade, holding it tight. Why else did combat knives have serrated back edges, blood channels and fret-cut blades, but to stop the knife sticking on its outward stroke?

Karo's knife'd had none of those. It was too old, too primitive. And she might have wiped the handle but, unfortunately for her, steel takes good fingerprints and when a blade is not withdrawn swiftly enough, it can leave echo prints inside the victim's flesh. Prints which fluoresce under a foreign-DNA scan. Classified or not, Angeli's *bot* had found him a read-out of the *WeGuard's* stab wound, and the prints were Karo's, perfect match.

But knowing that wasn't getting him anywhere.

Black hair in need of a wash, dark almond eyes bruised with lack of sleep, mouth still swollen where her lower lip was split, she just sat and glared at him. As interrogations went, it was a non-starter. Angeli knew what she looked like: pretty. What she smelt like: dirty. But that was all he knew.

He'd kept her in the security cell at the back of his office for three days and she still wouldn't give him her name. She'd accepted his original offer of new clothes with a snarl, grabbed the paper sweats and retreated into a fecal recyc to change. Dumping her leather suit into the recyc rather than give it to Angeli. And that was it. Total silence from there on in. She wouldn't even comment on the molywire.

Withdrawing rations hadn't helped. She didn't complain. In fact, Angeli got the feeling she was relieved. She didn't look the type to eat slop, though she drank the water Angeli offered her night and morning before he made his rounds.

Locking off her washroom facilities hadn't helped either. She'd just dropped her sweats and left him to deal with the mess. After the third time, Angeli handed Karo a disposable trowel through the bars, keyed out the electronic block from her door and told her to clean it up herself.

She did.

Now he had her out of the cell and in his airless office, dressed in a paper top and no bottom, on a seatless steel chair, hands cuffed to the bare frame. There was a FujiLara vidding everything she did or said, which wasn't much. She was meant to be answering his questions and Angeli wasn't getting very far. He could beat her about, of course. Bring out the 'trodes or his taser. Maybe rape her. Spin that chair away from the grey metal table, kick it over and ream out her pride. Mess up her emotions.

That's why the seat was missing. To give NVPD officers easy access to a prisoner's genitals – male or female, it didn't matter. Bruising the fruit was allowed in the rule book. Angeli just didn't like doing it, never had.

Moving in, until he stood close behind her, Angeli waited. Karo could turn her head, but not far enough to see where he was, or what he was about to do. The cuffed hands saw to that.

'Tell me your name,' Angeli suggested.

There was no answer, but then he wasn't expecting one.

'You killed the *WeGuard*, knifed him in the Doge's own throne room. How did you get in there? What were you doing in the Palazzo?'

She didn't answer those, either. A kid from the Suites, a murderer, locked in his precinct. And with all the answers Angeli needed to prove he could make Vice Questore locked away in her head. The little bitch wasn't leaving him many options. Had she been anyone else, he'd have turned her over already.

One hand, then another rested on her shoulders, lightly. The girl didn't flinch, didn't even look round, though every muscle in her upper body tensed at his touch. Casually, as if he wasn't really thinking about it, Angeli dropped one hand to her small left breast, cupping it through the paper of her sweat top, feeling her nipple harden under his fingers. Fear, not lust: he knew the difference. Everyone in the NVPD always did.

Not a sound left her lips, not even when his fingers twisted, viciously.

She was rigid now, anger and fear, every muscle locked. He could take it further, Angeli knew that and so did she. Alternatively, he could just beat it out of her. For a second, Angeli almost considered it. But that wasn't the answer. He didn't know how he knew, but he did.

Releasing her nipple, he walked back round her shaking body and sank tiredly into his own chair, which at least had a seat. She was crying, silent sobs. Her face turned away from him.

'Enough already,' Angeli said quietly. The idea of giving her back, letting CySat finish the case was getting more attractive by the day. He'd been brought in, offered the post of Vice Questore if he could solve the case – and now he had. It wasn't his fault they wouldn't like the answer.

Let them get their own confession.

That CySat wouldn't forgive Angeli for doing his job went without saying. No good work goes unpunished, or so the proverb said.

'Look,' said Angeli. He touched a Matsui panel inset into the cell table, switching off the overhead vid recorder. 'Help me on this one.' Switching off was a bluff, of course. Angeli had a private back-up vid, a fly-speck lens set into the wall that ran all the time, without an on/off option. It had fuck-all to do with the NVPD: the grabs uploaded into his private dataA/C, time-clocked and click-tracked. Insurance in case NVPD ever decided Angeli needed to be framed.

'Tell me your name.'

The girl said nothing. Didn't even seem to notice he'd turned off the vid. If anything, her heart-shaped face was even more impressively impassive than before.

'This isn't helping either of us,' Angeli said, ignoring her silence. 'Tell me your name and I'll see if I can get you bail. Maybe let you go home to your family. I mean, they must be worried by now.'

That got a reaction, finally. Her smile was bitter, as if the idea of going back to her family was a sick joke. Perhaps it was.

Sweet fuck, Angeli thought suddenly. He could hit himself. She was here because she needed to be. This was her choice. Angeli didn't figure in this at all. 'He knows where you are, doesn't he?' Angeli asked suddenly, as everything tumbled into place. 'Your father knows, *everything* . . .' Which was more than Angeli did.

The word was stacked up between them.

She didn't deny it, but then in three whole days she hadn't denied anything. Hadn't admitted anything, either. Which didn't mean it wasn't all true. All she'd done was watch the fucking clock.

'Look,' Angeli said, as he pushed himself up off his chair, walking back round the table to stand near Karo. Only this time he stood where she could see him and he kept his hands behind his back. He'd got it right, and she knew it.

'I needed to know where that door was,' said Angeli. 'How you got past the wall. Okay, it was a nasty trick. And I probably shouldn't have sent Paco in either . . .' Angeli shrugged, crossly. 'Fuck it, he'll manage.'

'He's already dead,' the girl said suddenly.

Angeli looked shocked. 'Paco? You psychic?'

She scowled impatiently, thick black curls swinging into her eyes. 'I don't need to be. That's standing orders, if outsiders come down those tunnels. Of course, I'm not meant to know . . .'

'Whose orders? Angeli demanded.

The girl looked at him in disbelief. As if only an idiot could ask that question. Angeli could see her reassessing him and he didn't like it one little bit.

'CySat,' Her eyes raked over him, filled with contempt. 'Why do you think *WeGuard* are there?'

'To protect newVenice from outside attack.'

It sounded lame, even as he said it. newVenice had been born with more weaponry than most countries. The JCIT deck had been upgraded to full Turing capacity within fifty years. These days, it interfaced with humans via a standard Gibson link only when it needed to. Otherwise it just got on with its job. There was nothing *WeGuard* could do the JCIT couldn't manage infinitely faster, not to mention more efficiently.

'Okay, then,' Angeli shrugged. 'To protect the Doge . . .'

Karo's expression soured, but there was real sadness in it. 'They didn't, though, did they?' Her eyes met his and Angeli suddenly realized she hadn't heard the news. Well, she wouldn't have done, would she? He'd kept her locked up in the precinct for the last three days.

'The Doge is back,' he told her.

This time Karo looked genuinely shocked. 'Not possible. We don't have cloning insurance, it's not allowed under CySat rules.'

'No,' Angeli shook his head. 'Not a clone. The real Doge. He's been found.'

There was a silence, as much as there was ever silence in the levels. A Niponshi airship hooted overhead, on its way to unload at Arsenale. A heavy thud of HiDub echoed up from a wolfbar two levels below, solid bass riffs carried along the bulkhead of what was once an old P & O cruiser. But there *was* silence, at least between them, and Angeli had the feeling the girl was fighting her disbelief, and losing.

'The Doge is dead,' Karo said flatly. 'Shot through the head. I saw his body.' Dead? In spite of his NVPD conditioning, despite everything he'd seen or done, Angeli still felt sick with shock. He realized, only too well, how long was the list of things she wasn't telling him, but he ignored all that, trying to wrap his mind round what she *was* saying.

'He was gunned down, at the Palazzo Ducale, by a crazed *WeGuard* . . . It was an accident, I think. There was a screen-induced fit trig . . .' Karo stumbled over her words. She was crying now. 'You know what happened next.'

Angeli looked at her, thought of a palazzo kid taking molywire against a trained guard. The odds were stacked in the wrong direction. He found it hard to believe Karo could come out alive, never mind win.

'The Doge? He was your family?' Angeli asked. That was the only thing Angeli could think of, that blind filial fury had somehow given her an edge.

'Of course not. Aurelio was an Orsela.' Karo said it as if Angeli should know what that meant. But he didn't, so through her tears Karo told him.

'I'm Karo DiOrchi, Aurelio belonged to the other side. But I knew . . .' She stumbled over her words and Angeli suddenly realized it wasn't Aurelio she was crying for, it wasn't even for herself.

'Did you know Razz?' Karo asked him.

Angeli shook his head. The name rang slight bells from an old CySat documentary, nothing more.

'Aurelio's bodyguard. We were . . .' Silence stretched between them as Karo searched for the right word without finding it.

'. . . Friends.' Angeli finished for her.

Karo nodded, sadly. 'She taught me to fight, Razz did. She taught me most things. The *WeGuard* was meant, I think the *WeGuard* was meant . . . ' Karo stopped, looking at him, her eyes holding his, searching. Angeli had no idea if she found what she was looking for.

'They're not there to protect the Doge from assassins,' said Karo flatly. 'That was Razz's job.' Her face was hard, angry: but at the turmoil going on inside, not with him. 'They exist to protect us from you.'

Angeli said nothing. He wished he was shocked, but he wasn't. His uncle had said as much once, long before, in the weeks before he got himself killed. Others said it too, but they were ignorable, dusted-out, lunatic or drifting.

'Look,' Karo said. 'We were staying with Aurelio when he was shot.' She caught Angeli's look of disbelief and reddened. 'What do you know about CySat's Council?' Karo demanded fiercely. 'It was our turn.'

'What do I know?' Angeli spread his hands. 'Less than nothing.'

'There's a war,' Karo said. 'Polite, well-mannered but still vicious. CySat's at war with itself, has been for as long as anyone can remember. My father is Count Ryuchi, he represents one faction, Count Orsela represents the other. Neither has enough votes to make final decisions. So they *negotiate*.' She made the word sound like the insult it was.

Ryuchi/DiOrchi/Orsela. Those were names he knew. As well as anyone on the levels knew them, from sites and newsfeeds, names that hinted at power without needing to spell it out. Everyone knew the Council existed, few knew who they were. Or rather, on the levels few knew who they were; but this girl did, she came from where the Council came from, and she'd ended up behind bars in his precinct.

And yet, something still didn't match up. No, Angeli amended that, there were a dozen things didn't match up, but the main one concerned the Doge.

'Look,' Angeli said. 'About the Doge . . . It's not like anyone tells us anything anyway. But the Doge is alive. I've seen him on the evening newsfeed.'

'Stock footage,' Karo insisted. 'Or a Lotusmorph'

'No,' Angeli was adamant. 'We're not stupid, we know a morph when we see one. This is His Serene Highness, Aurelio, Doge of newVenice.'

The girl was looking at him in bemusement. 'You don't believe that stuff?' Karo asked at last, her dark eyes never leaving his. And despite his silence, she seemed to be waiting on his answer. Even chained to a chair and dressed in paper she was in control, Angeli thought bitterly.

Did he believe? In Izanami, Cú Chulaind, Santa Passionata. In loyalty to a child who'd never even heard of him. Did Angeli believe that stuff? Not too long ago, he'd have said yes without having to think about it. Now, after this? Absent-mindedly he told her cuffs to unlock.

'Yes,' Angeli said at last. 'I suppose I still do.' His voice was gentler than she'd heard him use before and his NVPD rasp less obvious. 'Not blindly, but yes. And I know he's powerless, a figurehead. That CySat controls newVenice . . .'

'You're telling me,' Karo said bleakly, then added, 'But he's not powerless, at least not on paper.'

'No?'

'No, but it is complex. The Doge ceases to rule at the point he reaches puberty. A panel of doctors is always on hand to identify that moment. Imagine it . . .'

Angeli couldn't.

'The baby born closest to that moment becomes the new Doge. You know what? Six babies were born within five minutes of the last child hitting puberty. That's natural births. Not a Caesarean among them, not allowed. Aurelio's mother got it to within three seconds.

'Boys get carried full term, girls are put out to womb unless they're like my mother . . . She carried me. For all the good it did her. You know what else? My aunt has an AI devoted exclusively to identifying the optimal point of conception for Aurelio's replacement.'

'Then why hasn't Aurelio been replaced, if he's dead?' Angeli demanded, asking the obvious question. At least, it seemed obvious to him.

Karo shrugged. 'Maybe because there's never been a Doge assassinated before. Or else the Council's going to wait until the levels have been cut free. Just think of it, whoever wins the power struggle can select the next Doge.'

Cut free, thought Angelo.

Karo nodded. 'Yeah, should have been on yesterday's incoming tide.'

Angeli didn't know what to worry about first. He decided to start with the fact he hadn't spoken aloud. Which meant . . .

'Psi,' said Karo, then grinned at his look of disbelief. 'So I lied,' she said. 'Sue me.'

Angeli groaned. All he fucking needed. He didn't know if she was natural or rewired, or even how to tell. The CySoaps were riddled with *psi* characters, and there were endless *alt* shows on the newsfeed on viral rewiring, bioClay implants, neural-frequency modulation, but he didn't know how much of it was true.

'All true,' the girl assured him. 'But I'm a natural. My father's enhanced, but *Psi* genes are dominant on my mother's side. Always have been, right back to Passion.'

She said the founder's name like it meant nothing, as if Santa Passionata was just some distant great aunt of hers. Which she was, Angeli realized. But if she was *psi* . . . ?

'How come I fell for that shithead scam with the subway?'

But Angeli knew the answer even before Karo told him. His NVPD helmet was optixed up for sound, night-sight and m/w-video.

Karo didn't deny it. 'Digital scribble, complex fooler loops . . . ' Karo shook her head. 'There's a knack to getting past the static. I don't have it.'

Angeli was trying to think back, over the things he'd thought while she was around. Rather too many of them concerned her breasts. And those that didn't touched closely on his uncle. Sweet Jesus.

Reaching into a Braun cooler beside his chair, Angeli pulled out two Tsing-taos. Karo took hers without comment.

'So, the Doge is really dead?'

Karo nodded.

'Why cut the levels free?' Angeli had to ask.

By the time she'd finished answering, Angeli wished he hadn't bothered. It's hard to sit and listen while someone tells you you're widely blamed for spreading disease, living like pigs and breeding like animals. And it seemed that, if Count Orsela and Karo's father Count Ryuchi agreed on one thing, it was that matters couldn't continue as they were.

What they did disagree on was what came next. Orsela had won, and his plan was to send in the *WeGuard* and re-establish a proper rule of law.

'I am the law,' Angeli insisted and was appalled to see pity appear in the girl's dark eyes. She smiled, sadly.

'You keep the peace, Orsela wants rule of law. There's a huge difference.'

It seemed that there was, too. CySat wanted taxes, repatriation of illegals, the closure of black clinics, an end to overcrowding. Those left behind would come under direct rule from CySat, housed in projects to the north of the city. The levels themselves would be cut away, then sunk, to free the edge of newVenice. A city open to the sea. 'That's how it was meant to be,' Karo insisted.

'What about the Council?' Angeli asked. 'Is that how it was meant to be?' He watched her, but for once Karo couldn't meet his eyes. Just as he thought, it wasn't only life on the levels that had looped into *abort, retry, fail* . . .

'Your father want the same?' Angeli asked.

'No,' The girl shook her head, black hair rustling against the paper shoulders of her sweats. 'He wanted to cut the levels free, let you take your chances . . . It's a better offer than being overrun by the *WeGuard*,' she said defiantly, watching Angeli's expression. 'You'd have water purifiers, solar power, slop boxes to compile food . . .'

'Weapons?' Angeli asked. 'AIs, Datacores? Comsats?' Flattened beneath his fingers, the Tsing-tao tube was being rapidly folded into tighter and tighter squares. Metal was cutting Angeli's fingers but he was too shocked to notice. 'How long do you think we'd last,' he demanded, 'without defences?'

Karo didn't answer. Instead she drained the last drop from her can, crushed it easily and tossed it into a recyc bin. The bin coughed, swallowed and the alloy scattered into its basic atoms, ready for reuse.

Angeli watched, thinking. Part of him wanted to do things the traditional way, call Orsela and offer him Count Ryuchi's murdering daughter on a plate. Then offer to help Orsela clear out the levels, in return for that post as Vice Questore. That was exactly what his uncle would have done: ream her out, then hope Count Ryuchi didn't find out his child had been raped, at least not until the Count was too weakened to do anything about it.

'But you're not him, are you?' Karo said. She was touching his wrist, her fingers cool against his skin. 'And you didn't, did you?' said Karo. 'Which isn't to say you didn't seriously think of it.' Her voice was brittle, out of balance. She'd just caught his next thought and she didn't like that either.

Angeli looked at her. 'Can you turn it off?'

The girl nodded, lifting her fingers away from his wrist.

She was right, he wasn't his uncle, never had been. Angeli didn't have the bastard's strength, guts or certainty. But he had street smarts and there was more than one way to get leverage.

'It was an accident, wasn't it? The guard killing Aurelio.'

Karo didn't, couldn't answer. Maybe she didn't know, but Angeli wouldn't count on it. Not if the look in her eyes was anything to go by.

'They were after Razz. You know that, don't you?'

If Karo didn't, she did now. 'Razz taught you how to fight, to kill,' said Angeli. 'And you killed her assassin.'

'Razz taught me everything,' Karo said simply.

'Then help me stop CySat cutting free the levels. Do something to really avenge her death,' Angeli suggested.

'I already did,' said Karo, and then she told him about Jericho Fever and Izanami, and how she'd infected the Dragon.

[The Gods In The Machine]

What Razz needed was a SAIR SanD zapper. Because, when you get down to it, there's nothing like a 2 million-volt electromagnetic field for fucking over an enemy vehicle's electronics.

Some nickel/aluminium foil would be neat, too.

A new vehicle was the other thing she needed. She'd have preferred a hover, preferably a Honda, but she'd already destroyed one of those and the only other one in the area was after her. In fact, they'd been playing cat and mouse for seventy-six hours but that game was about to end.

Razz was almost out of gas. There'd been one tank slung under the mission's huge 4 × 4, two extra bolted to its side as spares. Useful but deadly. The Colonel didn't need missiles when one shot from a Browning could blow Razz to fragments.

So she'd had to ditch her spare canisters, burying them under a cairn of stone deep enough to hold back the sun's heat. Razz wanted to be able to collect them, not have the bastards explode as the noon temperature topped 100 degrees.

But then the Colonel blew them, to let Razz know they'd been found and hey, she was almost out of gas . . . That wasn't how Razz would have done it. She'd have hid up by the buried supplies and waited. Gone for a turkey shoot.

But that wasn't how this guy worked. Though whether he'd come after her, the dead priest or the Doge, Razz couldn't quite work out. The Doge, probably.

Razz knew it was the Colonel, at least she did now. She'd found that out yesterday morning when she watched him glide to the top of a dune on a cushion of red dust, climb arrogantly out of his hover and stand – legs spread, arms behind his back – staring down into the rubble wilderness of the red desert below, his eyes hidden behind ×8 RayBans.

He should have seen her. Razz was there, the blond boy cradled fretfully in her arms as she tried to hold him tight, stop him from running. But the Colonel missed them. Either that or he was toying with Razz. Not a thought Razz wanted to deal with.

But then, it was amazing how many thoughts she didn't want to deal with these days, how many decision trees she couldn't be arsed to climb. Nothing like getting pinned down in the desert by a lunatic for simplifying life's options, Razz thought bitterly.

'Move it,' Razz told the boy. But he didn't shift, just looked hurt.

It was almost dawn and the boy was shivering with cold. Stars glittered down at them like cat's eyes. On a dark clear night the Kalahari was one of the coldest places on the planet, and the boy still had on a thin hospital shirt with no coat.

'Come on, honey,' Razz said, more gently this time.

Aurelio just stared at her, his blue eyes full of tears. *Oh well,* Razz thought tiredly, *at least tears should wash out the sand and grit*.

'We need to move.' Razz insisted.

'Please . . .'

Razz shook her head. She didn't need to ask *please* what. She knew. Please stop running, stop moving, stop burning up your nerves. Most of all, stop taking it out on me. Combat tension: it wasn't a side of her Aurelio had ever seen.

'No,' said Razz. 'We keep going.'

'Why?' the boy asked plaintively. 'Where are we going?'

It was a good question, one without a good answer. He believed she was Razz now, just not the one he remembered. It wasn't only that this version was younger or didn't have her old silver skin, there were subtler differences, though Razz was too tired, too rushed to remember what they were. The sun was rising in long horizontal streaks of red, and they were almost out of time. All the clocks were heading towards zero.

'Twigs and branches,' Razz demanded, ignoring the hopeless way he pulled himself up from the cold rocks and went to search. An hour from now, that sun would be so hot, black rocks would char the worn soles of his cheap sandals.

Razz needed the sun's heat to make their next run. The Geep didn't have asynchronous, round-the-clock thermal camouflage. Run it at night and the engine stood out like a cancer on a CT scan. And Razz was willing to bet Colonel Carlos had an expensive little spySat link in that hover of his, not to metion asynch thermal. The Geep, of course, made do with old-fashioned daytime shields.

Run under normal temperatures, the ceramic sensors on the front fender could analyse upcoming ground heat, then match it to thermal panels on the Geep's roof and hood. The system was twenty years out of date, but it still went a long way to explaining why they were still alive.

Only problem for Razz was that what constituted normal daytime temperature in the mind of the Geep's original designer fell inside a twenty-five minute window, first thing in the morning and last thing at dusk. At least it did out in the Namibian desert. Twenty-five-minutes.

The boy was back with his meagre collection of twigs.

'I'm sorry,' Aurelio said, 'there isn't very much.'

'It's a desert,' said Razz and the boy smiled sadly.

'You could give me up,' he said. It sounded like he meant it.

'No way.' Razz didn't even stop to think about her answer. 'They'd kill me anyway,' she added crossly, seeing the doubt in his eyes. 'We're better off together.'

Aurelio knew it was a lie. He knew that Razz knew, but the girl didn't push it. Of course she'd be better off without him. But then, as Razz kept reminding herself, she'd taken the job what seemed like years ago, back when she was some burnt-out fuckhead and he was a sad and spoilt small boy.

It was up to her to get him back to newVenice, to keep him alive.

Razz tied the twigs loosely to the rear of her Geep, so they just brushed the ground. The main advantage a hover has over a 4 × 4 when it comes to desert warfare is that hovers don't leave tracks, not clear ones anyway, just dancing sand devils.

But a 4 × 4 with brushed tracks ends up looking much like a passing hover to anyone who comes after. Razz had no idea if it was working. All she knew was she'd been hiding for what felt like days and Colonel Carlos still hadn't found them. All the same, Razz was attritioned out. She was a realist. It wasn't just her Geep 4 × 4 that was running on empty.

'Into the Geep,' Razz told the boy, her voice harsh with sand-burn, lack of water and fear. The sun was almost up, they were out of gas. The decision was making itself for her.

So she told the boy. She felt she owed Aurelio that.

'Honey, we can't keep running, we've got to attack.' Razz reached under the dashboard and ripped it away, revealing handfuls of silicon and cable. The Geep had a suicide-destruct, all APVs did: using it was usually better than falling into the hands of an enemy. Like everything else, the s/d option was open to serious abuse. At least, Razz hoped it was.

Sorting through the cables, Razz swapped a couple, reset three jumpers, borrowed the internal clock from an MS Routesoft console and began to knit the dash back together. For the first time in days, Razz felt, if not happy, then calm. Which wasn't necessarily good news.

Splicing the clock chip to the front fender's ceramic sensors, Razz reset the sensors using the Geep's fingerboard, pulling crude code out of her memory. If it worked, if she hadn't been too drunk at that *Last Boer* bar to remember the details properly, the chip should run from five to count zero, then self-destruct, but only when it came within three paces of the hover.

As theories went it was a beaut. But knowing her recent luck, the Geep would probably blow the first time they passed a boulder with a high enough metal content.

Time to roll. For a second, Razz considered leaving the boy

where he was, putting him in the shadow of a rock and just driving away. If everything worked she'd come back for him. If it didn't, she'd be dead but at least he wouldn't.

No, Razz told herself crossly. He'd only die of thirst or heat-stroke. Same choice. Anyway, she needed him with her. These days, Aurelio was her reason, her driving force. Maybe the only thing that stood between fighting on and squatting in the dust to die. Which was what she'd wanted to do when that bastard blew her gas canisters.

'Let's go.' Razz stuffed the cabling back inside the dash and hit the ignition. The hazard diode for low fuel flashed in a slow steady rhythm, but Razz ignored it as she pulled out from the deep gulley and headed north, towards a spot where she'd last seen the Colonel.

Survival depends on timing. Razz understood that. But she understood, too, that sometimes it's just down to luck. And luck was with Razz. At least, it was at the start. Her Geep topped the edge of a barren volcanic crater and there, on the other side, maybe two klicks away, was the Colonel's camp: two inflatable huts tucked in under the crater's lip. The man hadn't even bothered to throw up thermoCam.

Razz couldn't see any defences either, but they'd be there. Trip wire and screamers maybe, or a couple of wide-angle, laser-tripped Claymores. If she got really unlucky he'd have seeded the area with Ghengis XIV crab mines. An inch of crawling six-legged high explosive, programmed to home in on enemy body heat. Bastards had green shells of infra-red proof chitin, not that it mattered a fuck. She didn't have infra-red goggles to look out for them anyway.

The Colonel hadn't bothered to hide, which meant he didn't consider it necessary. And that upset Razz. She didn't like not being taken seriously: it upped her aggression. Razz felt he should have known that.

She had the sun at her back. Always come out of the sun, Miyamoto Musashi had said. That was, if you couldn't come out of the darkness. And Razz couldn't do that, not without decent thermal camouflage.

Backing up, with Aurelio hunched in a neophrene bucket seat beside her, the stolen Sig Sauer rifle cradled in his small hands, Razz dipped behind the crater's outer rim and hit accelerate. But all that happened was the 4 × 4's skidded, worn and toothless treads failed to bite into the loose gravel.

The Geep tipped precariously and Razz spun her steering wheel, moving into the skid. Only to find herself sliding straight down the crater's outside slope.

'Shit, shit.' Pounding her foot on the brake, Razz pulled the Geep to a long, slow halt. Behind her was a gravel scar dramatic enough to be seen ten klicks away. 'Try again,' she told herself sadly. It was the politest thing she'd said to herself in years.

Razz flicked the ignition, pushed accelerate and held her breath as the Geep began to climb back up the crater's outside edge. Then all she had to do was drive round the edge without being seen.

It took twenty minutes to reach a point Razz reckoned was just the other side of where the Colonel had his camp. Twenty minutes of being a sitting target, during which the sun began to hardbake the ground. Two diodes now flashed on the Geep's dash. The rapid beat of her fuel warning light, and a tolerance-failure diode for thermal camouflage. They weren't just pushing against the window of safety, they'd punched right through it.

'Okay,' Razz said. 'Get out now and hide, over there.' She pointed to an outcrop of lava that stuck through the red earth. The shadow under its overhang was as black as night and half as safe. Too bad.

'What if you don't come back?' Aurelio said plaintively.

'I will,' said Razz. Then laughed grimly at the boy's expression. She wouldn't have accepted it at his age either.

'I'm going over the ridge,' she said swiftly. 'To point the Geep at them. I'll come straight back.' Like most impossible things, it sounded almost true if you said it fast enough. If you ignored the flashing diodes, the heat radiating up off the Geep's hood like a thermal beacon. Not to mention the shakes that racked her fingers or the rank signature of fear that rose from them both like old sweat.

For someone who'd made a living looking death in the face, Razz was only too aware that she was finding this tougher than she should. Everything turned on whether Colonel Carlos Don Carlos wanted them alive, and if he wanted it bad enough to let her Geep come in close. Of course, if he scanned the vehicle for human life and found none, then her plan was buggered anyway . . .

Having hidden Aurelio under a ledge, Razz clambered back into her seat, set the cruise control, straightened up the steering wheel and ripped the cover off the Geep's fusebox. A metal blade across the electronic wheel-lock and all the Geep could manage was straight ahead anyway.

What had she got to lose? Except Aurelio. And Razz would lose him anyway unless she did something fast . . . Half sitting in her seat, Razz stayed with the Geep as it crested the lip of the crater and, as it slowed to breast the top, she stepped neatly from the moving vehicle and grabbed for its swinging door.

It was close, but Razz caught it, slamming the door shut with a thud that echoed off the far wall of the vast crater – the desert's silence had some uses. At the same time, Razz hit the ground, rolling in under a large rock.

Below her, two soldiers bolted out of a tent, alerted by the slamming door. One raised a rifle to his shoulder, squeezing off a shot that whined past the Geep, burying itself in the earth near where Razz was crouched.

Terrific: she was in a direct line of fire. But it was the only shot that headed her way, the second soldier dropping his g2g launcher, missile unfired, at the first shouted order from the Colonel.

'Sweet fucking Nazarene,' Razz thought happily, as the Colonel watched the Geep approaching. He thought they were coming in, surrendering. Seeing him standing there, Razz regretted not putting a white flag on the comms whip. It might have let the vehicle get in closer.

Razz was holding her breath, busy watching the Geep slowly decend the rim towards the tent, when feet crunched on gravel behind her.

'Wait!' Aurelio shouted, as she flicked round, molyknife at the ready. When he was certain she wasn't going to hurt him, he slid into the depression beside her. He was carrying her rifle.

'Wanted to see if you were okay . . .'

'Get down,' Razz ordered, but not harshly. She was busy willing the Geep to keep its line, willing the Colonel not to fire, willing . . .

An end to it all, if she were honest. She was tired, her face belonged to someone else. Drugs no longer worked. Sex was empty. The world around her was a mess. Disparate, dissolute, pitiful in its despair. Only Aurelio kept her pinned to wherever the hell it was she was.

The Geep was fifty paces from the edge of the Colonel's camp when Razz got the first indication her luck had just run out. A soldier, screaming his head off as he ran, hurtled towards the Colonel, holding a flat box above his head, waving it frantically. The bastard had a Sanyo L/S scanner. For a second, Razz wished she'd trapped some desert animal, anything at all, a buzzard, a sackful of meerkats, just something to give a positive reading, however odd. But it was too late to wish.

Instead she grabbed the Sig Sauer from Aurelio, squeezed off a shot, trigger finger slippery with sweat as she dropped the screaming soldier in his tracks.

'Stupid,' she told herself, 'stupid shot.' She should have taken out the Colonel but it was already too late. Colonel Carlos had hit the dirt at the sound of her first shot, talking rapidly into his throat mike. Razz snapped off two more rounds and watched him roll away from their ricochet but he was too far away and Razz's hands were shaking too badly to make the bullets count.

Stupid, stupid. Instinct and training cut in as Razz made herself do nothing for three whole seconds, counting each one off like the countdown to eternity, so slow the life of everyone she'd ever met could have scanned in front of her eyes.

It was in those three seconds that a g2g missile was launched, its tracking system locking instantly onto the lumbering Geep. The vehicle had no anti-lock system and even if it had, no one was inside to initiate the sequence. Her vehicle blew apart in an orange fireball that made glass of the silicon-rich desert floor.

'Fuck it.' Razz wasn't panicked any more, just angry and hopeless. Risks had to be taken. And all risks have probability against them, or they wouldn't be risks . . . Razz could recite the Langley mantra as well as any fifteenth-century Zen warrior could recite his *koan*.

But it didn't help. They were fucked. On the run, out of water and with no food, in a desert that could melt rubber or desiccate flesh as swiftly as any furnace. Already the Colonel and his remaining mercenary were sweeping up the slope towards them, hover engine whining with the climb. The craft carried Colt pulse rifles, laser-sighted. Maybe Colt p/Rs couldn't drill through rock in quite the way the ads on CySat suggested, but it was a close-run thing.

Well, she wasn't going to let the Colonel take Aurelio. 'Honey,' Razz told the boy, 'I'm so sorry.' She raised the Sig Sauer – but Aurelio was busy grinning, staring at someone over her shoulder.

Razz flipped round, hard and fast, refocusing her rifle, then froze as time stopped dead. When it jerked back into being, the Sig Sauer was at her side and Aurelio was sitting cross-legged in front of a bare-breasted old woman who was smiling at something the boy had just said.

The crater was gone and with it the Colonel and his hover. They were sitting in a small cave, in front of a fire, and the air was thick with wood smoke. The woman nodded politely to Razz and held out her hand in a very Western gesture. When she spoke it was in a Boston accent redolent of old families and older money. 'I'm Nzigé. You were looking for me . . .'

'You're American?' Razz asked.

The old woman smiled, 'No, I'm a god. Not yet the same thing.' Her voice was mocking, but not unpleasantly so. 'Actually, I'm several gods.' And as she spoke her sunken features changed slowly. Until a short, slightly flat-faced, soberly-dressed Japanese woman sat before her, hair straight and black, parted neatly in the middle. Around her neck was an intricate spearhead, hung from a thread of light.

'Izanami,' Aurelio said.

The woman smiled. 'Sasumi,' she corrected the boy. She turned to Razz. 'You have something for me?'

Wordlessly, Razz unwrapped the wafer-thin fear-feather she'd taken from Alex and, taking care not to touch it, passed it to the Japanese woman. Sasumi nodded, looking relieved. If a goddess can look relieved.

'Good,' she said. 'Now we can start to take down the walls. Karo will be happy.'

'Karo?' Razz asked.

Sasumi nodded. 'I'm sorry, it wasn't ever Alex, you know. Karo borrowed your memories, Alex was just in them. Your job's over,' she added. 'You can rest, if you want . . .'

'We're dead,' Aurelio told Razz sadly. 'I did wonder.'

'Dead?' Razz said slowly. Maybe that was why she felt so stupid.

'I'm information,' said Aurelio. 'At least, that's what Sasumi says. And the Colonel is a data protection unit . . .'

'And then what am I?' Razz asked.

Aurelio looked at her. 'Oh, you're Karo's virus.'

[Dar as-sin'a/House Of Industry]

'Vampyres,' Karo said in horror. For a killer she was easily shocked.

Angeli nodded. Karo was right: there were vampyres, wolfBoys too. Out in the open, where morning sunlight reflected from pink-bricked walls. But then, when Sabine spoke the levels listened, and it was to Sabine that Angeli had turned. Getting Karo to crypt a call through to her lair.

They came, drawn by the rumour of riots, of war . . .

Karo wore Angeli's second jacket, unbuttoned, stripped of NVPD insignia, and a pair of NVPD boots. He could hear the whispering, feel the strange glances, but Angeli shrugged them off. The girl could hardly go out in paper sweats, could she? Beneath the jacket, she wore a white crop top. Black Levis covered her legs. Both came from a market, free. Angeli just pointed. That was all it ever took.

They met Sabine, as the elderly kohl-eyed vampyre suggested, under the shadow of *Arsenale*'s huge carved inner gate. And as Sabine also suggested, she brought her brood with her.

Dar as-sin'a was the city dock's official name. But everyone called it *Arsenale*. The original Venetian *Dar as-sin'a* had been a production line for wooden ships, able to turn out a whole galley in a hundred days, or so Karo told Angeli. Now, of course, ships grew themselves to patented, carefully crafted templates and cargo arrived at newVenice by air anyway, slung in pods below vast helium-filled Niponshi airships.

At each end of a wide, 450-yard-long canal known as Arsenale Cut, laser-cut marble lions stood guard over huge Renaissance gateways. The lions were fake, of course. So were the great marble gates. Perfect in every detail, but still fake. The warm water in the wide canal was real enough, though. It stank and lapped sluggishly against the canal side. This was where Niponshi airships dropped their pods, ready to be passed through electrified inner gates to be taken by canal into the city proper. Except that these pods wouldn't get that far.

And both inner and outer gates were no longer electric . . . Not just dead, but waiting already open. Swung back, ready to let them stream in from the levels. Hardened titanium deadbolts withdrawn into their sheaths, the gates free to swing in the hot breeze. If any wind, hot or not, could have moved such a weight of metal, ceramic and protein/polymer mesh.

At first Angeli thought that was Sabine's doing. That she'd found a way of disrupting the current or else tricked the locks. But Sabine denied all knowledge of it. Though that meant nothing. Besides which, Sabine's smile was sly. And something in her green eyes said that if she wasn't exactly lying, then she wasn't telling the truth either.

The vampyres of San Michele sacked the pods coldly, quickly, cleanly. And because Sabine's brood rarely strayed from their own deep sets, Angeli had no idea how many of the dreadlocked, white-faced girls there were. Silence surrounded the brood as tightly as their ceremonial black cloaks. Like the drakuls, the vampyres were a race apart, genome-licensed. The fifty who sacked Arsenale might have been them all, or this could have been a fraction of the true number. Angeli had no way of knowing.

But the green-eyed, red-haired old woman walking towards him knew only too well. They were hers. And as she navigated the cobbles with the aid of a silver-topped cane, Sabine watched darkly as her brood claimed the Niponshi cargo containers, pulling white kevlar-skinned pods up onto the cobbles to let them stand and drip like giant glistening wasps' eggs. Casually hauling the containers out of the water by hand.

Angeli tried not to think how much strength that took.

If myth lied, and Sabine didn't create her *get* by letting acolytes drink virally-mutated blood (and Angeli seriously doubted it), then no matter, because these albino children were still hers, body, soul and patent rights. Sabine held the patent on toothbuds, on genetically-inherited night-sight, even on induced phobia to sunlight.

In her hand she held a bag of sugared white mice, and each time she popped a mouse into her mouth, it wriggled and squeaked.

Angeli smiled and slapped his electric baton against the leather sides of his boots. He was fifth-generation NVPD; he knew the value of trademarks as well as anyone.

'So,' Sabine said, looking round at the torn-open containers, at the self-chilling boxes of peaches, haunches of venison and p/styrene-wrapped crates of Cuvée Napa. 'Who wants to tell me why we're here?'

She knew, of course. Angeli'd told her already. But Sabine wanted to hear it again. In public. She wanted other people to hear it.

'Tell her,' Karo hissed, pushing Angeli forward through a group of *TripleHelix* regulars who'd gathered round him for safety.

The old vampyre smiled.

'Sabine,' Angeli said. He nodded politely and tried not to flinch as the woman's green eyes examined his face, then looked at the girl beside him.

'Rosso Rispoli's boy,' she said finally. 'I hope you don't take after your uncle.' Angeli opened his mouth, and Sabine held up one hand to silence him, silver rings adorning long, knotted fingers, her black-lacquered nails curled and bent with age.

'It doesn't matter,' she said.

'No,' said Angeli flatly, 'it doesn't.' He fingered the taser in his belt, his eyes not leaving the old woman's hooded face. 'And you?' Angeli asked. Two could play dumb. 'What brings you?'

'Apart from your interesting message?' Sabine's voice mocking his NVPD growl. 'Tell me . . .' She waved her hand at a group from the *TripleHelix* using a Braun laser to slice open a kevlar pod, its skin peeling back from the flame like split fruit. 'You could have done this a hundred years ago. Why do it now?'

'I wasn't born a hundred years ago,' Angeli snapped.

Sabine sighed heavily. 'You know what I mean.'

And she was right, he did know what she meant. So why now, not then? It wasn't a question Angeli could answer. Event horizons? Improbability theory? Divergence fields . . . ?

'Luck,' Sabine said shortly. She snapped her fingers at a kinderwhore who was pulling an antique chair from a pod. 'Napoleon V,' she said to Angeli and beckoned the child over. Patting the faded velvet, Sabine sank into her new chair. Elderly queen, vampyre elder, raddled whore – it was hard to know which was right.

'All three,' Sabine told Angeli, her cold green eyes holding his. She smelt of dusty cloth and old talcum powder. There wasn't much Angeli could say, so he didn't bother.

'They have your boy, you know,' said Sabine suddenly, her voice low but pleasant. She could have been discussing the weather, rather than sitting in the shadow of Arsenale's outer gate watching a filthy child gleefully lance open another Niponshi pod.

'Paco?' Angeli asked. 'He's still alive?' The strangest feeling surged in the NVPD officer's gut. If Angeli hadn't known better, he'd have called it guilt, or relief.

Sabine nodded. 'He makes a good Doge. Paco has . . .' She struggled for the word, ignoring the fact that both Angeli and Karo were staring at her aghast.

'. . . *Simpatico*. He'll do well, if CySat let him live that long. Which they would be well advised to do.' She turned to Karo. 'By now, even your father must realize Paco was the accident waiting to happen. And he was an accident, of course. A whore/suites cross. But you knew that . . .'

Angeli knew nothing of the sort.

Sabine sighed, irritated with his stupidity. 'Systems change, sometimes they mutate, sometimes they change themselves . . .

Elective evolution, something Darwin didn't cover.' Sabine grinned darkly, and Angeli had a nasty feeling she was serious.

'The game gets bored,' Sabine said. 'The Doge is its amusement. Plus CySat need a human face, to keep the levels in check, to keep you compliant.' Sabine's face grew sardonic as she gazed round at the docks, at the split pods, the gyro-cranes ripped off their standings by sheer brute force.

'Well,' she said to Angeli. 'You're an NVPD officer. Do these people look compliant?'

There was little Angeli could say. Equally, it was obvious his input was no longer needed. Karo and Sabine were suddenly eyeing each other up, not aggressively but thoughtfully.

Did *psis* shield their thoughts from each other, Angeli wondered. Could they think faster? Something told him this wasn't the moment to ask. The answer, of course, was yes to both. But they had another trick, also not known to Angeli: *thought splicing*. Like two people simultaneously writing live code for the same CPU, it was fast and messy and its main potentiality was to go badly wrong. But when it worked, it worked.

By the time Angeli had coughed once, tapped his baton against his boots in irritation and begun to open his mouth, the decision had been taken away from him, though neither Sabine nor Karo presented it like that.

But by then no one was talking much anyway. A low grey hover, its bow a fan-shape of fractured stealth surfaces, was prowling up the Grand Canal towards them, the *WeGuard* logo tri-D'd across its cabin in a gold hologram . . .

'Time for you to do your bit,' Sabine told him. She was smiling.

[Lampedusa's Dictum I]

The Doge was cross. He was also hungry, dirty and bored. If he'd wanted to get locked up he'd have stayed around Angeli.

Paco's head hurt, he had the worst hangover he'd ever had and now he knew French burgundy made him sick. Added to which, the silk of his ridiculous suit was stiff with grease from yesterday's CheezeRoyale.

The last real food he'd had.

'At least try,' Paco demanded. The small winged monster sat high on a rock preening itself in a half-hearted fashion. One hooked front claw scratching at purple scales under one wing, scraping away parasites. The LearningCurve division of CySat were pleased with that little bit of code.

If Paco put on the gold headband he was meant to wear, he'd be in there on the floating mountainside with Lucifer's Dragon, ready to battle, but Paco was fed up with the headset and he was fed up with the dragon, too. It was sulking and wouldn't play. Paco wanted to go back to the old days when the Dragon wiped the floor with him first time.

So instead of wearing the headset, Paco looked down on the kitten-sized dragon where it sat in the middle of the old marble-topped Louis Napoleon table, centre stage above a Sony tri-D showunit. And because Paco didn't know the dragon was meant to freeze when the headset wasn't being worn, Paco didn't think it odd that the dragon remained in real time.

Besides, if the dragon wouldn't play, then Paco wanted it to talk, because he had a question for it. Actually he had dozens, from why didn't it just rip the shitty little angel to shreds and have done with it, to where the fuck was everybody. But Paco had another question. A serious question.

Paco wasn't even sure why he was bothering to ask, since no one else had ever been able to answer. But, tugging at his Izanami talisman, he asked his question anyway . . .

'Hey!'

The winged lizard didn't move and it certainly didn't reply but from its sudden stillness Paco was sure it was listening. 'What are the rules?' Paco demanded.

The dragon looked at him as if it didn't believe what it had just heard. 'We fight each other,' it said shortly. 'I win, eventually . . .'

'I know that,' replied Paco crossly. He took an apricot from a vast Italian silver bowl. What he wanted was tacos, but the door was locked, the kitchens shut and no one answered when he pushed the bell. In the last twenty-four hours, he'd eaten more fresh fruit than in his entire life before that. Small wonder he had gut-rot.

'What's the point of a game no one can win?' Paco demanded.

If the dragon hadn't been a three-dimensional fuzzy-logic construct, Paco would have sworn that it grinned at him. Of course, he didn't think of Lucifer's Dragon as a construct at all: the dragon was just the dragon. It wouldn't occur to Paco to question what made some logic systems intelligent and some not, because it never occurred to him that most computers were thick as shit. The dragon, however, had no such illusions. That was one reason it tended to talk only to Izanami or to itself.

'Heard of learning curves?' The dragon asked hopefully.

Paco shook his head.

'Lampedusa's dictum – always change if you want things to remain the same?'

Paco stayed silent, half sulking. He didn't like feeling stupid.

The dragon sighed. It was going to take longer than it thought. 'Lock the door,' the dragon suggested.

'It is locked,' Paco said crossly, getting up to key another random sequence into a numeric keypad on the wall. Nothing worked. The door stayed shut.

'You use the handle,' the dragon said. The boy looked blank and the dragon sighed again, a puff of white smoke curling out of its mouth. 'The metal circle, turn it.'

Paco did, and the door swung open. It was heavier than he expected. And it didn't say anything to him when it opened and shut. Paco shrugged. With all CySat's billions he'd have thought the Count could afford decent doors.

'Now lock it,' suggested the dragon.

Paco stared at the door, looking for a clue. He was still looking when felt his mind swallow the door whole and spread its construction out in his mind. It was simple enough, Paco decided, once you knew what went where.

He decided to think about that.

A second later, there was a click as tumblers fell, and the reinforced door into the Doge's private games room locked at the top, the middle and the bottom. Carved oak laminated onto a sheet of bonded tungsten/polymer micromesh. No one was going to get the door off at its hinges either, given that they were tungsten-cored with a surface designed to refract laser.

It went almost without saying that if Passion hadn't actually commanded them made herself, they were at least constructed to her design.

'Stick on your helmet,' the dragon demanded. And then when Paco looked doubtful, the dragon softened its voice. 'Direct mind interface eats up capacity,' it said quietly. 'I don't have that much spare, not at the moment.'

Reluctantly, not yet understanding a word of it, Paco did as he was told. And gasped as his optic nerve adjusted not to the familiar rocks of the dragon's floating lair, but to a strange, desolate island, fashioned from rusting steel. They were ships, Paco realized. Thousands of near-derelict vessels, different heights, strange colours. Paint peeling back with age from superstructure walls. The decks were buckled, rails bent. A wind blew across the deck but did nothing to relieve the blistering tropical heat.

'Welcome to the true story . . .' said the dragon as Paco stared wildly around him. 'You wouldn't believe the interest we've had.'

[All Bodies Fall With The Same Acceleration . . .]

It was hard to say what *WeGuard* were expecting. Not much, to judge from the fact they had two Chinese soldiers riding shotgun on the approaching hover.

What they got were two shots from Angeli's NVPD-issue Colt that blew them away, flipping the guards off the small Mitzubishi hover before dropping their bodies into the stinking waters of the canal. And another two shots that etched ornate stars into the surface of the gun-turret window.

The Mitsubishi spun 180 degrees and vanished the way it came, through the inner marble gates, retreating into the narrow canyon formed by high, red-stucco warehouse walls, back towards Riva Ca di Dio. Angeli slammed another two shots into the hover's neophrene skirt, and when that failed to do anything, watched the hover retreat around a corner in the narrow feed canal.

'You've just declared war,' Sabine said, glancing between Angeli and a white-faced Karo. 'I hope you realize that . . .' To Karo it felt like stating the obvious.

'I realize,' Angeli said shortly. 'Got any better ideas?'

Sabine smiled: she didn't need them. Without it ever being said, all three knew that Sabine was running this show. Just as surely as she'd always run the *TripleHelix* and God knew how many other bars and brothels. Invisibly, by reputation alone. That was the way with vampyres, Angeli decided. Puppet masters, all of them.

Sabine's silent decision, to let Angeli lead, had nothing to do with his being a man or Karo being little more than a girl. The NVPD officer knew that.

No, it was the cold logic of trademarks. As a member of the NVPD, Angeli's blue uniform commanded the attention of the crowd. Few of the kinderwhores, drakuls or vampyres bothered to look past the kevlar cloth to the man inside.

'Just as well,' Sabine muttered to Karo, who frowned.

'You like him, don't you?' Sabine said in surprise. Taking Karo's hand, the old woman paused, tapping her long black nails on the girl's slim wrist. Listening. Karo blanked her mind and fought down disgust, trying not to notice that Sabine watched her pulse the way a cat watches a bird.

'You should be one of us,' Sabine told her. 'Oh . . . don't look so shocked.' The old woman's laugh was short and brittle. Around Sabine, a few of her brood looked up, curiously. Their hard eyes raking over Karo. The old woman shook her head slightly, and the brood turned away.

'Do you really think your generation is untouched, unaugmented?'

Yes, she did. Karo nodded. And Sabine's answering smile was almost human in its pity.

'Just because you don't have these teeth . . .' Sabine bared her canines. 'Or bioClay implants wiring together both halves of your cortex, doesn't make you natural. No matter what your father likes to think.'

Karo looked puzzled.

'No one alive is untouched,' Sabine said sadly. 'Only the dead are still normal. Think about it, about joining us.'

The young girl looked away, not trusting herself to reply. Instead she concentrated on watching Angeli, sun in his eyes, try to convince the crowd they had to fight CySat. Not just here on the edge, or in the levels, but in the city itself. Angeli wasn't working the crowd to a frenzy, or even playing with it. He was just telling them what he believed to be true – and they listened because he was NVPD.

All the same, to take on CySat . . . Karo shook her head.

'Better now than too late,' Sabine said, before adding, 'if anyone can manage, that boy can.' She stroked her nails lightly across the white underside of Karo's wrist, making no pretence of not caressing the blood that flowed beneath her skin. 'You have a strong pulse, a good heart. You could live here for a long time . . .'

'If this fails, no one will live,' Karo said sharply, grabbing back her hand. Her voice was shrill, her dark eyes angry. But her fury didn't last, not in the face of Sabine's amused smile.

'Life/death?' Sabine shrugged, with the calculated insouciance of someone who'd chosen both at once. 'But if I were you, I'd think about my offer . . .'

A middle-aged tattooed rent boy cheered, drunkenly, as the two bodies Angeli'd blown off the hover finally bobbed back to the surface. His almost-empty bottle of Mouton Rothschild arced into the dark water with a splash, nearly hitting one of the dead *WeGuard*. Others began to throw bottles, peaches, beer tubes, whatever was nearest until a barrage rained down on the sodden, broken bodies. But from her gilded chair Sabine had already picked two unwilling Lascars to swim out and bring her back the corpses.

Red scarfs wrapped tight round their shaved heads, heavy gold earrings, curved knives stuck in thick leather belts, the Lascars looked deadly. But one look at Sabine's haunted face, her ivory-yellow fangs unsheathed under her top lip, and they dived into the murky water anyway.

Both imagined Sabine wanted the bodies for food. Pretty bizarre, Sabine thought, for people who drank blood from slaughtered chickens. Anyway, she didn't eat meat, she just knew Angeli wanted the rifles still hanging from their pulse packs.

One thing you could say for Heckler & Koch, Angeli thought, as he checked the read-outs on a pulse rifle still wired-in to a dead guard's belt, the company knew how to make weapons that lasted. Though it probably helped that it was the marine-assault model Angeli was admiring.

With the *WeGuard*'s weapons, that gave Angeli his own Colt, the two H&K pulse rifles, and whatever anyone in the crowd might be carrying. It took the crowd a second to realize just what Angeli was asking, and when they did most gaped at him in disbelief.

Weapon-carrying was a capital offence, at least in theory. Having learnt for years to keep their weapons hidden from the NVPD officer, his uncle and grandfather, the crowd was suddenly being asked to produce them openly.

They weren't going to do it. The conditioning was just too strong. Angeli would still have been shuffling and looking worried if Karo hadn't have stepped up beside him.

'This is an emergency,' she said, her voice as clear as a newscast. 'And besides, there's a weapons amnesty. Right?' She glared fiercely at Angeli, who nodded, repeatedly.

'So who's got what?' Karo demanded. She moved towards the crowd, who began dipping hands into their pockets before they fully realized it. Even so, the haul was pitifully small.

Knives mostly, ceramic blades with fractal edges, a handful of Chinese shockblades, a couple of pairs of expanding nanchuks, roughly what Angeli would have expected if he'd ever been brave or stupid enough to organize a strip-search at somewhere like *PolyRiptides*.

Enough to start and finish a Saturday night brawl, other than that . . . Nothing there to take out a hover or three. What they needed were real weapons, and fast.

'Greek fire,' Sabine said loudly. Everyone in her immediate area stopped talking, but no one knew what she meant. Angeli certainly didn't.

'Where are the nearest *vats*?' Sabine knew damn well where they were, but she wasn't going to admit it. She pronounced the word with distaste, as if her brood were too elegant, too sophisticated to eat cultured protein. But they did. On the newVenice levels, retex was as good as it got. Fermentation vats of genetically-amended bacteria turned out complex proteins with absolute precision: from spider's silk and basic polymers to food . . . And on the levels, the choice of food was slop, dried krill or clone-protein. Retextured protein tasted best.

'Over there,' Angeli said, pointing to a round ceramic tank about two storeys high near a small water-filled berth that led off Arsenale Cut. From looking at it, Angeli couldn't work out if the vat was meant to produce slop or plastics. Some of the vats fed *A. eutrophus* bacteria with propionic acid and glucose, to synthesize biodegradable polyester.

'What are we meant to do with it?' Karo asked.

Sabine explained, throwing in two parts history to one part chemical formulae. Her plan was to mix the protein mash with brandy, vodka, olive oil – whatever from the Niponshi pods might burn.

Kinderwhores and tattooed rent boys gutted the white pods together, drakuls and vampyres sliding back through the levels to ransack bars, empty shops, turn markets inside out. The only thing that stopped outright war was a solitary vampyre girl bothering to explain that CySat was about to cut free the levels. Once they believed this, Sabine's brood was allowed to storm back with vodka and flasks of industrial alcohol, followed by new clans, stick-like Edgar Allans, endless metal-head Ishies.

Sabine smiled grimly. 'The olive oil alone would do.' She pointed to casks of Spanish oil being rolled from a pod towards the ceramic tank. 'But then,' her green eyes swept over the swelling crowd, picking out eight different subsets of human, 'pointless self-sacrifice, nothing beats it for binding people together . . .'

Angeli stalked away, black leather boots clashing on the cobbles. A huge drakul, busy rolling the barrel, stopped and moved aside to let Angeli pass. Angeli nodded, as if he expected no less. All the same, he couldn't rid himself of the feeling that Sabine's eyes were drilling into the back of his head. Karo's too, come to that.

'Fuck it,' Angeli muttered, hearing their laughter. That was an unholy alliance if ever he'd met one.

The drakuls tipped oil, vodka and industrial alcohol into an open hatch on top of the fermentation vat. And Angeli had compressed air blown through a vent at the bottom to curdle the

mess. There was glucose too, in an automated feed hopper overhead. Angeli had it broken open. Glucose burnt and it stuck, what
more could he want?

'Pump it up,' Angeli ordered a chalk-faced Edgar Allan, and
watched as the tank was put under pressure. When the read-out
reached danger, and diodes began to flicker frantically, Angeli
told the Edgar Allan to stop. All it took to complete the plan was
a flat kevlar firehose run out from the tank to the edge of the
dock. Sabine's Greek fire was ready.

'Old ideas never die,' she told Karo cheerfully.

And nor, Karo realized, had the original hover, its windscreen
still starred from Angeli's shots. With it were two others, skimming
over the narrow canal leading up from Riva Ca di Dio, leaving
only the faintest flicker of a wake on the brackish water. No guards
rode shotgun this time, the gun turrets in battle mode, the craft
slung low over the water.

Heavy munitions or extra crew, Angeli decided, reaching Karo
at a run, Colt already unholstered. He had the gun held in combat
readiness, without even realizing it. He'd have gone for extra
weapons, but then he wasn't a *WeGuard*. Nodding at a dark-
skinned rent boy next to him, Angeli sent the child scuttling
back towards the huge protein tank, dodging between torn-open
containers.

Angeli needn't have bothered. None of the Mitsubishis opened
fire. Instead they skimmed into the Cut and swung outwards, until
they faced in three different directions. And then started to slide
slowly sideways, keeping within a tight circle, like rotating petals
on a flower. It was classic APV/H tactics.

'Go for the obvious, why don't you!' Sabine muttered.

Angeli almost pointed out that either good ideas never died or
else they did: Sabine couldn't have it both ways. But he had better
things to worry about, like staying alive. Crouched behind a
broken pod, Angeli flicked his gaze between the slowly circling
formation of hovers and the fermentation tank, waiting.

But there was no right time, there was only now. Raising his hand, Angeli waited until the Edgar Allan had raised his own in acknowledgement. This was it. Angeli swung his down, hard and fast. Immediately the waiting Goth slammed more pressure into the vat, setting alarms screaming, and seconds later tripped open the fire hose.

The flat hose bulged along its length, like an obscene worm, kicking in the hands of the spike-haired drakuls who held its open end, and then Sabine's protein mix was spewing over the hovers, burying them under lethal goo.

Mix flooded off the hovers' fractured surfaces, running into the canal, thousands of gallons a minute. Not that anyone had a minute or anything like. All three hovers had already begun to bring round their gun turrets, laserRadar scanning the dock for weapons.

Not yet: wait.

'Ceramic.' Angeli snapped off a couple of shots which ricocheted harmlessly from the nearest hover. He fired in bursts of two, because that was what he'd been taught. It was a hard habit to break. The turret on the hover he'd hit slid to a halt, its semiAI picking up his shots and identifying Angeli's position. On cue, one of the Ishies opened ragged fire from the other side of the dock with a captured pulse rifle, missing more times than she hit. But it did the trick, stopping the second hover's turret before it swung towards the protein tanks.

'Come on, fuck you,' Angeli was spitting. He needed that other H&K. Just as Angeli was about to give up hope, the second captured H&K opened up, from the far end of the Cut, out towards the levels and the sea beyond. Whoever Karo'd selected, they'd crawled right out along the roof of the marble gate.

It was brilliantly done. If any one of the hovers tried to take out that second rifle, they risked trashing both nV's priceless heritage and the Matsui smart gates. Replacing the electronics would cost more than CySat paid *WeGuard* in a year. It was impossible to know what rebuilding the outer Arsenale entrance would cost.

Angeli glanced round to congratulate Karo and realized with horror she wasn't there. Listening to the crack as a second low-level pulse reflected off a hover's side, Angeli groaned. It didn't take intelligence to work out where she'd gone.

When he looked back, there was an Ishie at his shoulder – Zeiss eyecam, Sanyo throat mike, Hayes belt pack with crypted satellite modem, the works . . . The Ishie was crouched, trance-struck, his head stock still so as not to ruin his close-up of Angeli.

'Move,' Angeli demanded, slamming a new multi-magazine into his Colt.

'No.' It was little more than a whisper. 'This doesn't need movement, it needs authority.' The smile on the Ishie's face wouldn't have disgraced an angel.

The beauty of semiAIs was that semi-intelligent was exactly what they were: all of their choices were obvious. An actual AI might have wondered why hostiles were attacking from three different directions and looked for an overall plan; it might have tried to analyse the thick mat of protein it now floated over. But the hovers just decided to react to the most obvious input.

A stream of shells wrote their signature along the pod Angeli crouched behind, whistling over his head. But the Niponshi cargo pod was simple kevlar and the shells were full ceramic jacket. Fragments of shattered kevlar scythed through the air, but no one got injured.

There'd be time for that later.

Inside the hover, a gunCam took note of the disintegrated pod, automatically switching to explosive rounds, but by then it was too late. As the hover sighted on where Angeli's last shot suggested he should be, Angeli threw himself sideways and rolled out from behind the wrecked pod, NVPD Colt held high in his hand.

'Phosphor.' Instantly the Colt switched magazines. Giving Angeli what he wanted, twelve shots, six bursts of two, all phosphoric/magnesium-cored explosive.

'Got it.' Angeli sighted, fired, rolled sideways over the cobbles and fired again, rolling back in the other direction. His first two shots caught a hover at the point where its neophrene skirt joined the ceramic of its rim. The neophrene swallowed most of the damage but the exploding rounds threw fragments of burning core onto the neophrene, where it adhered and began to burn through the skirt.

Black smoke filled the air, stinging his eyes, catching at the back of his throat. But Angeli kept firing, his next two shots and the two after doing the same to the other hovers, but by then no one on the Arsenale was looking at where his shots landed.

Most were retreating from the smoke, but a few stuck it out, gripped by static images of retina-burnt freeze-frame, too fast for memory. Only Sabine took everything in, but then she'd had practice. Schwarzchild's Radius defines the critical point in space curvature from which matter no longer escapes, its point of no return. And as the black smoke spiralled up into the afternoon air, Sabine knew such a radius was being drawn around time and events at Arsenale.

The silver-grey surface of the canal was slowly, inexorably begining to burn, turning into a river of molten steel. Nothing in the spinning hover's memory had prepared it for floating over fire and none of the *WeGuard* officers wanted to be the first to retreat. It was a fatal, inescapable loop.

By the time the guards trapped inside the burning hovers realized their Mitsubishis were doomed, they were too late to fight clear.

Nevertheless, all of the hovers tried to reverse at once. Someone, it seemed, had finally operated an AI override, but the override couldn't be obeyed. The neophrene had melted under the barrage of Angeli's phosphoric rounds. Smoke thinning out as the hovers' skirts turned to tattered webs, epoxied to the floating mat of burning protein. The Mitsubishis were trapped. All the *WeGuard* could do was come out fighting.

Angeli didn't give them the chance. He hit the first hover to raise its hatch with two rounds which exploded off the hatch, showering burning metal into the craft below. Closing up would just have locked the fire inside, and the pilot couldn't lower the hatch anyway. The gunner who'd been climbing out was jammed in the way, his body flailing as flames raced up the hover's side.

Angeli blew the screaming man apart with another round. It was partly mercy. He might be NVPD, but that didn't mean he liked to see people suffer. But it was mostly common sense. The shuddering, thrashing puppet of a man was shocking the crowd to silence with his death agony. Angeli needed them with him, not running scared or weak with doubt.

'Get down!' Angeli shouted frantically. 'They've still got guns.'

A few ducked behind boxes or walls, but most still stood there, dumb with horror at the craft that settled lower and lower into the flaming canal. No one else tried to climb from a hover, which was just as well. Angeli didn't think the crowd would stand for him taking out the guards one by one, not if that flame-patinaed stick figure was what death really looked like.

Out on the canal, Sabine's Greek fire burnt as fiercely as ever. What would he do, trapped in that situation? If life reversed to pin him down by *WeGuard*? The answer didn't take brains, it just took gut instinct. He'd try to take out as many of the fuckers as he could.

'Down!' Angeli shouted. 'Now. Get the fuck down!' He slammed a fresh magazine of ceramics into his NVPD Colt and emptied it in one deadly burp over the head of the watching crowd.

They got down, hitting the cobbles in a screaming mass. Even Sabine ducked, settling lower into her chair with a scowl.

The only problem was that Angeli didn't get down, not in time. The blast of the first hover blew him backwards, slamming him into a wall. He was down, hunched into a ball, his back to the canal when the other two machines exploded, fragments scything over his head. It was like getting kicked viciously twice in the small of his back: no bones broke and none of his major organs ruptured, but all the same . . .

[Hack & BackSlash]

It was the tsunami mechanism of his uniform that saved Angeli, shielding him from the blast, stiffening itself into a rigid carapace a nanosecond ahead of the shock wave to protect his spine and ribs.

Angeli's link was turned off. He didn't want NVPD Central able to order him back to base, but he wore the helmet from habit anyway. And habit saved his life, the helmet's honeycombed cellulose lining forming a baffle between Angeli's skull and the blast.

Someone not in NVPD street dress would have been killed. As it was, Angeli was alive, shocked but not concussed. Though his right shoulder was dislocated, his leg twisted under him. And the hovers were gone, sunk beneath flickering flames.

The whole scene already uploaded by an Ishie into the newsfeed.

'Here,' Sabine materialized at his side, unscathed, pulling him to his feet. She flipped up his visor, took his face in her hands, black nails pressing against his skin. Angeli looked into her green eyes and shivered. 'Let me see that,' Sabine demanded. Unzipping Angeli's jacket, she tried to pull it off his shoulders.

Angeli screamed.

Tutting to herself, the old woman pushed his jacket back into place. 'Oh, well,' she said coldly, 'If you're going to make a fuss about it . . .'

'He needs a hospital,' said Karo, sliding to a halt beside them. She wore the H&K p/R slung over one shoulder of Angeli's old jacket and a pair of Nikon OutBounds she'd found in the pocket.

'Oh, fuck it,' Sabine said crossly, tapping her cane on the

cobbles. 'What this boy needs is to stop fussing and get to Paco, before it's too *late*.' Her voice was harsh, hissed through thin, black-painted lips.

Both Karo and Angeli stared at the elderly kohl-eyed vampyre in shock. Sabine showed her yellowed fangs, and around her fifty drakuls stopped in mid-stride. 'So you've got Karo,' she snapped at Angeli. 'How long do you think that will stop Ryuchi from blowing the bolts? Well . . . ?'

Sabine shrugged off Angeli's outrage, then stilled, green eyes already distant. Wherever she was, it wasn't down under the blazing sun, where the acrid stink of burnt neophrene overlaid the canal's usual sour tang.

'Who is she, really?' Karo demanded, one hand brushing softly against his. Angeli glanced from the girl to the elderly vampyre: they had identical eyes, the same slightly too heavy face. It occurred to Angeli how little he knew.

'Enough questions,' Sabine said. She was back, ancient fingers dipping inside her velvet cloak to pull out a pearl-hued square that unfolded itself in her hand like a waking butterfly. Sabine flipped the little knife round and caught it neatly. The moment the handle touched her hand, its blade lit along the edge with cold blue flame.

Before Angeli had time to protest, Sabine was gripping the uniform cuff of Angeli's injured arm, slicing up the sleeve, supposedly indestructible spider's silk and kevlar peeling back before the blue fire like burning parchment. With a quick twist of her wrist, Sabine cut around the weld of his sleeve, ripping it from his NVPD jacket.

Fingers passed briefly over the blade and the knife folded itself away. Sabine dropped it casually into Karo's hand, smiling at the girl's startled confusion.

And while Angeli was still staring at his ruined uniform, Sabine gripped his wrist with one thin hand, slammed the palm of her other hand hard against his injured shoulder and nodded as the joint popped back into place.

It made a sucking click, lost beneath Angeli's hiss of pain. But he said nothing, not even when Sabine grinned.

The fire in the Cut was down to a flicker, ghost flames of palest blue. Nothing remained of the exploded hovers and, looking round him, Angeli was shocked to realize how badly the inner Arsenale gate had been damaged. And not just the marble gate. Steel cranes were bent, warehouse windows ripped out, the narrow docks littered with what looked like stars of rough diamond.

'Wrong way,' Sabine said shortly, glancing at a steady line of the shrapnel-hit being carried back towards the levels. 'We should be heading towards the city.'

'But the wall?' Karo asked. Nothing got through it alive, everybody knew that. In fact, using the sonic wall to commit flash-suicide was a favourite with depressed Edgar Allans. How better for a true poet to go than to be turned to dust in a sheet of flame?

Sabine looked at Angeli looking at Karo and sighed. 'Oh, work it out,' she said crossly. And stamped away towards an injured vampyre child, cane clicking on the cobbles.

Karo followed, helping load the injured onto makeshift stretchers, slashed from ripped-open pod. There were maybe twenty people badly hurt. There were dead, too, six or seven. But those remained where they had dropped. All attention was on the wounded. A wolfBoy, scalp ripped open, strips of opaline skin peeling from his burnt chest, struggled to crawl to his knees as Karo tried to help him up.

He stank of singed hair and fear.

'We need fresh skin,' Karo said, 'self-stitching wound dressing. Proper analgesics.'

'Out here? On the levels?' Angeli snorted. 'Maybe where you come from.'

Karo tried to stare him out from behind her shades, but couldn't. When Angeli looked again, the girl had her back to him, her arm under the wolfBoy's shoulders, helping him towards a new stretcher.

Angeli had a nasty feeling she was crying. But what could he say? Slop was free on the levels, medicine wasn't. Legitimate medical and recreational drugs *were* the ghetto's economy. It wasn't just tooth buds, or the other tawdry tricks of elective surgery that you had to barter for, it was antibiotics and analgesics. The Kartels had pharmaceutical design sewn tight. And there wasn't a hospital to be found on the levels. Unless you included the Geneticists' clinic. The girl had no fucking idea . . .

A hand gripped Angeli's arm, tough as steel, and he turned to find Sabine's face close to his, eyes cold as ice and twice as deadly. Dark threads of thought brushed against the edge of his mind, forcing the NVPD officer to blink back tears, Karo's tears.

Despite the heat, he felt suddenly cold.

'You . . . *you* have no fucking idea how little you know about the Suites,' Sabine said fiercely. 'None. So why expect that child to understand this?' Her sweeping hand took in the cracked Arsenale gate, the sliced-open pods littering the cobbles and the metal chaos of the levels behind him.

That wasn't a question Angeli could answer. It wasn't a question he'd even considered asking. He was still thinking about it when Karo returned, her jacket stained with the wolfBoy's blood.

'Flood the tunnels,' Karo said to Sabine. 'Short out the maglev's coil pairs.' Sabine smiled in approval.

Angeli might not have been there for all the attention Karo paid him.

She was getting thinner, Angeli realized, watching her not watching him. Strung out on worry, wired with grief for Razz, buried under the whole weight of still being young. Sabine was right. He knew nothing. Not her life, nor her family nor how she fitted into the war with *WeGuard*. If she did . . .

'Flood them,' Karo repeated. 'Give CySat something to really shit about.'

'You getting this?' Sabine hissed at Angeli, but it was Karo she took by the shoulders, turning her to face the NVPD officer. 'Tell him,' she said.

Karo did. 'All the cabling runs through there. The air purifiers, water cisterns, fecal recyc, electric storage, it's all cut into the coral. All accessed from the tunnels.'

'Mainframes too?' Angeli asked.

Karo looked at him as if he were stupid. 'No. In the Palazzo Ducale. You think CySat's going to put them where they can be reached?'

'And the tunnel gates . . .' Sabine prompted.

'Can be locked open. Mind you, that would take s-user access.'

'I can't do stuff like that,' Angeli protested.

Sabine looked at him with thinly disguised contempt. 'You couldn't boot up your own smartbook if it didn't do it for you. Karo'll do it . . .' Sabine reached for Angeli's belt and casually ripped free his NVPD Librex. It came away with that familiar velcro rip.

'Karo?' Angeli was puzzled.

'Fighting and hacking. She was taught by the best.' Sabine turned to Karo. 'He never met Razz, did he . . . ?'

Karo took Angeli's book gingerly, as if it might disintegrate in her hands. But once she'd opened its scuffed cover of synthetic suede, Karo realized the book was little different to hers, except his page was scratched and the words and pictures weren't as clear.

Karo ran one finger swiftly over its surface and a page woke beneath her touch. She made the small, quick scraping action needed to flick it over and was startled by the shortness of his *Contents*.

Most of the headings were subtly different, too.

Rapidly, Karo set about changing it. There was an appendix at the back that held Angeli's options, and Karo flicked across. It made good reading, though she was shocked to discover he'd been orphaned at seventeen and was now thirty (she'd thought him older than that). Besides his NVPD career to date – pretty depressing: CySoaps made the NVPD more exciting than it was – the appendix had a frame with his name, birthdate and ID number. Fingers dancing over the page, Karo began swapping his details for hers.

Then, when the book queried the change, she soothed it with a password her father sometimes used.

And though her father had taught Karo polite children used traditional finger passes, she toggled the Librex into voice mode, ordering it to return to *Contents*. Elegance was for people with time to burn: Karo was beginning to learn that.

'Subway,' Karo ordered and *Contents* dissolved as letters and colours rearranged themselves into a chapter opening. 'Plan,' she told it, and there was Cysat's precious subway, laid out in front of them, all gates open; a broken spider's web of lines, each line a different tunnel system, all linked by connections and short walkways.

'Shit,' said Angeli, looking at the hidden maze beneath his feet.

Sabine smiled. 'It's bigger than I remember. But then . . .' She looked at the terracotta-tiled roofs in the distance, then behind her to the sprawling, sun-baked metal city that was the levels. 'Everything's bigger than I remember. That's what happens when you take a nap.'

The old woman leant over Karo's shoulder and tapped the page with one long, black-lacquered nail, tracing a purple line that led from the Palazzo Ducale out to Arsenale. It looked like a vein. 'Lock back the gates and then try this one.'

The girl's fingers blurred as they flicked across the darkened page, pulling up options and icons, linking objects, collecting code. And then she was looking at a pictogram of Arsenale, its lion gates clearly marked, a service entrance flashing. But no options lit to allow her to lock open the tunnel's flood-barriers – no digital scrawl wrote itself across the page.

The library was open, but she couldn't get from there to CySat's database. It was busy.

Karo tried again.

And again . . .

'Shit,' said Sabine softly, mostly to herself.

'Either they know what we want,' said Angeli, 'or the central system's down.' It was obvious from Angeli's voice he feared the first.

'I'll create a *bot*,' Karo said, fingers already moving. And she did, sending it out to watch the gates and cancel any attempt to shut them. It was to use Karo's access code as authority.

'You,' Sabine said, nodding at Angeli. 'Blow the tunnel, while you still have time.' She shrugged. 'You might as well do something useful.'

It was a tenet of NVPD training that revolutionary cells flourished all over the levels. Only the forces of law and order – such as Angeli – stood between such cells and social collapse. *Terrorists*, *cells*, *social collapse*: each one had its own chapter in the training manual. Angeli was only just beginning to get his head round the idea that maybe, just maybe, social collapse had already happened, and it was the Suites who were responsible.

The fact that no explosives were forthcoming from the crowd didn't surprise him, though he asked twice. In the end, Angeli ran back to his precinct, taking the first two *TripleHelix* regulars he saw, a thin white-faced Edgar Allan and a large middle-aged whore dolled up like Marie Antoinette.

The armoury door recognized Angeli, hissed out compressed air and slid back to reveal less than Angeli would have liked, maybe less than they needed. He tossed a box of magnix to the thin Edgar Allan who bent almost double under its weight. The Goth held the explosives gingerly, his nervous scowl stating clearly that he'd rather be somewhere else.

The whore snorted, picking up two boxes of the magnetic mines. 'Back to the Arsenale?' she asked Angeli.

He nodded briefly.

The whore snorted again, this time at Angeli. 'Say please, why don't you?' Her words drifted away as she ran, boxes in her arms, leaving Angeli staring after her in amazement. Saying please to whores wasn't a concept he'd considered before.

But then, shit, there were a lot of things Angeli hadn't previously considered. Like ransacking his own armory.

What he needed most were *hotkeys*, wafer-thin sheets of bio-Semtex for slipping between a door and its frame. Mind you, as

Sabine warned Angeli darkly when he arrived back at Arsenale, gasping for breath, sweat streaming down the inside of his jacket, *hotkeys* probably wouldn't work anywhere *bricolage* wasn't the preferred method of building.

But they did . . . spectacularly. Shearing a door in a small deserted Customs building right off its hinges, in one clean burst. At the bottom of a spiral stairway, Angeli found a small work bay thick with dust and cluttered with empty cases. Through an arch beyond that a long room stretched away, empty and echoing, its walls on both sides studded with rivets and red with rust.

The NVPD officer rapidly checked the right bulkhead, trying to calculate how far to the water outside, how thick the steel and how much that water must weigh. Every building at the edge of the coral mass rested on what had once been a ship. And if the newer buildings of marble and stucco rose proudly above ground, they still rested on Passion's original foundations. And those foundations were metal.

He was in a hold, that much was obvious: a single-skin steel bulkhead curving along both sides, to join in the distance. The east wall was all that stood between them and the Cut, the west was tight to the coral. A large circle had been thermo-lanced into its side to provide entrance to a tunnel that dipped away into darkness, lit only by floor-level strips of bioluminescence that eventually vanished, swallowed up by darkness.

'It was to be a loading bay,' said Sabine, staring around her. 'But it never happened.' Angeli didn't ask how she'd managed the steps with her cane, just nodded. The NVPD officer wasn't really listening, he was too busy examining the eastern, waterside bulkhead. Steel plate, riveted together through turned-in seams. Its condition was good, or as good as it could be, given that it had once been a Panamanian rust bucket.

CySat would expect them to come in by the tunnels, would have guns waiting, but it wasn't going to happen that way. Angeli tapped the seams with the handle of his Colt, listening, looking at the rivets. They were hand-fitted, at least some of them were.

Rivet-gunned and hammered flat. Angeli shook his head in disbelief. God, but the ship must have been old when it finally reached new Venice.

Pulling Karo's molywire from his belt pouch, Angeli flipped it rigid and began to cut away surface rust, ignoring the girl's horrified gaze. Let the fucking wire do something useful. What was the point of keeping it in an evidence bag? He was going to have to lose it anyway when this was all over. If he ever got that far.

It took precious minutes to cut back enough rust to slide a dozen hotkeys between a seam. Each key looked like a small black playing card, with a break-off primer at one edge. Invites, his uncle had called them. Used handfuls at a time when the mood was on him.

Without being asked, the whore in the Marie Antoinette dress dumped her boxes at Angeli's feet and looked on grimly as Angeli positioned three of the magnetic mines up the first hotkeyed seam, parallel to the rivets.

Now what? Angeli wondered. He glanced round for the Edgar Allan but the Goth was gone. His box of mines was there, though, placed neatly against the bulkhead.

Taking the last of Marie Antoinette's mines, and two from the box the Goth had managed to carry, Angeli staggered along the bulkhead until he came to the next seam. The mines in place, he scraped rust out of that seam and slid in as many hotkeys as he could.

'Thanks,' Angeli said to the Marie Antoinette. 'Now get out of here.'

She grinned, not kindly, and did what he suggested, backing hurriedly out of the hold, her heels clattering on the spiral stairs as she made for the surface and the blazing sun.

Karo and Sabine stayed put, examining Angeli's handiwork. They had a brief, pointless argument about how much time Angeli should allow, until the NVPD officer pointed out that hotkeys worked on a five-second countdown: that was what there was, it wasn't negotiable. You broke off the tab and then you hid. End of story.

'I'll do it,' Sabine said, her voice matter-of-fact. And before Angeli or Karo could argue, the elderly vampyre was already shooing both of them out of the hold. For a second Karo resisted, but when Sabine hissed in irritation and lazily pulled back her upper lip so that two sharp teeth unsheathed and dropped into place, Karo decided she'd be better off elsewhere.

'She's dangerous,' Angeli insisted quietly. He was following Karo up the spiral stairs, trying not to notice how tight the 501s stretched across her ass. Hell, he kept reminding himself, he'd seen a lot more of her than that.

'She's not.' Karo shook her head and stepped out into the blinding sunlight. 'There's no way Sabine would touch me.' Karo's smile was ripe with private amusement.

It was midday. Angeli could tell by his shadow. There wasn't one. The Pacific sun was almost directly overhead. It was too hot for a cop to be in full uniform but Angeli didn't dare take off his NVPD helmet. It wasn't the thought of shrapnel that worried him, it was the idea of Karo listening in on his thoughts.

They were standing side by side, not just with each other but with a fresh, rapidly expanding crowd. The old crowd had gone, mostly back to the levels with the wounded. But more thronged into Arsenale, drawn by the smoke of the burning hovers, by Ishie uplink and rumour. No longer just punters from the *TripleHelix*, either, or even dwellers from the Third District, there were gangs whose colours Angeli didn't recognize. Sets and subsets he didn't even know existed. Thick-shouldered black wolfBoys boasting vast smoke-grey manes, fashion-victim cyborgs, even a pack of girlKats from Giudecca, naked except for their thin coating of fine fur. It made Angeli realize just how ordinary the Third District was.

'If I ditched the helmet . . .'

Karo looked at him. The NVPD officer had a nasty feeling she already knew what he was going to ask, but Angeli asked it anyway.

'. . . would you stop listening in?' Karo seemed on the brink of answering. But instead she just smiled. Problem was, Angeli wasn't sure if that counted as a *yes* or a *no*.

He never got the chance to ask. Simultaneously but unconnected – that is, as unconnected as anything could be in a world defined by fractal logic, quantum need and chaos – the hold beneath their feet blew with a dull *crump* that echoed off the warehouse walls. Down below, the bulkhead sheared free from its rivets and began to blow out, only to be pushed back and crumpled by the weight of water from the Cut.

'Sabine,' Angeli and Karo shouted, racing towards a white swirl on the water's surface where the sea was being sucked through the hold into the open tunnel. Panic filled their voices, but Sabine was already standing behind them, smiling grimly, her velvet cloak settling neatly around her. As ever, she smelt of old talcum powder but this time overlaid with acrid smoke and the organic stench of burning bioSemtex.

Some trick. Even the kats were watching, though not one of them came near her. That was power, Angeli thought.

'How . . . ?' He caught the tiredness in the old vampyre's green eyes and instantly swallowed his question. His blood beating too fast, a sick knot of bile in the top of his stomach, Angeli wasn't sure he wanted her answer anyway. There were other things to worry about, like what happened next.

CySat weren't going to hand Paco back. And holding Karo wasn't going to be enough to stop Ryuchi cutting the levels free, not now. But at least flooding those tunnels would stop *WeGuard* using them to get out to the levels. At least, Angeli hoped to fuck it would.

'Okay,' Angeli announced loudly, clambering up the top half of a sliced-open Niponshi pod, 'that'll slow down the guards.' He sounded a lot more confident than he felt. 'But it's not enough. Not yet. Not nearly.' Angeli stared around him, catching the eye of the crowd. 'We've got to fight . . .'

Sabine smiled. 'He'll do,' she said shortly, and Karo nodded.

He would, too. Angeli's voice rang out over the heads of the crowd, as he told them about CySat's plan to clear the levels. 'They'll try to cut us loose. There are explosive bolts fixed to the outer rim of the coral.'

It was more a guess than fact, but it seemed possible. Even likely.

'The bolts will be blown from the central computer,' said Angeli.

Sabine shook her head, but softly so only Karo noticed. 'If that were true, it wouldn't happen.'

'Why not?' Karo kept her voice low.

'Because that's Sasumi, what's left of her.' The elderly vampyre shrugged, 'A passion for tidiness, you see. Probably came from leading such a messy life as a child.'

'What?' Disbelief was written across Karo's face.

'You know her as Izanami,' said Sabine, then shook her head. 'Actually, you probably don't, but he does . . .' Sabine nodded towards Angeli standing on his pod. 'Whatever, she makes a good database. It was her choice, too. I'd have hated it, but what do I know . . . ?' Sabine's green eyes were bright, her smile thin. 'I didn't even make a decent saint.'

Sabine shook her head. 'But no, it's not the central computer that blows the levels. There are four bolts, independent semiAI. Each one has to be coded by hand.'

'Which means *WeGuard* have to come out to the edge,' Karo exclaimed as Sabine stood and then began to limp towards Angeli.

'Certainly does. Apart from anything else, they'll need to chop the optix and lance through all that cable binding you to the coral.' Sabine clambered uncertainly onto the pod, draping one arm across the NVPD officer's back to steady herself.

When the crowd saw who it was, they shuffled uneasily. But they listened to Sabine, even if most were unable to meet her gaze. 'They'll kill you,' Sabine told the silent crowd, 'if they can. Cut you adrift if they can't . . . The question is, what are you going to do about it?'

Sabine paused, waited for her answer.

It came from a wolfBoy, who was casually swinging a spun-carbon baseball bat. 'Stop them?'

Sabine nodded. 'Go into the city,' she suggested.

'What about the wall?' Sabine was almost buried under the demand, a hundred people asking it at once.

'Ah, yes. The sonic wall.' Sabine looked at a tall, mournful-looking Edgar Allan and grinned, thinly. 'Has anybody tried it recently . . . ?'

[All Of It's True . . .]

It was Karo who suggested a small party should brave the after-noon heat, go in over the boiling roofs to get Paco back, while the rest fought their way in at ground level.

Angeli assumed, everyone but Karo assumed, it would be quickest, easiest and safest to use the canals and the Riva di Schiavoni. To go in strength and rely on Angeli's remaining *hotkeys* being able to blow the ornate wrought-iron gates that blocked entrance into the Piazza San Marco itself.

It was only after she'd warned them the wrought iron was electric, that it wasn't wrought iron anyway but high-tensile molycable with a conductive finish, that anyone started to listen to her.

Getting in to the Palazzo Ducale wasn't going to be easy. No one had ever said it would be. And it wasn't going to be quick, either. *WeGuard* would fight. In all probability they'd win: they were professionals. Angeli knew that, he just wished Karo hadn't said it.

Sabine was gone, taking half her brood with her, a feral cat clutched in one thin hand. She was off to try the sonic wall.

Karo glared round at the remaining vampyres and drakuls, at the Ishies and Edgar Allans. She was avoiding looking at the kats and the kats were ignoring her, all except one black girlKat who hadn't taken her hungry eyes off Karo since she'd replaced Sabine on the Niponshi pod beside Angeli.

'Go in over the roofs,' Karo suggested shortly. 'Not everyone, just a few.'

'What about the panels?' someone protested.

Karo nodded. 'Not all the panels are silver, not like the levels. What silver panels there are, we'll walk over. They'll hold, most of it's just binary sheet slapped onto felt. Sunlight doesn't kill you, you know . . .'

A small crowd of drakuls growled their disagreement. 'All right,' Karo corrected herself, 'it's not *meant* to kill you. I know . . .' She held up her hands. 'But melanoma's not instant.' Karo glanced at the drakuls and grimaced. 'Most of us won't shrivel up and die.'

The crowd looked doubtful. Angeli didn't blame them, he was feeling pretty doubtful himself. From space, newVenice and its levels reflected like a silver disc set in a blue sea. It was one of the great tourist sights at Japan's Kyoto2 holiday resort on the Moon.

All aerial shots of newVenice were computer-created (CySat copyright) and satellites no longer watched the city: mirrors in sunlight didn't photograph well, and that was what newVenice had become. A marble city surrounded by Japanese solar panels and Lucas thermal glass, designed to reflect the sun towards heat collectors, sparkling out into space.

Somewhere in Osaka, over a 100 years before, the first strip of sheet steel intended for newVenice had been fed through a series of fifteen high-pressure rollers, each one depositing a separate layer of amorphous silicon, with a final protective layer of clear polymer on the top and a non-conductive layer on the bottom. And then the photovoltaic sheet had been bundled up like a roll of paper and shipped out to line every roof in Passion's new city.

There were no complicated fixings. The stuff could be nailed, epoxied or staple-gunned into place and gave a forty-five per cent sunlight conversion rate. It could even be shaped and dyed to mimic clay tiles for buildings that fronted onto public areas, such as the palazzi stretched along the Grand Canal.

The only problem was that, cheap sheeting or expensive tiles, it needed regular replacing, but that was only four times a century and the contract was still running to the satisfaction of both parties.

But none of that mattered a shit to Angeli. They were running out of time. He just wanted to make sure each clan got its own job, and then kept busy. Just one subset off on a looting spree and the levels would implode. Angeli was fucked if he was going to let his people do *WeGuard*'s job for them.

His people. Angeli grinned at the irony.

The drakuls weren't keen, but then, drakuls didn't like talking to outsiders, never mind taking orders . . . Yet they'd watched Angeli arm in arm with Sabine and that made him almost drakul in their eyes. In the end, Angeli was able to send a small group off to steal a splice into the nV newsfeed. Drakuls would provide muscle, the Ishies the upload. Scrambling the intraNet should keep CySat's techies tied up for a while.

Angeli even managed to persuade a pack of wolfBoys to go and start fires at Campo Ghetto Nuevo, on the far side of the city proper. Actually, they came to him with the idea, lolloping up, their overlarge tongues hanging from between exaggerated jaws. Knowing their uneasy relationship with fire, Angeli was deeply impressed.

The kats insisted on coming with him over the roof, pointing out they were better at jumping and climbing than he was.

'Quieter, too, Shit-for-brains,' said the black girlKat and Angeli suddenly remembered where he'd seen her before. At least that explained why Karo had gone quiet.

The girlKat was Neph, queen of the pack. She looked maybe twelve but had a single newborn kit curled in her arms. Neph saw where he glanced and slid out her claws, lethal hooks that recessed into soft fingertips. She grinned, too, a small cat snarl that drew her lips back over her needle-like teeth. Okay, so she was protective: Angeli took the point.

So did Karo, who was watching him closely as he looked anywhere except at Neph's svelte, tight-muscled, completely naked body. Angeli scowled and looked away, going red despite himself. Could he help it if the girlKat was a shorthair?

Anyway, they needed kats, Angeli told himself quickly. As Neph had already pointed out, only the kats knew their way round the roofs of the outer City, where the levels and the red buildings met.

'At least we know the centre,' said Angeli. It sounded like bluff, but for once it wasn't. Santa Passionata's city copied the original. And Angeli had a map of the real Italian city. Only it wasn't cached in his book, it was loaded into his helmet. And he really didn't want to wear that thing. Not up on the roofs, with heat hitting 100°F.

'I'll take it,' Karo offered.

Shit. Angeli glared at the girl. He'd asked her not to do that.

'The helmet?' Angeli looked down at the carbon, kevlar and plexiglass monstrosity clutched in his hand.

'Not the helmet, the map.' Karo smiled sweetly. 'I can download it direct, if you let me.' She reached for his NVPD-issue, semiAI battle-vision head protector and ripped out its lining, scattering honeycombed cellulose baffles. Karo reset the compression ratio on its control panel, toggled a couple of virtual jumpers and slammed Angeli's helmet hard and fast onto her head, tipping down the visor. To Angeli, it looked like Karo wasn't giving herself time to protest.

'Maybe d'bitch has uses after all,' Neph said, appearing at Angeli's side. They both watched Karo carefully, but there was nothing extraordinary to be seen. Anything happening was taking place inside the helmet, where Karo was downloading a map from the visor's screen into her memory, not as a picture but as straight binary code. She'd uncompress what she needed later. All the same, she couldn't resist surface-skimming the caption.

Venice had been – as VeniceDisney still was – a port in north-eastern Italy. Originally built on 120 islands, with 177 canals and 400 linking bridges, situated in a lagoon at the mouths of the Po and Piave rivers, at the northern end of the Adriatic, next to what had once, briefly, been Yugoslavia

'Want it back?' Karo asked, offering him the helmet. One look at her face told Angeli she didn't like finding Neph there.

'No,' Angeli shook his head, so Karo tossed the helmet onto the cobbles, pretending not to notice as everyone turned to look.

Neph grinned and stalked away, twitching her small tail high to reveal the crease of her neat buttocks.

'Engage your brain,' Karo suggested with a scowl. 'While there's still time.'

[. . . Written in Silver]

Ready to move, Angeli dipped into his pocket and came up with a couple of grit-covered NVPD blues. Not much, but it was what he had.

Neph shook her head at his offer, reached into her small waistband and extracted a foil packet of wizz, the crystals not grey nor discoloured but clear as diamond. Class merchandise. She crunched one between sharp teeth, tossed one to Angeli and handed the twist to Karo, who hastily shook her head.

One of the other kats laughed, far back in her throat, and spun rapidly, knocking the packet from Karo's hand. Someone else caught it before it had time to hit the hot cobbles. Within seconds, the packet had gone round Neph's kats and then, as synapses clicked and NTs altered sequence, the kats started to stretch and arch their backs. Even more disconcertingly, they started to purr. A quick-fire low rumble.

'Spare me,' Karo whispered, glancing at Angeli. But all the NVPD officer's attention was on the black girlKat.

Neph grinned. 'What we waiting for, then?' she demanded and crouched lazily, then squat-jumped straight from the cobbled dock to the nearest roof, a pink kit still cradled in her arm. It was only one storey, but it was still a shock.

'Need a hand?' Neph asked Karo sweetly. She leant casually over the edge, still clutching her kit, and reached down to grip Karo's wrist. Karo was pulled roughly over the edge. Other kats helped pull up Angeli, a small crowd of kinderwhores and even the Edgar Allan who'd reappeared, his black cloak replaced with more orthodox Levis and teeshirt.

From the one-storey clearing house, Neph moved not towards a terracotta-tiled warehouse roof as Angeli expected, but back onto the levels, to the deck of what had once been a Taiwanese fishing trawler. From there, with the Cut and the outer Arsenale Gate already behind them, it was a short climb to a hot polyglass roof, thrown over the deck of an aircraft carrier. Designed for warehouse units, the space below had been converted to a flea market years before.

The levels were simple: design didn't enter into it. Newcomers moored alongside established boats, bullied or bribed their new neighbours into letting them bolt themselves to the main mass, and then set about splicing themselves into the information feeds. Osaka sheeting was free, about the only thing other than slop that was.

The installation rules that came with each roll of Osaka sheeting proclaimed that six hours of sun on eighty square metres of photovoltaic sheeting would provide twenty-four hours' power for the average family. No such mythic grouping existed in new-Venice, except maybe up in the Suites, but that didn't seem likely. Not, Angeli decided, if Karo was anything to go by.

The girl was scrabbling up a metal ladder, its rungs baked oven-hot in the sunlight. Even behind shades, Karo had her eyes half-shut against the afternoon glare. She was picking at the download from Angeli's helmet, worrying it like a scab, pulling off little slivers of information.

The levels grew, year on year. A floating metal mat now housed over a million and the number continued to grow: biology saw to that, even though less ships came than before.

'Here,' Neph hissed.

They stopped on the edge and looked down at a row of ceramic studs set in the ground. This was the sonic fence, the invisible firewall separating the levels from the City. The gap from ship to landside warehouse was narrow, but still more than Angeli could ever jump. Not that he'd have dared try. Even looking at the ceramic studs made his mouth dry. Two kats had appeared, carrying a long metal ladder wrenched from the side of a ship. Lowering the ladder, they positioned it so it crossed the gap almost exactly, resting on a low parapet at the far end. Angeli gulped, literally. Fear tightened his throat. Nothing he'd seen or done, none of it, covered a situation like this.

The ladder would be fine, untouched. But then, it wasn't alive and the sonic wall only unravelled living things. Stopping their heart mid-beat.

'It's going to be okay,' Karo whispered, hand brushing Angeli's shoulder. 'The wall must be off, remember what Sabine said . . .'

Neph grinned at Karo, an evil light in her yellow eyes. 'You really trust Sabine?'

The young girl nodded. Yes, more than anyone except Razz, and that had been different.

'Really trust?' Neph smiled, happily. 'Good, then you be d'first.'

The other kats were watching and Angeli looked appalled, but Karo was already stepping out in front of the ladder. Shrugging off Angeli's old jacket, she screwed it into a ball and tossed it across the gap, hearing it land with a thump on the other side, out of sight.

Then she took up a stance somewhere between combat and ballet, and flipped across the ladder in a blur of twisting, cartwheeling limbs. She was on the other side before anyone had a chance to protest.

'Your turn,' Karo told Neph, and turned away, not bothering to watch the girlKat make the same journey.

To outsiders, Passion's original plan for the central city looked insane, a chaotic jumble of sunken ships, grounded rigs and concrete pylons surrounded with random coral groups. Except it was far from random. Its template had been imposed two thousand years before, on another continent, when the tribes of the Venetio fled out to the mudflats in the face of barbarian invasion.

For Passion's coral template followed the exact plan of the original city, down to the last twist in its smallest canal. It had taken thirty years to cut and carve the coral, to lay foundations, to slice ships off at ground-level and erect squares, basilicas and palazzi. The *Palazzo Ducale*, *Real* and *d'Patriarcato* came first, along with the basilica of San Marco. Everything else followed. The new city was built with stolen money in the face of outside threats, but then so was the original republic.

And when newVenice was finished, Passion sprang her final surprise, running CySat for less than six months before stepping out of public view. The new ruler, her godson, was supposedly chosen at random in a public lottery held in the Piazza San Marco. No one was surprised by the result.

Karo smiled grimly. Some things never changed.

From the outer gate of Arsenale to the Piazza San Marco and the Palazzo Ducale was less than a klick. To get there, they'd go over the roofs to the great square, then along the edge of the square and into the Palazzo. That was the theory, anyway.

The first bit was easy. Although, as Karo reminded herself as she clambered along a narrow ledge and in through the broken window of a warehouse, it was all relative.

The cats led, a furious Neph prowling ahead, jumping from gable to gable, landing on the tiles in near-silence. Her eyes were half closed, pupils shut down to slits against the sunlight. She panted slightly, her mouth just open, tip of her pink tongue just touching her lips.

When she could, Neph kept her back to the sun, making shade for the kit. All kats liked the heat, she told Angeli shortly when he questioned her, but only when they could laze in it. From choice, all of them would have moved in the shadows. But here there were no shadows, just a head-splitting glare as sun reflected off tiles.

'Smoke,' Neph said suddenly. And there was. Spiralling up in the distance, out on the other side of the city. Not white or pale grey, but the black, chemical-laden, carcinogenic smoke of burning polymer. The wolfBoys had found something to torch. There was gunfire too, the sound of loud hailers, security sound systems. The levels were moving in on the city, which meant the sonic wall was down everywhere, its nanite horde gone from the control field, blown away like dust.

Beneath them the buildings were changing, from red-brick warehouses to neat communal CySat houses of grey stucco. Ahead in the distance, where the Grand Canal cut its reversed 'S' though the city, they changed again to the bright primary hues of new-Venice's famous palazzi.

They were moving high above sea level, five floors, maybe more. Climbing uneasily from overheated roof to overheated roof on their way towards the Piazza San Marco. Shuffling across the reflecting tiles was easy enough, if you didn't mind going nearly blind in the glare. Staying hidden was another, deadlier problem.

Not that the city's inhabitants would be looking skyward, Karo reminded herself. They'd be glued to the newsfeeds, or watching the battle on the ground. If it was a battle, and she thought it must be from the volume of the distant gunfire. Anyway, the bigger houses had roofs that dipped into a vee in the middle, providing shelter. Others had traditional tent shapes of terracotta clay, faced at the lower edge with low parapets, behind which Karo and the others could crouch, moving single file. But too many were simple, sloped roofs with no obvious cover at all. Those were the ones the kats hated most.

'Don't worry,' Karo materialized beside Neph, her voice dangerously polite. 'Keep to the shadows, where you belong.' She patted one hand lightly on the girlKat's shoulder, and left Neph's fur bristling, fine black hair prickled upright.

Karo shrugged. Rounds one and two to her.

'I tried talking to . . . that thing,' Karo said, returning to Angeli. 'She's worried we'll be seen.'

'We won't, not yet,' said Angeli. And he went to tell Neph why, dropping into a crouch beside her, so close he could almost taste her sweat . . . Angeli could do line of sight in his sleep, any NVPD officer could. Hell, sight-lines even got checked out in his dreams.

Provided the groups kept to the centre of roofs where possible, to the edge of narrow canals or *calle* where not, there'd be too little gap for anyone to look up and see them. Besides, attic floors were usually deserted – the heat saw to that – and the angle of sight was too sharp to be seen on the roof from the next floor below.

Neph smiled, at what Angeli wasn't sure.

'You okay?' he asked.

Neph nodded and turned to go, then glanced back and caught Angeli gazing after her with unashamed interest, even hunger. He scowled, but not fiercely enough to hide his blush, and Neph smiled sweetly. Her buttocks wriggled slightly as she climbed away up a hot roof, her tail lifting briefly to reveal the pink gash of her genitals as if by accident.

'Enjoying the show?' Karo asked, sliding alongside. Somehow Angeli didn't think she'd like the answer. Hell, he knew she wouldn't. Didn't like it much himself.

They'd gone maybe a third of the distance, Angeli reckoned. No more. And already the heat was burning into everyone. All those with shades wore them against the glare, even a couple of the kats had wrap-rounds, velcroed neatly to their face. But everyone still squinted into the sunlight.

Maybe the drakuls were doing better, splicing the Ishies into the nV newsfeed. Angeli hoped so, and he didn't care what kind of revolution they were preaching. It didn't really matter. CySat wouldn't like it whatever it was.

Angeli had been watching Karo push ahead, scrambling up a roof, refusing to be left behind by the girlKat. What, Angeli wondered, drove her? She didn't belong on the levels, but then, from what he could see, she didn't really belong in the city, either.

Oh, her voice was right. Perfect manners, too, when she forgot to be rude. But she was too spiky, her mind too angular for the neat, fettered elegance of life in the Rialto. Ill at ease inside her own skin. All the classic clues to meth hunger, just without the ice.

So where did Karo's father think she was now? More to the point, could Karo be trusted when it really came down to choosing sides? Angeli stopped himself short: *would Karo pick his side?* was what he meant.

Jesus, what a life.

Angeli rubbed his raw eyes, shivering. If he knew why he was crying, maybe he'd be able to stop. But he didn't. And the only cure for meth come-down was more meth. Except he didn't have any. Angeli scrabbled in his packet, looking for the grit-covered NVPD blues he'd found earlier. They weren't there.

'Here.' Karo passed him not meth but a handkerchief, white cotton, for God's sake. He glared at her, but the girl was pointedly looking away, staring towards the gilded dome of the distant basilica, with its weird multi-sided, ball-studded three-dimensional cross, looking like a model for some complex atom. 'We should move,' she said.

'Yeh,' Angeli agreed. 'Before we all die of fucking boredom.'

[Base Pairs]

The room was vast, curving round at one end like the stern of a ship, though the walls were made from stone, not steel. Metal was there, of course, ferroconcrete formed its core, brick and marble were just facing materials.

The room was cool, too, chilled down to an elegant sixty degrees by huge silent Mazda air-purifiers. But the silence was colder . . .

There were windows, vast expanses of glass that stretched from floor to ceiling, but there was no view to the city outside. The impregnated yttrium-hydride glass had already switched from clear to an oily, sun-reflecting sheen.

It was late afternoon, but without natural light or heat it was impossible to know that, not without looking at the huge sunburst Venetian clock inset into a gilded oak panel on the wall.

There was coffee in an eighteenth-century silver jug on a small table by the door. Pure Colombian, freshly ground, grown high in the mountains. The coffee jug's dark scent filled the room, heavy as earth and rich as chocolate. Nobody touched it. The meeting had started at noon, nothing had been decided. And other than administrative *minutiae*, dealt with by the Council's most junior members, little had been discussed.

That was going to change. Count Ryuchi was going to see to it.

Count Ryuchi sat at the table, tapping one purple lacquered nail slowly on its polished surface. Very purposefully, he never sat at its head. Always choosing the first seat on its right-hand side, a bow-legged Louis XVI chair with scrollwork carving. The table he sat at was huge, hand-cut and polished. The fact it could seat a hundred made it the largest burr-walnut dining table in the world.

Sitting opposite Ryuchi, also not at the head of the table, was Count Orsela, Aurelio's father. He wore black. Beside Orsela, sitting in a silent row down the table, were five other CySat executives, just as five sat alongside Count Ryuchi. Anyone, even a child, even Paco had he been present, would have seen immediately that the Council of Twelve was still split down the middle. As it had been for decades.

But Paco wasn't there. And the Regent, the Doge's representative, was riddled with Creutzfeldt3Jakob. So the Regent's ornate seat sat empty, and the child who might have occupied it stayed locked behind titanium deadlocks in his room, playing.

A wind-up tin robot was in his hand, very old, impossibly valuable. Paco was making the Japanese toy climb a slope of ancient books and then tumble off the other end. He had to amuse himself; the dragon was still busy thinking.

No one had fed him all day, but then no servant could have got through his locked door, not that they had tried. He'd eaten the apricots, found and virtually finished a box of Belgian truffles. Sneaking out of his room, in search of something as ordinary as bread, Paco discovered the truffles and ate them instead.

He was forgotten, a discarded puppet in the game between the divided executive and the levels. Not that Paco minded being forgotten. Anonymity was safety, that was a basic lesson of life, at least it was if you were a street kid. Besides, he'd never seen so many toys. Come to that, he hadn't seen many toys, full stop . . .

'Gentlemen.' Count Ryuchi's voice was cultured, his yakuza accent barely perceptible. His words carried effortlessly over the strains of the Bach concerto playing in the background. Had it been necessary, the Count would have been heard without trouble at the other end of the huge table. Voice training was expensive, but always useful.

'We must end our deadlock.' The Count's dark eyes were haughty as ever as he stood to address the table, staring round at his own side as well as Orsela's. But his voice was more measured than usual, less grating. He paused, adding weight to his coming words.

'The Niponshi containers have been robbed. Arsenale's inner gate seriously, irreparably damaged.' One manicured hand flicked up to hush the murmurs of outrage rising automatically from executives on his side. Count Orsela didn't find it necessary to still his side: they sat in bleak, stony-eyed silence, which was how they'd been since entering the Great Chamber.

'Unless CySat acts,' Ryuchi said smoothly. 'There will be damage to *all* of us. And, of course, for our families. Our differences must be sunk, now.'

Count Orsela sneered, a smile flicking across his round, self-satisfied face. It was sometimes easy to forget Ryuchi had not been born neoVenetian. Indeed, Count Ryuchi worked hard to achieve just that. But no one born in newVenice would use *sunk* in that way. Not in a maritime city, where the young Doge yearly betrothed himself to the Ocean with a gold ring. No one who *really* understood would risk the bad luck.

'Count,' the Japanese nobleman was speaking direct to Orsela now, ignoring the other man's sneer. 'We have a duty to CySat, to our shareholders.' Ryuchi conveniently forgot the fact that CySat's biggest shareholders, or at least their proxies, sat around that table. He was drawing on the Council's sense of duty, instilled, ingrained. 'We must act to protect the company against its enemies.' He smiled at Orsela, calmly. 'I'm sure you agree?'

The two men stared at each other, then Ryuchi sat and reached for a wine-filled Murano glass, an original. Its value would have bought the *TripleHelix* six times over. Ryuchi had nothing more to say. It was Orsela's turn.

The squat Italian rose and tugged at his grey jacket, pulling it straight. His heavy brow revealed his family origins, poor Sicilian made better than good. To buy thinking time, Orsela stared round the Chamber, at the huge Venetian-glass mirrors and the rows of long-haired naked women, trapped in ornate gold frames. Above the Titians, a long frieze by Barsano showed gaunt men in dull armour, thin hunting dogs, weeping women. Dark pictures for a dark republic.

'Enemies, you say. Where are they?' His words were fluid, powerful but still raw. A dozen episodes of microsurgery and the world's finest musicians had tuned his vocal chords. But no amount of aural trickery could disguise his anger, or the frustration he felt at the unsolved death of his son.

'Breaking down doors. Burning warehouses. Even moving over the roofs of San Zaccaria towards this chamber,' said Ryuchi.

Orsela looked startled, then caught himself. 'Is this conjecture or fact?'

Fact, cold and hard.

'It's true, Ryuchi said shortly. 'Take a look.' He ordered the windows to clear and pointed to smoke rising on the horizon.

'But the fence.' Orsela protested, 'It's impossible.'

Ryuchi smiled grimly. 'Nothing's impossible. Or have you forgotten how this city was founded? It's happening. The fence has gone.' He paused, twisted at a silver ring on his finger, wondering how to tell them the rest. 'But it gets worse. The tunnels are flooded, the maglev is at a halt. No supplies can come in, no men can get out . . .'

For once, Ryuchi had the undivided attention of Orsela's side as well as his own. He intended to use it. 'If we let this division between us continue,' announced Ryuchi. 'We will lose this city to illegals.'

There. It was done. The Japanese nobleman had said the unthinkable.

'I admit there are substantive differences between . . .' Ryuchi hesitated. 'Between our views, but these should be put aside in the face of bigger, more basic conflicts.'

Count Orsela's face was dark, but he said nothing to disagree. The levels had always been an irritation. Now they were a danger, that much was obvious. If this was a trick of Ryuchi's, it was a convincing one. Looking at the tall man one could almost imagine he was afraid.

'Very well,' Orsela said. 'What do *you* suggest? Although, obviously,' Orsela opened out his hands like a cheap actor so even some on Ryuchi's side of the table smiled, 'this must go to a vote.'

Ryuchi nodded, a sardonic smile on his thin face, his grey hair spilling elegantly back onto his shoulders. Even past his prime, the Count looked good, and he knew it.

'What do I suggest . . . ?' Count Ryuchi shrugged, languidly. But when he spoke again his message was as hard as his voice was soft. 'Kill them. In desperate times, good men demand desperate measures. Send out *WeGuard*.'

Orsela looked into the narrow face of his opponent. Fifteen years of hatred stood between them. Walking through that barrier wasn't easy for either of them.

'You're worried,' said Orsela.

It was a simple statement and a true one. For a second Count Ryuchi prepared to deny it and then didn't. 'This is the first-ever open challenge to CySat's authority. It should be taken very seriously. After all,' Ryuchi said, glancing round him, 'it's not as if we're well armed.'

'Not well armed . . .' Orsela was on his feet, heavy torso bent forward, strong arms pushing down on the table, his palms flat on the polished burr-walnut. It was a habitual pose.

Ryuchi caught and held the man's eyes. Demanding attention. 'Two hundred members of a new, untried security franchise against,' Ryuchi shrugged, 'a million inhabitants of the levels?'

'But not all that million are in the street or on the roof,' Count Orsela protested quickly. His followers smiled from habit, but for once they listened to both sides of the argument.

'Not now, not yet,' Ryuchi said baldly. 'But have you seen the newsfeed? The Doge belongs to them, they want him back. The city is theirs, too, apparently. If we send in *WeGuard* we can cut this nonsense short.'

'At what loss? Can we afford the loss?'

Ryuchi paused, something close to pain crossing his narrow face. He twisted his silver ring, not answering for a second. But whatever decision he took, he took it himself, inside. Karo was his only link to Lucrezia, but his duty was to the city. He could only hope that idiot police officer still had her safely locked away. As for the rest . . .

Counts Ryuchi and Orsela looked at each other. No words were said. None were needed. The answer was unspoken between them. Let the guard and the levels kill each other. After all, CySat's security franchise could always go to re-tender.

'Send out the guard,' Orsela agreed. 'And put some on the roofs. Not,' he added almost hastily, 'the roofs of this palace. Put them on the *Prigioni Nuove*.' He nodded his head in the direction of the old prison next door.

'Agreed.' Ryuchi reached again for his glass. 'Also, enforce an immediate curfew to clear canals and *calle*. Bring out the JCIT and prepare the guns in the courtyard, should they be needed.'

[Out On The Tiles]

'Shit, sweet fucking sh—' The ceramic bullet took Neph in the shoulder as she skirted San Zaccaria, scouting for the best point to jump a narrow canal blocking her way. It flipped her sideways, punching her back onto the tiles. And then Neph was up and hurtling towards a stone chimney, blood running between the fingers clasped to her arm.

'Went straight through,' Neph shouted across to Angeli, her voice raw with pain. The kit was still in her arms, but no longer asleep, its narrow face staring around it. Neph was purring reassurance even as she tried to staunch the blood, bright red drips baking to black as they congealed and glazed on the hot roof tiles.

'Shit, shit, shit.' Angeli was up and running, Karo keeping pace with him as they jumped gaps and gullies, dodging from side to side, only just avoiding crashing into each other. And then the shots started to hiss past, not touching, and they both hit the tiles at the same time, rolling down a slope into safety. Away from the bullets. Hidden behind a parapet.

'Move,' Karo demanded fiercely. Angeli did, rolling off her. He was smiling, she wasn't. Sweat was slicked across her gut under Angeli's old jacket, her back stuck to the kevlar lining every time she moved her shoulders. She smelt not just hot but burning. Even the sweat-soaked cropped top had rubbed raw just beneath her breasts.

She was too uncomfortable to be afraid.

Whoever was out there was firing on single. Stupid, really, when automatic could have chopped them off at the hip. Unless, of course, the guard had orders to take them alive. But that didn't seem likely, and it wasn't an idea Angeli liked.

A hundred, maybe one-fifty paces from the Palazzo Ducale. Too far from the palazzo to storm forward, and much too far into the city to get safely back to the levels.

'Suicide,' Angeli muttered. That's what the whole thing had become.

Beyond the narrow canal ahead was Calle delle Rasse and just past that, the Prigioni and the back of Palazzo Ducale, where Paco would be. If the boy was still alive, Angeli reminded himself.

And between them and Paco? The sun was too bright to see, direct into their eyes from the west. Even squinting, eyes hidden behind his NVPD-issue RayBans, Angeli couldn't make out much more than shards of light reflecting from the tiles ahead.

WeGuard were out there, though how many Angeli didn't know. But *WeGuard* were there, between where he crouched and where he needed to be. And what did they have to go through them? Two H&K pulse rifles, an NVPD Colt locked to his DNA, which only Angeli could fire, and half a dozen cheap handguns, plus any number of home-made monofilament garottes. Oh yeah, and Karo's molywire.

Fucking great.

'You get to that kat, I'll take the snipers,' Karo said, and was gone before he could protest. Not that he intended too. Angeli hadn't forgotten how well she'd positioned herself at Arsenale, how she'd pinned down that hover. *Lessons*, he thought suddenly.

He stared after the girl as she climbed a sloped roof behind him, H&K slung across her back, moving in the shadow of a huge red-brick chimney stack, careful to keep dead ground between her and where she thought the *WeGuard* snipers might be. *She'd had lessons*.

Karo looked back and grinned, then returned to clambering up the hot tiles, wiggling her Levi-clad buttocks at him for good measure. Angeli blushed.

Jesus. He'd forgotten about Neph! He ducked out of cover and ran along the parapet towards the girlKat. Not that he was needed when he got there. The bullet had spun clean through her *pectoralis* muscle, scraping ribs but not breaking anything in its path. Already another girlKat stood behind Neph, closing the exit wound with slow steady licks. The neat entrance hole was already sucked clean, Neph busy stuffing it with handfuls of spider's web brought up from a dusty, deserted attic below.

'No problem.' Neph arched her arms back, taking the strain off her injured shoulder. 'We mend fast, you know. One of our better mod'fications.'

Angeli backed away. He wasn't needed there, anyway. Shots were coming from behind them, as Karo squinted into the sun and began picking off anything that moved. It was the wrong day to be a pigeon. She killed three birds and one *WeGuard* in as many seconds, splintering tiles and punching fist-sized chunks of rock out of the walls as low-burst pulses burnt straight through her targets.

'All right,' Neph said loudly. 'Keep them busy. Keep her busy, too.' The Kat's voice was abrupt and a raised strip of fur down her spine told Angeli he wasn't yet forgiven for forgetting her.

It was agreed, without a word being spoken. Neph and her followers would prowl ahead towards the Palazzo Ducale, moving at their own swift pace. Neph was bored and the girlKats could no longer afford to be held back by the others. Karo, the Edgar Allan and Angeli, and anyone else left would follow after.

Angeli settled himself high on a cornice, below the bas-relief belly of a winged lion that held an open book. *Pax Tibi*, read its slogan. Somehow Angeli doubted it. He was on the wrong side of a narrow canal, under the lion's slight overhang, looking down at the white-tiled roof of the Prigioni Nuove, the New Prison. Santa Passionata's perfect copy of the seventeenth-century original.

That narrow canal was all that stood between him and the Prigioni Nuove. And all that stood between the New Prison and the Palazzo Ducale was the enclosed bridge of *Ponte dei Sospiri*, CySat nV's elegant logo, the infamous Bridge of Sighs. If nothing else, Angeli thought bitterly, one couldn't hope to die in more famous surroundings.

Looking behind him, the NVPD officer tried to work out how many from the levels were up there, strung out across the burning roofs. Not many, certainly nothing like as many as started. The milling crowd had seemed like hundreds, when everyone was ripping open the Niponshi pods back at the Arsenale, but two-thirds of those had stayed at ground level. And God knew were they or the others now were, because Angeli sure as fuck didn't.

Neph had with her maybe five, not counting those who were little more than kits. Other than that? The Edgar Allan. An overhot, panting wolfBoy busy staying well away from Neph's tribe. No drakuls, obviously, not in this sun. The Marie Antoinette and two *TripleHelix* kinderwhores. Ten, maybe, plus Karo and himself. Every one of them blistered by the sun, exhausted by their trek across the burning roofs. It wasn't much with which to take on the might of CySat's Grand Council. Added to which, they'd probably rather cut Paco's throat than hand him back anyway.

Of course, Angeli reminded himself, it was anyone's guess what the wolfBoys were doing over on the other side of the city: except it still involved serious damage, to judge by the black smoke rising from Ghetto Nueve.

Slung there, below the stone lion's belly, Angeli swapped RayBan Smarts, pulling out a pair of ×4s. Balancing the standard-issue shades at his feet, Angeli slid on his magnifiers and brought up his Colt. The handle rested comfortably in his hand, diodes winking as the gun authorized use. Everything about it had a reassuringly familiar feel.

Over there . . . The flat-lens magnification reduced the distances significantly. And there was no sighting conflict, the Colt had already recalibrated itself to allow for ×4 mag in the first simple exchange between gun and RayBans. Basic training.

Single shots, don't waste rounds . . .

'Ceramic.' Angeli squeezed off a shot mid-breath, and watched the head of a *WeGuard* explode to fragments of splintered cranium, blinding a female guard behind him. Blood pumped briefly from the opened skull, the guard thrashing on the hot tiles like a dying fish, but Angeli had already moved on.

'Flechette.' He shot the blinded woman through her left eye, his flechette ripping through her eyeball, shredding *rectus* muscles and optic nerve as it spun into her brain then exploded from the back of her skull, still spinning. She staggered backwards and went down in a tumble of twitching limbs.

Angeli nodded, satisfied. It was easy to forget, until you'd seen throwback in action, that flechettes dropped victims with more impact than a baseball bat.

Angeli took out three more, two clean ceramic headshots – clean, that was, if you ignored the blood and bone – and one that caught a guard in her elbow, spinning her round. She might have survived, but in her panic stepped back and dropped herself neatly off the Prigioni's roof, landing not in a canal but on a narrow cul-de-sac below. Angeli could hear the wet thud from where he crouched.

Shots whistled round his head. Two, maybe three ploughed into the bas-relief stone lion, gouging gaping wounds in its side and showering Angeli with white dust. Time to move before one of those shots ricocheted in his direction. He slid down the roof to kneel beside Karo.

Angeli sighted again, as someone dodged swiftly over the Prigioni Nuove roof in front of him. Gun sighted and trigger finger already whitening at the knuckle, Angeli frantically threw his shot wide. It was a ginger girlKat, almost a kit, dodging swiftly across the dangerously open area. She had a rifle in one hand, a pistol in the other. As Angeli watched she grabbed a second rifle without pausing and flipped round to land on her feet, already heading back towards Angeli's roof.

Behind her a *WeGuard* rose from his hiding place, unslinging a cheap copy of an Uzi micro, its stuttering barrel already beginning a deadly sweep. Angeli fired and so did Karo and the Edgar Allan, flechettes and pulses ripping into the man's head, heart and gut. Angeli hoped it was the poet and not Karo who shot the guard in the gut. As wounds went, gut shots were painful as fuck and deadly in the long term. But as a short-term solution they stank.

'Aim for the head,' Angeli shouted.

'I was.' The white-faced Edgar Allan's elegant, rolling voice was mournful.

'And keep firing.' From his new position, Angeli squeezed off two more ceramics to give the ginger girlKat covering fire as she sprinted across the white roof, cleared a narrow *calle* in a single leap and landed near Karo. She was holding two *WeGuard*-issue H&Ks and the clone Uzi. Karo glanced round, looking for likely people for the weapons. Marie Antoinette got one, as did a rent boy, his whole body a web of cobalt-blue spiral. The clone Uzi went to a skin-stripped boy who had slunk up from beneath a hatch. He held out his hand silently, and it looked from the awed expression on Karo's face like she didn't dare refuse him.

She'd never met a corpse before. And though it irritated Angeli to admit it, neither had he, not a live one, anyway. Named for an Italian city that once kept surgeons supplied with flayed cadavers carved from wax, Florentines were the extreme end of elective surgery.

The Florentine had been stripped of his epidermis. Surface skin had been ripped away, as had sections of the middle skin layer, cut back to reveal the purple muscle, veins and organs beneath. The lost skin had been replaced with a clear layer of synthetic protein, bonded with f/nectin. Leaving the boy looking like a living anatomical model.

Beneath his synthetic skin, the boy's heart beat as healthily as anyone else's, better probably. His body was so toned he undoubtedly worked out, avoided drugs and ate whatever fresh food he could get his hands on. But then, all corpses were notoriously vain: it came of having their muscles permanently on show.

The corpse cradled his Uzi micro, and then scuttled back through his hatch. He'd been trailing them from below, down in the deserted attics. Seconds later, a staccato burst ripped from below their feet and two guards spun backwards off a ledge where they'd been balancing, out of Angeli's line of fire. The corpse had good sight, enhanced probably, along with his long-loop reflexes.

Shouts ahead caught his attention and Angeli cursed, slammed up his Colt and took out the knee of a guard racing straight towards them, sprinting across the hot tiles of the almost flat roof. Angeli needn't have bothered. The man was terrified, blinded with fear and sweat, on the run from someone.

It didn't require much thought to work out who.

Neph rounded a heat-converter and skidded lightly on the Prigioni's tiles, her bare feet shifting position in mid-slide. Somewhere in the last few minutes she'd lost the small kit she'd been cradling, and gained dripping red gloves that stretched to her elbows.

Seeing the man's splintered knee Neph hissed, furious someone had touched her prey. Blood dripped down her pointed chin, and her thin lips were pulled back in a snarl as she moved in on the shaking guard, hauling him to his feet.

Instinctively, the man threw up his hands, trying to protect his throat . . .

And Neph struck, arms blurring as her fingers shredded his uniform jacket, cutting bloody weals into his exposed stomach.

Oblivious to the bolts and bullets hissing around her, Neph struck viciously at the helpless guard, right leg rising rapidly, her foot open-clawed long before it reached his hairless skin. The man never stood a chance.

He was still trying to protect his throat when her hooked toes reached up under his ribcage, ripping through his diaphragm, shredding corded muscle to mangled red meat. Neph curled her feet, hooking nails down into his gut, and pulled. Grey coils of intestine, wine-dark liver, bag-like stomach, Neph gutted them all out of his body in a single blow. Dropped them wetly onto the sizzling roof.

His sickening howl of pain lasted until his lungs were emptied. Even Neph looked surprised, halting for a nanosecond before raking her open hand down the front of his screaming skull, ripping his face away like a wet grey mask.

All but dead, the guard was still breathing, still trying to scream as Neph thrust fingers into the opened cavity of his chest, reaching for his juddering heart, sharp thumb bursting it open like a blood-filled balloon.

Stepping neatly back, Neph raised her dripping hand to her face, sniffed in the rich salt scent of blood, then gave her cupped palm a slow lick.

Angeli vomited.

Then vomited again, until his gut was emptied down to bile. Grabbing his Colt, he began to squeeze off shots, taking whatever ammo came, firing at any movement, killing guards, windows, pigeons, whatever . . .

Karo was still hunched nearby, behind a low marble parapet, cradling her rifle, face slick with fear and sweat. He could smell her panic, sour and ugly as his. Their eyes met and then slid away. The girl had nothing to say to him.

'We're running out of time,' Angeli said.

There was no reply, just a sick, dangerous quietness. Angeli recognized shock when he saw it. At least, he recognized it in others.

'Move it!' He tried to pulled at her arm, then jumped back as Karo swung at him. But he didn't move soon enough, her bunched fist catching him hard under the jaw, jolting his skull. Her own face was hollowed out with anguish. She was shivering, deep-to-the-bone shivering, despite the heat.

Angeli was appalled. But quite obviously, not as much as she was.

'Have you ever felt someone die?' Karo demanded. Without even realizing it, she was nursing her fingers, rubbing her knuckles.

'No.' Angeli hadn't felt someone die, he couldn't and never would, that much was obvious to both of them. He could kill, but he wouldn't truly know death until it finally happened to him.

'It freezes you,' said Karo. 'It's a void, bottomless.' There was horror in her dark almond eyes and her lips were bitten through, but she wouldn't let him put his arm around her. Crouched there, dressed in his jacket, she looked the child she was, or at least had been until not that long ago.

It was all Angeli could do not to hate himself for dragging her into this.

'I dragged myself,' Karo said, sticking up her chin. 'On the end of a bit of molywire.' There was pride in her shaking voice, and fury and a sadness, that was for neither of them. 'We shouldn't have met, ever. I should never have gone to the *TripleHelix*. Shouldn't have launched that virus. Shouldn't have molywired that *WeGuard*. But then, he shouldn't have killed Razz . . .'

Angeli wondered if Karo realized she'd just admitted to murder. But what did it matter? It was outside his jurisdiction. Always had been, if he were honest.

Karo stared at him, head turned to one side, then looked across at the ornate roof of the Palazzo Ducale. And Angeli suddenly realized two things at once. She was crying again, and she was looking at her home.

'Okay,' he said, sadly. 'You tell me. Where do we go from here?'

'Down to ground level,' said a voice above them. Serious and sonorous, it was the poet, a H&K slung under one arm, an open-bladed swordstick under his other, its silver blade tipped with blood. 'Neph cleared the way as far as Sospiri Bridge.' Edgar Allan twisted his lips at the memory. 'But then we hit a wall at the far end . . .'

Angeli looked puzzled.

'Sospiri's a closed bridge,' said Karo crossly, rubbing away her tears. 'We can walk across its roof okay. But the Palazzo is higher than Prigioni Nuove. We'll need ladders to climb.'

'Or go in through a window,' Angeli said.

'No need.' The poet's voice was solemn, but then it was probably always like that. 'CySat are offering talks . . . Message from the corpse. What's left of *WeGuard* are trying to stop Sabine leading her brood into the city. They're not winning.'

'Then we go down,' Angeli said. Standing slowly, he instinctively tensed, ready to dodge gunfire, but none came. Across the tiled roof, he could see the wide-open waters of the Canal di San Marco. It was a long way to have come by accident.

The quietness unsettled Angeli as he scrambled down the side of the Prigioni on a wrought-iron fire ladder, dropping onto the dark asphalt of Riva degli Sciavoni. Sitting target, that's what he was. Angeli could almost feel fear prickling at the back of his neck, though it could have been sweat running into the open blisters of his sunburn.

The Canal di San Marco was the *only* open stretch of sea between the city proper and the silver levels in the distance. The levels held back by razor-edge molywire netting stretched from the end of the Grand Canal to the tiny island of San Giorgio Maggiore. And from the island to where Arsenale's feed canal met the Ca di Dio. And even then, Canal di San Marco was no wider than a big river.

Maybe, Angeli thought, maybe he was seeing everything for the last time. Seeing it truthfully. If so, shouldn't he have felt more angry?

Facing onto the Canal di San Marco, the side of the Palazzo offered shade beneath its colonnades and marble fountains that bubbled with ice-cold water. It was there Karo and Angeli met up with Neph and what was left of her small group, three adults, two half-kits and the newborn now back in her thin arms.

From there they had to round the corner of the palazzo, turning right into St Mark's Square. The entrance to the Palazzo Ducale was through an arch leading off from the square. Karo stalked arrogantly through the piazzetta, the little piazza, towards the entrance, walking between the two great columns of St Theodore and the Lion, knowing this was where executions once took place, that to walk between the columns was to invite death.

'And why not?' Karo demanded grimly. The jacket she'd borrowed from Angeli was slick inside with sweat, but she'd stopped at a fountain to wipe down her gut and tie back her black hair, splashing cold water onto her face.

Every step she took towards the Palazzo Ducale stiffened her gaze. She had her chin up, determination etched across her face. Karo was back on home ground, Angeli realized, feeling a hollow sadness.

[Shit In A Silk Stocking . . .]

Count Ryuchi was waiting for them in the courtyard of the palazzo. He was every bit as imposing as Angeli remembered from their last brief meeting. Count Orsela stood two paces away, a bull-like man with a barrel chest and shaved head.

The two of them stood at the far end of the courtyard, in front of a carved well-head, covered like an altar with a purple cloth. Between them on a golden chair, with two bodyguards at his back, sat an old man with dead hands and dull eyes, one side of his sunken face flash-frozen by a stroke. The ten remaining members of the council were arranged behind the well-head, in the shadow of a colonnade.

And except for the Regent in his heavy red velvet robes, and the Regent's two bodyguards, the rest were dressed simply: dark double-breasted suits, cotton shirts, enamel chains of office around their necks.

The bodyguards didn't wear suits, silk or otherwise, making do with body oil, rubbed into torsos that shone obsidian-black in the sunlight. And round their necks were not chains of office, but neophrene straps taking the weight of quad-barrelled Martin machine-guns.

Angeli had expected the Council to be gathered in St Mark's or waiting somewhere inside the Palazzo Ducale, had expected them to use the stark white backdrop of the vast Byzantine Gothic palace to overawe the rebels streaming into the city.

But the whole sprawling elegance of the Piazza San Marco had been deserted, echoing and empty. Café shutters pulled tight over polyglass windows. The vast square's grey paving slabs occupied only by strutting pigeons and litter. Even the *Atrio Foscari*, that open-ended stone corridor leading from the square to the Palazzo's inner courtyard, had been unguarded.

With the gilded dome of San Marco at his back, Angeli looked down the courtyard at the silent, waiting figures. They exuded authority, pure absolute power. If, as Napoleon said, St Mark's Square was the grandest drawing room in Europe, then this courtyard was its office, the place where decisions were taken.

Fingers brushed Angeli's wrist even as trails of thought brushed at his mind. Karo! She was, she was – what . . . ? From the sweat broken out across her forehead and the ugly tension in her jaw, it looked like Karo was already fighting her battle. One he couldn't see.

'Power. Authority. It's what they want you to think,' she whispered sharply. 'Don't let them into your head.' But try as he might, Angeli couldn't shake free his growing feelings of unworthiness, of doubt.

So Angeli did what he always did when doubt hit . . . Pointed his NVPD Colt at someone. 'Phosphor,' he stated, sighting the pistol on Ryuchi.

Breathing deeply, Angeli let the certainty he held the Count's life in his hands steady his nerves. Feeling the panic ebb. Not a pleasant trick, but an effective one.

'We're the winners,' Angeli told Karo fiercely, but she knew he was really reminding himself. Not that it felt true to Angeli. He didn't feel as if he'd won anything.

Next to him, Karo rocked on her feet in the heat, her black hair plastered close to her skull with sweat. The skin across her nose and forehead was raw, mottled into angry red patches. She stank like an animal. They all did.

Angeli risked another glance at the walls surrounding them, at the double row of stone arches, one above the other. The Palazzo's famous colonnades and high carved pediments that framed the courtyard.

Mocked up in a thousand virtual studios to provide the stage for balls, love affairs and deadly duels, that double colonnade with its row of high windows above it was almost as famous as the Taj Mahal or the sublimating carbon dioxide ice mountains of Mars. What was really amazing was that the tri-D constructs didn't come even close to capturing its real power.

But all Angeli knew was that he didn't belong. That he shouldn't be there.

'Leave,' ordered a cultured voice, the command carrying effortlessly across the courtyard, though the executives were too distant for Angeli to be sure who'd spoken. Beside him, Karo tensed. And, once again, Angeli reminded himself of the obvious, that one of those men was her father.

Sweet fucking Jesus. How would he have felt at her age going up against his uncle? Angeli tried to imagine it but couldn't. He wouldn't have done it. Wouldn't have had the guts. Didn't have that much of a death wish.

Without looking down, Angeli gripped Karo's hand, twisting his fingers into hers. Though just who most needed the reassurance, he didn't know.

Karo pulled back her shoulders. Steadied herself so obviously that Angeli almost smiled. Together they walked slowly across the stone slabs towards the waiting men, the girlKat padding beside them; with them, but no longer quite of their number. More than distance stood between them. Neph was jumpier, more highly strung since she'd started killing. And every time Angeli looked at her blood-crusted fingers he remembered the gutted, still-screaming body of the *WeGuard*.

Their walk seemed endless, the stone colonnades more elaborate, the marble statues richer than Angeli could have imagined. And if Ryuchi was worried by the Colt pointed at his gut, then it didn't show. None of the CySat executives looked worried, none flinched. Brave or stupid, the Council were living up to their own standards.

Angeli tried telling himself the courtyard was fake, not even two hundred years old, a laser-cut, ferroconcrete frame resting on scrap metal and dead coral, but it was no use. The copy Passion had ordered was as perfect, as powerful as the real thing.

As he got closer to Orsela, Angeli could see disbelief in his eyes as the barrel-chested man looked at the filthy, exhausted group dragging themselves towards him. In a flash, Angeli saw the levels through CySat's eyes. Walking wounded, elective freaks, badly-armed refugees. From a rusting, lawless, floating barrio that should long since have been cut free from the edge of a perfect city.

And here they were, walking unhindered into the courtyard of the most beautiful palazzo in the world. Trespassing on the headquarters of the world's biggest, most powerful metaNational, while its executive stood defenceless. Beside him Karo nodded and Angeli smiled. The human mind was adaptable; it could cope with almost anything, even being listened in to.

But Karo shouldn't have let her mental defences down. Without a filter in place, her thoughts tripped over into the public domain. And before Karo realized it, her father had picked her memories out of the crowd.

'God, Katherine!' The tall Japanese executive's cultured voice echoed around the courtyard, shock tinged with open horror.

Karo froze.

Around the Count, CySat's other executives stared in disbelief, one after another, as they slowly realized the truth. That it was Ryuchi's daughter who limped half-naked towards them, sunburnt and bloody, a blue NVPD jacket slung over one shoulder, her frame wrapped in a man's torn Levis and an indecent white top, rendered almost see-through with sweat.

And because Angeli had looked away as he checked the 'rounds-remaining' read-out on his Colt, he had missed the horror revealed in the man's face. But wired alert by that simple calling of Karo's name, Angeli had time to see the tall nobleman's expression shade from worry into rapid thought.

He'd seen that calculation before, in every bluff he'd ever had called. Someone trying to rewrite history's code on the fly, and suceeding. Neural paths, hardwired in by hard experience, kicked up Angeli's adrenal level. Axons rapid-fired. Seratonin levels rebalanced. But all Angeli felt was a sudden searing unease, fight flicking to flight in a nanosecond.

To one side Neph prickled, a ruff of dark fur running suddenly across her hunched-forward shoulders. She felt it too. Logic wasn't a kat thing, and neanderthal sentimentality they left to the wolf-Boys, but kats were hot on pure emotion. And razor-sharp on instinct. The balance of power had changed against them. And while the Count called again to Karo, both Neph and Angeli tried to work it out.

Taking a deep breath, drawing on every hated voice lesson she'd ever had, Karo straightened her shoulders and threw her answer back at him.

'Father.'

Projecting her single word across the dwindling gap between the groups. Her reply was effortless in its arrogance. The girl's voice was as clear, as studiedly cultured as his.

Shit, thought Angeli. Knowing this wasn't the Karo he knew. Not one he'd ever seen. But if Angeli was shocked by the confidence in her voice, Count Ryuchi looked shattered.

'Come here!' His order was peremptory, but this time even Karo could hear worry underwriting it.

Karo shook her head. That she was disgraced in his eyes, in the eyes of his colleagues, Karo knew without even having to think about it. Whether or not he'd known about Razz no longer mattered, at least it didn't to her. She'd made her choice, weeks before, when she molywired the man who had killed her lover. And even if Karo pleaded ignorance, youth, stupidity, no marriage would ever be arranged for her in hushed whispers between dowager aunts.

'No.' Karo said. 'I'm sorry, but no . . . It's too late.' She sounded shocked, as if she couldn't really believe the choice she was making.

Angeli certainly couldn't. Between the sombre elegance of

CySat's executives and those who trickled into the courtyard from the levels stood more than the mere distance between the city and its floating barrio. The gap was cultural, aesthetic. There was more to it than just Neph's sweating feline nakedness, the Corpse's visible heart, Angeli's torn uniform: their emotions were stained and tattered too.

His NVPD Colt was still pointed straight at Ryuchi's heart, an explosive round still jacked into its chamber, but the Count had dismissed him completely, cut him out of the equation. Such arrogance was suicidal, unless the Count really was so unbelievably certain of his own safety. And if he was? Then Angeli had missed something, something vital . . .

Even deadly.

'Go,' Angeli told Karo. 'While you can.'

'I need your permission?' Karo asked icily. Her chestnut-flecked eyes burned into his and Angeli wilted. When he glanced away, breaking the link, the young girl's gaze swept over the waiting Council, her father included.

'I'm here,' Karo indicated the spot where she stood. 'I don't need anyone's permission. This is my choice.' For the first time, even Neph looked vaguely impressed.

Count Ryuchi stepped forward, away from Count Orsela, the two bodyguards, the Regent sitting drooling in his chair. His thin, silver-ringed hands were open in friendship, held low. As he glanced at Karo, Angeli and the kat, a tolerant smile was fixed on his long, narrow face. But it didn't even come close to reaching his eyes.

Somewhere in there, Ryuchi was balancing out that equation. Angeli and Neph already counted for nothing, Karo didn't. But what the NVPD officer needed to know was, what else was being equalized out?

'Karo,' said the Count. The pet name came clumsily, uneasy on his lips.

Standing beside Angeli, the girl bristled.

'Count,' Angeli said, stepping in front of the girl, blocking her

father. His NVPD Colt was almost against the Japanese nobleman's gut, its automatic sight reduced to the tiniest pinprick on
the man's black silk jacket. Count Ryuchi had no option but to
acknowledge him.

'You're trespassing,' the Count said calmly. 'The campus of
newVenice is off-limits to all non-CySat personnel . . .'

Angeli said nothing. What could he possibly say?

The Count sighed, stepping back slightly. And if the Count
stepped away from the gun, he made it appear that he did so by
accident, as if that were not his main concern.

'Look,' he said. 'CySat are not insensible to the needs of . . .'
The Count paused to consider his words carefully, '. . . our
suburbs. The levels have grievances. We understand that. But this
is not the right way to address your problems.'

And what was the right way? It was hard to know if the man
referred to the H&K rifles, to Angeli's floating-breech Colt still
pointed at his gut, or to the poet's bloodied swordstick. Or whether
his quiet, measured words took in the screaming of drakuls in the
distance, the crunch of explosives and the pall of grey smoke
beginning to obscure the afternoon sky around them.

Sabine was moving through the city proper.

'We must talk,' said the Count. 'That much is obvious, but it
cannot be under these conditions. CySat will not be held to
ransom.'

He was staring at Angeli now. Eyes peering deep into his.
Flickers of thought were catching at Angeli's mind, but they
couldn't grip, couldn't get hold. Karo was keeping her own father's
mind at bay, Angeli realized with shock. The sick, tottering young
girl beside him was all that stopped the Count from reaching into
his mind and snuffing it out like a candle. No wonder the girl
burned with real, physical pain.

'End this now,' the Count said. He sounded concerned, serious.
And when the NVPD officer said nothing, the Count shrugged
slightly, as if disappointed by Angeli's response. As if disappointed
by Angeli himself. A pose, Angeli knew that, but all the same he

couldn't stop a sudden lurch of doubt, the automatic cut-in of an ingrained desire to defer.

It was all the NVPD officer could do not to holster his Colt on the spot and salute. God, if *he* felt like this, what must Karo be feeling? Glancing sideways, Angeli saw she was holding her own, hanging in there. Sweat might slick her hollow face, her mouth might be tired and drawn, but her eyes were like ice, her jaw set like steel, unbending.

'You have Paco,' Angeli said, loudly. He'd found his voice and it sounded better than he expected. 'We want him back. And there must be changes . . .'

The Count stared at him in amusement, and Angeli stared right back, ignoring the sweat that dripped into his eyes, the stink rising from his own body. His aching, sickening tiredness.

'Did you really think CySat could try to cut us loose,' Angeli asked, 'and not cause a riot?'

'Cut you loose?'

In silence, Angeli watched the Count reassess, noted the exact moment the man realized his daughter was the only way Angeli could know about that. The NVPD officer enjoyed the shock that flickered into the Count's eyes, the way he glanced suddenly at his daughter. It was a small victory and a cheap one. But Angeli needed to get inside this man's skin, before the man got inside his.

'Katherine,' said the Count softly, his voice low, reproachful. 'You know that wasn't policy. It was the barest idea, a potentiality that we . . .'

'Wasn't the alternative killing them?' Karo asked through cracked, blistered lips, her voice almost a dried-out croak. Dark eyes slid past her father's shoulder to settle on the squat figure of Count Orsela. 'Things are about to change,' said Karo.

'Too fucking right, mon,' Neph spat. 'Already have, wouldn't you say?'

She nodded at the seated Regent, then to a small pack of drakuls slinking in through the *Atrio Foscari*, looking around in amazement, impressed despite themselves. The girlKat's thin smile was ironic, as ironic as she could make it. 'When was the last time the levels met the Regent to discuss policy?'

Even Karo smiled.

'Well,' said the Count, 'perhaps so.' He shrugged, elegantly. 'It's getting late, we'll discuss it in the morning. Karo, you come with me. Your friends can use the Procuratie Vecchie.' Ryuchi said it as if putting up elective species in one of the Piazza's grandest buildings was commonplace.

He moved easily towards his daughter, one arm reaching up to rest lightly across her shoulders. The man intended to shepherd Karo away from Angeli. And looking at the dark certainty in Ryuchi's eyes, Angeli knew instinctively that Ryuchi's distaste for the levels was not his only reason.

'Karo,' said Angeli, but he needn't have bothered. She was already twisting out of her father's grip. Whether consciously or not, Karo had unslung her rifle, as if putting the H&K into easier reach.

'Come,' the man said abruptly. 'Enough. Stop being stupid. Your place is here with me.'

'No,' Karo said, her voice a dry, furious whisper. '*This* is my place . . . At least I belong here.' She met her father's gaze without flinching, her eyes every bit as cold as his. Fear shook her body until her fingers trembled on the trigger of her rifle and an ugly *tic* pulled at the side of her sun-blistered lips. But her gaze never faltered, nor did the hate now open in her eyes. When Karo spoke she was calm in spite of herself.

'I know what you did to my mother . . .'

There, it was said.

'And I know what you had done to Razz . . .'

'You know nothing.' The Count's answer was abrupt. 'Your stupidity over that woman has caused all this.' He looked at his daughter in scorn. As though her stand against him was a weakness, a flaw for which he was not responsible. All kindness was gone and with it his offer to negotiate.

Already he was backing away from their group. Silk jacket still uncreased, unstained by sweat. A light citrus cologne still fresh on his skin. Of course, the suit was made from smart silk, MIT-patented, with built-in thermal adjustment. The cloth so dark it practically swallowed light.

From his clothes to his voice, everything about the Count was a statement, Angeli realized. One that elegantly, politely, calmly said *Fuck You*.

And then Angeli took another look around and suddenly realised why the man was not afraid.

He was the predator, they were the prey...

[Machine-Guns & Poses]

The Count had wanted to cut his daughter from their group. Now that had failed, Karo was dismissed, and with her all of them. Digital dust, footnotes in history.

'Rispoli . . .' The voice addressing Angeli was rich with contempt. 'Take this rabble back to the levels while you still can.' The Count nodded once to his daughter as she stood beside the NVPD officer, shrugged and turned to go, his cold gaze flicking briefly to the walls surrounding them all.

'Take it,' the Count said coldly over his thin shoulder. 'You have no idea how good an offer it is.'

Angeli had.

Count Orsela was helping the Regent to his feet, holding him upright, head half turned away in disgust at the spittle dribbling from the old man's lips. The Council were withdrawing. Falling back under the arches, into safety.

If Angeli'd had anything left in his gut, he'd have been sick. But instead he concentrated on staying upright, on not looking at the stone circles cut above each arch. Behind each stone porthole was a gun, hidden in shadow . . . How many portholes, how many guns? Fifty, a hundred. It was impossible to say without looking, without making it obvious he knew.

The *WeGuard* might be gone, but the defences weren't. Any half-competent semi-AI could cut the crowd into bloody meat in a few seconds. And CySat had the JCIT, a Turing-standard AI. *That* was why Ryuchi had been so certain of himself.

Watching the retreating figure of a man who could command their deaths with a simple nod, Angeli realized that everything that had just happened made sense. Or, at least, it did to Angeli. Even knowing it was Karo who'd killed the *WeGuard*, the man had wanted to save his daughter. Maybe that was love, or what passed for it in the Suites.

But he'd abandoned her, walked away at the mention of her mother. It made Angeli wonder if Karo understood her own father had just condemned her to death.

'Hey, don't look so grim. We can take d'bodyguards.'

Neph grinned, but even Karo knew it wasn't true. From their loose stance to their watchful eyes, those two were true professionals. And their rotating quadMartins were heavyweight weaponry, of the kind usually bolted to the gunpods of a Mitsubishi.

Faced up by quadMartins, surrounded on four sides by a wall of linkless Brownings. It was going to be a turkey shoot, and Angeli had delivered the crowd to the guns.

'Get the fuck out of here,' Angeli shouted, swinging round. 'Move, get out of here.'

He might as well have been shouting at the waves. Ignoring the CySat executives at his back, Angeli flicked into combat stance, squeezing off two shots over the heads of the crowd. Screaming at them to leave. Windows splintered, raining glass down on the crowd below. Good idea, bad move . . .

A wolfBoy howled. Instinctively, an Ishie began to push towards the wounded boy, going for a death scene. And as Angeli brought up his Colt again, a flechette hit, took him in the back, punching him forward. The second flechette flipped him round in a half-circle before he'd even hit the ground. Grey stone came up to meet him and Angeli could hear Karo's anguished scream over the sledgehammer thud of his own heart.

He wasn't dead, though: reinforced kevlar and clone spider's silk saw to that. His NVPD jacket was in tatters, its shoulder guards cracked right though. 'Shit,' he whispered, sounding stupid even to himself, and scrambled to his knees.

Karo stopped screaming.

And then, just as rapidly, Neph was grinning. It had nothing to do with joy at Angeli's survival. Neph had the seven-coloured sight of all girlKats, rod-cells in her eyes tuned for movement, not detail. And Neph saw instantly what Angeli and Karo hadn't.

'Flat dead,' Neph said, her voice a rapid hiss. 'No fucking movement at all. Those AIs should sight us, shouldn't they?' Her voice was fast, impatient.

Karo nodded. Of course they should. Every static-mounted weapon in the city was now operated by the JCIT deck.

'You're sure?' Angeli demanded. He'd pushed himself to his feet, swung round to face the Council who stood under the colonnades in silent amusement, as if watching a play. He'd fallen into combat stance, without even realizing it. Not that it looked that lethal. Anyone not in the know would have thought Angeli was just slouching, hand on belt.

'Am I sure?' Karo sucked her teeth hard in disgust, sounding so like a girlKat that Neph laughed. 'Beltless Brownings,' said Karo, 'laser tracking to pick out key personnel . . . First through the arch, who's carrying the biggest weapon, who's doing the talking, stuff like that.' Karo grinned.

She was trained, all right. 'Then why aren't the Council worried?' Angeli asked.

'Cos,' Neph interrupted sweetly, 'they don't fucking know. Do they?' She spat expertly onto the flagstones. 'You going t'start this, or me?'

'Me,' Angeli said. And dropped deeper into a fighter's crouch, Colt already drawn and raised, the ornate splendour of the Foscari Arch, the polychrome tiles, the colonnades – all forgotten.

'Flechette,' he snapped, and sighted in on Ryuchi without even pausing, his Colt ready-lit for distance. It was fluid, Zen-fucking-perfect.

Just too late, one of the Regent's two bodyguards began to swing the barrels of his quadMartin. The other slid into a back-up move, flipping sideways to draw fire from the Regent and give himself greater killing space.

Bead already drawn on Count Ryuchi's head, Angeli heard Karo's high-pitched wail and switched mid-shot to Orsela. No point at all in snuffing the Regent, he was senile, brain-dead already . . .

The flechette took Orsela through the throat, ripping open the cartilage plates of his voicebox, spinning like a little black copter from the back of his neck. The fat man spilt onto his back, already dead.

Angeli's finger was tight again on the trigger. He could almost feel the whiteness of his knuckles. The bodyguard with the raised quadMartin was his: the other would kill *him*.

There were worse ways to go.

'*Wait!*'

Angeli froze, as a child's voice suddenly flowed through the courtyard, echoing off the high walls. Even the two bodyguards stopped in mid-stride.

'*Listen* . . .' The voice came from everywhere. It filled their heads and flowed from between the stone colonnades, from the windows. The crowd fell into silence. And Sabine's brood stopped trying to force their way into the now overcrowded courtyard. Which meant the commanding voice obviously reached out as far as the Piazza San Marco. Angeli didn't know it, but it reached everywhere. Legal or illegal, every newsfeed in newVenice, every Website, every tri-D, every CySat channel streamed it.

Neph hissed softly, for the first time truly afraid.

Even Ryuchi looked shocked, more shocked by the echoing voice than he was by Orsela's ugly death. It was obvious, from the disbelief scrawled across the Count's narrow face, that the child's voice was not part of any plan – at least, not one of his.

Frantically, the Count grabbed the Regent by his arm, hauling him from the safety of the colonnade, across the flagstones, out towards the well-head.

Holding the Regent upright, Ryuchi ripped the purple cover from the well-head to uncover a large mahogany box, inset around the sides with carved panels of ivory, its top a riot of beaten gold and garnets.

'Shit.' Neph was on her toes, her head pushed forward as if she couldn't believe her pale yellow eyes. She wasn't the only one to recognize the box. Angeli knew it instantly, despite the decoration. He'd seen the box in *Saints & Synners*, seen what it could do. It was Declan's JCIT deck, the central control for every weapon in newVenice.

Count Ryuchi pushed back his white shirt cuffs, fingers extended like a pianist. He was a man in love with his art, and his art was power.

'*Won't work.*' The voice spoke again, no longer all around them. This time people could identify its source, as they were meant to. It came from a vast flight of marble steps behind the crowd, leading up to the first-floor colonnade, opposite the Foscari arch.

The steps were designed to impress.

They did.

But not as much as the young boy standing at the top, dwarfed by colossal statues of Mars and Neptune: War and Sea, all of the city's history caught in two lumps of marble. The boy wore gold robes of office, threaded with precious metals and glittering, spider's-web-thin filaments of optic fibre. At his throat was a button mike, his computer-enhanced voice issuing from a speaker hidden somewhere high behind him.

'Paco,' Angeli said in shock. And Paco it was, though it was obvious from the intense expression on the boy's face that this was not quite true. It was Paco but not . . .

Behind Angeli, someone groaned and Angeli spun round in time to see the Regent, senile and drooling, fall to his knee. Whatever else Creutzfeldt3Jakob had wiped from his mind, it seemed his image of the Doge had been left undamaged.

Paco smiled, sadly. Then stared straight down at Ryuchi. '*The deck doesn't work,*' Paco announced. '*It won't work.*'

Over one shoulder, Angeli watched Ryuchi drag the Regent back to his feet and ram the old man's fingers hard against the deck's touch pads, until the old man moaned. But the JCIT deck remained lifeless. A beautiful, ornately-decorated impotent relic, belonging in the basilica like other religious relics, not there in the courtyard of the Palazzo Ducale.

The Count was swearing, his cultured voice stripped back to the vicious obscenities of his yakuza youth. It was not Ryuchi's day. The taller of the Regent's bodyguards reached over and began effortlessly to prise the Count's fingers off those of his master. In fury, Ryuchi pushed away the bodyguard, hands sliding on the man's well-oiled skin.

It was a bad mistake. One chop with a chiton-edged hand was all it took to drop Count Ryuchi to the ground, his windpipe crushed flat, his brain not yet so oxygen-starved it couldn't recognize pain.

Paco smiled.

And before Karo could scream, or any member of CySat protest, the bodyguard stamped once on Ryuchi's neck, cracking apart his vertebrae with an audible pop. The Count's already-dead body shat itself, twitched violently and then subsided into an inelegant heap.

It was over.

[Lampedusa's Dictum II]

They had a room under the roof. Paco insisted. A high room with huge uncurtained windows that reached from floor to ceiling.

When he put them in one chamber together, Angeli was surprised, but not so surprised as when Karo didn't immediately protest. Their room was not as ornate or well-kept as the chambers on the floors below but it was still gilded, with a view out across the city to the levels and the darkening sea beyond.

In insisting that Angeli's view be the level's silver sheen, instead of the stone grandeur of the Piazza San Marco, the young Doge was telling him something, Angeli knew that. But whether Paco's message was as basic and childish as *This is where you came from* or whether it was deeper and darker, telling him *Look where you are now, these people will become your enemies* – Angeli couldn't decide.

Karo was behind him, asleep now, her breath low and steady. Angeli could smell lanolin on her sunburnt body and the heavy musk of recent sex. It was a rich scent, reassuring, dark like chocolate.

She was a killer, like him. He knew that. Knew that Razz had been her lover. That what she'd done in the Doge's chambers weeks before, and what she'd done up there on the roof, owed more to the silver-skinned exotic than to genetics or any *Fujibishi dojo*.

She was dangerous, erratic, damaged – much like him.

Angeli didn't fool himself. There had been women before, a string of them, but Karo was something else again. He was more used to the fake pheromone-stoked lust of the *TripleHelix* whores than to her slow, burning passion. This was real, if anything was:

not the sour fear of a woman who needed something, not from him but from the NVPD – Neph's empire now. Let her sort it out.

Mixed in with Karo's warm scent was the subtle, insidious smell of black orchids. A vase carved from muttonfat jade stood on a small marble-topped table by their wooden bed, real orchids resting in rain water. The vase came with a brief note addressed to both of them, from Sabine, delivered by a drakul direct to their chamber under the roof.

Angeli shivered. Then smiled.

This was a night which had seen more changes than any since newVenice began. And yet, looking out over the darkened water, Angeli knew how little had really changed. Micro and macro, sets and subsets – no matter how often you rewrote the code, life always came back to the same templates. Seven sins, seven virtues. Even the unexpected had always already happened.

His own life was changed beyond recognition, way beyond wildest dreams. Glancing down at the naked young girl beside him was enough to tell Angeli that.

And he, one jump up from the ghetto, anger hidden behind a cheap kevlar uniform, was now Regent of the Council at thirty, elected for life. For, as Paco had pointed out, if Karo was sixteen and on CySat's new Council, then at nearly twice her age, Angeli must be Regent, CEO and City Elder.

And who the hell knew how old the girlKat really was? Whatever, seven or seventy, she was Paco's new head of police. And Karo? Not just a Council member but Chancellor, also for life.

Karo didn't look like Angeli's idea of a Chancellor, sprawled out naked under a linen sheet, her soft arms hugged in around her head, one pink-tipped breast exposed to the Pacific night. But then, even with the silk suit slung across the back of a Louis Napoleon chair, Angeli didn't feel like a CySat executive.

Then again, if Paco could be Doge, anyone could be anything.

Though what Paco was these days was anyone's guess. A god, maybe, except Angeli didn't believe in gods. Some things made sense, most didn't. One that did was that *Lucifer's Dragon* was more than a game, it was the JCIT deck's continuous training program. One that didn't, concerned what the Dragon was to Paco, and Paco to the Dragon. But that question the new Doge wouldn't even begin to answer.

Angeli draped his arm across Karo, feeling the heat of her naked skin, the soft curve of her body beneath his hand. She was beautiful, more beautiful than he'd ever imagined, more than he deserved. Her youth scared him. So, too, did the sudden tension that pulled at her face, even in sleep.

The quickness of her mind and the tendrils of thought that she slid, without thinking, into his head worried him also, but not as much as her dry-eyed anger. She hadn't cried once all evening at the death of her father. If grief was there, it was locked tight inside that mind of hers.

She'd wept once, though. In Angeli's arms, slow racking sobs he'd pretended not to notice. And as she had rolled away from under him, lovemaking over, she'd looked deep into his eyes and told him crossly that sharing a bed wasn't permanent.

Never occurred to him it would be, Angeli had answered.

Both had lied.

These Jon Courtenay Grimwood books and other Simon & Schuster/Pocket titles are available from your book shop or can be ordered direct from the publisher.

0 671 02222 9	reMix	£6.99
0 671 02260 1	redRobe	£6.99
0 671 77368 2	Pashazade	£6.99
0 671 77369 0	Effendi	£6.99
0 671 77370 4	Felaheen	£6.99

Please send cheque or postal order for the value of the book, free postage and packing within the UK; OVERSEAS including Republic of Ireland £2 per book.

OR: Please debit this amount from my

VISA/ACCESS/MASTERCARD ....

CARD NO: ....

EXPIRY DATE ....

AMOUNT£ ....

NAME ....

ADDRESS ....

Send orders to SIMON & SCHUSTER CASH SALES
PO Box 29, Douglas Isle of Man, IM99 1BQ
Tel: 01624 677237, Fax: 01624 670923
e-mail: bookshop@enterprise.net
Please allow 14 days for delivery. Prices and availability subject to change without notice